# The Last Great
# Wild West Show

For Aurora & David —

Hope you enjoy the trip

Jeff Stonull

# The Last Great Wild West Show

A Novel of Alaska's Salmon Fishery

Jeff Stonehill

| Library of Congress Control Number: | | 2011902524 |
|---|---|---|
| ISBN: | Hardcover | 978-1-4568-7056-0 |
| | Softcover | 978-1-4568-7055-3 |
| | Ebook | 978-1-4568-7057-7 |

**To order additional copies of this book, contact:**
Xlibris Corporation
1-888-795-4274
www.Xlibris.com
Orders@Xlibris.com
94627

# CONTENTS

For Liz

And in memory of Brian King, my Alaskan guru.

# ACKNOWLEDGEMENTS

I give many thanks to Martha Kendall, Barbara Quick, Liz Stonehill, Laura Stonehill and Skip Walker for generously volunteering as my editors, proofreaders and literary advisors.

Special thanks also go to Sylvia Lange Meyer for sharing her family stories and recollections of Cordova and the Copper River Fishery, and to Andrew Smallwood for his writing tips and bush pilot expertise.

I also wish to thank the quirky and wonderful people of Cordova who make a living from the waters of the Copper River Delta and beautiful Prince William Sound, for their inspiration, understanding and forgiveness, and to reassure them that while some local historical figures are mentioned by name, this is a work of fiction.

# CHAPTER 1

## Happy Trails

Brutus died in Geyserville. In a way, it was for the best. He'd been ailing for a time and I guess he just didn't have it in him to make such a long journey to the promised land. At least it was quick. He was tired. He was old; a 1959 Plymouth with a gearshift operated by push buttons on the dash. After a joint or two, passengers would mistake these for the selector buttons on the car radio. This had led to some startling downshifts.

I culled my vital gear into my backpack. I put on my puffy down jacket and grabbed my guitar in its crappy cardboard case. The rest of my stuff was entombed in Brutus' trunk like grave goods buried with ancient kings. I removed his Colorado license plates and tossed them into the blackberry brambles on the side of the road as I walked north in the golden California sun with my thumb out. Rest in peace Brutus. An unknown soldier, your fate is to lie in an unmarked grave, your dog tags lost forever. No one will ever trace you back to me.

Vineyards awash in yellow mustard and orchards in clouds of white blossoms lined the highway. Cars blew by with no sign of stopping, each one trailing a lonely gust of warm, dusty wind. "Maybe it's not meant to be. Maybe I should cross the two-lane and hitchhike back the other way. Go home. Wimp out. No! Screw that! Press on!"

I reached the edge of town. An auto wrecking yard. Some old winery with an Italian name on the metal barn roof. Then the Geyserville Church of Christ: "Expect a Miracle!" the sign said. And lo, one did appear! A black '53 Chevy panel truck rolled to a stop. It looked to have been painted using several dozen cans of flat black spray paint. The passenger side window rolled down. Very furry heads with huge bleary grins peered out at me from the front bench seat. The closest one, a pretty girl with a great curly strawberry Afro, asked, "You goin' very far?"

"I'm going to Alaska."

"Whoa, man! We aren't goin' that far, just to Port Angeles."

"Los Angeles is the other way," I said.

"Nooo!" she giggled, "PORT Angeles!"

"Where is PORT Angeles?"

"It's in Washington."

"Any place north of here works for me."

"Far Out! Hey, you guys in the back. Is there room for one more with a backpack and shit?" Muffled grumbles and scuffling came from the back of the vehicle.

The redheaded girl opened her door, jumped down and padded back to the back of the truck. Her bare feet were hardly visible under the voluminous frayed ends of her bellbottom Levis. Originally intended for life on legs several inches longer, the jeans had been abraded to their present length by long contact with the planet. They scuffed and snuffled along the surface of the highway like a pair of inquisitive Scottie dogs. Above her knees, however, the jeans hugged her thighs and her lovely round bottom as though the fabric had been spray painted on. I followed her along the windowless side of the truck to the aft-facing back doors. "Happy Trails" along with a couple of jaunty music quarter notes, was painted in white, fluid longhand beneath the little rectangular windows.

The back box of the van was bare metal with a piece of orange shag rug covering the floor. Covering the rug were sets of legs like faded denim sardines in a can. Four, no, five people were sitting, legs extended into the center, their backs against the side wall panels. Hands grabbed my guitar and pack and piled them on top of the other gear against the bench seat up front. Buttocks grudgingly scrunched forward to create a little more space and I assumed the position, my hiking boots next to the thigh of the guy opposite me. He was very skinny with a dour frown, a wisp of beard and heavy black-framed Allen Ginsburg glasses. Next to me was a plump girl in a wool US Army dress jacket with a black and yellow air cavalry horse head insignia on the shoulder. Beyond her, two blonde people, a man and woman I guessed, were bundled under a parka jacket they were using as a blanket. Across from them a guy with shoulder length yellow hair, an African print dashiki shirt and a blissed-out expression rocked in time to some music only he could hear. The back doors slammed shut, the red cloud of hair reappeared in the front seat, and we began to roll. The Grateful Dead launched in to "Truckin'" through loud but low-fidelity speakers somewhere up forward. A joint made its way back from the front seat. I took a deep toke and passed it across to Allen Ginsburg. I sat for a while grinning ecstatically at my good fortune in securing what was possibly going to be a 6 or 7 hundred-mile ride, a hitchhiker's mother lode.

After a couple of hours, reservations set in. First, my back was not enjoying the metal backrest, and the occasional bump or pothole elicited a drum-like thump of the head against the side panel. Another drawback was the view, or lack thereof. If I craned my neck I could see a tiny frame of sky out the front windshield far ahead, but most of that view was blocked by the two red and one brown cumulus clouds of hair up there. Looking back at the diminishing road behind was an option if I got up on my knees high enough to see out the rear windows. Otherwise I was relegated to watching the sky and an occasional treetop flash momentarily past my oblique 11 o'clock view out the back window.

I felt the van slow down, then swing to the right and stop. The red haired driver from the front seat liberated us from our incarceration, and sang out a rapid-fire chant like a carnival barker:

"Piss stop! Burger up! Stretch yer legs! See the sights! Smoke 'em if ya got 'em!" We were at the far end of the metal-roofed parking awning of an Arctic Circle Drive-in. Twenty or so angle parking spaces faced each other across a raised concrete promenade graced with garishly painted wooden picnic tables and benches. The promenade led inexorably to the order and pick-up windows of an equally garishly painted 1950's style burger emporium. The scent of fries and hamburger grease is genetically encoded in the pleasure center chromosomes of my generation. Resistance is futile.

I was seated at one of the picnic tables, powering my way through a double cheeseburger, bag-o-fries and an Arctic Blast. I heard a rhythmic mopping sound and the red-haired girl plunked down on the bench across from me.

"So I'm Julie? And the other two are Peter and Charlie. Charlie is my brother," she said between pulls on the straw in her giant lemonade.

"Aha, Charlie the Red!"

"Yeahhh, we're both pretty red."

"Well, I'm Matt." I extended my hand across the table and Julie tilted her head quizzically and pumped my arm up and down with exaggerated seriousness.

"Charmed, I'm sure," she intoned in a mock upper class British accent.

"No, really, the pleasure is all mine," I replied in my best faux-Knightsbridge. And it was! She really was pretty. Sparkly blue-green eyes with laugh crinkles at the corners when she smiled. Creamy skin with just a hint of freckles lurking beneath. Bra-less round breasts brushing against the gauzy white peasant blouse.

I lapsed back into Californian. "But hey, thank you guys for this totally cool ride. This is really groovy!"

"Hey, it's what we do. It's good karma? So where are you going in Alaska?"

"A little town called Cordova."

"Oh, far out!" she squealed. "I know someone there! Do you know Anna? Vasiloff?"

"No, I've never been there before,"

"Oh! Well, you'll notice Anna," she said mischievously, "she's like a raven-haired goddess. Boys worship her. She went to high school with me for a while when her family lived in Port Angeles. We were soul sisters. Plus, I'm Vaughn and she's Vasiloff, so we were always next to each other in the alphabetical prison lineups they make you pull in school. Then they moved back to Cordova all of a sudden." She reached over, took one of my fries, dipped it gingerly in ketchup, and popped it in her mouth. "Gawd, I love these greasy things! I don't eat meat, but, friiiies . . ." She got a far-away look in her eye, then launched into a passable imitation of John Lennon, singing: "*All we are sayyy-ing, is give grease a chance.*"

I snorted with sudden laughter, nearly blasting a mouthful of Arctic Blast across the table at her. "You almost made me do the elephant trick!" I blurted between sniggers of laughter.

"The what?"

"You know, the elephant trick. When you laugh with a mouthful of drink and blow it out your nose by accident?"

"Oh Gawd, that's disgusting!"

It was, too. What a stupid thing to say to her! Like something an eight-year-old would come up with. So much for my cool hippie-drifter persona. And why, exactly, do I care about the impression I make on her? 'Cause she's a fox! That's why, you idiot! I was saved from further recriminations and self-loathing by Charlie.

"Roll up! Roll up for the mystery tour! Step right this way!" He was chivvying his charges back toward the *Happy Trails*.

"Cool your jets, Charlie!" said Julie. "We're not done eating."

"OK! But hey, Jules, I say we take the blond couple and that Dashiki Dude up to Humboldt State like we promised. Then let's roll for the border. We can camp at one of the beaches up by Bandon or Coos Bay tonight."

"Did you talk to Peter?" she asked.

"Yeah, he's in one of his silent moods."

"Tell me about it! I wish he wouldn't smoke so much pot!"

We loaded back up and began traveling north again. By now we were launching into the third pass through somebody's bootleg recording of a Dead concert highlighted by a very stoned Jerry Garcia's endless noodling guitar solos. The Dead precluded all but the most perfunctory shouted conversation with my fellow travelers, so I took my Canada and Alaska maps out of my coat pocket and studied on just how freakin' far it was I had to go.

# Chapter 2

## And Free Beer Too!

After we dropped off the blond people at the college, the Happy Trails made another pit stop at a Taco Moe's in Arcata. Julie and the Air Cav girl used the restroom. Ginsburg and I stretched our legs behind the panel van. He looked up at the grinning serape-clad Mexican caricatured on the sign.

"Man, I hate these places."

"Don't like Mexican food?" I asked.

"Nooo, I don't like American corporate plastic fucking racism!" he hissed. "I don't eat at Sambo's either"! For a moment I had a strange urge to defend the indefensible, at least to say something nice about Aunt Jemima, but I swallowed it.

At dusk we stopped somewhere on the Oregon Coast. The campsites were in a big grove of pines above a vast sandy beach that looked like it ran all the way north to Canada. A funny-looking haystack of rock stood out in the ocean beyond dozens of parallel lines of breakers. Peter and Charlie pitched some sort of army surplus green tent. I kicked the pinecones away to make a flat spot and strung my flimsy red plastic tube tent on a rope I tied between two trees. I flopped my foam pad and down bag inside and stuffed a couple of shirts inside a tee shirt to make a pillow. We gathered up sticks out in the woods and built a fire inside a cement fire ring. Julie put an aluminum coffee pot of water on the fire.

"Chamomile tea," she said sweetly. "Helps you sleep." Ginsburg and the Air Cav girl surprised the hell out of me by setting up a couple of sleeping bags together off in another campsite. Shit, they hadn't said two words to each other all afternoon. Who knew?

Now it was dark except around the crackly pine fire. It was cold enough that we'd put our jackets on. Another joint went around while the water got hot. Peter, Julie, Charlie and I drank the tea and I ate some of my granola. Everyone volunteered as how they had the munchies. I offered my dried fruit around. It turned out they had some stashes of food in the van. Mostly avocados. They were returning from a pilgrimage to a big outdoor Grateful Dead concert down south, and had scored a monster bag of avos at a roadside stand. They were really ripe. We ate salted avo halves, slicing the flesh into strips and fishing it out with our pocketknives. It was rich and delicious.

"It's like nature's peanut butter," said Peter.

Charlie pulled out a bag of Granny Goose brand potato chips. "Organic Goose Chips?" he offered wryly. As she munched them, Julie got the same far-away look I recalled from her afternoon fry high, and she licked the salt and grease from her fingers.

"So, the guitar? You wanna play something?" Charlie asked.

"Sure, let me see if I can warm my fingers up." I held my hands to the fire for a minute; then I went to the truck and got out the black cardboard guitar case. Inside was my old nylon-string Goya, with its fat neck and easy action. I hadn't dared to bring my big Yamaha steel-string on such a risky voyage. I tuned up and started a song. Easy rock stuff to get going. "Me and Bobbie McGee," Simon and Garfunkel's "The Boxer," "Up On Cripple Creek" by The Band. Charlie and Julie both had nice brother-sister voices and harmonized on the choruses. We got going good on some old Stones: "Sympathy for the Devil," "Honky Tonk Women." Then we launched into some soul R&B and ended up doing old girl group songs from the early 60's. Julie had a great time singing along to my falsetto versions of "My Boyfriend's Back" and "Be My Baby". After that, I figured I'd quit while I was ahead and put the guitar back in the case. Charlie and Julie did some acapella versions of old 50's songs. It was obvious they had sung together since they were kids. It was kinda cute.

After a while I got up and walked down onto the beach. There was half a moon off to the south, so the white of the breaking waves was all luminous. The slow roll of the long lines of surf made a continuous fuzzy hissing sound like a radio with the volume up but not tuned to a station. The kelpy ocean smell filled my head. I felt someone walk up behind me. Julie. I heard a little whisper. "It's so cosmic, the beach. You're right on the cusp between the land and the unknown sea." I was a bit irked that she was launching into some stoned-out Aquarian philosophizing. I couldn't resist the urge to quote Lewis Carroll:

> *"When the sands are all dry, she is gay as a lark,*
> *And will talk in contemptuous tones of the shark;*
> *But, when the tide rises and sharks are around,*
> *Her voice has a timid and tremulous sound."*

She gave me a puzzled look, then she said: "When I'm high I can feel the tide pulling my insides right down the beach toward the water. Back to the Mother."

That was pretty cool. I thought about the moon overhead, pulling the sea toward her in their endless courtship of mutual yearning. "I love the ocean," I said. "As a kid I was afraid of a lot of things, of heights, big dogs, but not the water. I would swim or body surf or paddle around on an air mattress whenever I could get to the beach.

I would stay in for hours; even when I was so cold I was numb. I was never afraid I would sink or drown. It's my element."

"It buoys you up," she said.

"Yeah, it does." We stood there just listening and watching for a while. Then she took my hand. I looked over at her once or twice but she was just looking way out to sea. After a bit she leaned up and gave me a quick kiss.

"I gotta go back," she said. "Pleasant dreams."

At first light, I heard rustling at the fire pit. I inch-wormed out of my bag and little three-foot high tent. I stood on the tops of my boots as I pulled on my pants so I wouldn't get pine needles and dirt on my socks, then sat down and laced up the boots. Up to the outhouse for a desperately needed pee. When I got back, Julie was squatting by the fire ring with a glum expression. She was poking a spoon at a pot of mush on a little fire made up mostly of the unburned stub-ends of last night's wood pushed together. Charlie and Peter returned from their treks to the outhouse, and then Ginsburg and Air Cav joined us for breakfast, looking smug.

Charlie started in: "So, you cats, I hate to do this, but the *Happy Trails* doesn't run on love alone. Can everybody throw in a couple of bucks for gas? I figure we can make Port Angeles tomorrow." He gestured at Ginsburg and the Air Cav girl. "These guys need to get off in Astoria, so we'll stay on the coast that far. Matt, you need to get inland to the 5. We could slide over at Grey's Harbor and take you to Olympia."

"Free beer in Olympia, well, Tumwater," mused Peter. I wondered what the difference was between beer and tumwater, and what tumwater actually was, but I didn't ask.

"Home tomorrow? That means another night camping out?" Julie whined. Maybe she wasn't a morning person.

"Hey!" Charlie said. "You think I like listening to you guys dance the horizontal polka every night?"

"Charlie!" Julie squealed. "We wait 'till you're asleep!"

Charlie snorted derisively, then said: "And Peter, man, you snore!"

"Only when I smoke pot." Peter replied dismissively.

"And when isn't that?" asked Julie.

To change the subject, Peter says: "So, Matt, do you seriously propose to hitchhike all the way up the Alcan?"

"Well, yeah."

"Bad plan, man! The Alaska-Canada Highway is *not* to be toyed with," Ginsburg says with a scowl.

"Why? People drive there, don't they?"

"Yeah, but it's a seriously long fucking way, man! Couple thousand miles of dirt road bulldozed through the wilderness during World War II. And it's March still. Like, a bazillion degrees below zero at Muncho fucking Lake right about now. I know this shit! My uncle drives truck for the Army. I've rode with him up there. It's so cold they leave the diesels run all night so the oil in the engines don't freeze up while you sleep. If you stop it, you gotta build a fire under the oil pan to get it started again. Brother, you try to sleep out in that and you'll never wake up. You'll be like a frozen burrito in a bag, man."

Peter piles on with an ominous: "And they're Canadians up there too, man." He makes it sound like vampires or something.

"What does that mean?"

"Well, it's not the Haight-Ashbury. Not many longhairs. I tried to hitch up to Kamloops once from Vancouver. No one would stop. Finally, this old farmer goomer stopped because he thought I was a girl. When he figured out I was a guy he said no one hitchhiked around there unless they were out of gas. So I got a gas can at a market and pissed a bunch of people off when they realized I had no car and didn't want to get off at the next petrol station."

Charlie chimed in. "Yeah, you'll probably get stranded in Fort Nelson or some place, spend all your money staying in a crappy motel so you don't freeze to death, and then have to marry some fat local girl and become a Canadian, eh?"

"You should take the ferry!" Julie added, brightening a little.

"You know, you *should* take the ferry," said Peter. "For seventy or eighty bucks you are all the way from Seattle to Haines or Skagway or wherever, then it's just a few hundred miles to Fairbanks."

"And you get to go on a cruise!" Julie added enthusiastically. "I wanna go!" Peter gave her a sour look.

"It sure beats freezing your nuts off in Toad River" Ginsburg added with finality.

"I'll think about it."

Well, there actually was free beer in Tumwater, which turned out to be a little town, not the local name for 3.2 beer. They had a huge Olympia mega-brew factory with a tasting room. It tasted like Olympia beer, but what the heck. They give you free beer then suggest you drink responsibly, which I could only assume meant not spilling it just 'cause it was free. Peter and Julie were down at the other end of the tasting bar. Charlie held up a can by the bottom, showing me the famous horseshoe with the river flowing out and the motto: *"It's the water."* He covered the *"the"* with his middle digit and intoned: "At least they warn you." Then he got serious for a minute. "Man, I'm in a rut in Port Angeles, and I'm sick of being broke. We grow a little pot in the greenhouse. I do some odd jobs, carpentry stuff, but I'm kinda tempted to go north myself. Here's our address. Send us a note if it works out up there, OK?"

"I will. You guys really helped me out here. Thanks Charlie."

I said goodbye to the *Happy Trails* travelers in front of the brewery. Beery soul handshakes from Charlie and Peter, and a nice long squeezy hug from Julie.

"Have a groovy trip, and give Anna a hug for me." They were heading northwest on 101. I was heading north on I-5.

I made a call from the pay phone at the brewery to the Alaska Marine Highway Office in Seattle. Ferries to Haines, Alaska via Ketchikan, Petersburg, and Juneau left weekly on Fridays at 5:00PM. Walk-on passengers to Haines, no car, no stateroom, were $73. It was Friday at 2:15PM. Seattle was 60 miles away. If I get there in time, I'm getting on the boat. If I don't make it, I'm not chilling out in Seattle for a week, so it's up the Alcan. Once again, Thuma Dactylis, the goddess of hitchhiking, smiled on me. I bought my ticket for the MV Taku with an hour to spare.

# CHAPTER 3

## Gimme Three Steps.

The Taku was a huge navy-blue and white steel vessel with gold stars on the stack cowling forming the Big Dipper and the North Star. A rectangular hole opened onto the car deck and vehicles were rolling up a ramp into the bowels of the ship. I purchased some road-trip groceries at a nearby store, then went up to the passenger lounge and staked out a deck chair. We turned loose from the dock and headed out into Puget Sound. Heading north. I felt great! I had tingly excitement bugs in my stomach, but mostly a warm mixture of adventure and well-being.

I watched Seattle get smaller; then a series of islands and headlands and little towns paraded by on either side of the boat. After a while it got dark so I wandered around the decks to check the ferry out. Coming from one corner of a big lounge area was music, obviously of the homemade variety. Four people were sitting on the floor in a circle. Someone was playing a pretty good harmonica. One guy had a little bowl-back mandolin. The other guys were clapping and singing. I had to check it out. As I got closer, I figured the one facing away from me, playing harmonica, was probably a girl judging by the long black braids. She had to be one big girl, though, with a thick neck and great broad shoulders. I listened for a little while, then went back to my deck chair and got my guitar.

When I got back Ed, the guy singing, waved me in. I sat down on the floor to one side and tuned my guitar to the E of the harmonica. Turned out the big girl was not a girl, but an Ojibwa Indian guy from Ontario heading to a logging camp near Petersburg. He wore his hair in long braids tied with horsehair, had the incongruous name of Melvin, and played a sweet French-Irish folk style harmonica. He knew lots of nostalgic old songs. "Whisperin' Pines," Hank Williams' "I'm So Lonesome I Could Die," sailor's hornpipes and sea chanteys. We played late into the night. Toward the end the Indian sang some lodge songs of his people in their alien language. I dozed off in my bag that night with the deep hum and vibration of the engines setting a drone accompaniment for dream memories of his ethereal chanting.

The next afternoon Ed, Ernie the mandolin, clapping guy Doug and I had a few beers in the Taku's bar. They were going to Fairbanks. Turns out they were going to be my hitchhiking competition for getting out of Haines at the end of the ferry ride. I got out my Alaska map. Haines was at the end of the marine inside passage at the top of the Southeast Alaska Panhandle. Cordova, where I wanted to go, was just three hundred miles due west of Haines, but separated by a range of 18,000-foot mountains and several glaciers 50 miles across. The only road out of Haines ran north about 100 miles into the Yukon in Canada to meet up with the Alcan Highway. From there it was a couple hundred miles more to the Alaska border at Beaver Creek and about three hundred miles beyond that west to Fairbanks or southwest to Valdez and the ferry to Cordova. So Haines was more of a waypoint than a destination. We were all hoping we would meet someone on the boat and hook up a ride to points beyond, but it wasn't looking too promising so far. We had an uneasy laugh when we realized that they had been hoping for a ride from me and I had been about to ask them if there was any room left in the vehicle they didn't have.

By Sunday afternoon, when we docked in Petersburg and said goodbye to Melvin the Ojibway, the snow had come down the mountains to the shore. The next morning we got to Juneau, and huge steep snowy mountains reared up right from the beach to cover half the sky, with glaciers oozing down the narrow valleys between them. The scene was incredibly beautiful, but we were definitely back into winter outside.

The next afternoon we were finally in Haines, the end of the line. Well, not quite in Haines. No one coming off the ferry in a vehicle gave any of us a ride. This was a very bad sign, as those cars, trucks, and Winnebagos rolling off the boat, extra tires and gear lashed onto the roofs, were the rides into the interior, where we all needed to go. So we started walking toward town under ominous grey skies. My heart sank further when I saw a mile sign up the road a ways. "Haines 4 m." The frickin' ferry dock was four miles from town! When we finally got to it, Haines was pretty minimal as towns go, but it had a cafe, so we decided we should have a good meal. A quick inventory of my cash stash had me just above the $300 mark. "SPECIAL! Hot Roast Beef and All the Trimmings! $4.90!" said the chalkboard in the window. Gotta eat to live.

Afterward, we felt a lot better physically, but I had an uneasy feeling as we walked out of town in search of a place to set up camp for the night. These guys seem OK, but who is going to pick up four guys hitchhiking? Forest or snowy meadows interrupted by an occasional tired-looking wood-framed house lined both sides of the road. A few fat, lazy snowflakes were beginning to fall. It was getting dark. After about a quarter of a mile I saw a place under some trees with no snow. I didn't want to get too far out of town. Don't want the potential rides to get up too big a head of steam.

"I think I'll crash up there tonight and start working my thumb again in the morning." I said.

Ed looked back and forth between the three of us. "I think I'll stay up there too."

Doug and Ernie sort of shrugged their shoulders and concluded they would go on a little farther and see what came up. Maybe they were thinking the same thing about four of us all together.

About an hour later, a big old boat of a station wagon heading toward town pulls to a stop, and then makes a U. Ernie the Mandolin sticks his head out of the passenger window.

"You guys wanna stay indoors tonight?"

"Fuckin'-a right we do!" says Ed.

"Well come on!" We scramble our gear together and toss it in the back of the station wagon. The driver is a kid about 16 with a bottle of Carling Black Label beer in his hand. He breathes with his mouth open like a Labrador retriever after a good run. We drive maybe 1,000 yards up the road and the station wagon pulls off onto a dirt driveway leading up to a log house with a big covered front porch.

"Bring up your stuff." The kid says.

Clapping guy Doug is sitting on the living room floor with a beer in his hand. Three high school age kids are draped on the couch and on an overstuffed chair. The stereo is blasting Lynerd Skynerd: *"I was cuttin a rug, at a place called The Jug, with a girl name a Linda Lou."* Most of a case of beer is sitting on a table in the main room. The place reeks of pot smoke and it feels like it's about 90 degrees inside. I set my pack down in a corner and someone offers me a beer. *"When in at the door, walked a big 44, and he was pointing it at you-know-who!"* The house looks like the Hollywood movie set of an Alaskan lodge. The varnished log walls are barely visible because there are animal pelts everywhere, hanging on the walls, draped over the furniture. Lynx, mountain goat, fox furs, minks. Between the pelts are gun racks with shotguns and rifles. *"I said wait a minute mister, I didn't even kiss her, don't want no trouble with you!"* A lever action Winchester 30-30 and a cleaning rod and rags are lying on the table next to the case of beer. There must be 40 or 50 weapons in the room. *"Gimme three steps, gimme three steps mister, give me three steps toward the door."* A huge rack of moose antlers on the wall next to the door serves as a hat and coat rack. In the corner is a grey iron safe. The door is open and I can see a couple dozen boxes of ammunition of various sizes. *"Gimme three steps, gimme three steps mister, and I won't bother you no more!"*

Over the music, Ernie yells out his story: "So we're truckin' up the highway, sticking out our thumbs at the two cars that pass in 15 minutes, when Billy here comes out on his front porch. 'Where do you think you're going?' he hollers down at us. 'There's nothing up that way but about 5 houses and then a whole lotta Canada.' So he invited us in. We started partying pretty hardy, but we were feeling bad for you two guys out there freezing, so we asked them if we could go get you."

Billy and his older half-brother Willy live here. Willie has a disconcerting rictus grin which shows off a front tooth made out of something that looks like stainless steel. His laugh is an alarming machine-gun staccato. I can't figure out if there are any parents, but certainly not tonight. Anyway, these guys apparently hunt game in the fall and trap furs in the winter and sell the pelts. Pretty soon a car full of more of Billy's friends show up with more beer. The party ratchets up another notch with the addition of several squealing teenage girls. By about midnight things finally quiet down, the friends go away and the boys tell us we are supposed to sleep out in the "skinning shed" in back. Then they look at each other for a second.

"Aw, fuck it! You can sleep on the floor in here, but just for tonight. Billy's mom gets back tomorrow, and you're gone!" When Willie talks, I'm mesmerized by the flashing of the silvery tooth, like a semaphore lamp blinking between ships. Then he says: "You guys are royally fucked, though, for getting out of Haines any time soon."

"Why's that?

"'Cause the run went up the creek already. Most of the people just passing through from the ferry already left. The big parade went by around five o-clock. People who live here don't have much need to drive to Burwash Landing on a regular basis."

In the morning we get out on the road at first light. There is fresh snow on the highway and more falling steadily. Two sets of wheel tracks are heading into town. No one has driven on the outbound lane at all. "Guess we didn't miss any rides this morning," I say brightly. We slog up the road a ways, lost in our own thoughts and hangovers, when we hear a car coming up from behind. It's the mad trappers, our hosts from last night, with very serious bad vibes looks on their faces. I'm thinking: 'who died?' Or maybe they want us to come back and help clean up before mom gets home? They roll down the passenger window and wave us up close. Willy informs us that someone ripped off a $100 bill out of the safe last night. No one has the combination so they never lock it. A big cannon of a nickel-plated handgun with a square barrel and a bore the diameter of a roll of dimes is sitting on the seat between them.

The four of us step off the road and have a little conference. None of us took it, we all claim. Still, we eye each other warily. Lots of their friends had been in and out, but we are the strangers. I own up to not being sure what a hundred dollar bill even looks like. I carry traveler's checks. Ed says he is carrying all his traveling money, over $600, in hundreds. We look at each other uncertainly. The station wagon rumbles, patiently idling, the exhaust sending up a plume of white steam in the frosty air.

"Well, I don't think they're gonna go away," Clapping Doug opines softly. "Did you see that fuckin' gun?"

"I'll go talk to them," says Ed and he gets into the back seat of the car. I spend some time looking straight up at the descending snowflakes and soon I have the sensation of levitating upward into the soft grey sky. Not a bad plan, actually. After a few minutes Ed gets back out. The tension has lessened a bit. "They say there's an abandoned building up the road a ways where we can stay. They'll take us up there."

I whisper to Ernie: "Maybe they don't want to shoot us here, right by the road?"

"Not funny, man! Did you see that fuckin' gun?" Still, we pile our stuff into the back and crowd into the back seat.

Up the road, when I get my pack out of the back of the wagon I ask Willie if they'd gotten their money back. "We'll never really know, will we?" he replies cryptically.

Once they're gone, Ed says he gave them a hundred dollar bill. "Did you see that fuckin' gun?"

"Yeah," I say, "it matched the dude's tooth." There was no way to ask him if it had been their hundred, or his.

# CHAPTER 4

## The Chilkat Hobo Hilton

The Hobo Hilton is a big two-story wooden frame building with no window glass and lots of holes in the walls. I think the place used to be a meeting hall of some sort. Just 30 or 40 feet up the hill from the road; it is a perfect hitchhiking base of operations. We make ourselves at home. We scrounge up a piece of roof tin and some rocks to make a fire brazier on the floor, build a fire, find ourselves some benches upstairs and get comfortable. The Fairbanks boys seem resigned to a long stay.

I stake out a corner of the room for my sleeping spot and stash my pack and guitar, but make sure my wallet and traveller's checks are in my pocket. I really don't know these guys that well. We all pitch in a few bucks and Ed heads back to town to get groceries and supplies. "Get a jug of wine!" yells Doug as Ed starts off.

While the boys seem content to hang out in the Hilton, I keep making futile attempts to get a ride. It's snowing a full-on blizzard now. I strap on the pack and guitar and stand by the road for an hour or two until my feet start to freeze, then slog back up to the house and warm up by the fire for a while. Clapping Doug comes down and waits with me for an hour or so.

"You're a persistent fucker, aren't you?" he comments. One car goes by, the guy glances at us but doesn't slow down. Low grey clouds begin to gather again and it gets colder. Doug shakes his head. "Call us if Ken Kesey's bus stops to pick us up, OK?"

"Yeah, no problem." I watch two or three cars go into town. An hour later, one of them comes back the other way. Grocery shopping perhaps? Quickie with the girlfriend? A little Ford Falcon with a US Post Office sign in the back window drives by, tire chains thrumming rhythmically on the snowy highway. A couple of hours later it heads back to town on the other side of the road. The postal gal waves at me with a quizzical look.

Hitch-hiking is best done by becoming Gary Snyder. My college buddy B.D. and I read a lot of Gary Snyder back in college. So I tried to stay in the zen-like bliss, or at least the OK-ness of the now and the here. Each moment is a bright bead, but it is better not to string them together. Don't keep checking the length of the necklace, as you have no control over how much longer it will get. But as hard as I try to maintain my zen *wa*, little "Oh Shit" moments of gloom and dread start to nibble at my confidence. I am truly stuck in the middle of nowhere. No, worse! The middle of nowhere would imply the possibility that other travelers would pass by, heading through or out of nowhere. But this is the end of the road to nowhere. Until next week's ferry, Haines is its own self-contained universe of nowhere.

What if Charlie's Alcan prognistication was right? Stranded, I'll run out of money. In desperation I'll marry a mousy local girl and settle down. Maybe the mad trappers will hire me as a part-time pelt skinner. Perhaps no one has ever intentionally chosen to be here. Maybe Haines is inhabited solely by drifted flotsam, left here by higher tides than we have now. Like dreamlike beings in a Franz Kafka story, they visualize leaving, but the struggle is so pointless the vision eventually recedes into myth.

That evening we cook up a hobo stew out of canned food and start making inroads into the gallon jug of Carlo Rossi Red Mountain Burgundy Ed got in town. The boys start up a poker game for matches, which have some small monetary value at first, but as the level in the jug goes down, the value of the matches goes up. Eventually, we are playing for major interests in each other's future prosperity. By the time we are ready to crash for the night, I pretty much own the rights to Doug's labor in perpetuity. He has become like my personal serf, and I am quizzing him about his skills so I can extract the maximum return on my property.

In the morning the snow has stopped and soon a low sun is peeking through a slot in the mountains. I pack my gear and prepare to resume my vigil by the highway, but first I walk about a bit in the crisp, still woods behind the Hilton. There are gravestones poking out of the snow between the trees. Old ones. Raven's heads, human faces and fishes incised in smooth grey stone top the pedestals. "—1876—Chief Donawock, Great Chief of the Chilkat Tribe." Black ravens are up in the white-flocked trees, like high contrast photos by Steichen or Ansel Adams. And when the sun is on them they flash molten platinum, not black at all. They make hollow clucking sounds in the still air, like beating a stick on a log, then a throaty wooden hoot-caw. When they move they start little sparkly avalanches of snow, which shimmer and glisten as they cascade from branch to branch.

Down on the road, time passes. The beads string together. I see the post office car go by again on her outbound trip. She's earlier today. A semi with a trailer comes along, my thumb goes out at a jaunty angle and I exert all my psychic powers in an attempt to make him stop through the sheer steely force of my will. His psychic receptors must be tuned to a different channel. The big rig reminds me of the time BD and I were hitching back to San Jose from the Mexico border. We'd spent a day and a half stuck at a God-forsaken four-corner in the Mojave Desert near Barstow. No one would stop. But at least vehicles came by now and then. Half a pre-fab house had wheeled slowly through a left turn, heading north. The open side was sheeted off with clear plastic. When the other half came, we talked about slitting the plastic, throwing our packs in and jumping in after. We figured we'd be living good in the living room until the rig rolled up to some empty lot in Fresno or wherever the hell the house was going. Back in the now I stamp my frozen feet and yearn for some of that desert heat.

A little yellow Fiat roadster goes by. It's got a ski rack on the roof piled with lumps of gear under a canvas tarp. A luggage rack on top of the trunk is similarly laden. Small and full, the Fiat is an unlikely ride. Still, I waggle my thumb hopefully. The driver looks at me curiously but keeps going. I resume my disconsolate pacing, trying to stay warm. About five minutes later the Fiat comes back heading the other way, flips a U in the middle of the highway and rolls to a stop.

"Man, you look stuck. I just had to come back. Where are you heading?"

"Cordova . . . Alaska . . . Outta here will do!"

"I'm going to Fairbanks. I think I could fit you in."

"Oh! Great!" He starts to rearrange some stuff in the little jump seat area behind the bucket seats.

"Guitar will fit back here. I'll strap your pack under the tarp on the trunk."

I yell up the hill to the Hilton. "Hey! Got a ride! No more room, though!"

The Fairbanks boys come out on the front porch. Ed yells: "Good luck, Matt!"

"Same to you! Hey, Doug! I'm forgiving your debt! You're free!"

They wave morosely as we ride away.

The little Fiat is piloted by a recently retired merchant marine sailor on his way to Fairbanks to start a new life far from the sea. He spent a couple of days in Haines waiting for better weather before heading in to the interior. We climb up and over the Chilkat Pass, past an unmanned Canadian Border crossing and into the vast wilds of the Yukon. The snow starts again on the pass. We startle a lynx in a snowdrift by the side of the road. In his mouth he is carrying a limp white bunny with oversized feet. Farther along we top the crest of a windy hill and are surrounded by dozens of large grey and white falcon-like birds, darting and swooping in the snow squalls blowing between the skinny fir trees. The sailor says they are Peregrines—falcons. The trees are getting smaller and sparser. The land is dropping into a huge valley. The snow stops and the air clears. We can see for a hundred miles. Far in the distance is a giant lake. Beyond that, another great rampart of mountains. Miles pass with no fences, no side roads, no sign that any people have been here since the last mastodon hunters camped nearby, except for whoever punched this dirt road through the middle of it. We reach the lake and drive alongside its frozen expanse, past jumbled piles of fragmented ice pushed up onto the shore by some irresistible force. We cross back into Alaska a little before dark. We are on a vast rolling plain dusted with blowing snow. The trees are wretched, malnourished-looking little firs, maybe 15 feet high. To the south, huge white mountains remind me of pictures of the Himalayas. We sleep that night next to the Fiat in his little two-man tent. My clothes and my jacket plus the sleeping bag barely keep me warm.

# CHAPTER 5

## Quinn the Eskimo

I'd come North to the Future, just like it says on the license plates. I was in Alaska instead of graduate school. I was breaking my parents' hearts. I hadn't really come up with the idea all by myself, however. It was mostly B.D. Clausen's fault.

Freshman roommates at Colorado College were assigned randomly to the double rooms. I had lugged my first load of stuff, my little portable stereo and an orange crate full of records, up the stairs and in the door when I met him. A plaid flannel shirt, heavy black Oshkosh pants, kinda short brown hair. A pile of his stuff was in one corner. Not the college student stuff I had, like typewriter, record player, and rock concert posters from the Fillmore West, but cross-country skis, downhill skis, snowshoes, ice skates, Sorel snow boots, a backpack full of clothes, a compound bow and a quiver of arrows. I'm thinking: a bow and arrows, fer crissakes! What the hell is going on here, the last of the Mohicans? He smiled, stuck out his hand.

"I'm BD, you must be Matt Mankiewicz? Hey, pick whichever bunk and closet and desk you want. I'll stow my gear in the ones you don't use."

"It's all the same to me," I said, but then I noticed the big south-facing window. "How about I take the desk on the west side of the window so the afternoon sun doesn't melt my records."

"Hey, great! You've got a stereo! Didn't bring one." Geez, the guy's got snowshoes but no stereo? "Got some albums, though. What kind of music you into?" he asked.

"Rock and Roll, Blues, Beatles, Cream . . . ?" I had a moment of anxiety. It was 1967. Music was the crucial litmus test of the culture wars. What if he had a box of Buck Owens or Lawrence Welk albums under the snowshoes? Things could get ugly fast.

What a relief when he said: "Mine are mostly Soul music. You know, Motown, Aretha, Otis. I used to listen to the Negro radio station from over in Anchorage."

B.D. Clausen was from the fishing village of Cordova, in Alaska. The Clausens were commercial fishermen. They lived part of the time on an island in Prince William Sound, where BD's grandfather used to have a fox farm, and part of the time in Cordova, a town of about 2,000 people with no road to it. Access to the town from the rest of the world was by a State-run ferryboat, which came twice a week, and an airport. BD's mother, very fond of poetry, had christened him Byron Dante, and his father had immediately abbreviated it to B.D.

After that first year we weren't always roommates, but stayed friends. When BD was around, the world was crisper, the colors a little more intense, little things seemed to have more . . . significance, or humor. Competent and self-contained, he was like some modern-day John Muir. On winter weekends we would take off on cross-country ski trips into the high country around Colorado Springs. He seemed to have been born with the long, narrow skis on his feet. I would struggle along behind him as he glided across the world with ten-foot strides. As a boy he had run trap lines in the winters, skiing a twenty-mile loop to check his traps. He knew how to fine-tune the wax on his skis until he could ski up slopes like a monstrous fly.

We read Gary Snyder and Thoreau and John Muir, Tom Wolfe and Kesey and Kurt Vonnegut. We were feeling around for a better way of being with nature and with other people. We wanted lives that were healthier, more harmonious, less materialistic than the American Way as we saw it, with its colonial war and fast food diet, its corporate conformity and its contempt for other cultures and their wisdom.

My sophomore year roommate was Barry Roake, who insisted we call him Roach. With a curly blond fright-wig 'fro and a backpack full of tie-dyed tee-shirts, he was a marijuana-smoking San Francisco kid who could play the guitar, drums, fiddle, you name it, and he sang like Jesse Colin Young. We started playing together, trying to be Simon and Garfunkel or Crosby and Stills. When we got the groove right and really played it was a rush. A high with no hangover. It transformed me out of one-ness into group-ness. I know it sounds kinda gay, but it was intimate, like dancing. Pretty soon we were doing little gigs at coffee houses and parties. We had big plans for rock-n-roll back on the west coast after college.

Roach and I and my self-styled hippie friends were becoming partial to pot, but BD was more of a beer guy. When the pressures of school began to build he would say: "Come on, Witz. Let's take a little barley pop break." Armed with our fake ID's, we would pile into Brutus and make a pilgrimage to the Kachina Bar in Colorado Springs. BD could drink as effortlessly as he skied, pacing himself like a marathon runner, saving a sprint for the last hour before the bar closed. When he got going he was extremely funny and, I suppose, quite charming, judging from the attitudes of various young lovelies who tried to keep up with him on these debauches. He explained that since the Alaska drinking age was 19, he'd gotten his fake ID at 16 and had been in training years longer than we had. In Cordova, where he went to high school, he was too well known to fool anyone with it, but whenever he was in Valdez or Anchorage he'd passed as a young-looking 19 year old.

Despite his competence and popularity, BD worried that he was a hick. He'd never had a TV when he was a kid. They didn't even have a phone on his island, and used the marine radio on their boat to get messages in to town. It bothered him that he was out of sync with the homogenized America the rest of us were busy rebelling against. But then he would embark on homesick stories of bears, otters, trapping beaver and lynx in the winters, vast runs of salmon in the summer, and pristine bays and forests which have never known axe or chainsaw. He told tales of the seasonal malady known as fishing fever, and of the staggering money that could be made in a few days of good fishing.

"Man, it sounds great! I'd love to go up there and do something real, like commercial fishing," I said.

"Yeah, we get *cheechakos*—greenhorns—coming off practically every ferry that comes to town. Heading to the Last Great Wild West show. They think they're Daniel Boone, wrass'lin the American wilderness, but most of them are just clueless goomers. North to the Future in a Winnebago. Or they're sociopaths who hate government, rules, and laws. The Land of the Midnight Sun is the last refuge of scoundrels, prophets, criminals and hermits. Now we're even gettin' hippies." He looked at me out of the corner of his eye and grinned. "'Course, even a hippie can get work in the canneries."

At college, we were insulated from the Vietnam War by our student deferments, but in the fall of our junior year, the war became real for BD Clausen. BD's little brother Will graduated from Cordova High School in May, was drafted and sent to Fort Lewis for basic training, and deployed to the Central Highlands of Vietnam. By Halloween he was in a grave in the military cemetery in Seattle. BD spent weeks brooding in his dorm room like a wounded bear. He rebuffed me when I tried to talk to him. He rarely went to classes or the cafeteria. But by Christmas he dried his eyes, harnessed his pain, and became one of the leaders of the anti-war movement on the CC Campus.

About that time he met Melissa. Lithe, blithe and blond, she had a smile like a warm embrace. Still, she somehow conveyed that she was the smartest one in the room. When she met BD, she saw something she wanted. At first, he even complained that she followed him around like a puppy dog, but he soon succumbed to her charms, or her persistence. Melissa had been raised by her mom. "My orthodontist father dumped us when I was little and started a whole new family with his slutty dental assistant."

The three of us and Roach and his girlfriend leased a big house off campus for our senior year. It was a faux-western Bonanza-meets-South Fork monstrosity on about an acre, owned by some rich Texans who were never there. The huge kitchen had a cattle branding-iron themed dinner service for twenty-four. Man, the dirty-dish pile-ups really got out of hand! That was the year I grew the beard and mustache, and my dark brown hair got longer and longer. Melissa thought it made me look like Jesus Christ. I told her no one actually knew what Jesus looked like, but she was still pretty sure he had the same intense brown eyes I did.

My folks fell in love with Melissa when they came to visit me that Thanksgiving. I think my mom secretly hoped Melissa would break up with BD and marry me. But she was my best buddy's girl, and I related to her more like a sister than a potential mate. That was probably for the best, as Melissa was pretty mellow about most things, but had no tolerance for infidelity, real or imagined. Despite the occasional temptation, usually magnified by what we called "having the beer goggles on," BD remained relatively faithful to her and usually left the Kachina with his relationship, if not his brain cells, intact. I, on the other hand, hadn't had a long-term girl friend since my soap-opera train-wreck with the lovely Gina, which had consumed my sophomore year. So I succumbed occasionally to the honky-tonk homily that the girls all look prettier at closing time.

At the end of his senior year, BD went back to Cordova to fish the summer salmon runs and think about his future. He had a degree in biology and environmental studies, whatever the heck that was. Melissa had graduated as well, and went with him. I really wanted to head up there too, but I was running a little behind on credits and completely behind on money. My plan was work a little during the summer and come back for the fall semester to try to graduate in the winter. I was on the 4.5 year plan and losing patience with my academic career. A degree in Psychology? I ought to have my head examined!

# CHAPTER 6

## Dodging the Big Burrito

When I finally graduated in January, I spent a few weeks boxing up and shutting down my life in Colorado. Most of my close friends had graduated last June. Other students I didn't really know were living in the big house. That extra semester had been a little strange and disjointed. I felt like the guy who drew the short straw and had to stay and clean up after a fabulous party. But I had met up with Sharon on one of those late nights at the Kachina. She worked at a western wear store and lived in a doublewide trailer on a few acres near town. She had a little dancer's body and fine, silky brown hair. I guess she was a cowgirl of sorts, at least she liked to play that part. To her credit, she did have a horse on the place. When we did it she liked to swing up on top and whisper little rodeo encouragements. "Cowgirl up!" "Easy, big guy." "OK, let 'er buck!" She was a couple of years older than I was, and she called me her college boy. Her husband worked at the college, in the drama department. She never really said, but I got the idea that he might have been at least partly gay. She said he wasn't too uptight about her "boys" as long as she didn't flaunt them around. I knew we weren't in love, but we were certainly in lust, and I was flattered, and pretty darned pleased to be her boy toy when she'd call me. When I told her I was going away, Sharon said she'd miss me but plainly there wasn't much pain. I guess I was mostly saddened by visions of my impending celibacy.

So Brutus and I headed back to San Jose to visit some of my old high school friends and, of course, the folks. The apricot and prune orchards of the bucolic Santa Clara Valley of my childhood had long ago been bulldozed into piles and burned. Instead of miles of fruit trees and tall, gingerbread Victorian farm houses, each with its even taller shingle-sided water tank, I rolled past miles of nearly identical cookie-cutter tract homes built in the housing booms of the 50s and 60s. As I pulled into the driveway of the one I grew up in, my father Moe was standing on the front lawn, examining the grass with a pensive look. He had on a pair of tan dungarees and a Hawaiian shirt. He was 50 pounds overweight. He had a passion for big, nasty cigars. Illegal Cuban ones whenever possible. A half-smoked one was planted in the corner of his mouth. I got out of the car.

"Hi Dad."

"Goddamn crabgrass, Matthew. It never sleeps, even in the winter. So, how's tricks?"

"Well, I'm done with school."

"Yes, *Mazel Tov*! Your mother is pleased."

He didn't sound especially pleased, though. It wasn't a degree in business administration, so what was the point? He was used to me teasing him that he was the archetypical fat Jewish cigar-chomping capitalist. He didn't mind. He'd say: "That's what I am. Shouldn't I look the part?" Other than the cigars, his true passion was his ever-expanding chain of fast food restaurants. Originating in San Jose, "Taco Moe's: Home of the Foot-long Burrito," had gathered investors and momentum, gone corporate, and spread its octopus-like franchise tentacles up and down the California coast. At some point in the 60's there had been an investor rebellion. As my Dad put it: "They got some smarty-pants marketing wizard who said the name didn't have 'pizzazz.' What the hell is pizzazz? We're selling tacos, not pizzazz!" They did market research on "Taco Mo`le" for a while, but too many gringos thought it referred to the rodents that infest your lawn, rather than the spicy Mexican sauce. "Taco Ole'!" didn't roll off the tongue right, so to my father's delight they returned to the original name, but insisted on a garish plastic logo of an inanely grinning Mexican in huaraches, serape and a floppy sombrero, "to add authenticity". A Taco Moe franchise could now be encountered in half the towns in the state. Now that big corporate money ran the show Moe wasn't getting rich on the deals, but he made a nice living with what looked to me like minimal effort. Still, as the only son, I had been groomed from childhood as a crown prince who would someday bestride a burrito empire.

Mom came out on the porch and launched into a gushing monologue of welcome, punctuated by increasingly insistent demands that I come inside and eat something. Chela, my Mexican/Portuguese mother, has never tired of pointing out to my father the absurdity of Moe Mankiewicz, a Polish Jew, making his living selling "beaner food". She had other aspirations for her son. I was the first college graduate ever in her family, and she hoped I would enter a profession.

I spent a few weeks at home; back in the same room I'd had as a kid. All my old stuff was still there. Psychedelic Jefferson Airplane posters on the wall, the old Revell plastic sailing ship models I had lovingly assembled and painted in my pre-teen years, pictures of my friends and me on backpack trips in the Sierras, the prized canoe racing trophy from Boy Scouts. My kid sister Sandra, who was still in high school, referred to it as "The Shrine."

"She dusts in there, but she never moves anything. Won't change it. It's like one of those weird cargo cults down in the South Pacific islands you read about in National Geographic. You know, where they think if they make a runway and some decoy airplanes out of brush, the transport planes will come back full of cargo like during the War? But hey, maybe it worked. You're back."

"Not for long, Sis."

The weirdest thing was how small everything had gotten. My room was now tiny. My street, that had seemed as big as a football field when we had played in it as kids, could be crossed in a couple of strides. When I walked down the block, the lots and houses were like miniatures in a museum diorama of the California suburbs. Somewhere along the line I'd nibbled the wrong side of Alice's mushroom. "How the hell am I going to stuff myself back into one of these little boxes?" I wrote BD a note and mailed it to his Cordova post office box, informing him that I would be rolling in to Cordova sometime in mid April, so he'd better hide the whiskey and the good silverware.

When things got too claustrophobic "at home" I would look up one of my neighborhood friends, or stop by to see Stephanie, my old sort-of-girlfriend. We had dated in high school, partly from a mildly lustful mutual attraction, but also because we were both in the same smarty-leftie going-to-college social group, so our dates were friendly and pleasant even when we weren't totally steaming up the windows of the old '55 Buick. It had been California, but before the 1967 Summer of Love. We were teetering on the brink of a sexual revolution, a psychedelic revolution, a cultural revolution, maybe even a genteel flower-powered political revolution, but we weren't quite there yet. Even though the Beatles had already urged us to "turn on your mind, relax, and float downstream," we didn't smoke pot in high school, though we were pretty sure we wanted to. Good girls like Stephanie didn't have sex with boys. They didn't even give them blowjobs like the Catholic School girls from Mother Butler and Presentation High School purportedly did. In some ways, the bedrock knowledge of these facts, "the rules," had been as much a relief as a disappointment to me back then. But there had been lots of kissy-face, lots of tongue. My hand had read the Braille edition of labia and clitoris through a damp, steaming layer of Capri pants. No hands inside the waistband! I had had the occasional guilty triumph of a dry hump orgasm against her sharp pubic bone. The background music was Hendrix's "Foxy Lady" or *Fast talkin', slow walkin', good lookin'* Mohair Sam." But the real theme song had been the Beach Boys lamenting: *"wouldn't it be nice if we were older, then we wouldn't have to wait so long."*
So now we talked about which high school friend was married to whom; who was working at IBM; who was at Yale Law; who was in Vietnam; who had come back from Vietnam in a box. She had a fiancée. I was going to Alaska. We looked at each other a few times with a wistful, woulda-shoulda look that said: I don't think we are ever going to have sex, are we? I guess that boat had sailed.
Back home, I floated around aimlessly, read a little, played my guitars. I'd put my Fender Stratocaster and the Yamaha steel string back in their same old corner of the bedroom along with the old Goya classical. I made a couple of trips up to San Francisco to see Roach and whichever rock gods were playing at the Fillmore West. The Cream concert was total bliss, helped along by the mescaline Roach had scored from one of his freak friends in the Haight. Roach was in a band too, but he

complained that the other guys were so loaded all the time that they could barely play. "That might work for the Grateful Dead, but not for us lesser mortals." He tried to convince me to stay and take over for the other guitarist, who'd just gotten drafted. I said I'd think about it, but my heart was set on Alaska.

I could tell from their sidelong glances that everyone in my family was wondering just what the hell I was going to do, and when. I had tried a couple of times to talk with my mom about my Alaska plans, but somehow she would out-segue me into her misty-eyed reminiscences of her abortive college career, and how she should have continued her studies.

Mom, Graciela Pacheco Gomes de Sa', was the last child and only daughter of Francisco Gomes de Sa', a Portuguese immigrant from the Azores Islands with a large dairy farm in the Central Valley town of Los Banos, and Maria Elena Pacheco, the daughter of a Californiano Mexican family that had been in California since before the Yankees came. If there is such a thing as a Latina-American princess she was it. She was her daddy's angel. When she enthralled my father's heart, Graciela (Chela for short) was a tall dark-haired beauty with a dazzling smile.

Moe was working evenings at the Buster Brown shoe store and Chela was attending San Jose State College, planning to get a teaching credential. My mother does a very funny Cinderella/Prince Charming routine about their first encounter over boxes of black pumps. Totally flustered and discombobulated by her presence, he never did produce a pair that fit, but she finally purchased one just to put him out of his agony. She exchanged them the next day to get a chance to see him again. Her sense of humor was a godsend during my childhood misbehaviors, as she generally succumbed to the hilarity of a situation before any serious punishment could be meted out.

After dinner one evening the conversation came gingerly around to my plans. Now that I had finally finished college, the Taco Business held out its arms in a greasy embrace. A whole franchise for my very own! Mom casually brought up the graduate school plans of her best friend's daughter. With great rhetorical skill I told my father that the foot long burrito would have to wait. I was going to Alaska the end of March. His jaw locked up so tight he bit the end right off the Cohiba Banker he was lighting. We went around and around about it for a few days. My mother reached the point of saying:

"Moe, let him go for a while! It's just a lark. He'll get it out of his system and be back in a few weeks."

"As far as I can tell, that four and a half years at that ski bum college was just a lark, too. What kind of bird did we raise here, Chelita? When I was his age I was working two jobs! I had a wife! I'd fought Hitler for two years! I was ready to start my own business! I tell you, its time for this *mishegas* to stop!"

"Moe, he's over 21. You can't force him."

And that was, after all, the bottom line. We were talkin' free, white and 21 here.

Finally he shook his head in despair. "For years I bust my ass building a business to give you a good life. I pay to send you to some fancy college. I try to make it so you won't have to start with nothing and struggle like I did! But are you grateful? Does a chicken have lips?"

As I was carrying my things out to Brutus, I received my father's parting benediction. "Call us now and then, or write. Your mother worries you'll freeze to death or be eaten by a bear."

# CHAPTER 7

## Cordova

The ferry ride to Cordova across Prince William Sound was a lot like the last half of the Inside Passage trip, spectacularly beautiful and wild. The bays and headlands were covered with virgin forests of great hemlocks and fir, not the pathetic little pecker trees of the interior. Steep snow-covered mountains reared up thousands of feet high, even on the islands. The ferry rounded the last headland and the town came in sight. It perched on the lower slopes of a crotch between two mountains on the east side of Orca Inlet. There were several canneries along the shore, clusters of corrugated steel buildings built on pilings over the water, with cranes and unloading docks and white plumes of steam coming out of pipes in the roofs. Hundreds of gulls were wheeling and screaming, diving into the water around outfall pipes underneath. I could see the masts and booms of fishing boats in a little harbor behind a boulder breakwater at the base of the town. The ferry dock was just before the row of canneries, not four miles from town like in Haines. That was a promising start.

I walked into town in a cold drizzle of rain, past run-down wood frame houses half buried in dirty snow. The tops of old vehicles, a kid's tricycle, fishing gear, and other unidentifiable objects poked out of oddly shaped mounds of it. It was 9:30 in the morning but the town seemed asleep, maybe still in hibernation. A couple of blocks of newer buildings built out of cement block or steel siding made up "downtown," but the sidewalks were long decks of wooden planks like some old western town. A raven was talking to himself like a burned-out wino, making wooden clucking and groaning sounds. The big black bird was the only other pedestrian walking along the wet sidewalk.

I'd heard stories of the Club Bar, BD's favorite hangout. The door was off a little alley, not on the main street. A grey and black speckled dog, some kind of mongrel mix of spaniel and lab and God-knows-what-else was outside guarding the door like the bouncer at a sleazy bar. He gave me a puzzled look as I went in. It felt like he was going to card me.

A wooden ship's figurehead of a buxom, bare-breasted girl dominated the low-ceilinged barroom. The walls were hung with antique outboard motors, propellers, a ship's wheel. Several men sat at the bar like permanent fixtures in the décor. Two others were shooting a languorous game of pool. A girl with a streaked blonde bouffant hairdo was chatting with the bartender. She was dressed like a vision from a Texas whorehouse, white cowboy boots, pink shorts and a short, fringed leatherette vest over a white shirt with puffy sleeves. I sat down a couple of stools away. She glanced at me, then returned to her agitated conversation with the bartender. "So Nick won't leave her, even though he likes me better! He's just a stubborn asshole!" The bartender nodded in mute disinterested agreement and gestured to me for my order.

"It's breakfast, how about a screwdriver?" He fixed me one; opening holes in the top of a big can of orange juice with a beer can opener. "I'm looking for B.D. Clausen. Has he been around?"

"I think he's out herring seining . . . hey Max, you seen B.D. lately?" One of the pool players said: "Didn't he get a job with Dickie Hanson for herring? I think Melissa, that pretty girl he's with, is cooking for them."

At this point the girl interjected, "His pal Duck might know. You a friend of his or something?"

"Yeah, from Colorado."

"Oh! I'm from New Mexico! We're neighbors!" she bubbled enthusiastically, "or is that Utah?"

"Both," I replied politely. I'm thinking, uh-oh a 25-watt brain in a 500-watt body. Still, she's friendly enough. "Where in New Mexico?"

"Las Cruces. You ever been there?"

"No, only Taos."

"Oh yeah, that's a groovy place!" She finished her drink. "I've got to get going now, I work down at the Cordova House?"

"So how would I find this Duck person?"

"He has an apartment right down the street from here. I'll point you."

I took the last pull on my drink and paid while the girl put on a huge shaggy coat over her outfit. "Take it easy now Vicki," the bartender admonished as we headed for the door.

"I'll take it any way I can get it!" she replied giggling.

No one was home at Mr. Duck's apartment. I scrounged through my pockets for a pencil stub and started a note on the back of my ferry ticket. As I was scribbling, I heard boots clomping up behind me. I turned to see a thickset, black-haired, round-faced guy in brown Carhart coveralls standing behind me.

"May I help you?" he asked with a wry grin.

"Uh, well, someone said the Duck, I mean, the guy who lives here is a friend of BD Clausen. I'm trying to find him."

"BD's out fishing. Actually, he's out waiting to be fishing, which is what herring fishing mostly is." He eyed my pack and guitar. "Just get to town?" He had a hint of some accent. His lower jaw stuck out farther than his upper, and it hardly moved when he spoke. His "the" and "that" sounded like "ta" and "tat."

"Yeah, just this morning. I'm Matt, a buddy of his from Colorado. When do you think he might be back?"

"Well, here's ta deal. They just went on 24-hour notice from Fish and Game, which means there are lots of herring, but they're not ripe yet. So the boats are all out on the grounds, 'cause fishing might open tomorrow, or it might be a week or so."

"So, herring, like, pickled herring? I wondered where they came from."

"No, the Japs eat the roe, the eggs. We catch 'em, salt 'em, squeeze ta eggs out and sell 'em to the Japanese trading companies. Big delicacy over there. Beaucoup bucks. But ta eggs have to be just right, so we wait for the Japs to say go. That's what they're doing. Waiting for days, maybe weeks, for a chance to fish for a couple hours, 'till the fleet catches the quota."

"They just eat the eggs, huh? What about the fish?"

"Into the grinder, into the bay. Crab food. Hey, I'm being rude, I was just coming home to grab a quick sandwich. I'm working on my boat. But come on in. I'm Duck Petroff."

"Matt Mankiewicz. Thanks, but I don't want to be a bother."

"Hey, suit yourself. You have someplace to stay till BD gets back?"

"No, not really. I was thinking about trying to get a cannery job, maybe stay in a bunkhouse?"

"Mmm, lots of cannery jobs, but not too many bunkhouses. Hotels will kill you. Too expensive. You can always stay out at Hippie Cove. It's warming up."

"What's Hippie Cove?"

"Shelter Cove, just past the Ferry Dock. Couple of old cabins and kind of a little tent city out there where transients and hippies camp out in ta summer. No one hassles you."

"Hey, thanks for the tip. So, you know if any of these canneries is hiring?"

"Well, they're just running crab right now. Too early for any ting else. Morpac has the most crab boats, so they're staying pretty busy."

"Thanks a lot, Duck!"

"Pleasure's mine, my friend. Best of luck with your endeavors."


The Morpac cannery was built on several acres of heavy wooden decking supported like a centipede on hundreds of pilings driven into the bottom of the bay. Old two story wood-frame, board sided buildings were clustered about a great barn-like corrugated metal warehouse. From within came a grinding, rumbling noise, the sound of running water and the occasional whooshing roar of live steam. The office was in one of the smaller buildings. I went in. A curvaceous woman with mink-brown hair in a shoulder-length flip was writing in a large ledger. Her fuzzy lime green v-necked sweater was an explosion of color in the drab office. She looked up inquiringly.

"Hello?"

"Um, any job openings here? I'm looking for work."

She looked me over for a moment. Her face brightened with a smile. "Oh you are, are you?" She appeared to find something amusing in this. "We're just running crab right now. Do you have any experience in cannery work? Ever butcher crab?"

"Well, no, but I'm sure I could learn."

"Oh, I'm sure you could too, but you'll have to check with the foreman to see if he needs anybody. Just go back in the plant and ask for George. If he gives you a job, you'll have to come back here and fill out a form. Leave your pack here, and the ukulele. Oh—and you'll have to wear a hat." This last part seemed to fill her with glee, and she sang it out in a honeyed Glinda-the-good-witch tone. I had a wool cap somewhere in my pack, but she instantly reached into a drawer and pulled out a paper soda-jerk hat. Grinning broadly, she dangled it tauntingly at the end of her fully extended arm. "Health regulations."

I felt like a total dork, walking through the place in the white paper hat. I approached a group of short Filipino guys with brooms and long handled scrub brushes, hosing and scrubbing metal gratings and equipment. I asked them for George. "Over there" one of them replied, pointing at a portly guy with a droopy moustache, suspendered rain pants, rubber boots and a yellow CAT Diesel cap. George was lowering a large steel basket filled with steaming hot crab sections into a metal tank full of cold water by means of an electric hoist on a steel track over his head. An inch of water was flowing across the cement floor. I sloshed over to him.

"The lady in the office told me to talk to you about a job."

He glanced at me for a moment with no apparent reaction, unhooked the basket from the hoist, and walked away, striding purposefully toward a large, square, stainless steel tank. I followed him around like a dutiful dog, splashing through the water on the floor. At some point I managed to step into a deeper channel, I almost fell, and frigid water poured over the top of my boot. George adjusted the control knob on some sort of steam line to the cooker tank, which was full of boiling water, then turned and eyed me thoughtfully. He lifted his hat and scratched his head. "Yeah . . . be here at 8:00 tomorrow." He turned and ambled off, bellowing "Florio! Get the covers back on these gutters before someone breaks a leg." I stood there for a moment while his first statement soaked into my brain like the icy water soaking into my boots. 8:00, that was easy.

I squished back to the office and told the woman that I was supposed to be back at 8 the next morning.

"That worked out well for you, huh?" She beamed at me as she handed me applications and W-2 form. "Just get to town?"

"Yeah, today's ferry. I didn't expect to get a job this easily."

"Well, we have a pretty quick turn-over here. Be sure to fill out this part." She leaned over the counter and indicated a section of the form, but my attention strayed up to her generous cleavage and the top of some black undergarment. She was probably in her thirties with a pleasant, lively face and little smile wrinkles around her eyes. She smelled warm, good. I wrenched my attention back to business.

"Do you have a bunkhouse for your workers?"

"Oh, of course, you need a place to stay." Her voice oozed concern. "Can't help you" she concluded abruptly. "We have a fisherman's bunkhouse, but it's not open 'till salmon. We have a few other rooms but our Filipino guys, our regulars have them. Don't you know anyone in town?"

"Well, I know BD Clausen, but he's out herring fishing."

"Oh, that cute little Clausen boy! He fishes for us during salmon. Anyway, good luck finding a place. There's always Hippie Cove."

"Well, thanks," I said as I passed my completed forms back to her and turned to squish my way toward my backpack.

"See you tomorrow," she trilled "and you can keep your little hat, it's on us." My hand shot to my head and crumpled up the paper hat. I felt my ears start to glow hot and red. Fortunately, my hair was long enough to cover them. Nerd exits, stage left.

# CHAPTER 8

## The Visqueen Palace.

Shelter Cove was a little lagoon at the mouth of a stream that poured down the steep face of the mountain on the north side of town. A small abandoned cannery building that had fallen off its pilings in the big '64 quake lay at an impossible angle at the edge of the lagoon. A very humble old bus with a smokestack sticking out of the roof was parked on a gravel spit nearby. Someone had tarred the top with aluminum leak-stop paint, which had run down the sides in places, making it look as though the roof had been subjected to metal-melting high heat in some past cataclysm. Up in the trees I spied a couple of little cabins, chimney smoke trailing up into the misty rain. I took a look around the area and could see places where people had camped and left their litter. It all felt a little too 'occupied' for my taste.

I went a little farther down the road, which crossed the mouth of the lagoon by way of a raised gravel-fill roadbed with two huge steel culverts punched through for the water to pass. On the far side of the lagoon a great rotting wooden barge rested on the mud flats. Three massive rudders, connected to each other with a system of metal steering bars hung off the stern. Beyond that was a little tree-covered hill, which the stream had cut away from the rest of the mountain. A bald eagle soared by and landed in a snaggly treetop. I could hear the whiff of wind in his wing feathers as he braked for his landing. His white head and tail and yellow beak and feet contrasted starkly with the dark body like someone had grabbed parts out of the wrong bins at the eagle assembly facility.

I walked into the woods twenty yards or so. Large trees stood every ten or fifteen feet, blocking the sky. Others had toppled, making long horizontal walls. Between them was almost no undergrowth, and no snow, but everything was covered in a soft carpet of thick green moss a foot deep. Man, this is great! It's like some troll's living room with a big shag carpet! I picked a spot with no nasty roots beneath and strung my tube tent between two trees. The moss made a soft comfortable bed of my thin pad and bag.

I slept well that night and the next morning I dreamed of Gina. Of her soft, round places. Of our early days when we had first discovered the thermo-nuclear mind-body meld of sex with each other. In my dream, we were making wonderful slow lubricious love in her dorm room. Then she needed to pee, then her phone rang, then her roommate came back, then she had to go to class, then I woke up with a tremendous hard-on and a sad sense of loss. I finished what we had started in the dream with the aid of a little fantasy and hand cream, then I lay in my bag a while and thought of her.

When we met we had both been technical virgins, but together we had changed the world by inventing sexual intercourse. We strutted around for several months acting as if we held the patent on it like Edison and his light bulb. But gradually, each of us had begun to inventory all the irritating things wrong with the other. I had recoiled in horror from the glimpses of my carefully hidden imperfections as they were reflected in the mirror of her dissatisfactions. Will she still want me when she finds out how cowardly and lame I really am? And if I love her, why does she bug me so? If she loves me, why won't she change just one or two of those things that she knows bug me so? We met each other's inchoate petitions for redress of grievances with stubborn anger. Unretractable words were spoken. We broke up. We were miserable. We had wildly passionate and tearful reunitings, followed a week or a month later by the sullen realization that we were still just as disappointed with each other as before. Finally, we realized that we had broken whatever it was, and that we would have to try again, elsewhere, for love.

It had gotten colder in the night. I pulled on my frosty pants. My rock-hard boot-sickles glittered evilly in frozen reminder of yesterday's soaking. I got a fresh pair of socks from my pack and was truly grateful that I could put on the new pair of X-tra Tuff rubber boots I'd bought yesterday at the hardware store. I dug out my navy watch cap so there would be no repeat of the paper hat caper, ate a banana and a handful of granola and headed off to work. When I arrived, George the Foreman told me to go get a time card from Donna and clock in. As it was Sunday, she began teasing me about missing church. She had on another of those soft cashmere sweaters she filled so nicely, and that pixie grin and flirtatious banter stirred a replay of my earlier tumescence. Geez, I'm turning into some sort of goat! But then I was out the door and off to the locker area.

Like a knight preparing for battle, I donned company-issued rain pants, hooded coat and thick rubber gloves. George then instructed me in the fine art of crab butchering. The live snow crab had been unloaded from the crab boat early that morning and placed into large wheeled tubs, one of which was located at my butchering machine. The machine, mounted on a waist-high pedestal, consisted of a small iron triangle and a whirling stiff-bristled brush. George held the crab by the legs, left legs in his left fist, right legs in his right. Then he rapped the center of the crab's body on the iron triangle. The top of the shell popped off and the crab was now in two sections. Each body portion, below where the shell had been, was topped by a row of pink gills, like little grapefruit sections. He rubbed these on the spinning bristle brush for a moment and they came off, along with some nasty-looking green guts. When the section was clean, he tossed it into a metal cage like the ones he had been hoisting around the day before.

"There ya go. That's all there is to it. Just try not to break the goddamn legs off. When your basket's full, holler for a new one. When your tote's empty, holler for a new one. Florio there'll keep you butchers stocked." There were five other stations just like mine. Every hour or so we would stop and clear the crab shells and guts piling up around our boots, shoving them into the gutter with a push broom. The gutter ran to the grinder, then to the seagulls circling around the outfall pipes.

At first, I handled the crabs gingerly, taking care to avoid the claws at the ends of their first set of legs, or arms, or whatever, but I soon caught on to the process and realized that these deep-water dwellers were functioning in slow motion up here on the surface. Once I got beyond my fear of pinching injuries, I had some moments of moral revulsion at slaughtering the hapless crustaceans. This was soon replaced by callous indifference to their fate. "People don't feel guilty when they eat these guys, so why should the executioner feel bad?" The movements soon became automatic, boredom set in, and the hours crawled by at dream-slow quarter-speed.

I started breaking the monotony with a little acapella singing with one of the other butchers. "Whoopee tie yi yo, git along little crabbies. Its your misfortune, ain't none of my own." He had a pretty impressive baritone to go with my tenor, and we did some renditions of old Sam Cook and Nat Cole tunes. "Ramblin' Rose" always made the other workers smile. The other half of the duo was named Greg, but everybody called him Walrus. He was a tall, skinny guy with a big droopy mustache that extended clear past his shaved chin. It really did make him look like a walrus who'd gotten carried away on some extreme weight loss program. His droll sense of humor harmonized perfectly with his appearance. It turned out Walrus lived in one of the old cabins out at the Cove, the one with the wood-fired sauna by the creek. When he found out we were neighbors he told me that any time I saw smoke coming out of the sauna I should wander over for a steam.

The only other monotony breaker was lunch hour. The cannery provided sandwiches and coffee. If it wasn't raining or snowing, and George Foreman (as we took to calling him) wasn't around, some of the crew would share a joint out on the back dock for dessert. After a few lungfuls of the Walrus's Alaskan homegrown, lovingly known as "Matanuska Thunderfuck," we'd sit and look out at the snow-shrouded islands across the inlet. The low sun of early spring pumped out a golden light. The air was cold crystal. God, it was all BD had said! The land was covered with mature spruce and hemlock. Bald eagles perched on the dead snags or flapped lazily along the beach. Sea otters paddled around the bay doing the backstroke and smacking clams on their bellies. The other side of the inlet had big sand flats that showed at low water. On the really low tides we would see people over there digging razor clams on the exposed sandbars. Higher up the mountains, open expanses of white showed where meadows of muskeg and shallow ponds waited for spring. The world still looked as it must have when the first natives paddled into the inlet.

Unfortunately, our stoned-out moments of reflection were often disrupted by Billy, an irritating, cocky little dick of a teenager who reacted to the repetition and boredom of the cannery by perfecting twisted forms of sadistic dementia. We would come upon strange, totem-like creations he'd formed by connecting several still-living crabs to each other, impaled together using their own, or other, claws and pincers. He'd secreted a little spinning rod and reel somewhere in the plant, and liked to "fly gulls" during the breaks. He would chum some seagulls in by tossing them little pieces of the herring the crabbers used as bait. Then he would put a piece on the little treble hook on the end of his line and cast it out. The gull would grab and swallow it in mid air and Billy, giggling hysterically, would fly the hapless bird like a kite. Finally, Walrus would bellow at him. "Knock it off Billy, you sick fuck!"

"Just watch, that little prick is going to grow up to be a serial killer," I intoned.

After my first day at work I stopped by the hardware store again. A big roll of heavy clear plastic Visqueen, a ball of 1/4" twine, a handful of nails and some round pebbles from the beach, and I had the fixin's for a palatial dwelling in the woods. I lashed a slender spruce spar to a tree up as high as I could reach to make a ridgepole. I flopped one end of the roll of plastic over it and pulled enough over so I could double it back to make a floor, then I lifted and lashed the other end of the spar to the other tree. I tied rocks into the outside edges of the plastic to make monkey fists to hold the ropes. These I tied to nearby trees to pull out my roof and walls. I now had a nice big plastic room 10 or 12 feet on a side. The fallen tree made a half-wall on one side. A large jagged muskeg-covered stump partially closed off one end. I could stand up to put my pants on in the morning. Anyone who has ever made a secret hideout as a kid knows the cozy, blissful sense of well being that comes from inhabiting a cleverly-constructed tree-house.

The next couple of evenings I came home from work, cooked up a little dinner on my tiny propane camp stove and kicked back on my sleeping bag reading or playing my guitar. I sent some postcards, informing my parents that I had survived, bragging to Roach and my San Jose friends about my adventures. I sent one to Charlie, Julie and Peter, keeping my pledge to "write if I got work."

The more time I spent there, however, the more I began to notice some minor flaws in my Visqueen Palace.

One, lack of footing. The floor, plastic over deep moss, was spongy and slippery. This was fine in the bedroom, but a problem in the living-dining room portion.

Two, lack of visibility. The term "clear" plastic was a misnomer. I had plenty of light, but could only discern vague shapes through the translucent walls.

Three, limited seating. I had no furniture, so my options were to stand, or to sit or lie on my sleeping bag.

The fourth day we had no crab boats, so I had a day off from work. I started my remodel project by scrounging around in the ruins of the toppled cannery. I found a small square table with a broken leg. Perfect. I broke off a second leg and nailed the legless side of the table to my fallen log to make a permanent table installation.

I found a rocking chair with all but one of the horizontal slats missing out of the back. Lacing some rope back and forth would remedy that. I took a small four-pane window off its hinges and mounted it in the lowest spot in my rotting muskeg stump. The real triumph, however, was my floor. A six-foot by six-foot stair landing made out of tongue and groove decking had hung off part of the cannery. This piece of ready-made floor was lying on the ground. But it was heavy. I struggled to lift it up on edge. Dragging it a quarter of a mile to my mansion was going to be daunting. Salvation came in the form of the Walrus, rolling into the Cove in his ancient VW bus. Together, we crab-walked the decking through the woods to my palace. "All you need is some cubist art on the walls to really tie this place together," Walrus suggested approvingly.

# CHAPTER 9

## Gimme Shelter

By Friday, it seemed I had spent half my life in the crab Auschwitz. I started looking longingly over the side of the dock at the godlike crewmen who bestrode the decks of the crab boats when they unloaded. I wanna be down there, not up here.

At the end of the day I went into the office to pick up my first week's check. "Find a place to stay yet?" Donna asked brightly.

"I've thrown together a little plastic palace out at the Cove."

"Ooh." She scrunched her nose sympathetically. "Well, if you want you could come over to my place and take a shower," she offered nonchalantly. "Lord knows you must need one by now." This definitely caught me off guard, but I recovered enough to agree to come by her place up on Third Street a little later that evening. I'd found out you could shower by the minute at the harbormaster building, stuffing quarters into a little meter. I'd actually done it, but I wasn't going to tell her that.

Donna lived in a comfortable newer house a couple of blocks up the hill from the main street. The interior was done in a modified trailer house décor, heavy on the photo veneer paneling and shag carpet. The heat was turned way up.

"You want a beer?"

"Sure, why not?" I set down my stuff sack containing a change of clothes.

"Sit!" She gestured at a bulgy leather sofa and went into the kitchen. "So, Matthew, what are you doing up here in Alaska, anyway? Planning a career as a crab butcher?" She came back out with two beers, handed me one, and flopped down on the other end of the sofa.

"I heard this was the land of opportunity so I came up to check it out."

"Oh, yeah, plenty of opportunities to come work your ass off or die of boredom. Sometimes you can even do both."

She had a disconcerting way of saying something negative or sarcastic, then indicating with her Glinda smile, twinkling eyes and fawning gaze that she was actually delighted by it all. It had me back on my heels a bit.

"You been up here long?" I asked lamely.

"Oh, maybe four years. Just since I married 'Captain' (sarcasm here) Nick. I used to live in Seattle. I hated the rain there, but it was the Mojave Desert compared to this place."

Married . . . Captain Nick. Uh oh!

"It does seem pretty moist here." I agreed. In fact, it had rained or snowed at some point every day since I had gotten off the ferry.

"Listen to me bitch," she giggled, "It's not so bad. But I didn't get to go 'outside' for a vacation this winter. Maybe I've got a touch of cabin fever." At the last sentence she hugged herself, put on a pout, and mimicked a case of the chills, which jiggled her invitingly. I finished my beer and set it on the coffee table. She jumped up. "Shower! So, let me get you a towel. The bathroom is right over here."

My God! I had almost forgotten the luxury of a long, hot shower! I was soaping down for the second time when I heard Donna's voice over the splash of the water:

"Would you like me to wash your back?"

I froze for a moment and attempted to master the grin spreading across my face. "That would be great!" I croaked, resting my head against the wall tiles in stunned amazement. A few moments later, the shower curtain opened and she stepped in. Her naked body seemed shorter than she had appeared before, but she was wonderfully full and round, like the girls in those Hindu sculptures. She smiled that radiant smile at me, then turned me around and began diligently scrubbing my shoulders and back with a washcloth. Soon she dropped the cloth and was exploring with her soapy hands. I turned and caressed her neck and shoulders, then down the curve of her spine to the flare of her butt. The water coming over my shoulder beaded on her upturned face and dripped from the ends of her hair onto her breasts. The water cooled noticeably, then ran ice cold.

"Oh! Shit! Out!" She shrieked and laughed as we stumbled out of the shower and toweled each other off. All perky nipples and goose bumps, she led me by the hand into the bedroom. No more giggling. She looked deadly serious now, and she reached up, grabbed a handful of my hair, and pulled my face down for a kiss all full of her tongue.

After, we were sprawled, sheets tangled around our legs, on the aircraft carrier sized bed that filled the room. My nerve endings were still softly bubbling with carbonated bliss. Donna's hand played with my hair. "I've never known a guy with long hair," she mused. "Long hair's not girly at all."

"It is on you." I nuzzled the damp strands at the base of her neck. She hummed deep in her throat and her hand wandered down to my groin and took hold of me there. Here we go again.

When we were done this time I felt a tinge uneasy. The thoughts I had been studiously ignoring crept back into my head. What about the guy who usually skippers this supertanker of a bed? The mysterious Captain Nick. "Your husband won't be home tonight?" Really a stupid line, but I felt I needed to know something.

"No chance. He's out crabbing. Icy Bay. You'll stay, won't you?"

"I'd like to."

"Good! I'm tired of sleeping alone. Besides, it's better in the morning anyway."
The pixie grin was back.

Better in the morning? I mulled this over with a flicker of anxiety, suddenly on
the lookout for signs she was less than ecstatic about our lovemaking. It seemed
pretty good to me, but then, that was me. I considered being a sensitive guy and
asking her if I'm not doing something that she'd like, but, coward that I am, I
thought better of it.

I took to stopping by the office at the end of the day to say hi to Donna as casually
as I could, hoping to get invited up the hill on some pretext or other. This resulted
in a couple more very pleasant nights in the big bed. The day came, however, when
I walked into the office, began my nonchalant chatting, and Donna looked at me
blankly for a bit, then she silently mouthed the word: "husband," spun on her chair,
and began to type. I was sad as I walked out to the Cove, feeling a little like a puppy
put outside for the night.

# CHAPTER 10

## Six-pack

It's late afternoon. I've got a crab-busting rhythm going, a transcendent state of repetitive motion altered consciousness, like a whirling Sufi dervish. A tap on my shoulder startles me down, or up, to the non-crustacean realm of consciousness and I turn. BD is standing there with a big smirk on his face.

"Hey, Witz! You made it! I see you already found a niche for yourself." He reaches forward and picks a piece of crab gill out of my moist, drooping mustache.

"B.D.! How ya doing?"

"Getting by, and you?"

"Well, Cordova's great, but *this* place is agony!"

"Oh yeah," he nods knowingly, "but all the time you spend here gets subtracted off the time you spend in purgatory after you die."

"You mean this isn't purgatory?"

"No, more like Dante level 5 or 6. Speaking of the eternal, where's Brutus?"

"The fucker died on me, man! I think he wanted to stay in California."

"Who wouldn't? Hey, meet me at the Club when you get off work."

The Club is full and rowdy when I get there. I see BD and Duck sitting at a table halfway across the smoky room, drinks in front of them. I sit down, order a vodka and grapefruit juice (known as a Greyhound) and get introduced to Duck Petroff again. The guys at the next table are pretty lit, especially a big, tall guy in a striped Ben Davis work shirt who is punctuating their conversation with loud whoops and hollers.

"128 Fucking Tons!" The big guy bellows. "Filled TWO tenders. They were pumping fish for hours. Whooo-hoo!"

BD is giving the play-by-play of the 20 minute long herring fishery, which had "gone off" yesterday morning, and he starts throwing in little explanations for my benefit. "So three boats are looking at this same school, big ball of herring, from three different sides. It's Gauer, Billy Jepson on the Amy J and us. The plane is telling us it's probably a couple hundred tons at least. (Each boat has its little Cessna spotter plane flying around, guiding the boat to the fish over the radio. You can see the fish in the water easily from up there.) Fish and Game is counting down on the VHF, maybe 10 seconds left to the opening gun, when Gauer firewalls his boat and heads straight for us, around the edge of the school. When he's just about to hit us he turns, let's his skiff go and starts setting his seine. (The skiff pulls on one end of the net, the boat is setting out the rest off its back deck, and you make a circle around the fish.) He starts setting maybe 1 or 2 seconds early, not enough to get busted, but he completely cuts us off from the fish. Jepson starts setting across from him and gets a little chunk of 'em, but according to Arnie over there it sounds like Gauer got over a hundred tons. We wander around, looking for another dab of fish. We finally make some goofy set and get about 6 tons, hardly enough to justify cleaning the fish scales off the boat."

The guys at the next table have gotten quiet for a minute, then they turn toward us and start to chant: "Six Pack, Six Pack, Six Pack Clausen!" The Ben Davis guy says: "We fucked you BD; the least we can do is give you a kiss and buy you a drink! Har har!" One of them shouts at the bartender to six-pack our table. The next thing I know, I have six Greyhounds in front of me. Duck, the poor bastard, has six White Russians, which strikes me as a guaranteed trip to the vomitorium. BD gives them a half-hearted salute over his six Bud longnecks and explains *sotto voce*:

"The short, weasely, middle-age one is Gauer. He's a refugee from some bad mob shit back in Chicago or somewhere. Been up here about 10 years. The bastard is a fishing machine. The burly guy is his skiff man, Arnie, the local Viet Nam war hero. The other guy is the deckhand. 128 tons at $600 a ton is just about an eight thousand dollar crew share. Each."

"Hurts yer head, don't it?" says Duck.

Just then a tall, slender serious-looking woman with short brown hair and a grey rip-stop nylon flight jacket comes in the door of the bar and glides serenely to our table. As she sits down she smiles wanly at BD and Duck, then glances at me briefly. Her attractive features have an air of remoteness, like her thoughts are elsewhere. "This is Ellen, our pilot," BD explains to me, "Duck's in love with her." Duck hangs his head and shakes it in hopeless negation. Ellen is unfazed. "Ellen, Matt Mankiewicz. How about a drink, Ellen?" BD gestures to the table brightly. "Take yer pick."

"Wouldn't want to leave you guys short," she says. "On second thought, I'll drink one of your Buds. I don't have to fly for a few days." She picks up a beer and downs about a third of it. "The fleet caught over the quota, so herring's definitely done."

"Thought so," says BD. "So Ellen, what do you plan to do now that you're independently wealthy? Buy your own airline?"

"You forget, BD, we have to pay for the Avgas."

BD slaps his forehead in mock despair. "God, that's right! And all those groceries you ate, you little piglet!"

Ellen blows out her cheeks and squints her eyes to mimic obesity. "Guess I might have eaten the profits this season. And I was in town most nights, not like you galley hounds lolling around on the grounds. BD fill you in on our tale of woe, Duck?"

"Yeah, he was whining about his $400 crew share, and then Gauer's deck apes gave us a recap too." Duck gestures to the next table, where they are now singing along to Clapton on the jukebox. *"She's all right, she's all right, she's all right . . . Cocaine!"*

"I thought I had you boys right where I wanted you to snaffle up about a hundred tons, but it was not to be. I guess that's what happens when you get between Marty Gauer and some fish he wants. Well, we'll get 'em next year."

"Yep, here's to next year." BD holds up a toast, and we all chug back one of our drinks.

"I just wanted to stop by and de-brief. Dickie said you and Melissa were staying on your dad's seine boat, but I figured I'd find you here tonight. He wants to take the herring seine off tomorrow, so don't get too shit-faced."

"Absolutely no chance of that if you help me drink my beer. Here, have another one."

"No, I gotta go get my boy up at 'Auntie Linda's.' See you, Duck. Nice meeting you Matt." And she's gone, gliding between the tables.

"She's a pilot, huh?" I blurt, belaboring the obvious.

"Oh yeah, and a lot of other tings," says Duck. "Her dad was a bush pilot back in ta early days. She must have started flying about the time she was weaned off ta tit. She's got a 3 year old kid, too. Kenny. Cute little guy. Rick, the kid's dad, drowned out gillnetting the flats last summer. She's still pretty broke up about it."

"Yeah, she's a tough one, though," BD adds, "she'll be OK, especially now that Duck's in love with her."

"Hey! Why don't you quit that 'in love' shit, OK? I'm not in love wit her! I just care what happens to her."

"Donald, my friend, you are welcome to delude yourself as you see fit. In fact, I propose a toast: 'To self-delusion, the guardian of self-esteem.' So, Matt, tell us some tall tales of your Alaskan adventures."

I filled them in about my trip, the cannery, the Cove. We drank. BD talked about getting his skiff ready to go gillnetting. Asked me to help on my days off. We drank more. Duck began a rambling dissertation about some problem with something on his boat called the OMC outdrive. The six-pack of drinks was gone. Duck fumbled up three crumpled dollars for one more round, then promptly lay his head down on the table and began to snore. I looked at BD, who I now loved like a brother. "Do you know that Donna, who works in the Morpac office?" I slurred lustfully. "Kinda round, sexy woman?"

"Donna Vasiloff? Oh, you poor bastard!" He chuckled ruefully.

"What? Why?"

"I'm too drunk to explain."

# CHAPTER 11

## Glass Over Your Problems.

BD's skiff was stored for the winter; along with 10 or 12 other gillnet boats, in a big old two-story barn of a building next door to the cannery. We had a short crab day, a boat with a small load. Donna wasn't in the office when I left, so I stopped by BD's boat to see what he was up to. He was wearing coveralls and a dust mask and creating clouds of fine white dust with a big grinder. He saw me and shut it off. "Dude, you look old," I told him. He was dusted completely white, his hair, his eyebrows, his skin. He nodded agreement and took off his dust mask. Now he looked like a white monkey with a tan muzzle.

"Let me give you a little tour of this fine not-quite-state-of-the-art vessel, Matt." The skiff was made of marine plywood, 25 feet long by 7 or 8 feet wide, with a flat bottom and a square stern. A cabin, with two bunks tucked into the V of the bow and a little oil stove and tiny table took up the forward third of the boat. The wheel and controls were mounted outside on the back of the cabin next to the sliding door, and the pilot stood and looked over the top of the house to steer. Amidships, the 'fish hold', a raised bin with hatch covers, ran from side to side. The aft third of the boat was an open cockpit with a large drum, or reel, supported on metal A-frame legs and operated by a little Briggs and Stratton lawnmower engine. The net was wrapped on this drum, and a set of wooden roller fairleads shaped like a big U was attached to the stern to guide the net in and out. The motor was a black Mercruiser 4 cylinder engine at the stern, which powered an outboard drive unit attached to the transom. The motor was covered by a fiber glassed plywood box to keep the engine dry and so the net could pass over it without hanging up. The boat name "Hard Rain," like the Dylan song, and hailing port of Cordova AK, were painted on the stern.

"It's a lot smaller than those seine boats and crabbers." I pointed out.

"Yeah, it's big as it needs to be. Gillnetting is a solo occupation, and the tenders pick up the fish every day, so you don't need to pack a lot of tonnage. In fact, you'd be damned lucky to fill the fish hold most days."

"So, what's with the dust storm?" I ran my finger through the layer of fine powder on the cap rail.

"Oh, the goddamn cabin leaks. I'm sick of fighting it, so I'm going to fiberglass it. Gotta prep it, grind off the old paint, round all the corners so the glass cloth will stick. I was actually hoping you could help out with that. It always seems like you need 3 hands when you're glassing."

"We won't have crab tomorrow unless something changes."

"Well, if I bust my hump here I could be ready around 10 or 11 tomorrow."

"OK, I'll be here."

"Wear clothes you don't like, the stuff is messy and nasty. I've got an old pair of coveralls you can use."

The next morning I showed up at the cannery a little early and swung by the office to say hi to Donna. She was sitting in her usual spot when I came in, and glanced at me briefly from behind a pair of dark sunglasses. It was sunny, but she was indoors.

"Hi!" I chirped brightly, "traveling incognito today?"

"I wish. Trouble on the home front." She spoke softly, her voice flat, none of her usual banter.

"What's wrong?"

"My life." As she turned back to her desk I saw that her cheek was bruised. I stepped around the counter and lifted up her glasses. She grabbed the glasses and swatted my hand away but not before I saw a classic shiner surrounding her left eye.

"Holy shit! I mean, oww!"

"Shhh!" Her finger came up to her lips. "Rob's in the back office," she whispered. Rob was the cannery supervisor, and his office was behind a door next to Donna's desk.

I had an empty, sinking feeling in my stomach, a strange mixture of anxiety and anger. "Is this about us?"

"This is about me and him. It's not your problem. You should leave now."

"What do you mean, 'I should leave now'?"

"This isn't the time or place. Just go!" she hissed angrily.

I went. So much for consoling her. This time I felt like the puppy had been spanked before being put out for the night.

I wandered over to BD's skiff, feeling all weird and remote. BD was laying out tools, scissors, paintbrushes, rollers, and rolls of fiberglass cloth. A 5-gallon can of fiberglass resin and several empty coffee cans were sitting by the boat. He tossed me a pair of old blue coveralls and some rubber dishwashing gloves. "Suit up! You're just in time." He poured some of the resin in a coffee can and squirted some clear liquid into it. A pungent chemical smell filled the air. "Need a little extra catalyst when it's cold like this." He picked up the coffee can and waxed poetic. "God, I love the smell of fiberglass! The people's plastic! Glass over your problems." He brushed a layer of resin onto the surfaces of the cabin, then we began fitting layers of the cloth and impregnating them full of the drippy glass.

"No air bubbles under the cloth, that's the key." Soon, the earliest work was starting to get sticky, then semi-solid like taffy. "Kickin' real good!" He said with satisfaction. "Don't stop now." In a couple of hours we had the cabin and the flat triangle of deck up at the bow and the little strips of deck on both sides of the cabin all glassed with 2 layers of cloth. We were cleaning up with some thinner called acetone. He looked over at me. "You on drugs or something this morning? You look kinda spaced out."

"I guess it's about my friend Donna. I think her husband beat her up."

"Ah, yes." BD said with a sigh. "It wouldn't be the first time. I'm afraid you've stuck your dick in a meat grinder, my friend."

"Nobody knows about us," I whined defensively. "I hadn't even told you!"

"And you see how hard it was for me to figure it out? This is a very small town, filled with a lot of very small people with nothing better to do than look out their windows and put two and two together."

"But, she's got bruises and a black eye!"

"Black Nick is a mean son-of-a-bitch. A little bit of a psychopath. I'd stay out of his way." BD paused thoughtfully. "Good fisherman, though."

The next couple of days I butchered crab and kept to myself. I didn't stop by the office. I walked the docks in the harbor, asking at every boat with a person on board if they needed a crewman. I started showing up early at the cannery whenever a crab boat was scheduled to unload. If George Foreman wasn't around I would ask: "You need a crewman?" No one did.

One time one of the crabbers said: "We don't need crew, but I'll give you twenty bucks to jump down in the hold and do my unloading for me." I spent the next hour down in the fish hold with another guy, tossing crab into a big square stainless steel bucket. When it was full it was hoisted up onto the dock and dumped into a chute that led to a holding tank full of seawater. Twenty bucks for a little over an hour was a lot better than the $4.00 an hour I got inside the cannery. I decided to splurge and go up town for dinner after the crab were done.

Once again, I put off stopping in to see Donna. I went by BD's skiff instead and talked him into meeting me for dinner. He said that Melissa was going to some baby shower for a friend, so he was free for the evening. I talked him into going to the Coho, which was an ancient greasy spoon dive attached to the equally ancient and dive-ish Cordova House Bar and Hotel. I'd been there for breakfast once and was fascinated by the unabashed sleaziness of the place. He hesitated, but agreed, saying: "Life is a risk, we might as well risk a little food poisoning now and then."

As I was truckin' in to town from the Cove a rusty pick-up stopped and the guy offered me a ride. "Going up town?"

"Yeah, thanks!" I climbed in. As we passed the canneries we overtook that grey and black spotted dog trotting along the road. The guy stopped the truck.

"Hey, Skipper, going up town?" The dog looked at him inquisitively for a moment, then leapt into the back of the truck. When we stopped at the first stop sign in town the dog jumped out of the back and trotted up the hill toward Second Street.

"Hey, your dog jumped out, man!"

"He's not my dog, that's Skipper," he said by way of explanation.

I got to the Cordova House before BD. I sat on a stool at the nearly empty bar, ordered a beer. Five or six round Formica tables and chairs and the mandatory pool table were scattered around the darkened room. The Coho Café was through an open doorway at the back and the rooms were up a flight of stairs in the hallway, by the toilets. While my eyes were getting accustomed to the gloom I did some mental tasting notes on the barroom smell. The dominant scent was stale beer, with a top end of Lysol and urinal cake unable to completely mask an undertone of urine itself, and moldy wood. A hint of male body odor and a wild note of fruity women's perfume (or was it those auto air freshener trees?) completed the olfactory mélange.

The front door opened. I expected BD to come in, but it was Las Cruces Vicki, the cowgirl cocktail waitress I'd met my first day in town. She was hanging on the arm of a dark haired, leathery-faced guy with a roguish smile and a neatly trimmed black goatee. He looked around the room. Hard, piercing eyes locked on me for a moment then he greeted a couple of guys at a table farther back. Vicki disengaged her arm and came over to the bar to order drinks. She looked at me in puzzlement, then gushed out: "I remember you! You're BD's friend from Utah or where ever! Did you ever find him?" Just then BD walked in the door, slipped onto the stool next to me and ordered a Bud.

"Yep," I told her. She turned to BD.

"Oh! Hi! I guess so, then," she said.

"I guess so, what?" BD asked her.

"Oh, nothing, just . . . hi." She waved at him absently and wandered down to the other end of the bar where the bartender had gone to fetch the beer from the cooler.

"I'd be confused if it wasn't Vicki," BD muttered. "Hey, let's take the beers in the café and order, before I lose my nerve."

When the food came, mine was meatloaf, mashed potatoes and gravy, peas and carrots (obviously canned). BD had the fish and chips. An old native guy at the back table, across from me, was the only other diner. BD got up to use the restroom. I felt the presence of someone behind me, then the back of my neck was caught in a painful grip, vise-like fingers digging in below my ears. My head was forced down into my plate. A face was next to mine, so close I could feel the unpleasant intimacy of stiff goatee whiskers against my cheek and smell tobacco and beer breath. "I think maybe you should stop fucking my wife" he breathed softly into my ear as he slowly massaged my face in the potatoes and gravy. "OK, hippy?" He blew a little kiss in my ear, tightened the squeeze a little more, and then he was gone.

BD came back as I was wiping gravy out of my eyes and hair with a wad of napkins, cussing impotently under my breath at the searing hot embers of anger and humiliation scorching my guts. The old guy at the other table was rocking in his chair, emitting a strange snorting laugh out his nose. "Whoa, what happened?" BD asked.

"I think I just met Captain Nick."

"And you lived to tell the tale? That's good!"

"Fuck him! This is bullshit!" I was getting a belated adrenaline rush, not sure what I should do with it. "Fucking asshole! I should kick his ass!" I said unconvincingly.

BD smiled at me. "Not wise, my friend. Or do-able. Even if I was of a mind to help you, which I definitely am not. Don't get me wrong; I'm not passing moral judgments on your sex life. But Nick Vasiloff has won more bar fights and put more people in the hospital than, well, you don't want to think about it." He closed his eyes and shook his head to drive away the unpleasant thought. "He's even worse since his brother drowned." I got up and went to the toilet to clean up a bit and try to calm down.

"I can't believe that guy is married to Donna," I said upon my return. I was cooled down a little bit now.

"She's not the first one he's been married to," he said through a mouthful of fried fish. "Excuse me if I finish my dinner?"

"Fine, I've lost my appetite."

"So, you know that woman Alice Swenson who works in the hardware store? They were married for a while. Nick was sleeping around and they had a fight one night. He punched her up, so she was screaming at him that she was going to divorce him and take half of everything he owned, half his house, half his boat. Nick told her they could start dividing it up right then. 'You want half this house? Fine! Take that half." He got out his chain saw and started cutting the house in two. You know, up the wall, across the ceiling . . ."

"Jesus Christ! He's a fuckin' nut case!"

"You and your Psych degree, Witz! Spare me the technical jargon."

# CHAPTER 12

## A Glorious Boat Ride

The next day BD launched his skiff. I had another day off. Crabbing was slowing down as the water warmed up, and some of the crab boats or their crewmen were getting ready for salmon season. "Let's take a little shake-down cruise, see what doesn't work," BD said. The dock foreman fork lifted the skiff off its blocks onto a heavy wheeled dolly, then towed it to a sling hoist. The hoist traveled out over the water on a steel rail that was supported by the building on the inboard side and a tripod of pilings out in the water on the outboard side. The boat was lowered down to the water with BD standing amidships.

Soon we were out on the inlet, planeing merrily along. The black skiff's flat bottom slapped rhythmically on the ripples from a light breeze. The smooth white V of wake hissed out behind, tailing us like a comet. The engine hummed in its little box in the stern. BD slowed to an idle, then speeded up again, listening intently. "Here, take the wheel while I screw with some stuff. Just follow the line of the channel buoys. Red ones on your left going out. She's running a little hot, fathometer doesn't work," blah, blah, blah. BD was fussing about little details, but I was having a glorious boat ride. After a while he sorted things out to his satisfaction and made up his "shit list" of things that had gone to shit over the winter and needed to be fixed. Nothing catastrophic. He took the wheel and we turned around and headed back toward the harbor.

I was all full inside with enthusiasm, happiness, a feeling of the 'rightness' of being here and doing this. I looked over at him and said: "This is what I want to do. I want to get on a boat, go fishing, not work in the cannery."

"Well, you can keep pounding the docks, maybe get on a tender or get a seine job when seining starts later in the summer, or you can just jump in and buy your own damn boat and a net and go gillnetting. Sockeye season opens May 15 if we don't go on strike. Stupider guys than you have done it and lived."

"How much would it cost?"

"Oh, a used skiff like this is a couple grand, but there is a lot cheaper junk out there. All you really need is an open skiff and a 40 horse outboard, but a cabin, at least a doghouse, would be nice to get you in out of the rain, and a reel, so you don't have to pull the net by hand. A used net will cost you 400 or 500 dollars and some net mending time. In fact, I've got one I would sell you for $400, P.A.F."

"What's PAF?"

"Pay after fishing. Pay me in the fall." BD throttled the skiff back as we passed the jumbled pile of stones of the breakwater. Our stern squatted down and the bow came up as we came off "the step" then we leveled out again and idled slowly between the long wooden floats and creosoted pilings of the harbor.

"I've got about $700, but I could probably borrow a grand from my parents if they didn't know what it was for." I grinned at him.

"Yeah, tell 'em you knocked some gal up or need to pay for a drug deal that went bad, something normal like that. Anything but going fishing. Or you can go talk to the packers, maybe the cannery will give you a little loan if you promise to sell 'em your fish and give 'em your first-born kid."

We tied up in a harbor stall alongside the Glacier Island, the Clausens' 46-foot seine boat. Melissa came out of the cabin onto the back deck, bare feet and a flowing, homemade granny dress with a paisley pattern. As always, her smile lit up the day. "How'd it go, boys? Break anything?"

"Nothing major." BD said. "Just the usual spring gremlins."

"Good. Hey, Byron," (Melissa had taken to calling BD by his actual name, something only she and his mom usually did.) "I talked to old Andy. In fact, I helped him mend nets for a few hours this morning. He is going to teach me how to mend gear so I can earn an honest living. I won't have to be your 'kept woman' or work in the Club Café again."

"Far out! Free net mending for your special boyfriend, right?"

"Maybe for him, but YOU will definitely pay retail," she teased.

BD pouted, climbed over the rail onto the deck of the seiner, gave Melissa a little kiss. "I'm gonna miss 'keeping' you as my personal love slave." She gave him a push in the chest and made a sour face. Then BD said: "Hey, I guess it must be new career day today. Witz here is thinking about going gillnetting."

"Good for you, Monkey!" Once I had foolishly told her about the way my little sister had mis-pronounced our last name as "monkey-witz" when she was a baby. So that had become Melissa's personal nickname for me. Fortunately it had never caught on beyond her. BD and my other pals had stuck to "Witz," or "dim-Witz" when derision was required.

"Why don't you boys come in for a cup of coffee and we can talk about all these career changes."

The galley of the seine boat was a cozy little kitchen, glowing with old teak. We plopped ourselves down on the padded benches of the built-in table on the port side of the galley. A counter with a little sink and cabinets ran along the other side. A cast-iron diesel-fired cook stove with a smooth flat top stood against the aft wall by the door, throwing out a mellow heat. A passageway and a couple of steps down led forward to the focsle with its double bunks on both sides. Melissa grabbed mugs from a row of cup hooks and poured from the old coffee pot on the stove. The mugs were those heavy, thick-rimmed white porcelain ones you see in old diners. The ones that always make the coffee taste better than it is.

Now that I had declared myself, my euphoria was waning a bit. "You really think I should go gillnetting?" I asked. "Other than a canoe, the only boat I ever ran was the little aluminum bass fishing skiff my uncles had. And that was on lakes."

"All I'm saying is that you have a perfect right to go out there and flail around 'till you learn how to catch fish, get scared and quit, go broke, or drown."

Melissa bristled at this. "Quit being so macho, Byron! You sound like Ernest Hemingway! You could teach him."

BD smiled at her. "It doesn't work that way. Of course I'll tell him stuff, but you can only hear what your experience has prepared you to hear. And no one will be there to hold his hand. He's got to watch and think and do it, figure it out for himself."

That afternoon I went up town to the bulletin board in the glass case in front of the Cordova District Fisherman's Union, the Union Hall. Little 3x5 note cards were pinned inside. "For Sale. 60 mesh deep Red net. Good Shape—$500"

"Charlie Mohr Cabin Skiff w 4 cyl Mercruiser. Spare Outdrive. $3500 OBO."

"Like new seine jitney, Chrysler Crown eng. $4,000 firm." Then I saw it, scrawled in fat pencil with a squiggly hand. "Sellin Out Gillnetting. 24' skiff w doghouse. 40 horse Evinrude. 45 mesh net. Lankard reel. $1,000. See Pete at APA."

# CHAPTER 13

## Some Enchanted Evening.

I was walking down Cordova's main street, enjoying the hollow clomp of my rubber boots on the wooden sidewalk, when I saw her. As she came out of the drugstore with a little bag in one hand she paused and tossed her head to clear her hair, which a breeze had blown across her face. Her other hand came up and held her black mane against the flopped-back hood of the fur parka for a moment, her chin raised and her eyes closed. Every fluid movement was exquisite. She turned and took a couple of steps toward me. I stopped. I was staring. She stopped. Her sapphire-blue eyes opened wide and she tipped her head in a silent query. I felt all watery and electric inside, a kid standing with his toes clinched over the edge of the high dive, willing himself to jump.

"You must be Anna."

"Why . . . must . . . I be Anna?" she replied softly.

"Because you're a raven-haired goddess." I blurted it in a breathy whisper as I plummeted, feet-first toward the water far below. She stood still, with her hands at her sides, feet primly together like a little girl, and a hint of a smile pulled at one side of her mouth.

"A what?"

Having jumped, and survived, I felt a giddy, triumphant surge of invincible confidence. "Julie says hi," I said nonchalantly. "Actually, I'm supposed to give you a hug."

Now she was smiling in a bemused fashion. Her full lips were dark and lovely against the slightly olive blush of her skin.

"Julie? Julie Vaughn? OK, who are you?"

"I'm Matt. You should come have a drink with me."

"So, Julie commanded you to give me a hug and buy me a drink? And she sent you all the way here on this 'quest'?"

I loved that she called it a quest! I went with the theme. "No, the drink was my own idea." Switching to theatrical declamation I continued: "And the quest is my own as well. I wear no lady's token," I crossed my hands solemnly over my heart, "until now." This elicited a melodic laugh. I continued in modern English: "Julie was right about you, though. Let's go to the Alaskan."

"What was she right about?" I could see her curiosity and humor was overcoming her reticence. Swept away by my own audacity, I pressed on.

"She said I would notice you, which I certainly have. And that guys worship you. Which I will do in any fashion you deem appropriate, fair lady."

"Oh, my!" Her hand came to her cheek again. The blue eyes probed mine for a moment in disconcerting silence while some distant thoughts seemed to possess her, then she smiled and said: "Then I shall set you many perilous labors, fair knight. The first of which shall be to procure me a drink with rum, and a paper umbrella. This you may do this evening at 7 at the Alaskan."

The Alaskan was next door to the Cordova House, and almost as funky. Another of the two story frame buildings from Cordova's golden age in the 1910s and 20's, when the town was the port for the Copper River and Northwestern Railroad; the Alaskan was saved from tawdriness by a stunning, ornately carved and mirrored bar and back bar, which had come around the horn to San Francisco, then later up to Cordova. I sat at this bar, elated one moment and wondering the next if she would even show up. Then she slid onto the stool next to me and slipped off her spotted fur coat, revealing a little electric blue cocktail dress with a deep v-neck. Perfect with her eyes. Matching pumps. A string of pearls plunged invitingly into her generous décolletage. She was marvelously, magnificently, completely overdressed for the Alaskan Bar, for Cordova, for Alaska in general, and she was reveling in it.

"You look stunning!" I practically gasped out the words.

"Yes, I know." Something in the way she said this was an invitation, no, a challenge to me to be bold enough to join her self-admiration. The furtive ogling with which we so often plague beautiful women, and which was being practiced by every other man in the bar, would not do. I caressed her with my eyes, frankly reveling in her loveliness. She watched me watch her. Our smiles grew bigger and bigger.

"I'm honored that you dressed up for me," I said.

"I didn't do it just for you. I do it to keep the rest of them baffled." I had passed some test of looking at the naked face of the goddess and now we were together, inside the joke she was playing on the rest of the bar, the whole town. I glanced at my plaid work shirt, jeans, hiking boots. At least they were clean.

"My butler left my tux at the cleaners. I had to speak sharply to him."

"Sometimes one must." She intoned.

I ordered two dark rums and pineapple juice, doubles, and gestured at the bartender to lean close. "Can you put 'em in a brandy snifter?" I whispered. "And how about those little paper umbrellas?" He got an odd smile on his face. I put a 5 on the table and pushed it toward him.

"I may have some in the back, left over from Luau Night. Lemme check." The drinks returned a few minutes later, complete with little umbrellas that skewered miniature fruit salads of cherry, orange slice, lime slice and pineapple chunk.

"Well done, Sir!" I praised the barman enthusiastically.

Anna lifted her drink to me in salute. "You have completed your first labor, Matt. I am pleased." She took a sip, shifted gears. "This Lancelot and Guinevere shit is fun, but who are you really?"

Another warm rush of happiness came over me. I would be honest and open. Nothing I could say to her would be wrong. No defensiveness or hiding. "Just some guy from California, a friend of BD Clausen's. I'm gonna go gillnetting. Who are *you* really?"

"I thought you knew. I'm a Russian-Aleut goddess. No, that's not fair. I'm a local girl who cooks at the Point Chehalis Cannery, and has a splendid wardrobe!" We laughed. I was hopelessly in love.

"You grew up here," I asked?

"Yea, mostly. My daddy fished. Seined salmon in the summers, crabbing and herring in the winters. So we spent some time in Washington, Port Angeles, for a while. Every time I got settled we would move again. But we were in San Francisco, well, Sausalito, a couple of winters for herring and crab. I love The City!" She said it the way the Bay Area locals do, like it is the only actual city on the planet. "All those great restaurants! And that's where I got these shoes!" She rolled her knees to one side and we both looked admiringly down her smooth calves to the spike-heeled blue pumps.

"So, what about you and Julie?" The question was laden with innuendo.

"She and Charlie gave me a long ride when I was hitching here from California." For some reason I didn't mention Peter.

"You hitch-hiked from California to Cordova?" She seemed impressed.

"Well, I took the ferry part way."

The drinks were done and now we were nibbling on the rum-infused fruit. I saw one of her front teeth, next to the canine, was crowded, turned a bit. An imperfection! All the better! Perhaps not a goddess after all, but a real live woman!

"Do you want another drink," I asked?

"No, this was good."

"Dinner?"

"Where would that be?" She smiled ruefully. "No, I've had my fruit salad." She gestured at her umbrella. We fell silent. Just looking at each other again, but now easily, taking in the little details the way one examines a famous painting.

"Take me home with you then," I asked her quietly.

"I live with someone," she softly replied. She saw me wince as the steely dagger slipped under my ribs and into my heart. Of course she lives with someone! What was I thinking? That she had just emerged, fully formed, from the forehead of Zeus the moment before she walked out of the Cordova Drug?

"Take ME home with YOU then," she said. I exhaled audibly. My relief was so transparent that I was embarrassed and hung my head and closed my eyes. She reached over and put her hand on my cheek.

"I live in the woods. In a little plastic house like a hobbit," I said, still not looking up at her.

"That sounds nice."

"It's a long walk. I don't have a car."

"Me either. It's a nice evening for a walk," she said as she reached for her coat and bag.

She's gonna fuck up those shoes, I thought to myself, but I'm done arguing. I threw a few more dollars on the bar.

"I'll just be a minute," she said as she picked up her coat and walked serenely to the ladies' room, followed by most of the eyes in the bar. When she came back she had the coat and a pair of canvas sneakers on, and the pumps were in a little bag. She caught me looking at her feet. "I had to walk down here, you know. I'm not about to screw up these pumps."

Now that it was May, the days were getting really long. Rather than just setting, the sun had taken to slipping obliquely below the mountains on Hawkins Island across the bay and skulking along behind there for hours, indirectly illuminating the sky to the northwest with a mellow half light, sometimes pink, sometimes old gold, then deeper and deeper blue. We walked through town and past the canneries in this underwater light. When we got to the gravel road beyond the ferry dock I took her hand and she smiled a little closed-lips Mona Lisa smile. As we walked we swung our clasped hands forward and back like two little kids. When we reached my woods, the Varied Thrushes were calling to each other with their one-note trills.

"They sound like someone's cordless phone ringing," I said as we walked into the trees.

"They do! Would someone please answer that damn thrush!" she demanded in faux irritation.

"Chez Hobbit" I announced as I held open the plastic door flap and gestured grandly for her to enter. All my nerve endings were tingling uncontrollably.

"Oh my God! This is sooo cute! I love your little window! And the dance floor!" She did a few little rumba/samba steps with one hand on her stomach and the other held up with the palm out, then turned to me. The delight in her face melted toward seriousness, her coat slipped off onto the floor, and she leaned up and kissed me fully on the mouth. Not hard, so I could feel the velvet softness of her lips. Our bodies came together then and the kiss went on a long time, exploring. Her breasts and hips pressed against me. She had a wonderful scent as well, on her skin, in her hair. She took my lower lip gently between her teeth, then she let go and said: "You're taller than the other hobbits I've known."

"You've been with other hobbits?" I spoke with exaggerated seriousness. "Then you are aware of our prodigious sexual prowess?" This took her completely by surprise and she snorted with laughter.

"Tolkein left that part out of all the books," she said between giggles. Then she saw my guitar. "Ahh! I've just thought of your second labor! You will play me a love song that will make me laugh or cry."

I wasn't too keen at first to detour from the luscious direction things were going, but I got it out and strummed it a couple of times. I sat on my sleeping bag bed and she sat in the chair, pushing her sneakers off with the toe of the other foot. What to play her? Something I knew well enough not to make a fool of myself, but something lovely, the way she made me feel. I plucked out the intro to Stevie Wonder's "My Cherie Amour." I can't do it like Stevie, but my heart was sure in it when I sang:

> *"My Cherie Amour, lovely as a summer's day*
> *My Cherie Amour, distant as the Milky Way*
> *My Cherie Amour pretty little one that I adore,*
> *You're the only girl my heart beats for,*
> *How I wish that you were mine!"*

When I finished she stood up and looked at me sadly. She actually wiped a tear, and spoke musingly. "Seducing a girl with a love song. It's not even sporting. Like fishing with dynamite." She unzipped the back of her dress and let it drop. It caught for a moment on the ample curves of her hips and she shimmied out of it. Blue bra and panties and a string of pearls, and her black hair cascading over her shoulders. I zipped open the bag so there would be room for two and kicked off my boots. We lay like that, kissing, until she said: "take off those scratchy pants. Take off everything."

"Only if you promise to leave those pearls on," I whispered as I hurriedly undressed. She sat up and took off the bra. Her nipples were dark burgundy brown, like her lips. I touched and caressed and kissed her in all sorts of random places, nuzzling in the wonderful silky feel and bouquet of her. Then I was on top of her, kissing her neck through the pearls, my hard-on between her legs. I rose up on my extended arms and looked down at her as she lay with her eyes closed and her lips slightly parted. She seemed far away. "God! You're so beautiful!" I felt a rush of nervousness, I wanted so to please her and make her love me. Then my consciousness was floating up and watching us from a place high above. 'Where am I going?' I felt my erection shrinking away. 'What the hell is happening?' I tried to will myself back to arousal, but some circuit was shorted out. 'What will she think of this?' I felt increasing panic. I rolled off her and lay on my back with my eyes closed. I blew out a couple of big breaths.

"Is something wrong?"

Waves of embarrassed self-consciousness rolled through me. "I don't know. This hasn't happened to me before." As soon as I said it I felt stupid and awkward.

She snuggled softly up against me, her breasts pressing my arm, and her fingers traced slowly across my chest and circled my nipples. Her tongue made the tiniest touches to the folds of my ear, then her warm breath whispered: "Relax. Don't be scared. I'm just a girl, who's going to make love to you, sooner or later."

The way she said it liberated me. She understood everything. She'd seen into my fear and it was still OK. I wanted to cry like a little boy being comforted by the mother. I turned to her and kissed her lips. The tips of our tongues touched and we breathed together for a long time until our breaths were completely in unison and our bodies were pressing in time with them. I touched gently between her legs and she opened for me. She made little ragged exhales as my hand moved there. She took my cock in her hand, big again, and guided it into her.

It was slow and gentle the first time, and I didn't want it to ever end but of course it did. Then we did it fast and hard and she cried out at the end, which made me feel wonderful. She pulled her coat over us and I think we dozed for a bit. Then she was straddling me, on her knees, making slow dreamlike love with her hips rolling like waves on the sea, her hair and the pearls swaying and her eyes closed. I cupped a breast in one hand and the back of her neck in the other, tighter and tighter until she collapsed onto me with little gasps and murmured "Oh, baby, baby," in my ear. We were still for a while. I could feel her heart beating against my chest. Her hair lay across my face so I inhaled her perfume with every breath. I was very happy.

"I have to go now," she whispered.

"It's the middle of the night!"

"I told you, I live with someone," she said gently but firmly.

"Who?"

"My boyfriend, or should I say my other boyfriend, now?"

"How about ex-boyfriend?"

"We'll see." She put her bra on and stood, one hip thrust out, bra, pearls nothing else. Like one of Toulouse Lautrec's dancers or whores. Her pubic hair was still damp and slicked down from sex. She smiled down at me. "You understand, sweetheart, that your most perilous labor of all is going to be putting up with me, if you even want to, now that you've had your little conquest."

"I'll walk you back, then."

"Maybe part way would be nice." We walked through the indigo light. There was just enough faint glow in the north to see our way.

# CHAPTER 14

## Felt So Good I Bought A Boat.

I woke up the next morning feeling so good I bought a boat. I walked in to the canneries wearing the shirt I had worn the night before. It still had Anna's scent on it and I kept sniffing at myself and swooning blissfully. I hope no one saw me.

BD was mending a net upstairs in the Morpac warehouse and we walked over to the Alaska Packer's Association, next door to Morpac, so we could take a look at Pete's boat and fishing gear. APA was one of the venerable old names in the salmon business and had been in Cordova since the railroad days. Pete Pappas had too. He was one of the last of a dying race of old Greek fishermen who had settled here but never got around to sending back to the old country for any wives. If old Pete had any teeth remaining in his head they were not visible from the front. He stood by his skiff holding a Styrofoam coffee cup and rhythmically gumming his lips together. He drizzled a long brown stream of tobacco juice spit into the cup and launched into a wheezy, gummy recitation: "Fished the flats 45 years. Tender used to tow us out, back when we rowed the skiffs. Just fished low and high slack. Pulla by hand. Had to be tough back then. Now, all motors. Motor on the skiff, motor on the reel. Not fishermen any more. Mechanics!" he spat contemptuously.

BD said: "So, you're done, huh Pete? What now? Back to the old country?"

"All spawned out. Time to go home and die."

BD clambered into the skiff and took out a pocketknife and started poking it gently into the wood of the boat here and there, ribs, stern planks. "If she goes in more than about a quarter inch then the wood's punky, dry rot, not good. She seems OK so far."

"Re-corked her seams 2 or 3 years ago," Pete mumbled. "All sound. No rot." Then he wandered off a bit and fished in his pocket for a re-load of the tobacco he was chewing.

BD looked at me. "Its an old APA clam skiff! Pre-plywood. Planks nailed to the frames and the seams caulked with cotton and pitch, then painted. Like they've been doing it since Noah." The "doghouse" cabin was pretty much what its name implied; a little flat-roofed plywood box bolted into the bow, just long enough for a person to lie down on the bunk on one side, with a tiny oil stove and stovepipe on the other, and two little square plastic windows set in with bolts. Too short to stand up in. Short enough that you could see over the house when you stood in the stern to run the 40 horse Evinrude outboard. The gillnet, a pastel shade of grey-green with bright orange and white floats like little footballs strung on a line, was wrapped onto the reel in the stern.

Pete wandered back over to us standing by the outboard. "Vern Johnson go through the motor this winter. New water pump. The net got two seasons on it but I don't fish too hard no more, and she's mended. Tell you what, I trow in my old Silver net, no charge. One boat, one kicker, two nets. So, you buy, or not? I don't wanna stand around all day. My feet hurt."

I looked over at BD. He smiled and shrugged his shoulders. "Seems fair."

"I want to, but I've only got $700 cash," I said. I knew I would need to keep a hundred for little things like licenses, groceries, rain gear, gasoline.

"No, it costes $1,000. Don'a Jew me down. Go get the rest from the cannery."

I got a sick clench in my stomach from the "Jew me down" comment, but I brushed it off.

"You go talk to the Merle. I go have coffee, in the bunkhouse."

BD explained that Merle was the Cordova APA boss. "He's old time, been here since Christ was a corporal, seen it all. You could give it a try, but ask for at least $500 so you have a little wiggle room in case you don't catch a fish for a while."

I decided to go see if Rob, the Morpac manager, wanted to loan me some money if I would fish for them. As I came up to the office door I thought about Donna. I was a little embarrassed that she had pretty much slipped my mind for a day or two. She was at her desk when I came in, the last little tinges of yellow and green discoloring one eye just enough to notice.

"Howdy, stranger" she intoned.

"Hi!" I didn't know what else to say. I didn't want to ask how she was, and walk into that minefield.

"Do you still work here, or what? We've been running crab all morning."

"Oops."

"You just ran off like a puppy with his tail between his legs, didn't you."

I didn't say anything to that, but the puppy analogy was painful.

"OK, so maybe you don't give a shit? Just another easy lay."

"Donna! What am I supposed to do? Kidnap you? You're married!"

"Yeah, kidnap me. Good plan." She paused, blew out a breath, then said: "Look, I'm not surprised you're avoiding me. Nick told me he had a little heart to heart talk with you. God knows what that might have been like. He seemed amused by it, whatever it was."

"So . . . are you OK?" I asked hesitantly.

"Sure. I'm fine. I'm married to a psycho, but I'm fine." She slowly forced her mouth into a big, closed-lipped, sad-eyed smile. "So, how can I help you?" she asked in a flat, professional tone.

"I'm buying a gillnetter, or trying anyway. I'm a few hundred dollars short. I was thinking about asking Rob for a loan."

"Well, I expect you *are* his favorite employee today."

Then the awkwardness of the whole situation got the best of me. "You know . . . forget about it." I turned to leave.

"Your check will be ready Friday, as usual, unless you need it sooner."

"No, Friday is fine. Thanks, Donna."


I went back to APA. I blew a few deep breaths on the way, but I was feeling a guilty relief at the finality of what seemed to have just happened with Donna.

Merle was in his office with the door open and waved me in. "Mr. Mankiewicz is it?"

"Yes sir, how did you know?"

"Pete Pappas tells me I need to loan you some money or I am going to be one fisherman short this season."

"Well, I would like to buy his outfit."

"How much does he want for it?"

"A thousand."

"That is a low price, but it is also a lot of very old equipment. How much do you need?"

"Five hundred would be good."

"50% is all I can loan you anyway, on a handshake, so that is a good number. Will you need purchase orders for anything else? If you sign with us we can give you an open purchase order at the fuel dock."

"Well, I will have a little cushion if I borrow $500, but the fuel sounds good."

"Have you ever fished before?"

"No sir."

"Everyone starts sometime. Stay out of the breakers. No drowning until you pay us back, OK? That's a firm rule here. We have a full fleet of tenders, so no chippying around to the other buyers. Tell Pete we will cut him a check for our $500 as soon as he has a signed bill of sale and you come back in here and sign a promissory note. You won't owe us interest if you pay us off by September. Oh, and we have fleet insurance. We'll have to insure your boat. Welcome to APA." He reached a big meaty hand over and we shook.

We took care of the rest of the details and by the afternoon I had bought a boat. I stood in the warehouse for a while admiring it and monkeying with a few things. The little motor on the reel started right up. The entire boat had been painted a dull grey, a long time ago, and it was flaking off in places. I decided I would slap a new coat of paint on, and maybe paint the inside of the doghouse, which was unpainted plywood, so it wouldn't be so dark and cave-like. BD convinced me that I should clean up and rebuild the sooty, rusty, ancient stove. Mostly I just reveled in the glorious audacity of my decision. I called Anna at the Pt. Chehalis cookhouse and told her the news. She would be off in a couple of hours and I would meet her there.

My stomach got all fluttery when I saw her.

"Hi Anna."

"Hi, baby." She said it warmly, but relaxed, like we were long time lovers.

"Missed you."

"Me too! What's it been, 12-13 hours?" She beamed at me.

"14, actually." Just walking with her I felt like a demi-god. Unbeknownst to the lesser mortals around us, we two were secretly members of some superior race sufficient unto ourselves. I cast about for something casual to say. "Where did you get that coat, and what is it?"

"It's harbor seal. Old Aleut craftsmanship" she said a little sarcastically. "Only native people, part native anyway, can take the furs. My cousins on my mom's side, Duck and Bill and Bobby, hunt them now and then and Aunt Ruthie makes the coats. They cost a lot, but feel!" I felt. "I've always wanted one. Arnie bought it for me with some of his herring money."

"So Arnie's the ex-boyfriend?"

Anna chuckled a little at my presumptuous use of the "ex."

Then it hit me. Could it be big, loud, six-pack Arnie? "You don't mean the Arnie who seines with Martin Gauer?" I asked incredulously.

"Yeah, why?"

"He seems like a big buffoon," I blurted.

"Don't go there, Matt, jealousy is beneath you."

"Don't be so sure."

We walked toward town in a drizzle of rain. We got to the wooden sidewalks up on First Avenue.

"I love these boardwalks!" I said. "It's like some old western town."

"When I was a little girl, us kids used to crawl under and look for coins that had fallen through. The best treasure hunting was always in front of the doorways to the bars."

I started thinking of the little 20 page Cordova phone book I had looked up the cookhouse number in. It had seemed like about a quarter of the names were Petroff, Ivanoff or Katushev, with a few Vasiloffs thrown in for good measure. I needed to ask her about her last name, but I decided to go in tangentially.

"How come everyone here has a Russian name? I didn't think the town was that old?"

"Ah! Our dirty little secret! Aleuts aren't native to Prince William Sound. They're from Kodiak and out the Aleutians. This place was just a few Eyaks. The Russians brought Aleuts here as slaves to harvest sea otter pelts. Of course they screwed all the women, but repaid them by giving the kids good Russian names. After America bought us, we just stayed. My mom's half Aleut and half Norwegian. My dad was half Russian, but his father came here after the Revolution."

Now came the moment. "So, are you related to Nick Vasiloff?"

"Uncle Nick? He's my daddy's brother. Why?"

"Just trying to sort it out."

"The bottom line around here is everyone is related to everyone else. Nick's first wife Alice is Arnie's big sister. Now she's married to Marty Gauer. My Aunt Sophie Vasiloff is married to Dickie Hanson, who's older sister Lucy is your friend BD Clausen's mom. My mom's brother George Petroff was Bill, Lily and Duck's dad. See how it is? Its probably a good thing we're getting hippies and hobbits now, just to mix up the DNA a little bit." She turned to me with a smirk and a hug and gave me a kiss on the lips, then leaned back and said: "Is the interrogation over?"

I held her hips tight against mine. "Yes, but not the physical exam."

"I'm afraid it will have to wait. I have a prior commitment this evening. Anyway, you probably want to go play with your new boat."

"I do need to do a few things to it. And I want to paint it."

"Oh good! Can I help pick the colors?"

"Maybe. But no pink, OK?"

"No, I'm thinking burgundy, or teal."

In the end I painted it a deep teal blue with white trim. I got all artistic and painted a Minoan eye on each side of the bow to guide me through the waters. She was still a pretty humble craft, so I gave her a humble name. "Muskrat" "Cordova AK" was painted on the stern in bold white letters. May 15 was fast approaching, which was the date that salmon fishing opened on the Copper River Delta. Three or four other skiffs were still in the warehouse, their owners frantically tinkering with some project or other to get them ready. A few more guys were mending nets in the loft upstairs.

We would wander into Vern's compulsively tidy old machine shop around 10 AM for "mug-up," coffee and donuts around the oil stove, and I would listen to these guys tell tales and argue about fishing the flats. They took an amused yet helpful interest in what "the hippie" was doing with "old Pete's skiff," and were quite forthcoming with all sorts of often contradictory advice about what a rookie should or shouldn't do to catch a fish or just keep from drowning out there. "Don't try to set into the wind or you'll blow back on yer net and get it in the wheel." "Take the prop off and unwind it when you do get yer gear in the wheel (and you will!), don't just start cuttin." "But keep a knife back by the stern for when you have to cut your net, like if it's sucking you into the breakers or caught on a snag." And the most vehement advice I got from several different guys was: "Whatever ya do, stay the hell away from me! Don't set close and cork me off from the goddamn fish!"

But mostly there were little tips about keeping an old skiff working. "Run a few inches of water into her bilge the day before you launch to soak up those dry planks so she won't leak so bad. You'll still need to bail her out a couple of times a day until she swells up." "Keep a can of WD 40 by that Briggs and Stratton on yer reel, so you can spray the spark plug lead and get her to start when she's wet." "Keep a little piece of 2x4 back by yer kicker (as they called the outboard motor) so you can block it up at an angle and still putt along slow if you get in too shallow." Nothing makes a person happier than knowing more than someone else does and sharing that superior knowledge, especially if the someone else actually wants to listen.

One guy, maybe in his late 30's with an unruly nimbus of sandy hair, didn't join in the talk. He leaned against the drill press nursing his Styrofoam cup of coffee and watching with a smile. As I walked back to the warehouse after mug-up he fell in beside me.

"Matt is it?"

"That's right."

"I'm Bob, Bob Thoreson. Did you find the seminar informative?"

"Yeah, I guess I have a lot to learn."

"Theory without praxis is dry science. You'll learn a lot more your first set than you would listening to those guys all winter. And fish talk in town is like sex talk in the locker room. The ones who are getting 'em don't talk about it."

"Is that why you were so quiet in there?"

"No." He smiled. "I simply don't find fish talk intellectually stimulating any more."

"You've been here a long time, then?"

"I grew up here. I escaped to academia for a while but now I'm back. For me, however, fishing is a job, not a school of Greek philosophy."

"So, what was your foray into academia?"

"I was a psychology professor at University of Idaho." I chuckled. "This amuses you?" he asked.

"I just got my BA in Psychology from Colorado College. I'm sure it will be a big help out fishing." I rolled my eyes with sarcasm. "We did some rat psych, but no salmon psych."

"Don't confuse useless knowledge with knowledge you just aren't using at the moment." We got back to my skiff and he started up the stairway to the net loft. "If you ever feel the urge to stop by for coffee and a chat, I live in the old trap barge on Odiak Slough, about a quarter mile out Whitshed Road. The door is open. Only rule is, absolutely no fish talk or out you go!"

I didn't get a chance to take him up on his offer for a while. Aside from 10 o'clock mug-up, it seemed like I was busy every waking moment. I was either painting and fussing with the skiff, racing up to the hardware store, or obsessing about Anna and stealing chances to be with her. When I could I would walk her to work or get her to join me for a quick lunch out on the dock.

On the 12th I launched the boat at the APA hoist and took it out for a little test run. The outboard pushed it along with little power to spare. I ran alongside a seiner for a bit, and could barely keep up. The skipper was steering from up on the open flying bridge on top of his cabin. I yelled over to him to ask how fast he was going.

"Maybe 8 knots" he hollered. "You ain't gonna win any races in that thing." I thought back to the long, flat wake BD's skiff left as it had planed on top of the water.

"Oh well, I'll get there when I get there" I said to myself.

I ran back to APA to tie up at the little floating skiff dock in front of the cannery. I came in a little hot and bumped against the float. By the time I put the engine in neutral and got to the rail to reach over to tie up, I had bounced away just enough that the dock was tantalizingly out of reach. I started the kicker and circled around and came in again, more slowly. I quickly leaned over and put a line onto a cleat at the stern, which I figure-eighted into place rather smartly. As I did so, I realized that the current was running against the bow, which swung gently yet inexorably out into the inlet until the boat was perpendicular to the dock and the outboard was rubbing up against the float like an affectionate cat. Cussing with frustration, I had to let the line go and do it all over again. This time I tied onto the bow cleat first.

Four or five other skiffs were tied up to the float, which was held to creosoted pilings by loose metal loops, so the wooden dock platform could ride up and down with the tides which can vary as much as 18 feet between high tide and low. An old guy standing in one of the boats had watched my docking performance with a bemused expression. As I started up the ramp to the dock he called out in a voice with a Texas drawl: "You better tip yer kicker up! This spot goes dry on a minus tide and that outboard will pile-drive right into the mud or jump off the stern and swamp. And you should lash her onto the skiff with a piece of line so you can get 'er back if she does. Goddamn! Some people don't have the brains God gave geese. I'm Buck. Buck Barnett. Who the hell are you? You gotta have a name other than 'The Hippie'."

I could feel my ears reddening. "I'm Matt. Thanks, Buck," I said as I headed back down the ramp. "I'll be the first to admit that what I don't know about all this is . . . pretty much everything."

"Well that's obvious, but the fact you admit it, that's at least a start. Hey, is that Old Pete Pappas' rig?"

"Yes it is."

"Well, you sure painted it up pretty, but paint don't catch fish. And one more piece of free advice: get yerself a boat hook so you can latch onto the planet a little easier 'til you learn how to aim that thing, or grow yer arms a little longer."

# CHAPTER 15

## When The Draft of the Vessel Exceeds the Depth of the Water, You Are Probably Aground.

Saturday was bright, warm and glorious. I arranged to take Anna on a little ride to show off my boat. She told me that Arnie was frantically rebuilding the engine in his skiff, trying to get ready for fishing, so she would not be missed. "He puts things off to the last minute. I think he enjoys being in a panic."

I picked her up at the Point Chehalis dock. She tossed me a blanket and climbed down the ladder with a wicker picnic basket on her arm. "Boat rides always give me an appetite," she explained, "and, who knows, we might end up marooned like those clowns on Gilligan's Island." Her smile made me think she was enjoying the idea.

"Then I hope you have a radio made out of a coconut in that basket. I don't have any electronics on this canoe." She folded the blanket under her and sat on the wide bench the fish hatch covers made, facing back at me as I stood manfully in the stern running the outboard motor like an old salt.

"Let's go across to Hawkins Island," I suggested. "I've heard dragons nest over there. Maybe we'll see one."

She didn't miss a beat. "It's a little early for dragons, but the pterodactyls should be out."

Orca Inlet is the transition between the deep water of Prince William Sound to the north and west and the miles of shallow flats, sandy barrier islands and little fingers of river to the southeast that make up the 50 mile wide Copper River Delta, the Flats. We ran toward the Flats for a while, passing the alternating red and green Coast Guard cans that marked the main channel, then I turned west, toward a cove on the tree lined shore of the Island. I had actually bought a chart and there were a lot of shallow sand spits on this side, but a little channel or swale led into this cove, romantically named Mud Bay. The problem was that the water was so muddy it was virtually opaque.

I slowed a little bit as we got closer to the shore, but then I noticed the engine speed up a few RPM's on its own. A group of seagulls were wading just off to my left. It was beginning to dawn on me that the fact they were wading indicated something important about the depth of the water when the outboard struck the bottom and kicked up. A shower of sand and spray shot into the air behind the boat. A nerve-jolting moment of panic washed over me, but I throttled down, shut the motor off and tipped it up. In the ensuing quiet, the boat drifted forward a few more lengths, then gently grounded. I watched my wake overtake us and softly break in front of me in about 8 inches of water. The beach was still at least 50 yards away, across a sheet of uninterrupted but very shallow sea. I grabbed my oar and pushed against the bottom as hard as I could, cussing under my breath. The stern swung about 10 degrees, and then stopped.

"Maybe I can jump out and push us off?" I wondered aloud.

"That sounds like a wasted labor. What's the tide doing?" Anna asked.

I had gotten a tide book when I bought my chart, and I produced it from my back pocket with a flourish. I opened it to the month of May, and Anna stood by me as I checked. "High tide was 3 hours ago. It's ebbing."

"You're looking at Cook Inlet tides, sweetheart. Let's try Cordova," she suggested gently. A little better, but the same problem. It would be more than two hours before the water even started coming back. By now, pushing was out of the question. A little current was rippling around us as the water pouring off the flats to our left drained to the right, into the channel I had missed. We were well and truly stuck. Anna grabbed my new boat hook on its 6-foot telescoping aluminum handle and poked it straight down over the side.

"Looks like you draw about a foot of water. It'll be gone soon and we can walk in and have our little picnic. I've got my boots on." She did have on a pair of calf-high black rubber boots with a red stripe around the top. I had on my trusty Xtra-tuffs. She snuggled up against my chest and took hold of my butt with both hands. "So, Gilligan, what should we do while we wait?" She looked up at me with wide-open, inquisitive blue eyes.

I reached down and unbuttoned her jeans. "I've always wanted to take Ginger's pants off."

We were lying naked on the blanket on the fish hold, watching the gulls and clouds roll by in the sky. A little breeze was rippling the water in the channel 20 feet to the right. The boat was sitting on a shiny plain of wet, sandy mud, which extended off in every other direction.

"That breeze is keeping the bugs off us," Anna said knowingly. "I love outdoor sex, but usually the no-see-ums eat you alive. So, picnic? 'Do we dare to eat a peach?'"

"T.S. Elliott? Where'd that come from?" I blurted.

"Screw you, college boy! You think I'm just an ignorant native? I read!" She was up on one elbow, glaring at me. "You weren't surprised I knew who Ginger was, but T.S. Elliott is out of my league?"

Whoa! I've pissed her off! Now what?

"No, you just surprised me. You always surprise me. That's why I'm in love with you." There. I said it. I didn't care if she was mad at me or not. It felt great!

She lay back with her arms crossed beneath her breasts, glaring up into the sky. She blew some stray hairs out of her face. Then she rolled over and looked into my eyes from about 3 inches away. "You would have to fall in love with me! It's going to make everything so damn complicated."

We got dressed and jumped into the squishy sea bottom. Our feet sank in with every step and made a mucky sucking sound when we pulled our boots out. After about 3 steps Anna stopped and looked at me. She was still steamed.

"Forgetting something? What did they teach you at that college, anyway? You need to set your anchor so the goddamn boat doesn't drift away and strand us here if the water comes back before we do." It was a really good idea. I pulled the anchor off the bow, tied the line on the bow cleat, walked the anchor and chain up the beach a way and kicked the anchor into the mud. When we got to the tree line we sat on a shelf of rock and she hung her head sheepishly. "I'm sorry I yelled at you, baby. Going stuck was fun. I bet you used to pretend to run out of gas on dates in high school, too."

"I didn't do it on purpose, Anna. I don't know what I'm doing with boats, but I know what I'm doing with you. I wasn't joking when I said I love you."

"That's sweet, but I wasn't joking when I said it was complicated. Anyway, look at what I've got in the basket. Cherries. Wild duck confit! Smoked salmon paté and homemade bread."

"God! Where'd this food come from? And what the heck is duck confit?"

"I make the food, well, not the cherries. But that's what I do. I love it. And confit is what the ancient gods ate after duck season. Here, spread some on this bread."

Just as Anna had warned, the bugs came out as we sat in the trees on the beach. There were big, lumbering mosquitoes the size of small bees. Fortunately, they were slow, and so huge you could feel the breeze off their wings when they landed on you. More insidious were the tiny "no-see-ums", and another little gnat-like creature she called "white sox," which weren't content with merely biting, but literally gnawed their way into your skin until their heads were completely submerged. The picnic was lovely, but short, and we slogged our way back out to the skiff well before the tide came back. I picked up the anchor as we passed and walked it out toward the water and re-set it so we could pull ourselves toward the deeps as soon as we floated. Anna smiled and nodded. I guess I had redeemed myself somewhat.

We clambered back aboard and kicked off the muddy boots. The doghouse cabin gave a little protection from the breeze. It was sunny and almost warm enough so we took our shirts off and basked in it. "God, I guess I need some vitamin D," she said, her head back and her eyes closed. I gazed at her profile in the sun. Her eyelashes curled up daintily. A perfect nose and full, dark lips. Her long neck with a tiny beat of pulse in the valley above her collar-bone. Then down to the delightful slope of her breasts. I leaned over and kissed the warm hollow at the base of her neck and inhaled the scent of her. The corner of her mouth came up in a little smile.

We heard an engine approaching and a sort of underwater hum transmitted into us through our hull. A white plywood skiff with black trim was running by out in the main channel. It turned into the swale leading toward the beach and slowed down as Anna scrambled to put her top back on. He approached as close as the water would allow. It was Duck. "You OK over there? You broke down?"

"No, we're fine Duck, just waiting for water," I hollered.

"Matt! And . . . Anna?"

"Hi Cuz," she called.

"OK" . . . big pause. "Not much of a tide for digging clams, eh?" His tone made it clear that he'd figured out we were not on any sort of legitimate business trip. "OK" . . . again. "See you out fishing, Matt." He backed his boat up a bit, hard over so she spun around, and headed back toward the can channel.

"Well, I guess I'm officially busted," Anna intoned. "It was going to happen some time."

"What do you mean? Who is Duck going to tell? And what? Just an innocent boat ride."

"He'll tell someone, and that's all it takes."

"So what are you going to say to Arnie?" As soon as I said this I realized that it was 'the really big question.' The one I'd been waltzing around in my head since our first night at the Visqueen Palace.

"I don't know yet, sweetheart."

That wasn't the definitive answer I was both hoping for and dreading, but I was actually relieved by the postponement of my sentencing.

The tide came back eventually, as it has done as long as there has been water in the sea and the moon in the sky. We floated off the mud and motored back toward town. Anna stood, hugging against my down jacket as we slapped along. A sharp westerly had come up behind us. It kicked up little whitecaps that bounced us about like an old car on a bad road, spritzing us with splashes of spray.

# CHAPTER 16

## Use Local Knowledge

There was a little pre-fishing dinner get-together on BD's seiner Glacier Island that evening. As I was coming down the harbor float, that black and grey spotted dog was heading up toward the ramp with a businesslike look on his face. Melissa had made a huge pot of Cioppino or Bouillabaisse, some kind of fish stew with halibut, crab, potato and herbs. There was lots of hot garlic bread, green salad and she had even baked a pie. BD and I, Duck and Ellen, and John, a dark-complected, brillo-haired fisherman who looked like a cross between Jim Croce and Groucho Marx, were all mooning and swooning around the galley, gushing on about how good it all smelled. Melissa had to beat our hands away from the bread with a wooden spoon. Duck and I were threatening to Shanghai her to cook for us, or propositioning her to open up a restaurant. Finally she made us sit at the galley table and drink beer until she was ready to serve dinner. Ellen's little boy Kenny, in a tiny pair of Oshkosh overalls and a haircut that looked like it was done with a bowl, was down in the focsle playing with a roll of net mending twine. Duck went down there to keep him company.

BD started razzing John about a bird. "We were gonna have chicken, but we were afraid it would upset you, John. Too much like seagull."

Melissa saw the puzzled look on my face and took pity. "John there has a pet seagull. Wherever he goes, the bird follows him and perches on the pipe rack on his truck."

"Truck rack hell!" BD laughed. "I've seen the damn bird perch on his shoulder!"

I had to ask. "How'd you come to have a pet seagull, John?"

"Just lucky, I guess. I was fishing bay crab last fall and always had frozen blocks of bait herring in the truck, some of 'em not so frozen. Day after day, I'd park at the harbor by the Anchor Bar and this immature gull started hanging out with me. I fed him herring and he kinda adopted me. One day Fish and Game came down and said it was illegal to keep a seagull as a pet and I'd have to let him go. 'OK,' I said, 'no problem.' I turned to the bird and said: 'you're free! Free to go. Go away! Scram!' I waved my arms at him and he flew up in the air about 5 feet and then landed back on the truck again. I shrugged my shoulders at the fish cop. 'There, I've let him go. Is it illegal if he hangs out with me?"

The game warden got all serious. 'You can't keep him, John!'

"OK! Don't arrest me! Guess I'll have to shoot him." I reached into the truck and got my shotgun.

'Stop! You can't shoot a seagull, they're protected. Besides, we're inside the city limits.' I shrugged, put the gun back. The gull jumped onto my shoulder. The warden looked at me for a while with a pained expression then got in his truck and drove away." John smiled his impish smile.

Then the talk shifted to the fish price, which had just been settled that day at 50 cents a pound for sockeye and 60 cents for kings. John was glad that we hadn't gone on strike like last year, when the fleet had sat on the beach for over 2 weeks while the Union and the packers had argued over a nickel a pound. "We lost a third of the goddamn run! We would have needed another 20 cents a pound to get that back!"

BD, always the radical, thought it had been necessary. "If you don't stick your anchor in the mud someplace we would still be fishing for a buck a fish like the old days! You've got to show them that you've got a spine. Why do you think we got 50 cents a pound this time? It hurts them to sit idle, too."

Then they talked about which of the little sloughs on the Delta they were going to fish for the season opener on Monday. John said: "6 AM opener, that's two hours after book low water. Tide'll still be slack at Grass Island or Kokenhenik. Perfect for a little clean-up."

BD did not agree. "You're so used to missing the first part of the season from being on strike that you forget, it's too early for the fish to be there. They're gonna be down here on the West end, Pete Dahl or Egg Island. Plus, the wind is coming around to southeast tonight, so it'll blow them down this way."

"Yeah, maybe I'll stay closer to this end," John waffled.

Duck popped up from down below with Kenny riding on his shoulders. "Watch the overhead up there, big guy. Don't bump yer head!" Duck said he was going to go to someplace called "Steamboat." "Steamboat, Kenny! Bbbbrrrrrrrrp!" He blew a loud, low-pitched horn sound like a huge ocean liner.

"Do it again, Duck!"

Finally, Melissa gave us the go-ahead to tuck in and things got quiet for a while. Then BD looked over at me. "So, what's your game plan, Witz?" he said between mouthfuls.

"Well, I'm going to consider it a victory if I can *find* the flats. The chart I bought at the hardware store has a big blank spot for the Delta and it just says: 'shallow and changeable, use local knowledge.' I showed the guy and asked him 'where the hell do I buy a chart of local knowledge'? He laughed and gave me a photocopy of a little Fish and Game drawing of the closure marker locations. 'This is all the local knowledge we carry,' he said. So, I was hoping I could run out with one of you guys tomorrow, just so I don't get lost or go stuck someplace."

"Nah, don't worry about it," Duck said. "It's a pretty big tide tomorrow evening. Leave a couple hours before high water. Follow the parade out ta can channel, then take a left and go till you see the tenders at Egg Island. Or, better yet, follow one of them out there. I'm afraid your 'blazing speed' will make them your best bet for a running partner."

"In fact," said BD, "why don't you plan on fishing right there at Egg Island until you get the hang of it. Take your low water sets as close as you can get to the Eyak or Alaganik slough closure markers. Flood and high water sets down in the main channel. Anchor up on the ebb and sleep. Remember, this is DRIFT gillnetting. Your net sails around with the currents, towing you with it. You don't want to go drifting out the bar on the ebb, or flood up behind the closure markers and get busted. Stay out of the breakers out on the point."

John finished his second bowl of stew and looked at us all with a guilty, wincing smile. "I've gotta go. I'm gonna eat and run. I've got so much stuff left to do on my skiff." He shook his head, jiggling his fright wig of springy black locks. "I don't even have my net on board yet. It's still up in the mending loft. I caught that nasty snag in Paulson's Hole the end of last Red Season. Tore 30 fathoms of leadline hangings. Gloria finally finished mending it."

"Yeah, that's a bad one," said BD. "It's part of the old Cordova, the tender that sunk there years ago. Something sharp on it grabs hold and won't let go."

"Isn't that the worst feeling?" Duck made a face full of pain. "Net makes a big 'V', yer picking like crazy to get up to it, or maybe you tow your end of the net back up stream to lift it off the snag, then you start feeling the hangings tearing. Pop, pop, pop, pop . . . tear your whole leadline off. You're hopping from foot to foot. You don't know whether to shit or wind yer watch."

"Stop! Stop the torture!" John cried, holding his head in both hands in mock agony.

"Now that she's mended, don't leave without it, John," BD quipped. They laughed knowingly. BD explained for Melissa's and my benefit. "A couple of seasons ago we were running out for a salmon opener. I overtook John's skiff near Mud Bay. I looked over and saw he had no net on his reel. I gestured at it until he looked back at the empty drum and got a stricken look on his face. He'd been mending the net on the dock. He'd left town in a hurry and forgotten to put it back on the boat."

John hung his head in embarrassment.

"Yeah, you were gonna be like a neutered Tom cat on a Saturday night," Duck added. "Just watching the fun."

Melissa was shocked that John was talking of leaving. "Don't you want some pie, John?"

"I'd give my left nut for a piece of that pie, but I gotta go!"

"Here, take a piece with you." She cut a slice, put it on a paper plate and wrapped it in a napkin. The rest of us all groaned and protested in mock outrage.

"Quit babying him, Melissa!" "He made his decision!" "If he doesn't like our company, he doesn't get our pie!"

Melissa put her foot down. "You guys shut up! I'm the pie Nazi around here. I decide who gets a slice. Maybe Ellen and Kenny and I will just eat it all ourselves! Isn't that right Kenny?"

Kenny's eyes got really big underneath his blond bangs, and he looked around with a concerned expression. "I think everyone should get a piece," he said timidly. "He's right!" We all agreed. Kenny's face lit with a radiant smile. Duck looked at him with a puzzled expression. "But the size of the piece should depend on the size of the person, right? I'm kinda wide, so I get a wide piece. Matt's tall, so he gets a tall piece? You're the littlest, so you get the littlest piece, right?"

"No! Same size for everyone!"

"OK, so be it!" Melissa concluded the discussion and began to slice. John took his package and scuttled out the galley door, sent off with a chorus of well-wishing.

"Good fishing, Johnny! Load 'er up! Don't ferget yer net!"

Once he was out the door, Ellen gave us a sour cherry look. "That John! Some people are so busy procrastinating they never get anything else done."

Duck picked up the last piece of crust from his pie, leaned his head back, stuck out his jaw and squinted at me across the galley table. He cranked up his Aleut accent a notch and asked, "So, what sup wit chew and Anna, Matt?"

Ellen and Melissa exchanged significant glances and BD's head snapped around toward me. I thought for a moment about some bullshit cover-up, then I said: "I think I love her, Duck, if you really want to know. I met her about two weeks ago. I think about her all the time. She's beautiful, and funny. I've never felt this way about anyone before."

BD rolled his eyes. "Jeez, Matt, he didn't ask you to write a sonnet! 'How do I love thee, let me count the ways!'"

"It's sweet, Byron. Be nice!" said Melissa in exasperation.

"It's trouble, is what it is," said Ellen. "That girl leads men around by the nose. And isn't she still living with Arnie Swenson?"

BD chimed in: "You seem to have an affinity for the Vasiloff clan there Matthew."

I gave him a dagger-filled 'shut the fuck up' look. Then I realized that I hadn't told BD about Anna. Maybe he was a little pissed about getting the news from Duck's question.

"OK," I said, "you guys are the local knowledge brain trust. Explain something to me. Who is Arnie? How do I navigate this?"

"He's just a regular guy, maybe with an elevated opinion of himself," said BD.

"He's a little bigger than regular," Duck added. I recalled the slab of wide shoulders in the striped work shirt as he sat with his back to us that night in the Club.

"And then there's the Silver Star." Ellen added airily. "He's a war hero."

BD scoffed. "Yeah, that's a big deal for the old vets like your dad, but this war isn't dubya dubya two. Nobody gives a shit what he did over there! If we win, they'll all be war heroes. If we lose, they'll all be criminals and baby-killers. Don't you think Agent Orange and napalm won't be right up there with Zyklon-B in the crimes against humanity list? The winners write the history."

Ellen seemed ready to respond, but Duck looked uncomfortable and Melissa fixed Ellen with a look and an imperceptible shake of the head. BD got quiet now. He set his mouth in a firm line and wouldn't look at anyone. I could tell he was thinking about his little brother.

"OK Byron," Duck said, "but Arnie's a highliner. Been fishing since he was 12. I think the bastard can *smell* fish. Leastways he always seems to catch more than his share." The two guys were an interesting contrast. BD was an arguer; Duck was an explainer.

Duck looked at me and continued. "After Anna's father died she had a hard time. Nancy, her mom, really lost it, and ended up in Anchorage for a while at the mental health hospital. So here's Anna, like 16 years old, no dad, no mom. She was in their apartment, waiting for her mom to come home, or staying with her aunties, my mom or auntie Ruth. She got kind of wild for a while, drinking, pot, too many boys. Then she got together with Arnie when he came back from 'Nam with his medals and a hole in his leg. He was good for her. Steady. She settled down, or she grew up, or someting. They didn't get married, but they've been together, off and on, four or five years."

"What do you mean by 'off and on?'"

BD stepped in here. "He means she's had a boyfriend or two along the way. Arnie always takes her back, though." A look of disgust crossed Melissa's face.

Ellen got her faraway, determined look then gathered up Kenny and grabbed his jacket. "Past your bed time, young man. We gotta go. Thank you Melissa, this was great. Good fishing to you, boys."

"'Night Ellen, g'night Kenny."

"That was kind of sudden" I mused.

"The beautiful Anna is not Ellen's favorite topic of conversation, Monkey." Melissa replied. "One of Anna's boyfriends 'along the way' was Rick, a little while after Kenny was born. She's still smarting from it."

"How did he die?"

"Rick?"

"No, Anna's father."

Now BD picked up. "Joe Vasiloff? Oh, man! A bad deal. He was out seining and his boat, the Nancy V, rolled and sank. They figure the lazarette hatch cover, back aft, was leaking, underneath the net. Stern filled up with water. The bilge pump back there must have failed and nobody knew. When she went he was trapped in the cabin and drowned. The other two guys got away in the seine skiff, but the boat went straight to the bottom, along with Joe and about half a season in cash. No insurance either."

It was time to go home. Duck offered me a ride out to the Cove in his pickup. As we walked up the float to his truck, he had an odd, sad smile on his face. His voice was low and flat. "My uncle Joe was a little bit of a legend around here. A real nice guy. A real smart guy. A leader. The Union, fish politics, boat building, he did it all. Half ta town was at his memorial service. He was more like my dad than my real dad." We got to the doors of his old blue GMC and he looked at me across the truck bed. "My real dad was a drunk."

# CHAPTER 17

## Helen Keller in a Strange House

On Sunday evening I dropped my anchor in among a great flotilla of boats behind Copper Sands, a bare hump of silt on the east side of Egg Island channel. The two-hour run out from town had been another lesson in humility. Bucking into a rainy southeast breeze I could barely make out the sticks, the tops of spindly trees stuck in the sand to mark the curving channel over "the hump" between the Coast Guard channel and Egg Island. I was overtaken by dozens of faster skiffs and boats. They streaked or lumbered past, leaving me to wallow over the wakes that climbed up the ass of my skiff. One 30 foot Roberts hull, the Marauder, came by real close and I could see Nick Vasiloff sitting comfortably at the helm inside the cozy cabin. My face was numb with cold and burned from the wind and spray.

As soon as my anchor was down I climbed gratefully into my sleeping bag next to the warm glow of my stove. I set my alarm clock for 5AM. I didn't want to sleep through the season opening at 6. Sleep wasn't easy, though. The sound of boat engines arriving went on for several more hours, along with the rattle of anchor chains running out through the chocks. The tide was ebbing pretty hard, and it set me crossways to the breeze and a faint swell rolling in from the sea. My skiff rocked back and forth with sharp jerks that threatened to toss me off my little bunk.

The wind had let down by morning, but when I stuck my head out the sliding door of the doghouse the world was a uniform seagull grey; grey clouds meeting grey, silty water at an indistinct horizon. Now that the tide was out, the land had risen like some Old Testament miracle. Hummocks of sandbar defined channels and sloughs where last evening had been a flat expanse of water. I could hear the distant sound of the breakers booming like siege guns out on the ocean bar. I ate a quick breakfast, a peanut butter and jelly sandwich. I was really too nervous to eat, but figured I should stuff something down there. Then I put on my down jacket and got into my hip boots, stepped out the door and put on my long, dark-green hooded raincoat. The outboard started up with a blue cloud after a couple of pulls. I bailed out several inches of water that had leaked in or rained in during the night. Goddamn planks might never swell enough to stop the leaks!

There was lots of activity in the anchorage, engines warming up and anchors coming aboard. Some of the bigger boats headed straight out to the ocean. Others scurried around picking their spots for a first set of the net in the channels inside. One hapless skiff was perched high and dry up on the sandbar, waiting for the water to come back in. The owner peered forlornly down at us from his cabin door. Must have anchored in too shallow last night. One less net to fight come 6 o-clock.

I putted slowly up the channel away from the ocean. Even though the tide was flooding, I had been warned enough times to stay away from the breakers. By a quarter to 6, boats were jogging on their spots along the upwind side of the channel, spaced a few hundred feet apart. I found a wide space between two of them. At 6, everyone nosed up close to the beach. Each of us had a big orange inflatable buoy on a short line, snapped onto the end of the net. I tossed my buoy over the stern, pulled the first few feet of net out between the rollers and into the water, and then I drove slowly out from under it, downwind and away from the beach. The gillnet payed off the reel into the sea. The row of white neoprene floats every three feet along the corkline grew longer and longer, a string of pearls laid out on grey velvet. The leadline along the bottom of the net pulled the web down into murky water. The fishing gear was like a 900-foot long 25-foot deep volleyball net. Occasionally the leadline would come off the reel looped over the corkline and I had to stop and shake it loose so it would drape cleanly down into the opaque, chocolate-milk water. I got to the end of the net and set the dog on the reel so it wouldn't turn. The breeze swung the boat off to one side and the flooding current pushed the net up the channel like wind filling a sail, and towed me along after it. The water on the flats is so silty that the fish don't see the net until they crash into it. The fine nylon meshes of a sockeye salmon gillnet are big enough for the average red to get his head in, but his whole body won't go through. A fish has no reverse gear, so once his head is in, he's stuck.

I had no idea if I was catching anything, and was tempted to pick the net up part way to see if this was all just a cruel hoax in an empty sea, when a white splash exploded on the corkline about 100 feet from the boat. There was no mistaking it. A fish! I saw another one way down by the beach end, which was lagging behind the rest of the net in the shallow water. Near the boat, two or three corks began to bob down all together.

The boats above and below me began to tow the end of their nets against the current, slowing the drift of the faster, deep-water end so that it made a big arc and the inside end in the shallows began to drag along up the beach. By the time I realized what they were doing, my net had swung almost parallel to the beach. The net below me was drifting up on me, so I gave up, put on a pair of cotton gloves and started my reel motor to pick up the net. I engaged the reel by stepping on a cable a few inches above the deck, which tightened a v-belt on a pulley. The reel was pulling the skiff backwards into the net as I guided the net back and forth onto the drum.

The first sockeye came aboard. Six pounds of streamlined fish muscle with an iridescent green-blue back and a silvery-white belly. The tail was translucent. Anyone who has landed a fish alive knows the elusive, subtle colors, which dull from flashing magic to dead pigment as the life fades away. I cleared the gillnet meshes from inside his gill plate cheeks and dropped him on the deck, where he gave a couple of shudders. It was an awkward task, especially with cold, wet gloves on. Now I came to the part of the net where the corks had been bobbing. Three or four were sunk below the surface. As I pulled these corks up the reel lugged down a bit. A great fish snout appeared out of the silty water, and then a gunmetal grey torpedo, a three-foot king salmon came up and over the rollers and landed with a great thump between my feet. He was rolled up in several wraps of web like a salmon mummy. I rolled and flopped him around, trying to solve the puzzle of how to unwrap him without tearing too many of the delicate nylon strands of gillnet. When he was finally loose I hefted him into the fish hold. "He must weigh 30 or 35 pounds. That's $20!" A couple more reds came over, and then I came to another big Chinook. I could see its head caught in the web, but as it came out of the water it gave a thrash and fell out of the net. I grabbed for my gaff hook on its 3-foot wooden handle, but I was too late and it slipped beneath the water. Gone. "Shit! I gotta be more careful!" When the buoy end of the net came aboard I had caught eight or nine reds and two big kings from my short little set.

I started down the channel, trying to avoid the nets laced back and forth across the slough. As I went around the end of one I managed to smack into a submerged sand bar. I tipped my outboard motor up part way and backed until I was in deeper water. A skiff running down the slough behind me slowed to an idle. It was Buck Barnett from the APA float. "You slow down to laugh at me Buck?"

"No, I didn't want my big-assed wake to push you back up on 'at bar," he shouted.

"Oh, thanks. Not too much water."

"Oh, they's plenty a water, it's jest spread a little thin. Until you can read it, or get a fathometer on that rig, you're just gonna learn the flats by bumping into 'em, like Helen Keller in a strange house. Well, good luck!"

I turned the corner at the tender anchorage and ran out the wide main channel until I came even with the navigation light up on the grassy hump of Egg Island. I could see the rows of white breakers on the point another half a mile out, and off to my left as well. I set out the net across the middle of the channel. I was flooding in at a pretty good clip. The tenders in the anchorage were getting closer fast. Something else to worry about. Don't want to wrap my net around their anchors. I snapped my other buoy on the end of the net and let it go. I ran over to the other end and picked it up with my boat hook. Now I could get a better line of sight on the tenders. Looks like I'll miss them. But now I was on the upwind end and the breeze was pushing my skiff around onto the net. Can't stay on this end, but I didn't dare put the outboard in gear for fear of getting the net in the prop. I let go of the buoy and blew along the corkline, then up against it. I tipped up the motor, thinking I would blow across, but finally I had to push the corks down with the end of the old wooden oar. Pete had cut a little 'v' notch in the end of the blade. Perfect for pushing the net down. Smart old guy.

I ran back to the other end of the net and sidled up to my buoy. I put the outboard into reverse to stop my motion and reached for my boat hook. The outboard stopped with a clunk. I had a bad premonition as to why. I tipped the kicker up and the end of the net was wrapped up in the prop and twisted around and around into a thick green rope. Disgustedly, I got out the rusty red toolbox and began to take off the propeller.

The boat ahead of me picked up his net. I finally got mine loose from the outboard and put the prop back on. A fish splashed on my corkline. Give it another minute to catch my breath. Then I noticed off my bow a tall bare sapling stuck in the sand, with a white sign nailed on the top. 'Fishing Closed.' "Shit! The markers already!" I could see another sign way off across the slough, beyond my end buoy. I started the reel and wrapped net as fast as I could. When I came to a fish, I wrestled him frantically out of the gear, not worrying if I ripped a mesh or two. "Goddamnit! Now I'm behind the markers! Illegal! Great, let's get arrested the first day!" I picked as fast as I could and kept looking around for the floatplane or Fish and Game boat coming to get me. The last half of the gear dragged through the shallows, and little black and white flounders started coming over the rollers. They were a hassle to pick out of the net, so finally I just wrapped them on the reel and got the hell out of there. I was totally frazzled and all sweaty under my raingear. I made the next drift a little farther from the tenders, and it took a while to lay it out, as I had to clear the flounders as I set. Finally, high water slack tide came. When it started to ebb I picked up and headed for the tenders to deliver my fish. "Christ, barely six hours and I'm fried! How do you do this for 48?"

I find the APA tender by the sign on the side of the wheelhouse. The Teal is an old wooden power scow. Basically, it is a barge made out of huge timbers with a flat bow, a square house aft, a diesel engine somewhere down below, and a bunch of wooden bins on the flat deck to hold the fish. As I pull up a short, middle-aged Filipino guy walks along the narrow edge of deck outside the fish bins and hands me a line to tie on to my bow cleat. "How you doin' there, easy-money?" he shouts genially.

"OK, I guess." He guides a brailer, a four-foot ring of iron with a deep bag of heavy netting sewed onto it, between my boat and the scow. It is suspended from a big dial scale on a line that passes up to a pulley on one of the tall booms mounted on the front of the wheelhouse. I start putting my fish into it and he counts them with a little mechanical clicker in his hand.

"Put the kings last, OK highliner?"

When I am done unloading the sockeyes, he yells up to the wheelhouse. "Weight!" The whole assembly is lifted up. He stops the swing of the bag, then shouts up a weight. "Now the kings on top." I flop my big king salmon in and he takes a second weight. Now I hear someone singing, doing Nat Cole: *"Roll out those lazy, hazy, crazy days of summer. Those days of sockeye that splash in the gear."* Walrus, from Morpac, is standing on the walkway above the fish bins on deck, grinning down at me.

"Walrus! Did someone free the slaves?" His baritone booms out a perfect M. L. King imitation.

"Free at last, free at last! Great God A'mighty, I'm free at last!"

"You know this guy?" the Filipino asks him.

"Shit yes! That's Hippy Matt! Matt, meet Ray Guerrero, bantamweight boxing champion and the best cook on the Copper!" I take off my glove and shake Ray's hand. Just then the skipper sticks his head out the wheelhouse window, waves a receipt at them to give to me, and says: "Gentlemen, tea party another time if you please. We've got a boat on the port side." Ray climbs up on the bin boards and disappears. Walrus passes me the fish ticket and shoots a monster burst from a 2-inch wash-down hose into my empty fish hold.

"Christ! Don't sink me with that thing! I gotta bail this out by hand!"

"Well, gotta keep it fresh down there. That's what she said, anyway. Har, har! Hey, come by on the ebb tomorrow, when things chill out a bit. Ray will feed you."

I drifted back behind the tender a way and dropped the anchor, got out of the raingear and crawled into my doghouse. I was ready for a meal, or a nap, but first I drooled over my fish ticket for a bit. "26 Reds, 153 pounds. 6 Chinook, 145 pounds." I'd just made, what, $160 dollars? A week's work in the cannery in one tide.

And so it went, bumbling around, crashing into invisible sandbars and trying to figure out how to catch invisible fish, until Wednesday morning finally arrived. Fishing closed for 36 hours to allow some fish to escape up the river. As soon as we had enough water on the shallowest hump in the channel home, we were headed for town.

Back in town, I took an endless shower at the APA bunkhouse, and then slept for a while down on the skiff. It was a real 4 hour-long deep sleep, recharging my batteries. It was the same bunk, but the sleep was totally different tied to the dock. The plaintive screaming of seagulls fighting over the cannery scraps was the only distraction. There was no worrying about dragging anchor, swinging into someone else in the anchorage, or not waking up in time for the productive low water set, when the fish were concentrated into the gutters rather than spread all over the flats. Out on the fishing grounds you didn't sleep so much as take shallow, uneasy naps.

When I woke, I called Anna at the cookhouse. The cannery seemed to be rocking back and forth as I stood by the phone. My feet were on land, but my brain, or at least my inner ear, was still on the ocean.

"Point Chehalis Cookhouse, Anna speaking." A feeling like warm honey filled my chest.

"Is this the kitchen goddess?"

A melodious laugh, then: "Hi Matthew. Home from the sea?"

"Yeah, I survived. Can I see you?"

"I thought you'd want to be at The Club, finding out where the fish were caught."

"I'm tired of thinking about fish. I'd rather think about you."

"Oh no! Real fishermen don't get tired of thinking about fish until September. But I'm flattered. We're pretty busy here. First day of salmon and all, but you could come up to my house for a late dinner if you want, around 9."

"Your house?"

"Yeah, Marty Gauer gave me a message that Arnie found a new snag at Grass Island, so he's staying up the slough this closure to mend his gear."

# CHAPTER 18

## The Softest Thing in the World.

Anna and Arnie's house was actually a big apartment up the hill; in the old High School building that had been converted to residences. Someone, and I guessed it wasn't Arnie, had done some pretty cool Gypsy/hippy-meets Ottoman seraglio decorating with a bit of Alaska trapper cabin thrown in. India print cloth was hanging on the walls, furs draped over the backs of chairs. One wall in the living room was painted a dark purple color she called "Aubergine." I had thought to bring a bottle of red wine and she opened it and poured.

"I cook all day, so I kept it kind of simple here, but the first red salmon of the season is not to be scoffed at." Dinner is broiled salmon steaks glazed with a lemon butter sauce, a green salad and a side of boiled red potatoes tossed in butter and parsley. It is heavenly and I tell her so. She says: "You know, my Aunt Sophie is the real cook! She used to cook at the Windsor Hotel before it burned down. I guess she got me started. But now I love to cook the fancy recipes from the French and Italians. This stuff." She picks up a hardbound cookbook covered with tiny fleur-de-lis, *Mastering The Art of French Cooking*, and waves it at me. "I don't get to do *duck a l'orange* at the cannery."

"In my family, we all love to eat, but the cooking was usually pretty basic. My mom does some good Mexican dishes, and Portuguese codfish stew. It's kinda like cioppino. That was my grandfather's favorite."

She got a wistful look in her eye, then said: "Someday I want to cobble up enough money to go to the Culinary Institute in San Francisco. Become a real chef. But fresh sockeye salmon? You don't need to tart it up like a streetwalker, just cook it right and it does the rest. I almost blew off the salmon since I figured you'd been eating sockeye for the last two days out on the grounds, but I was too selfish not to bring one home."

"You know, I didn't even think of eating one out there. I sold them all. If I'd known how red and moist and good they are I might have eaten every one. I've had salmon before, but these are awesome."

"That's 'cause these Copper reds are going 400 miles up the river. They're loaded up with fatty oil 'cause they don't eat once they start the trip." Then she gave me a quizzical look. "So, fishing, what do you think? How did it go?" For some reason I list all my failures, rather than try to make myself look good. As if I'm confessing my sins to gain absolution.

"Didn't catch much. Probably *could* have eaten them all. I got the net in the prop. Then I caught a snag, but I came off without tearing too much. Drifted up above the markers the first tide."

"Oh, God! Did you get pinched?"

"No, not that at least. And I do like the money part. But most of the time I feel like I'm just flailing around straining water through my net."

"Well, that's what you do! Keep it wet. Can't catch fish with your gear on the reel." When we finish eating she goes into the kitchen, to the sink, washing something. I clear the dinner plates and set them down by the sink, then snuggle in behind her and nuzzle her neck. She presses backward against me for a few moments, then says: "You want to feel something wonderful?"

"I already am!"

"Come in here." She leads me by the hand into the bedroom, festooned with even more tent-like draperies. On top of the bed is a coverlet of some sort of fur, like mink only lighter brown and longer hair. She sits on the edge of the bed, rubbing her hand through the deep nap, like petting a cat backwards. "Sit!" "Feel!" I sit down and rub the sensual, thick fur. Long guard hairs on top, then deeper and deeper, softer and softer levels of exquisite downiness. She looks into my face as I rub, and her eyes open wider and wider, mirroring my obvious amazement.

"Oh my God!" I gasp. "What is it?"

"The softest thing in the world! Sea otter pelts," she whispers with conspiratorial delight. "Now you know why the Russians brought us here! Take your clothes off and lie on it. It's heaven!" She started to undress. She didn't need to ask me twice. We rolled and luxuriated around on it for a while, then crawled under and made slow, sensuous love with lots of touching and licking.

"Where did you get something like this?" I ask her, as we lie spooned together under the fur. "I though there were hardly any left."

"It was my mother's dowry. After my dad died, she gave it to me. Said she couldn't bear to ever touch it any more."

"I've never had anyone close to me die. I can't get my head around it. Do you still . . . how is it for you now?"

"I miss him every day. I loved my daddy. I'll never forgive them." She says the last in a venomous rasp.

"Who?"

"Uncle Nick and Marty Gauer. That pair of psychos. All I know is they got in that goddamn skiff and he didn't."

"You don't get along with your Uncle?" I still haven't said anything about my relationship with "Captain Nick" or Donna.

"No, not really, Dr. Freud. He's my daddy's older brother, and I guess he was pretty mean to Dad when they were kids. I don't think he liked it that my father was

smarter than him, more popular. My daddy made excuses for Nick, though. For why
he was so mean. He always said that Nick took the lightning from Grandpa Vasiloff,
who was the angriest man who ever walked. Joe was the good son and Nick and my
Aunt Sophia took the heat. My grandma just tried to stay out of the way and keep
from getting beaten. Arnie hates Nick's guts 'cause he used to beat up Arnie's sister
back when they were married."

"Is he mean to you?"

"Nick?" She looks at me funny, like she doesn't want to talk about it, but she does
anyway. "No, he's nice to me." She almost sounds disappointed. "Maybe too nice.
When I was a girl, a teenager, he used to creep me out. Looked at me with that wolf
grin. He wanted to fuck me, if the truth were known. Tried to a time or two. But
after dad drowned he sort of looked after mom and me, off and on. Once he bought
me a car, but a boyfriend crashed it into the lake. For my eighteenth birthday he
bought me and my best girlfriend Paula airplane tickets to San Francisco. Put us up
at the Mark Hopkins for a week. Gave me $500 for fancy restaurants and shopping."
I think about the blue pumps. "But I think he's just trying to make up for letting my
dad drown. So, is our hour up yet Doctor?"

"I'm sorry, Anna. You don't have to tell me stuff if you don't want to."

"Of course I don't have to! But there's something about you, Matthew, that
makes me *want* to talk to you."

I snuffle my face deeper into the cloud of her black hair. "We're soul mates,
Anna. You can tell me anything and I will still love you." I feel her nod ever so
slightly. Then she rolls over to look at me.

"If we're soul mates, when were you planning to tell me about you and Aunt
Glinda, The Good Witch of the North?" Of course I know who she means, and I'm
amused that she uses the same Wizard of Oz metaphor that had crossed my mind.

"You mean Donna? How do you know about that?"

"That little bitch isn't near as sneaky as she thinks." Then she adopts a
melodramatically ominous tone. "And my winged monkey spies are everywhere!"

"Well, Anna, Donna happened before I met you. And it's not happening any
more." This appears to tally with the intelligence her simian spies are providing.

"I have to work early," she says. "Let's go to sleep now."

I did get up early, helped along by a little oral sex wake-up call. Then Anna poured
a cup of black coffee into me, gave me a housewifely kiss and I was out the door and
floating down the hill in the morning sun. I hit Main Street and turned toward
the canneries and the Cove. The last block of commercial buildings contained the
bakery. At 5:30 AM it was going full on, emitting tantalizing odors of baking donuts
and breads. The door was locked, but I pressed my nose against the glass. One of
the bakers saw me, came up closer, looked at me quizzically and made the universal
shoulder-hunch palms-up gesture for "what the fuck do you want?" I pointed at my
mouth pleadingly and he rolled his eyes, snapped the lock and opened the door.

"Oh, Man! This place smells great! Sell me something!"

"No! The first batch isn't cool yet. We open at seven. Here, take some day old. No charge." I proceeded down the road with my bag of mixed donuts, munching on a maple bar and buzzing from strong coffee and morning sex. Life is just great!

The sound of a loud motor rumbled up behind me. It was Chuck the Truck, BD's 14-year-old station wagon with its monster V-8 engine and perforated exhaust system. When someone would point out that Chuck was not, in fact, a truck, BD would quote Humpty Dumpty: "When I use a word, it means just what I choose it to mean—neither more nor less. The question is, which is to be master—that's all." The truth was, BD used the wagon as a truck. Today he had a gillnet coiled onto an old metal retort tray stuffed in the back. He'd tied the side-hinged back door partway shut with a piece of line to keep it from falling out. He rolled up beside me and I jumped in the passenger seat.

"Brother Clausen! You are a godsend!"

"So the ladies tell me. You're up bright and early, Mister Mankiewicz. Or is it actually the end of a very late night?" He raised his eyebrows suggestively.

"Only a cad kisses and tells. Have a donut?" I offered him the bag. He steered with one hand and fished around with the other. "You got a minute to run me out to the Plastic Palace and back? I just need to grab a few things there. It would save a lot of walking."

"It must suck to be vehicularly challenged as you are," he garbled through a mouth full of powder-covered cake donut. A fine drift of white confectioner's sugar hung suspended like dust motes in the sunlight, and settled on the steering wheel, the dash, and BD's Levis.

"Yeah, the demise of Brutus has left quite an emotional and transportational void in my life. So, Great Guru, where are the fish going to be next opener? Where should I go?"

"You think you could find your way in to Paulson's Hole? Run out to the Egg Island Light. Put her right on your stern, then head east up the channel that runs behind the ocean bar. Just keep going to the Steamboat markers and slap the net out. Wait 'till it opens at 6 PM, of course. Low water is around 8:00, but the fish are going to have to come pouring off those flats before they go dry." He licked the last sugar off his fingers. "Oh, hey, don't forget! There's gonna be a big barbecue Saturday evening out at the 15 mile lake. The CDFU, the Fisherman's Union's putting it on. Half the town will be there. Check in with me at the Glacier Island around 4 and 'Lissa and I will give you a ride."

# CHAPTER 19

## Corked.

$A$ glance at a tide book shows a curious thing. There are two high tides and two low tides every 25 hours, a little more than 6 hours apart. That means that low tide, for instance, will be about an hour later each day than the day before. After 6 days, high water slack will be at the same time of day that low water slack was 6 days ago. And so the tides walk through the calendar.

The late week fishing periods were 36 hours, from Thursday evening to Saturday morning. High tide was in the early afternoon that Thursday. I headed out from town along with the rest of the big parade: through the Coast Guard cans past Mud Bay and down toward Little Mummy Island, which sits on the edge of the flats like a gentleman's top hat blown off in a gale. Then past the fuzzy little knoll of Shag Rock and into the grand slalom of the stick channel. This time it was a sunny and cheerful trip. To the north of the flats was a massive range of snowy mountains with glaciers slithering down between them. It hadn't even been visible the last opener. I managed to find my way into Paulson's Hole and up behind a long, high sand bar to the Steamboat anchorage.

Someone with too much time on his hands had created a series of whimsical driftwood sculptures up on top of the sand island separating us from the ocean. A doggie. An ogre with graspy hands made from the root wads of upside-down trees. A Viking ship. It all seemed rather pleasant and civilized here at Steamboat. A couple of smaller tenders, actually just seine boats with big resale gas tanks on the stern, were laying in the anchorage, along with a couple dozen gillnetters. A few more boats were already camped on their spots up by the markers. A steady stream of skiffs poured through and on into the Racetrack, the narrow, winding channel across the top of the flats to Pete Dahl, the next big system of sloughs to the east.

Six o-clock came. I drove up into the shallows a couple of sets down below the markers and off to one side, left myself a nice gap below the boat above me, and set the net, laying it at an angle up stream and back toward the deeper water of the channel. The net was going to block off a big expanse of shallow water draining back into the deeper slough, and there was still almost two hours until slack low water. The boat end of the net, in the deeper water, started to drag down a bit in the last of the current, then seemed to grab onto the bottom and stop. Fish began to splash into my net. Three, four, five fish splashing along the cork line. A nice-looking skiff with a grey hull and white cabin, the Valhalla, came slowly up the channel. It was 5 minutes after six and he hadn't set his net yet. The skipper was a tall guy in orange raingear with the hood up, looking up and down the nets as he passed them, weaving around the end buoys and the boats. As he pulled past me he veered over into the shallows up above me, over half way down the length of my net, then tossed his buoy over and began setting his gear back toward the channel. He was way too close to me, cutting me off from the fish. I was getting corked! "Hey!" I hollered. "What the fuck are you doing? Give me a little space!"

Arnie pulled back the hood of his raingear but didn't say anything; he just looked at me contemptuously as he came past, maybe 50 feet from my skiff, still setting his net slowly off his reel. Fish were splashing on his corkline pretty steadily, and I could see that my new splashes were slowing down. I still had some good action down at the far end, where I wasn't in his shadow. When he'd finished setting his net he watched it for a minute then went into his cabin.

I thought about picking up my net and moving, but once I got it onboard it would be hard to find another spot to set it. I didn't want to miss the change of the tide when the fish move around or come up out of the little potholes they've been hiding in to keep from washing back out to sea on the ebb. So I grumbled a few more curses, left it to soak and went in my cabin and cooked up a couple of pork chops on the stove. I'd put a potato wrapped in foil on the hot spot by the stovepipe a while back. I opened a can of peaches, the good Elberta Freestone ones, and dinner was served.

I heard the sound of Arnie's Briggs and Stratton on his reel. It took him quite a while to pick the first half of his net. Lots of fish. I felt like most of them should have been mine, and I didn't want to see, so I stayed in the cabin a bit longer. When he was almost done I started to pick mine up. What a nice surprise! I had three fish on board before the leadline came up over the rollers. Soon I got into a fish-picking trance. Fish were coming over the rollers each time I stomped on the foot wire to turn the reel. I had to stop every now and then and put them into the fish hold so I wouldn't walk on them on the back deck. Every so often the snout of a big king would come up and I would gaff him in the head before hefting him up and over. This was what it was all about! A big set! When I was done, I had over a hundred reds and 8 or 9 kings on board. The fish hold was half full and the little boat was down in the water. I wallowed down the slough about a mile and made a quick flood set for maybe half a dozen more fish, then headed for the tender to unload.

The tender was a seine boat with a big gas tank on the stern. When I was along side I could see right across its low deck. Duck was tied on the other side, pitching fish into the brailer with an intent look on his face. He got done before I did and came across to my side while I pitched off my fish. "Looks like there's a few around, eh? Don'tcha love ta see yer corkline all dotted with heads and tails?"

"Yeah, I had a good set, should have had a lot more."

"Arnie laced you pretty good, huh? I was set just across the slough and up a bit from you guys. You aren't the first guy he's corked when he needs to catch some fish, but tat was pretty rude. Maybe he thinks you owe him for corking him with Anna back in town."

"What, did you tell him?"

"No, but plenty of people have seen you two walking around making goo-goo eyes at each other."

"Well I hope he doesn't follow me around corking me all summer."

"I don't expect he'd want to waste his season like that. He'll probably just fuck wit'chu now and then until you leave her alone."

"Duck, he could cork me every set and I'm not going to leave her alone."

"Then maybe he'll kick your ass. War wound or not, I expect he could do it if he wants to."

"Arnie really got a Silver Star over there?" I asked. "What did he do?"

"Oh yeah, it was in the papers and everything! He was a grunt, infantry, in some hellhole in the jungle. Their platoon was part of an operation to move in and hold this little valley. They were at one end of their battalion, which was spread along this narrow clearing with jungle and mountains on each side. The VC hit their end of the valley from the mountains on both sides. The platoon next to them got so shot up that the ones who could fell back down the valley. Now Arnie's platoon is cut off and getting overrun. The lieutenant is dead, Arnie's buddy the radio operator is hit. Arnie is shot in the leg. The VC turn out to be a North Vietnamese Army unit, real pros. They start mopping up, going around shooting the wounded and the guys who are just playing dead, and gathering up their gear. Before they get to Arnie, he crawls over and grabs the grenade launcher, finds a machine gunner and a couple of other guys and organizes a little fire team. They start launching grenades and shooting like hell so it looks like a full-on counter-attack. Like it's a couple of dozen of them instead of just 5. The North Vietnamese pull out, melt back into the trees. 10 or 15 guys are alive today because of what he did. So Arnie gets a Silver Star, a permanent limp and a medical discharge."

I didn't know what to say. I was finished unloading, waiting for my fish ticket. I changed the subject. "You think it's worth staying around here for high water slack tonight?"

"Not me. I'm going out and drift in ta ocean. Make a night set out there and take a nap. It's like a millpond with the good weather. Plus, you can fish on the ebb instead of anchor up."

I must admit; the thought of making money while I slept had a certain appeal to me. "Maybe I'll go too."

"The only thing, you need to be sure you go far enough out you don't flood in the bar, through the breakers, and don't wrap the whistler buoy."

# CHAPTER 20

## Drifting and Dreaming

Fishing out in the ocean was a whole different deal. For one thing, the water was clearer. In the day, you could see down the net a few meshes, and the fish probably could too. A lot of guys kept the last few fathoms of their net towed back in a sharp hook, so that fish that had seen the net and were leading down it to go around the end would get caught in the bight of that sudden turn. And there was all this room. It kinda made me wonder how the fish were going to find my net with all the ocean they had to swim in.

I ran out the deep, wide Egg Island Channel, past the line of breakers on the point to my right, and out and east a few miles. I clipped a Styrofoam float with a blinking light powered by D-cell batteries onto the end of the net and set it out. Then I sat on the fish hold for a bit, just drinking in the quiet immensity. The ocean against the hull slurped softly like a big dog at his water dish. It was almost the middle of the night, but not dark. Mid-summer midnight in the 60's of latitude is maybe too dark to read a newspaper by, but still so light you can't really see the stars. The Egg Island Light was flashing way in and to the west of me. A royal blue scrim of sky backlit the Chugach Mountains to the north, and the glaciers running off them gave off an eerie blue-white glow in the light of the moon.

After my spell of mountain gazing I went into the cabin for a snooze. Duck had said that the current in the ocean went west all the time, but the flood would push you in toward the beach as well, or in the bar entrances, and the ebb out the mouth of one of those entrances would push you way off shore. I figured I was far enough out to be OK for an hour, and we were nearing high water, so I set my alarm and went to sleep. When I woke up the sky was lighter, but I could still see the Egg Island Light blinking, a little closer now. The net had a dozen fish in it. I ran back out and up current a mile or so, passing a couple of other skiffs with their little mast lights on. A red light over a white means, "I'm fishing, gear in the water, don't run over it!" My crappy little boat didn't even have an electric bilge pump, let alone a light.

I made another hour set, took another little snooze. In the middle of it somebody ran by, close enough to throw a pretty good wake, and shouted, "Get a light on that goddamn boat." When I hauled the net back I'd caught 8 more fish. This was really too easy. I decided to try one more, and then to go back inside to Steamboat while there was lots of time before low water.

I was lying in the bunk, boots off but clothes on. I dreamed. Nick and Arnie were chasing me in skiffs. Their skiffs were a little faster than mine. They chased me up a slough that got shallower and shallower. Pretty soon I was up on the dry land, but I kept making headway as long as I had the outboard wide open. The propeller was throwing up sand and clattering against cockleshells and stones. I knew I was ruining the motor, but I was going to go stuck and they would catch me if I didn't keep going.

The alarm awakened me and I took a quick look out the little window. The sea was oily smooth on top, but a slow lazy lump was rolling now, regular as a metronome, making a bottle of something in my little food locker under the bunk clunk back and forth. Then I heard it; a loud, low-pitched breathy moan. The exhausted exhalation of a great leviathan? "What is it? It sounded so close!" Then it sounded again; huge, but infinitely tired and sad. I pulled on my hip boots and was out the door. To the northeast, the mountains were backlit with pre-dawn gold, but a cool wispy mist lay just above the sea. A third groan and a little slap on the water spun me around. A 15-foot tall metal tower on a great cylindrical base was just off my bow, slowly rolling back and forth in the swell. The action of the waves pushed air through some sort of bellows when it rolled a certain way, making the pathetic moans. "The whistler buoy! Oh shit! I just missed it." My net was drifting off my stern as the buoy went by the bow. I had the sick, weak feeling in the stomach which comes from disaster narrowly averted, mixed with a sort of embarrassed elation at my dumb luck. A few fathoms farther off the beach and my net would now be doubled around the barnacle-covered buoy and the chain that attached it to its anchor on the bottom of the sea. The buoy passed by me at the speed of a stately walk, rolling its head and shoulders back and forth like Ray Charles playing one of his slow, groaning songs.

It took a long time to get back to Steamboat. The tide was ebbing hard out the channel. Just getting back to the Light took almost an hour, and then up the Paulson's channel was slow bucking too. 'The driftwood doggie on the beach could probably walk faster than I'm going' I thought as I crawled by. It was one of those dreams where you are running but it feels like slow motion, like running in molasses. I finally got my net out, just in time for the low water set, but it was no repeat of last evening. Maybe half a dozen reds and a couple of kings. The first flood set yielded a grand total of 1 fish. Hmm. Now what? Back out to the big water? It was another bright, sunny day.

As I went to the tender I passed Bob Thoreson, just getting ready to pick up his net. I stopped alongside for a moment. "Hey, Bob! Where'd they all go?" He pointed to the tenders.

"They're in there. Can't catch 'em twice."

"No, I guess not.

"Since you're new around here, you need to know about the snag where the old Cordova sank. It's down where my boogieman is up on the beach. Don't let the boogie man get ya!" So Bob was the guy with too much time on his hands.

"OK, thanks. Well, good fishing!"

"And to you. I expect that westerly will come up this afternoon and make us all miserable."

Bob was right. As I headed out the Egg Island Channel around noon a stiff breeze started up out of the west. Literally, out of a clear blue sky. By the time I was out by the breakers on the point, it was kicking up a two-foot high chop and starting to whitecap in the channel. I could see them, bigger and whiter, marching east out in the ocean. Guess I'm not going out there after all, I decided. Make a flood set in the channel instead. I could see there were four or five boats making short little sets all around the breakers on the point. I set my net one net length out from them and drifted by and watched the show. They would set out along the edge of the waves, and the flood tide would push them in around the corner into the channel. It seemed like there would be a half a dozen splashes in the net as soon as they set along the breaker line. One guy had his net in an eddy, just inside the point, and it was holding still while the others drifted in.

I spent the rest of the opener messing around inside Egg Island. The next morning fishing was going to close at six, but the tide was dropping then and we would be stuck waiting until noon to get enough water to get to town. A huge exodus began about 4:00 AM, just after high water. It seemed like the thing to do, so I pitched off my little handful of fish at the Teal and ploughed my way homeward. By six-thirty I was tying up at the APA float and heading up to the bunkhouse shower.

# CHAPTER 21

## Tithing the Sea Lions

That afternoon I clomped down the float to the Glacier Island's stall. John and Melissa were mending John's gillnet. His skiff was backed into an empty stall, and a blue plastic tarp was draped over the edge of the harbor float so the net wouldn't catch on the bolts, nail heads and splinters of the float's wooden beams and decking. John was pulling the net off his reel hand-over-hand and piling the cork line on one end of the tarp, and 25 feet away Melissa, barefoot in another one of her paisley print granny dresses, piled the leadline at the other end so the web was pulled full length in between. The pale green of the gillnet, the blue tarp, the bright red skiff, it looked like a cover photo from a National Geographic Magazine. 'Picturesque Alaskan fishermen repair their nets.'

"Bummer! There's another one, Melissa." John held the cork line over his head with both hands, displaying a tattered hole in the netting big enough to step through. "That's four already."

"Mark it with a ribbon, so I can find it. God, what have you been doing with this thing, anyway? It's only been two openers."

"Some big logs came floating out at Grass Island the first period and then the sea lions worked me over Thursday night down by Kokenhenik. I must have had half a dozen fish heads come aboard, no bodies, just heads! And who knows how many they just ripped out and ate the whole thing. Losing the fish is bad enough, then I have to pay you to fix the damn holes!"

"Well then, learn how to do it your own self!"

John turned his head to me standing behind him and winked. "I'd rather look at her, while she does it," he said in a conspiratorial whisper.

"I heard that, you horn toad!"

"Are these crude fishermen bothering you, sweetheart?" BD had come out on the deck of the seiner.

"I'm a big girl, Byron, but thanks for asking."

"Let's go on out to 15-mile, before the bankers and bartenders eat all the fish."

"The preachers!" said John. "They're the worst! Back when I was born-again I used to tithe Pastor Williams 10% of my season."

"Whoa! That'd be enough to make me an atheist right there!" I said.

"Yep, it's amazing how much sockeye a man of the cloth can eat. And did he ever consign me to hell for all eternity when I stopped the tithing!"

"Well, it looks like you're tithing the sea lions at least 10% now." Melissa said. "Let me just grab a sweater and some bug repellant, and I'll be ready."

BD looked at me as Melissa climbed onto the seiner and disappeared into the cabin. "You know, it's an interesting fact about this town, but we are a perfectly balanced little society."

"How so? There are twice as many men as women!"

"No, I mean we have exactly the same number of bars and liquor stores as we do churches. It's true, I counted. 'Course I counted the bars from the inside and the churches from the outside, but I counted! Makes for a perfect balance between the divine and the profane. God and the Devil arm-wrestling for our souls. Ever since John came back over, I think we may be gainin' on the God-fearing people just a little bit, though. Couple more hippies show up and that just might put us over the top and the town really will go to Hell." Melissa came back out with sweater, sandals and a macramé' purse, and John started back in on her.

"So, Melissa, Matt here says Cordova has twice as many men as women. That's pretty good odds! How come you're settling for this guy?"

"You know what Ellen says about that, don't you?" she replied.

"No, what?"

"She says: 'Yeah, the odds are good, but the goods are odd.'"

We loaded into Chuck the Truck and rumbled "out The Road". "The Road" was the old roadbed of the Copper River and Northwestern Railroad, which had once run from the seaport of Cordova to dead end at the huge ore deposits of the Kennecott Copper Mine. During the Depression, cheap copper from Chile had closed the mine and the railroad. The town was left to sink or swim on fish, the tracks were torn up, and the railroad grade became The Copper River Highway, a dirt road to nowhere. Well, not quite nowhere. It ran along Eyak Lake, past the trumpeter swans that always hung out where the lake dumped into the Eyak River at 5 1/2 mile. The airport was at 13 mile. Slipping down between the peaks of the Chugach Range came Sheridan and Scott glaciers, with their crevassed 100 foot high faces terminating in little lakes, gravel bars and streams that ran down to the delta. The barbecue was taking place on a big expanse of gravel and sand next to one of these ponds. Beyond them, at 27 mile a big bridge crossed the main stem of the Copper as it entered its delta, and clear out at 52 mile was the Million Dollar Bridge, crossing the Copper again to dodge two more glaciers.

The bridge had been the engineering marvel of the first decade of the 20th century. But one of its huge steel spans had dropped off its pier during the 1964 earthquake, and the bridge with its fallen span was now the end of the road, but just the beginning of the fevered dreams of Cordova's business community. "If only we were connected by a road, to somewhere, it would bring wealth and blessings beyond our wildest imagining!" The merchants wanted a road so they wouldn't be wedded to the damn fishermen and their roller coaster seasons for a living. Some of the fishermen wanted it so they wouldn't be wedded to the damn local merchants with their inflated prices. The other half of the town was dead set against a road, swearing that the last thing they wanted was to get invaded by Winnebagos filled with sport fishermen cleaning out the salmon and disrupting the solitude. Still, every election cycle some politician or other harvested a big chunk of the town's votes by coyly promising to "really get things going about looking into studying the feasibility of punching your road through to the interior."

We stopped off at Pierre's Powderhouse, a tavern which was actually the living room of Pierre and Kit's ramshackle old house on the lake, piled high with cases of liquor and beer. A little bar with 5 or 6 stools huddled in one corner, by the wood stove. We had a quick greyhound, listened to old Pierre tell a few lies, then bought a case of cheap beer and headed out to the Delta. John fired up a joint and passed it around.

Once we got past Eyak Lake in its bowl of mountains, the terrain opened up into a sea of grass and meandering, sandy streams. Mountains to the left and the flats to the right. Hundreds of Arctic Terns were fluttering delicately about, like swept-wing white and black butterflies. A beaver dam plugged one of the streams with a jumble of sticks, creating a pond behind. A grove of young willows grew along the banks. The dam builders had gnawed several dozen of them to stubby pencil points and in the middle of this palisade a moose cow and calf were browsing on willow shoots. John looked out at the primeval scene with a soft, stoned-out expression. "Wouldn't it be great if we could just keep driving, all the way to Fairbanks if we wanted?"

"No! It would suck!" BD replied immediately. "If we could go there, they could come here."

Melissa rolled her eyes. "Now you've done it! You got him started about the road!"

But BD was off and running. "Why don't people get it? That road will ruin everything! Fish and people don't mix. The only reason we have huge salmon runs is that nobody lives upstream. Gulkana is the only place they can even get to the stream. No dams, hardly any logging, hardly any sport fishing. Salmon are the canary in the coalmine of wilderness. Look at the Columbia. Used to have runs bigger than Bristol Bay. Nineteen hydroelectric dams later and they're lucky to fish a couple weeks a year." BD's tirade was cut short when he made a sharp left turn off the road onto a gravel track at milepost 15.

It looked like half the town actually was there at 15-Mile Lake. Lines of pickup trucks with gillnets, engine blocks and dogs in the back were parked along the gravel road. Skipper the spaniel was walking from truck to truck, making the dogs in the trucks bark at him as if on cue. A surprising number of the younger dogs looked a lot like him.

On the big open beach by the water several 55-gallon drums, cut in half the long way, served as barbecue grills. A large flatbed truck was parked at one end of the pond. It served as a stage, and bore the drum kit, microphones, guitars and keyboard of the Humpy Tones, the town's pick-up rock band. A little Honda generator was hidden behind the big dual rear wheels, gamely pumping out the watts to keep the music pouring out loud and happy from the waist-high amplifiers. Jimmy Buffet and Bob Marley tunes seemed a little incongruous in the land of the midnight sun, but the feeling worked.

I stuck a beer in each jacket pocket and we waded into the crowd. BD was immediately sucked into the small town vortex. He knew virtually everybody, and stopped to talk to most of them. After 20 or 30 minutes we had only advanced a few yards toward the enticing smell coming from the barbecues and the folding tables laden with big bowls of salads and bread. John and I looked at each other.

"Let's eat."

"Damn straight!"

"Me too!" Melissa pleaded. "Got the munchies!" BD gave us a distracted look and waved us on. The salmon was filleted whole sides, grilled with the skin side to the heat so that the skin on the bottom got all crispy. The grill master was slathering some kind of soy/ginger/teriyaki sauce on it, then serving it up in big slabs, maybe a quarter of a side each. It was superb, paired up with potato salad, green salad and a fresh roll with butter. I ate a few bites, but we were feeling hemmed in by all the people clustered around the barbecues.

As we set off to find a place to sit down I bumped into Donna. Literally. I almost spilled my dinner on her, just barely saving the paper plate from folding up like a taco. We exchanged profuse apologies. John and Melissa waited for a moment then wandered away and we stood looking at each other. Donna tilted her head to one side and gave me what I would have to call a carnal look.

"How have you been, Matthew?"

"Oh, busy. You know, fishing. How about you?"

She mimicked me: "Oh, bored. You know, all work and no play." She said the last line with her flirtatious twinkle. The invitation was so unsubtle that I felt a little tingle of arousal. 'Don't even think about it, Matthew!' Nick Vasiloff was talking with a couple of guys a few feet away, occasionally glancing over at us with an ominous look.

"Hey, I better eat this while it's still hot, and still on the plate. Enjoy the day, Donna."

"Mm-hmm." She crossed her arms, pursed her lips, and just stared at me as I walked away.

Melissa and John had found Duck, Ellen and Kenny sitting on a blanket. I headed over and joined them, and started scarfing down my salmon. Melissa gave me a sly look. "Donna seemed glad to see you, Monkey."

"That's ancient history, Melissa," I snapped. Instantly I felt a little chagrined at speaking sharply to her. Ellen picked up on it too, and looked at me disapprovingly. Then her eyes swung out toward the parked cars.

"If Donna is history, here comes Miss Current Events," she said archly. I followed her eyes. Anna and Arnie were walking down toward the crowd, hand in hand, like the homecoming queen and the big football hero from my high school memories. Despite the little hitch in Arnie's gait, they looked like the beautiful, popular people I hadn't been back then, and wasn't now, either. As they walked past our blanket Anna glanced over at us.

"Hi Duck, hi guys."

"Hi Cuz," Duck replied. The rest of us nodded. Arnie's hand came up in a minimal greeting and Anna's eyes glided past mine with a mere flicker of acknowledgement. My warm rush of pleasure at seeing her quickly morphed into a queasy feeling. The bold confidence I had always felt about her seemed like a bizarre delusion. I realized I was staring, and had a sick, stricken look on my face. Now everyone on the blanket was watching me watch them. Shaking my head in embarrassment I gave a little self-conscious snort of a laugh and looked away, then instinctively over at Melissa, whose sweet disposition was always a form of refuge. She had a concerned look on her face. Then it turned to a little smile of relief.

"You're stoned, Monkey!" It was as good of an excuse as any.

John was grinning at me and nodding in agreement. "Pull yerself together, dude! It's pot! Not like a bad acid trip."

"Sometimes it makes me paranoid," I heard myself reply in a hollow voice. "I'm not in a very good head space right now."

Ellen looked over at Melissa. "Pot or not, I think your 'Monkey' here just had a premonition of having his heart broken. Anna has her cake and eats it too. Matt doesn't know if he's gonna get to *be* the cake or if he's just gonna 'eat it'."

"Where's the cake, Mom?" Kenny asked, suddenly interested in the conversation. "Can I have some?" Everybody laughed, but Ellen's play on words had brutally summed up my mood, and taken me down another notch.

I'd heard enough for the moment. "I'll go see if there's some cake for you over at the tables, Kenny." I popped the tab off a beer and got to my feet. A beautiful, full, female voice came out over the Humpy Tones' amps. A large Mamma Cass of a woman with the voice of an angel was up on the stage fronting the band and singing a slow Bonnie Raitt ballad.

> *"They all said Louise was not half bad.*
> *It was written on the walls and window shades.*
> *And how she'd act the little girl*
> *The deceiver, don't believe her, that's her trade."*

On the way to the dessert, I came upon the Walrus, talking to Buck and some of the other regulars from the APA mug-up. "I just talked to my tender skipper. Fish and Game just announced it. No seine season this year in Prince William Sound." The salmon seine season usually ran for 6 or 8 weeks. "Maybe a few special openers later on if there is a big build-up somewhere, but the Humpy forecast is so crappy they are telling us right up front they need them all for spawners."

"Just like the parent year, 2 years ago. Ever since the earthquake, the even-year pinks have been all fucked up."

"Have you seen those bays down at the south end of the Sound? That land rose 15 or 20 feet! Those tidal spawning grounds were left high and dry."

Old Buck got right to the point. "So if you ain't gillnetting, you ain't fishing salmon this year. And if you are gillnetting, you're gonna have a lotta company that usually goes seining by the end a June."

"It's gonna cost me my tendering job," Walrus added. "The skipper's kid, that little nut-case Billy, was gonna go seining. Now he's gonna go tendering instead, in my spot." I slid away from the cussing and disgusted looks and found some cupcakes. I put half a dozen on a plate and carried them back to my people at the blanket. Kenny was pleased.

"What's the big buzz all of a sudden?" Duck asked. I told him what I'd heard.

John seemed to care about it. "Oh man! That sucks! We built a whole new seine last winter, and I was going to be skiff man this year, with a 20% share!"

BD finally wandered over, eating a piece of salmon and salad greens between two slices of white bread. He gave us a quick look-over and said: "You heard about seining, then?" John continued his litany of woes.

Melissa, of course, found the bright side. "So Byron, if your Dad doesn't go seining we won't get evicted from our boathouse in the harbor?"

"Yeah, he'll probably just stay out at the Island and putter with his oyster farm, maybe gillnet at Coghill. He and Mom have their gillnet boat if they need to go to town. He'll be OK. He hasn't cared much for seining since he doesn't have Will to go with him any more." BD's gaze focused stubbornly on the peaks of the Chugach Mountains. I could see his jaw muscles working.

I was standing up near the bandstand truck listening to a pretty good blues harp player, trying to cure my own blues, when Buck Barnett found me. He pointed to his ears and said: "Let's take a little walk. I wanna talk to you."

"OK Buck."

When we could hear, he said: "My seine boat's in the harbor. Big 48 footer. It's gonna be about as much use to me this year as the tits on a boar hog. You still camped out in a teepee like a renegade Sioux?"

"Yeah, no bunkhouse rooms opened up yet."

"So here's the deal. You pay my moorage for the summer, and the electricity. Pump the bilge once a week, and she's your house, 'til next seine season if you want. Got a nice shower, oil stove, big captain's bunk up in the wheelhouse, 3 bunks in the focsle. Now don't take it nowheres! And I'm renting it just to you and yer girlfriend if you got one. Don't turn it into a hippie commune or a cathouse! I've heard some stories about you longhairs."

"I expect they exaggerate. So how much is the moorage?"

"Oh, around $30 a month. It's cheap rent, and you got room to tie your gillnetter alongside."

"I think you've got a deal, Buck."

"It's the Sally B, about halfway down C-Float. Meet me there at 9 tomorrow for a look-see."

On the way back to the blanket I passed by John and a circle of guys laughing hysterically at something. I peeked over someone's shoulder and there was Skipper the Dog mating with a little taffy-colored Pomeranian. "Hey! John! What's so funny about two dogs fucking?"

"It's Pastor Williams' wife Ellie's precious purebred Pomeranian," he explained through snorts and guffaws. "Ellie's gonna go to meet her maker fer sure when Fluffy there gives birth to a litter of grey and black spotted pups." They all dissolved in laughter once again.

Later in the afternoon BD and I took a walk into the woods for a while to get away from the noise, and let the beer fumes in our heads settle out a bit. I explained my deal with Buck's boat. He thought it was a good idea. "We'll be neighbors." Then we were quiet for a while.

"Witz, yer brooding. What's up? You got second thoughts about giving up your Palacio Plastico?"

"No. I guess it's my love life. Why do I always pick someone who's already taken? Why can't I have a simple relationship with a normal girl, like you and Melissa have, instead of all this fucking drama all the time?"

"There's nothing simple about me and Melissa, man."

"What do you mean?"

"Melissa puts on the sweet face, but she's got issues. She flips out if I even look at another girl. Loyalty tests. I don't know, maybe she never got over her dad abandoning her. Whatever it is, she needs a lot of reassurance. It's challenging."

"Huh? You guys always seem so in the groove together. I guess you can't judge until you walk a mile in a guy's hip boots?"

He glanced at me with a wry smile. "I do my share of walking on eggs, bro, hip boots or no. You'd think someone as smart and pretty as her would have more self-esteem."

"Well, at least your woman sleeps in the same bed with you most nights, not with someone else."

"True that! How do you handle it?"

"I don't. It sucks! I guess I'm just gonna have to wait it out, and see what happens. I can't stop wanting what I want."

# CHAPTER 22

## Nagoon Berry Jam

I got my mail, what little there was, at the Post Office, General Delivery, Cordova AK. If you don't send mail, you can't expect to get much, so mostly it was letters from Mom, in her perfect schoolteacher longhand. That Saturday I got one filling me in on my sister's triumphs getting accepted at prestigious institutions of higher learning, and on my dad's bitching about Tricky Dick Nixon and his crooked cronies. But it was suffused with an underlying anxiety. They all wondered when I was coming home, and hoped it would be before, not after, I suffered death or debilitating injury on the high seas. Christ! I'm in Cordova, not Quang Tri!

But there had also been a little post card, with a picture of a place called Dungeness Spit, Washington. It was from Charlie and Julie, informing me they were embarking (had embarked, by now) on the epic journey up the Alcan in the Happy Trails, and would be in Cordova in a week or so.

The next fishing opener was uneventful, grey and drizzly. I scratched up maybe 60 or 70 fish total. But I spent the midweek closure enjoying my luxurious new accommodations aboard the Sally B. While not as lovingly cared for as BD's Glacier Island just a few slips down the dock, it was still bliss to have electric lights and hot water. Pt. Chehalis Packers was just down the road from the boat harbor, so I stopped in and told Anna my new address and the news that her old pal Julie was heading north.

"Julie? And Charlie? Here? That'll be different." I didn't detect quite the enthusiasm I'd expected. She was pleased about my improved housing, though. I invited her for a visit. She said she'd try to stop by after work. "Gee, I'll miss your little hobbit house, but not that hike," she mused.

I had my skiff tied alongside the boat. I pulled some net onto the spacious stern of the seiner and spent some time trying to figure out how to mend the holes. Melissa had given me a few pointers, but it was still confusing. At least it distracted me from the hollow feeling of disappointment as the evening wore on and I realized Anna was probably not coming by after all.

Early the next morning I was sitting in the captain's chair in the wheelhouse with a cup of coffee, surveying the sun-drenched harbor from my lordly perch. Down the dock came a vision in a white sundress with bold blue polka dots, matching white strap sandals and a straw purse. Her black hair was held back by a pair of sunglasses pushed up on her head like a barrette. Her graceful, sexy walk swung the skirt from side to side. I opened the portside window and leaned my head out. Anna stopped and looked up at me. She saluted smartly. "Permission to come aboard, Captain?"

"Permission granted." She came up the steep stairs to the wheelhouse and I swung in the swivel chair. "My, you look all summery!" I told her.

"We don't get many days like this. Gotta take advantage of them!" She glanced at my coffee cup. "Got any left?" I nodded and slid off the chair. She moved between me and the stairs. "Good morning kiss?"

"If you insist." My false reluctance wasn't very convincing. She was squeezy and luscious as always. After a bit we came up for air and she gasped her request for coffee again. Down in the galley, the pot was on the hot spot of the stove. I poured her a cup and she slid into the bench seat at the table, next to her purse.

"I brought you a housewarming gift." She pulled a jar of homemade jam out of the straw bag. "Nagoon berry jam. Picked it last fall at my secret spot. Got any bread?"

I pulled a loaf of whole wheat out of the cupboard and we each slathered up a slice to go with the coffee. "Mmmmoah, thaaas good!" I said with my mouth full. She beamed and bobbed her head in agreement, held her piece in both hands and took a big bite.

"God! Where do you get these berries?"

"Matthew! I said it's a secret spot! If I tell you, I'd have to kill you."

"It might be worth it!"

Breakfast over, we sat licking our fingers and looking at each other with silly grins on our faces till I said: "Come help me christen the skipper's bunk." She nodded. It was glorious morning sex, with the sun pouring in the wheelhouse windows. Whoever said women were bad luck on a boat never spent a morning like this.

But after, I felt myself plunging from bliss to blackness at the thought that she would go back home to someone else. Desperate boldness welled up inside me. "Anna, I'm dying here. I'm sick of sneaking around, being the back-door boyfriend. I love you. You love me. Something's got to happen."

"Matt, it's difficult . . ."

"No, it's simple! Tell Arnie to move out, or come live here with me."

Anna bit her lower lip. "I'm scared."

"Scared of what?" Her eyes closed. She didn't say anything, for a long time. "Look, Anna, I've gotta leave to go fishing or I'll miss the tide. Let's talk about this on Saturday. But you've gotta decide. Be brave. I love you." She still didn't say anything, just nodded her head like a little girl getting a scolding.

I spent much of the next fishing opener second-guessing myself. Maybe I shouldn't be so demanding. Why did I push her into a corner? Am I right to make her choose? What right do I have to give her an ultimatum? What if she breaks it off and stays with him? Aaaahhhggg! Don't even think of it! (Deep breath, deep breath.) Why can't I be cool about all this, and let her have both her men in some sort of open relationship deal if it makes her happy. After all, what was all this free love stuff we've been preaching if it isn't . . . No Way! I LOVE HER! I WANT HER! ME! MINE!

"You Fucking Idiot! You ran right into my net! You longhaired moron! Are you blind?" He was screaming and hopping on his deck like a demented troll. I had, in fact, run right into his net. Fortunately, the net wasn't wrapped in my propeller, but my outboard had torn the web loose from 15 or 20 feet of his corkline.

I tipped up the kicker and cleared the corkline. Then I putted over to Martin Gauer's boat. "Oh, man, I'm really sorry! I was distracted."

"Distracted? More like unconscious! Ya dumb shit. Didn't you see me waving at you? It's broad fucking daylight!"

"I'll pay to mend it. Let me know what it costs. You can find me down on the Sally B."

"I thought all you goddamn draft dodgers were going to Canada. What the hell are you doing here, anyway?"

Now the guy was pissing me off. "Man, I said I'm sorry."

He shook his head in disgust. "You need to paint bigger eyes on that sonofabitch!" he shouted as I motored away.


I was still burning red with embarassment as I bucked up the Paulson's Hole channel. It was just past half tide on the ebb, and I figured I'd make a low tide set in Steamboat up past the tenders. I decided to try to get a set up by the markers on the left side of the channel. I was a little early. The sand wasn't showing yet but I could see the white closure marker signs maybe half a mile farther. The outboard speeded up, then clunked to a stop and kicked up. "Shit! I hit a sandbar." My wake overtaking me bumped the hull on the bottom a couple of times. I dropped the outboard partway down, started it up and tried to reverse but it just threw sand and water up in the air. I grabbed the oar and started pushing the boat back the way I'd come, but then the hull scraped and the boat swung sideways. The ebbing current started flowing by on both sides of the hull, pinning me against the hummock of sand. "Can't go stuck or I'll miss the low water set!"

I pull up my hip boots and lower myself over the upstream side. The water almost comes over the boot tops. If I can just push over toward the channel, maybe 30 feet, it should get deep again. I swing the bow around. I'm making a little progress when my feet find a low spot and the water comes over the boot tops. "Oh! That is cold!" Then I'm past the low spot and the hull grinds in solid again. As hard as I can push, nothing moves now. Game over. Stuck. I pull myself back up into the boat. The boots are heavy now. Full, they jiggle like water balloons. I'm soaked up to the crotch. I sit on my fishhold and take the boots off and dump about a gallon out of each one.

A boat drifts slowly by in the channel, his net off his stern dragging him along, his bow not more than twenty feet away from me. The skipper waves, grins and shrugs. I can see sand now, off my bow, as the last of the water uncovers the bar I'm perched on. I think about getting out of my wet jeans, going in the cabin. The current is slowing down. Another boat, farther up the channel, has stopped moving. I see a white splash in his net, then another. I'm already wet. Tide is almost stopped. You can't catch fish with the net on the reel.

I toss the end of my net over the stern rollers, pay off a few fathoms and slip back over the side. My stocking feet splash into a couple of inches of water. At the stern, I drag the end of the net down into the channel. The water gets deeper, and as more net comes out the leadline dragging on the sandy bottom gets harder to pull. I can hear my reel squeaking as the net pays off. Once I get out about waist deep my teeth start to chatter. One of my socks comes off my rapidly numbing feet. I have maybe 60 or 70 feet of net out now. I tug it out a little deeper, and start bending it up the current. When the water reaches my chest it's just too damn cold. My legs are numb and I almost lose my balance a couple of times. It would suck to fall over and get tangled in the net so I let go and start slogging back toward the boat. The net stays put. I hear a skiff coming up the channel. By the time I'm back to about knee deep the skiff slows down. It's Bob Thoreson. "Matthew!" he calls as he goes around my end buoy. "Is your mother aware of your dangerous behavior?"

"No, but I expect she'd be glad to know I'm bathing," I tell him.

He shakes his head and laughs. "Think about her, and stay in the boat."

I take off all my wet clothes, heavy with grey silt. I turn up the stove and crawl in the sleeping bag. I'm shaking all over, but pretty soon I can feel my feet again. I hear a splash in the net and I start to smirk. The net may be short, but it's fishing.


Back in town on Saturday morning, I tied up to the Sally B and took a nap for a couple of hours. When I woke I lay musing about how this life was like a bi-polar disorder, a couple of days of intense fishing, by yourself, then back to town and a whole world of people and social interactions. Some of the guys couldn't handle the changes and just stayed out on the grounds over the closures and mended their gear rather than come to town at all.

I got up and was just getting out of the shower when there was a knock on the galley door. My heart leaped wild in my chest. Anna? I wrapped the towel and peered through the porthole in the door. Donna Vasiloff was standing there with a crazy, distraught look on her face. Shit . . . "Just a minute!" I pulled on jeans and a tee shirt, and let her in.

"That slut! That little whore!" A vicious hiss through gritted teeth. "I've had it! I'm done! My marriage is over!"

Whoa! Which slut is that? What's going on?

"Donna, settle down. What happened? Who are you talking about?" Totally shifting gears, she smiled up at me, face all wet with tears. Little black rivulets of mascara were running down her cheeks. She pleaded with a honeyed tone.

"Matt, let's go to Seattle, or even to Anchorage. I've got to get out of here. Come with me. We're good together." I needed a minute to process what was going on.

"Sit down. Here, wipe your face." I gave her the towel. She sat at the table and daubed her cheek, looked at the black mascara stain on the towel.

"Oh, God! I'm making a fool of myself," she said in the hopeless voice of the damned.

"No, you're not. But tell me why you're so upset?" Her anger came back.

"I came home at lunch and that big-titted cow Vicki was bouncing up and down on my husband, in my bed! I knew she was fucking him, but this was too much." I didn't think this was the time to remind her of the bouncing we had done in that same bed. "I'm getting on the plane to Anchorage, Matthew. I'm not gonna stay here and put up with the smug look on the face of that stupid slut." Now her voice assumed an acid, biting tone. "But I'm not just going to crawl away without giving Nick Vasiloff a little taste of the grief he's given me, that bastard! I made a couple of phone calls. I told that gangster Marty Gauer, and your little Anna, about the $20 or $30,000 Nick has stashed. The cash he took off the Nancy V before it sank. Marty's crew share. Anna's inheritance. The cash he told everyone was lying on the bottom of the Sound. Let's see him explain it to them now."

Then she softened a bit. "My suitcase is in Nick's Bronco, at the end of the pier up there. I'm not waiting around for another black eye, or worse. Take me to the airport, Matt, even if you won't get on the plane with me. Then drive the truck back and leave it downtown, with the key in it. Will you do that for me?"

I spent the trip back to town trying to regain my composure after the emotional barrage of taking Donna to the airport. The passengers and staff people in the little log waiting room had watched our awkward scene with unabashed interest as Donna practically dragged me onto the 727 with her. I was parking the Bronco on Second Street by the Moose Lodge when Byron and Duck walked up the street.

"What's this?" said BD. "Your good buddy Nick loan you his truck? You know, there's a nasty saying around here: 'Two things a fisherman don't need are a wife and a pickup truck. While he's out fishing, someone else will be borrowing both of them.'" Duck snorted with laughter.

I lifted up my hand to fend them off. "Don't start with me, Clausen. I've had a rough morning."

"*Pobrecito!*" "Hey, come in the Moose with us. It's taco day. A couple tacos and a beer will make you feel better."

"I'm not a member."

"It's OK. Duck's a Moose. We're his guests, right Duck?"

"You betcha, boys. Let's eat some tacos." The Moose was done in the low-ceilinged, unpretentious warehouse style that most of the buildings built in Cordova after the 30s tried to pass off as architecture. As we sat in front of our plates of greasy hamburger, cheese, iceberg lettuce and tomato tacos, the boys resumed quizzing me about my puzzling choice of transportation.

"So, why did you steal Nick's Bronco, Matt?" Duck asked. I figured I'd better just tell them the story.

"Donna showed up in a big tearful huff and asked me to take her to the airport. She says she's leaving Nick and leaving Cordova. I guess she caught him and Vicki doing the wild thing in her bed."

"Bummer!"

"The weird thing is she said she got back at Nick by telling Gauer and Anna that Nick actually had the money from the Nancy V, hidden somewhere."

Duck was aghast. "Oh shit! Gauer's been making funny noises about tat money ever since she sank. He's gonna come unglued! The guy don't take kindly to getting screwed. I heard his temper got him in trouble with some mob guys back east. Rumor is he was running a little chop shop operation with stolen cars, and someone didn't pay him what he thought he was gonna get for some of them. Whatever he did about it is why he had to come up here in the first place."

BD was puzzled. "What I don't get is why would Nick hide that money all this time? Why wouldn't he just spend it? And how can you prove where money came from, anyway?"

"Yep. It's not like Nick Vasiloff never caught a fish and made a dollar that he didn't wanna tell the IRS about," Duck added.

When our taco feed was over, Duck and BD headed down to the harbor. I told them I needed to go by the Post Office, just up the street in the stately old building that also housed the courthouse and Fish and Game. Then I was gonna keep on going to Anna's apartment.

Once again I had mail from home. This time it was from my sister Sandra. Odd, why would she write me?

> "Dear Big Brother,
>
> Do you have any idea how freaked out your parents are? Well I do. I am hearing about it every day and it is making my life miserable too. You have not called them once since you left several months ago, and have only sent 2 postcards. Our father is alternately morose and enraged at your lack of interest in the business he has built *for you!* (italics by Sandra). He wants you to come home soon and grow up. Our mother is consumed with anxiety that you *will drown or be eaten by bears!* (Sandra's italics again.) I personally don't really give a rip if you think you are Captain Ahab. I am used to your delusional states.

What I am miffed about is that dad is so intent on giving you his empire, when you don't even want it. I have been accepted at several very good colleges, not that anyone here has noticed with all their hand wringing about you. I am interested in going to business school and being "the son Moe never had." I've tried to bring it up with him, but he seems to think I'm just going to college to find a husband. He sees you as his heir, can't get beyond it. Perhaps you can put in a good word for me with him the next time you tell him you don't want a Taco franchise. He's such a sexist that he probably won't consider it otherwise. Be safe.

Your sister, Sandra."

Arnie's truck wasn't there. Maybe Anna was with him, or gone out somewhere, but I went up the stairs and knocked. I heard water running. The kitchen sink maybe? Then it stopped. I knocked again.

Then Anna's voice came in a funny singsong: "I hear you. I do-o. Who is it?" The door opened. She looked startled. "Hi there, Matt."

"Hi Anna."

"I'd invite you in, but . . ."

"No, probably not a good idea."

"No. Let's go for a walk. Let me get my shoes on."

We walked on the muddy gravel streets. Down to Railroad Row. Past the little old frame houses built for the foremen and mid-level people during the railroad days. Then out Lake Avenue, past the new Coast Guard apartments all in a line. We didn't say much. My ultimatum from our last visit hung heavy between us. Anna finally broke the silence.

"I got an odd phone call today."

"Yeah?" I was pretty certain which call that would be.

"Yeah, it was from your pal Donna. She sounded like she was losing it, but the gist of it was she wanted me to know that Nick actually had the money from the fishing season when my daddy drowned. I don't know why she's telling me this now, but if it's true, I suppose some of it is my Mom's. The boat share and the skipper's share too. Maybe fifteen, twenty thousand dollars. She could drink herself to death a lot faster if she had all that money."

"Christ, you could buy a house with 20 grand!"

"But how do you make Black Nick give it to her if he doesn't want to, that bastard! What would you do, Matthew? You're the college boy."

"I don't know. You can't sue to get something you can't prove even exists. Maybe Martin Gauer will solve the problem for you."

"She told Gauer too? Wait, how do you know all this?"

"Donna told me. She was flipping out about Nick and Vicki. She made me drive her to the airport. Said she's leaving town, leaving Nick."

"Hmmm. Made *you* drive her? She'll be back, just watch." We got to Nirvana Park, off to our right by the lake. A strange creation built by a Yogi mystic back in the 1940s, its dark little paths and odd structures all covered with muskeg lurked between overgrown trees. "You know, you may be on to something" she mused. "That Marty Gauer has about as bad a temper as Nick does. He hates to have anyone disrespect him. This could turn into the battle of the ticked-off titans."

Finally, I just had to ask. "Did you talk to Arnie, Anna?"

"Not yet." She looked at me out of the corner of her eye to gauge my reaction. I guess that was what I expected to hear, judging from her demeanor. I was bummed, but I tried not to show my disappointment. We walked a little farther. Up on the hill to the left was the Pioneer Cemetery, the native cemetery. The old wooden Russian crosses, with their diagonal second crosspiece like a polite afterthought to support the feet of Christ, leaned at drunken angles in the tall grass and wildflowers.

"Come up here, Matt. I hope it's not too early." I followed her up through the high grass between the old graves. "Oh, here's some! See? Chocolate lilies! Look at these things!" The thin stalks, a couple of feet tall, ended in three or four delicate trumpet-shaped flowers a deep, rich burgundy-mocha color. The color of Anna's lips. "These are my favorite wild flower. They like it here with our dead people." I took her hand. We stood in the meadow for a while among the grave markers and the wildflowers until Anna said: "I want those lilies planted on my grave when I die."

# CHAPTER 23

## Cut The Net

We were into Friday afternoon of the sixth fishing opener. Fishing was pretty good but the weather forecast was bad. I'd made a couple of flood sets in the channel, getting half a dozen fish each time. An obese mass of black clouds filled the sky to the southeast and dark skirts of rain hung from their distended bellies. The southeast gale they'd forecast was still only a stiff breeze, strengthening little by little. The channel was getting rougher and there was a big swell rolling in from the ocean as well, but I figured I could get my high water set in before it was blowing too hard and then I'd go anchor up for the ebb and let it blow if it wanted to. I tossed the buoy and began to lay the net out, jogging slowly downwind toward the beach just inside the point. The squeak of the reel and the clatter of the corks going out through the rollers next to me made a nice, busy sound. When the net was about half way out I saw the first splash. "Got one already!" Big seagull turd size drops of rain began to splatter the deck.

I finished setting and stood gauging my movement against the log debris on the beach. The flood had just about stopped for high water. A steady stream of boats was coming in from fishing out in the ocean. It must be getting pretty shitty out there. I ducked into the doghouse for a cup of coffee and to get out of the rain. I found a dirty mug, dumped some instant coffee into it and grabbed the pot of water steaming against the stovepipe. There was only enough water for half a cup of really thick mud. The sea seemed to be getting rougher by the minute; soon I felt the slap and hiss of a bigger wave.

I scrambled out of the cabin to see the other end of the net swinging out toward the angry line of white breakers. Going out, not in! The ebb was early, or the ocean current was swinging in the bar and pushing me west. I pulled the starter cord on the Briggs. The reel can get an empty net back in under five minutes, plenty of time to avoid drifting into the breakers. But the first sockeyes came over the roller in a little cluster. Uh-oh! I could see a couple of spots along the cork line sunk down from fish. I was picking as fast as I could, breaking meshes with a finger to pop the fish loose. The pile around my feet and in the hold got higher, but the remaining net continued to drag the skiff toward the surf. From the top of each swell I could feel the wind and see the angry 15-foot breakers humping up and crashing, closer and closer. Those monsters would fill the skiff up like a bucket. The only other boats still down by the bar got their nets aboard. One more was coming in from the ocean.

"Where did all these little bastards come from? Christ! The one piece of advice everybody gives is 'stay out of the breakers.' So how am I gonna do that now? Set it all back out and let it go? Lose all those fish and the net too? No, maybe I can make it. Keep picking!" I stopped even trying to pick them, just giving them a hard shake and then wrapping the ones that didn't come out right onto the reel. "Oh, shit!" "Oh! Shit!" I chanted under my breath as I shook fish loose as fast as I could. I was drenched from water trickling inside my rain gear, and from the sweat prickling under my t-shirt. My mouth tasted like rat fur. My stomach was churning. A big wave, a mountainous wall of grey, came humping up higher and higher as it advanced along the cork line toward me. Fish and net hung suspended in mid-air over the deep valley between the wave and the stern of the boat. Then it lifted the skiff up its impossibly steep face. We crested over the top and onto the broad back just before it folded and broke behind me into a booming mass of white water.

"Cut the net!" My end buoy rose on the crest of the next breaker. I started the outboard and fumbled for the knife to cut the remaining net loose and get the skiff away into quiet water. The knife slipped out of my gurry-coated glove and into the bilge. I felt around frantically between the fish floating in the bilge water. Got it! Too late. The suction of the approaching wave was like a rug being pulled out from under the boat. "No! Don't break! Please don't break on me!" The wave crested just as it reached me. It loomed over me and seemed to hang there. Everything was still for an instant as the wave blocked the wind. I dropped to my knees and hung on to the transom as the avalanche thundered down. I closed my eyes. This is it; this is how I die. I was amazed at how time slowed. I braced myself for pain the way you do when the dentist advances toward your face with the big steel novocaine needle. Then the sound of crashing water and crunching wood exploded in my ears. Tons of water almost ripped my hands from their grip on the stern.

Gas cans, gaff hook, hatch covers and other equipment bobbed in the hissing calm behind the wave. The breaker had blown the doghouse completely off and the surf was rolling what was left of it in toward the beach. The boat was full of water. The panic I'd felt as I tried to avoid disaster was gone. Now I viewed the totality of the catastrophe with calm clarity. My boat's ruined. I can't stay in it. The breakers will use it as a club to beat me with. Get away. Lifejacket? Probably under the bunk somewhere, rolling in the surf. I waded forward and unsnapped my spare buoy from the submerged gunwale and snapped it to my belt. As the next breaker loomed up I kicked off my hip boots and raincoat and splashed over the side, hugging the buoy to my chest. The wave lifted me, rolled me over and over, and the white water pushed me toward the beach. But the current was flowing out and to the west, through the breakers. My teeth began to chatter. I kicked my rapidly numbing feet in a feeble attempt to reach the beach. It felt like I'd been kicked in the belly by the cold, and my nuts were all sucked up and aching like I'd been kicked there too. The rope from the buoy sawed into my armpit, and I kept rolling upside down. Eventually I just hung there on my back with the buoy by my shoulder, trying to keep my head out of the water.

What is it . . . thirty minutes in this water before you freeze to death? I've heard of guys making it longer than that. Is it a bad way to die? Wait, who said anything about dying? The longer I was in the water the more unimportant it seemed. I was amused to see the occasional absurd object from my boat float by. I started feeling warmer, drowsy even. Every so often a big white foaming wave would bat me toward the beach, but the steady current kept moving me west, around the point to the outside. I thought about my mom, and how disappointed she will be when I drown. I should have written to her more. I wondered if Anna will feel bad for me, or if her sadness was all used up on her daddy. I was getting more and more remote from the whole scene. Just feeling stupid and a little sorry for myself, maybe. The way I'd feel if I put a dent in my new car, or pulled some other dumb stunt like that.

My legs were lead. They stopped at the knees. I tried to force my hand to move, to perform a simple task, and the inability to do so was inordinately funny. My whole body felt like a leg that has gone to sleep and now I was trying to use it too soon. It had been a while since a big wave came by. I heard a strange high-pitched whine like an eggbeater. The sound was more in the water than in the air. It grew louder. "A boat. That's a boat!" I tried to tread water and wave the buoy in the air to attract his attention. Couldn't do it. Head went under. But the boat changed course slightly and headed toward me, the bow throwing up sheets of spray.

When he was almost up to me he backed down in reverse and heaved an orange ring with a line attached. It landed a few yards to my left. I reached for it, but it was too far. He pulled it back and heaved it again. This time the rope landed across my body. I clutched it under my armpit and I felt the ring buoy come up against my shoulder. By now the boat had blown sideways and was wallowing heavily. The skipper began pulling me toward him. The hull rose threateningly over my head and crashed down beside me. On the next dip I felt a hand grab my belt and the back of my pants. On the rise, my rescuer took advantage of the upward momentum to pull me up to the rail. I got my arms over and smacked my chin on it hard. "Throw your leg over!" he commanded. I slammed my knee against the hull a couple of times, far below the top. On the next rise he grabbed behind my knee and rolled me onto the deck with a thud.

My mind exploded with the most intense feeling of bliss and love for this magnificent human being, this saint, this demi-god who'd saved me! I rolled over onto my back, opened my eyes and looked up at Nick Vasiloff's sharp features and black goatee. "Well, if it ain't Johnny Longcock." The mocking voice came to me through a haze of exhaustion.

Nick moved quickly to the Marauder's forward outside controls and spun the boat out away from the beach. I lay on the deck, blasts of salty water squirting through the scupper hole near my head dousing me repeatedly. The wind was really howling now. Over the wind and the roar of the big gas engine I heard Nick shout: "You'd better get into the cabin and take those wet clothes off. There's a sleeping bag on the bunk. Wrap up in that and sit by the stove." It seemed like too much hassle. I didn't really give a damn, I was just glad to be out of the water, but my teeth were chattering uncontrollably so I forced myself up on my hands and knees. A raw, burning sensation filled my sinuses as a stream of seawater gushed from my nose. Violent contractions of nausea shook me and the burning tore through my throat as I retched up a couple of gallons of acid, salty water.

"Yeah, pump the bilge! Pukin' beats dyin' any day!" Nick hollered back at me. When I was empty I crawled up to the sliding cabin door and fumbled at it with spastic hands. He reached over and pushed it open and I tumbled down the two steps into the cabin. It took an eternity to shuck off the thousand pounds of sopping jacket, shirt and pants and to drag the sleeping bag off the bunk. I sat on the deck by the stove and absorbed the warmth. My arms and legs began to tingle painfully, probably the only thing that kept me awake. I felt the boat entering calmer water, then a while later it throttled down and I heard the anchor chain rattle. The anchor grabbed with a jerk and the boat settled in to a steady bucking into the wind. With every big gust the stovepipe whistled a loud note like a huge flute.

Nick took off his raingear and entered the steaming warmth of the cabin. I was still huddled by the stove. He reached up and turned on the big AM marine radio. "They call'em weather forecasts? The goddamn things aren't even weather reports! Gale warnings my ass. It's blowing all of 50 knots out there right now!" He switched channels and a nasal female voice came on.

"Cape Fairweather to Cape Suckling, Storm Warning, Storm Warning, Storm Warning. Winds southeast to 55 knots, seas to 18 feet." "Area 2 C, Cape Suckling to Gore Point. Notice to Mariners. Gale warnings upgraded to Storm Warning, repeat Storm Warning. Winds southeast to 50 knots with higher gusts. Seas to 20 feet." He turned the radio off.

"Well, at least Peggy figured it out. No one's going anywhere for a while in this shit." Nick picked up my soggy pile of clothes and tossed it out onto the deck.

He opened a cabinet and pulled out a half gallon of Canadian Mist whiskey, poured a coffee mug about half full and handed it to me. "Here! Take a good snort of this. It'll make you feel better." He sat down on the bench seat on one side of the little galley table and poured one for himself. I took a sip. Mount St. Helens exploded in my mouth. Firebombed Dresden's 150 mile per hour winds burned down my throat. Hiroshima was incinerated in my stomach with the heat of a thousand suns.

"Tastes a damn sight better than sea water I wager," he laughed. My eyes were closed and I was exhaling spasmodically. "Oh, I see, the salt water puke has you kinda raw? This'll fix it." He filled my mug the rest of the way up with Bailey's Irish Cream. Hoping for relief I took another sip. Better. A warm glow, probably fatal radiation burns, filled my belly. Nick ducked into the little focsle a moment, and then tossed me a red sweatshirt and a pair of long johns a funny shade of pastel pink. He saw my expression and smiled. "I washed them with the sweatshirt and they came out all faggoty like that. Too manly for ya?" They were way too short but I put them on and sat at the galley table, my head in my hands, feeling weak.

"You had a close one, kid. I saw you picking into the breakers as I come in. You shoulda let that net go. Got a little greedy, huh?" He didn't seem to notice my silence. "I saw you swamp and figured you'd puke out the other end of the breaker patch, so I ran back around to pick up the pieces." A harder gust struck us and the stovepipe flute modulated up half an octave. "Jesus, it's gotta be blowing 60! I hope those poor bastards who decided to stay out in the ocean find something to hide behind. Guess we can kiss off the rest of this opener. 'Course, you'll have to kiss it all off till you find another skiff. Won't be much left of that old piece of shit you were fishing." He mused for a moment and took another pull on his mug. "You know, you ain't as dumb as you look. Snapping that buoy on your belt probably saved your life. 'Course, they've got such a thing as a life jacket, you know."

I finally roused myself to speak. "They're so bulky. I had one in the cabin."

"Hell of a lot of good it did you in there!" he snorted. "You warming up yet? Have another pull, and then we'll put some hot soup in you, and some pilot biscuits." He opened a can of something, dumped it in a pan and put it on the stove.

"You know, I lost a skiff once like you just did. True story. It was fall, silver season, coming on night, nobody around. I made a set on the outside beach. After a while I ran in to tow on the inside end of the gear. The swells were pretty good size, not as big as today, but a couple of big sneakers came in and they broke right where I was. The first one fills you up and the second one rolls you over. I made it in to the beach, but it was blowing and raining and I was wet. Damn cold too. I figured I was going to freeze to death unless I got out of the wind, so I dug me a hole behind a dune and covered myself up with sand, just my head and one arm sticking out. Held my jacket over my head to break the wind. Spent the whole night like that. Warm enough, I guess. The next morning they saw my busted-up skiff on the beach and came and got me. Wool! Gotta wear wool. Stays warm when it's wet."

"You have insurance on that skiff?" he asked me.

"Yeah, I do. The cannery made me."

"Well then, you'll be back in business in a week or two."

"I don't know." I was shaking my head in disgust. "Maybe I ought to get out while I can still walk away. I don't know what I'm doing anyway."

"What the hell's the matter with you? You think this is supposed to be easy? Everybody fucks up out here, especially when they're green." He took another pull on his mug and warmed up to a subject obviously dear to his heart. "That's what's wrong with people these days. No guts! Raised up too easy! First time life shits on them they run back to the titty. Find some nice brainless job in an office or a factory and start counting down to retirement. Now fishin', you got nobody to depend on but yourself. When you start out you don't know shit and nobody going to tell you much, either. How many fish you got in so far?"

"What, for the season? About 600 reds and a couple dozen kings."

"Well, shit! That's respectable enough, who for it is." He put a bowl of beef barley soup in front of me and a box of pilot biscuit. "Here, eat some of this and then we can get down to some civilized drinking." The bowl slid with the bucking of the boat until I grabbed it with one hand.

A boat appeared out the port side window, with a figure up on the bow, his raingear flapping wildly in the wind. He tossed an anchor over and the boat blew back astern as he paid out chain and line with one hand. He gestured at us with the other and shouted something unintelligible but obviously angry. Nick was not pleased. "It's that idiot Martin Gauer. Anchoring too fucking close! Might as well hook his anchor onto my transom, the moron."

"Where were we? Oh yeah, toughness! My old man was the toughest bastard I ever met. Stubborn and mean into the bargain, but tough! Momma used to say he'd never die, 'cause God wouldn't take him and the Devil didn't want the competition. He was a White Russian in the Revolution over there, the losers. He got sent to Siberia to some camp. Him and two other guys escaped somehow and they walked halfway across Siberia and across the Bering Strait to Alaska. Took 'em over a year, but two of 'em made it to the US. I shit you not!"

"How'd they get across the water?"

"He said they waited for winter when it froze and walked over the ice, but I suspect they might have stole a boat. He used to joke about the third guy, the one who died on the way. He'd say that the two of them would never have made it through that winter if they hadn't taken a sandwich. The third guy, the weak guy, was the sandwich!" He bared his teeth and took an exaggerated bite out of a crisp pilot biscuit. "Sometimes Papa'd get shitfaced and start looking at one of us kids with this evil kinda look, and I'd remember the sandwich guy and it would give me the creepin' fantods." Even when his Latigo leather face smiled, Nick's steel blue eyes stayed icy hard, like the devil himself.

The bounce of the boat began to change. Instead of a straightforward bucking, it started to surge from side to side like a fractious horse on a long lead. Our heads and shoulders snapped left or right with each surge. "The ebb's trying to lay us sideways, but the wind won't have it. Gonna be miserable for a couple of hours. Might as well drink up!"

"No, I'm fine!" I said as he reached over and sloshed my mug up again anyway.

# CHAPTER 24

## I'll Tell You The Real Goddamn Story.

"**Y**ou know, I considered throwing you back like an undersized halibut, but I don't ever wanna see anyone drown on my watch again. I lost my brother that way. Still, you never did me no favors, 'less you consider helping a guy get rid of his wife a favor. I understand you even drove her to the airport for me. By the way, if you're gonna borrow a guy's truck, the least you could do is put some gas in it for him." I shifted my position uncomfortably. Being around him made me nervous, a little scared, and now we were on to a subject that might just get me punched in the nose. Nick grinned at me; obviously delighted at the discomfort his remarks had produced. "And now you're chasing after Anna, too. You're a pesky fucker, you know that? I can't keep you away from my women." He gave an amused laugh.

Despite my fear of him I bristled at this one. "I don't think Anna would like it if she knew you thought of her as one of *your* women. You're right at the top of her shit list."

"Me? I treat the girl good! What's she mad about?"

"There's a lot of stories about what really happened when the Nancy V sank. And now Donna says you stole Joe's share. Gauer's too."

"They don't know shit," he growled. "Least of all Donna." His face had a bleary whiskey expression but his eyes gleamed intently. "You wanna hear the real story? I'll tell you the real goddamn story. Get it off my chest." He started to rock back and forth. His voice changed timbre, as if he was recounting a dream, or a Homeric epic from memory.

"We've been seining at Gravina Point, Joe and me and Marty Gauer, on Joe's big seiner. But the weather is getting too crappy, blowing Southeast maybe 35 knots, so we decide to run around Knowles Head to Galena or someplace in Valdez Arm where we can keep fishing but get out of the weather a bit. So there's this nasty following sea, a big chop really, maybe 5 or 6 feet high. Joe calls me up to the wheelhouse, says: 'she's feeling sluggish, Nick, not steering right. Go check the back deck. Maybe the skiff is swamping or something.' He throttles back a bit.

As soon as I open the galley door I can see the stern is awash, the seine pile starting to slop around. 'Shit! We're sinking! The stern's under!' Marty gets in the skiff. We're going to try to lighten the stern up by setting the net. But just about the time he gets the skiff going and we pull the pin a wave washes the whole seine pile over to one side. A hatch cover floats off. Now we're listing 30 degrees to port and water is pouring into the hold. We're fucked! I yell to Marty to turn the net loose and come get us. Another wave washes half the seine off the stern, then the engine stops. I don't know if it flooded, or the seine got into the wheel, or what, but we're dead in the water. Joe is on the radio, sending off a Mayday. I wave Marty around to the downwind side of the boat, hoping to keep the skiff's prop away from the seine, which is washing all around us now. Deck's so steep I can barely get back in the galley door to yell up to Joe.

'Joe! She's gone! We're getting off, Joe! Right now!' He comes down through the galley, practically sliding down the deck. He tosses me a life jacket, has one on him. I put on mine. He comes out onto the deck and hangs on to the mast. Then I say: 'Have you got the money?' Over half our season is in a plastic bag under his bunk. We've been selling for cash to this new buyer from Seward. The fucking bag has got almost $30,000 in it. We look at each other; then he turns and goes back in. Marty is screaming at me to jump in the skiff. I take a step toward him but right then the whole port side goes under. She rolls over so fast! The mast and the power block hit the water, barely missing the skiff. I'm in the water. It's cold. I can't swim. None of us local kids ever learned. Where are we gonna swim without freezing our nuts off?

I pull my way along the cork line of the seine back to the boat. Now the forward half of the hull, upside down, is the only thing out of the water, sticking up at a 45-degree angle. I work my way along to a porthole still above the water. Someone left it undogged. I can stick my head in but I don't fit through. I'm screaming for Joe. I see him splashing up over the mattresses and crap floating in the upside-down focsle. He's got a big gash on his head and blood running down his face. He gets to the porthole but he's not gonna to fit through either. He hands me the moneybag, stuffs it in my shirt. "There, got yer money." He pats my chest.

I say: 'Joe, you've got to dive down through the galley! Out the door or the big galley windows.' He just shakes his head. One of his pupils is way bigger than the other and he has a far-away look. The water is coming up in the focsle. I think about closing the porthole to hold in his air, but I can hear it wheezing out through the anchor locker way up forward. I reach in and hold his arm. He looks at me with the saddest face, the look he used to give me when we were kids and I did him some dirt he didn't think he deserved. Not mad, disappointed.

'Take care of my Anna, Nick,' he says. 'Take care of her!' Then the water comes up over us and the life vest pulls me up to the surface and his arm slips away."

Nick is quiet for a while. "Why'd I make him go back in?" he mutters softly. Then he flashes his evil grin. "OK college boy, you're the smartass. What would you have done different? Forget about the money? Just piss away half our season?" I didn't dare say anything. He watched me for a bit, then a look of triumph came over his face. "See? I never did tell Marty I got that money. Greedy fucker don't need it. Joe's wife would just drink it away. That money is for Anna, if she ever grows up."

I got a sudden burst of courage from somewhere. "And you're gonna be the judge of that?"

"Yeah. I am."

"So, why'd you tell me about the money if it's such a big secret?" His grin hardened back into a nasty, threatening grimace.

"What money? The money's on the bottom of the Sound, remember? It's all sea stories. Blackbeard's buried treasure. Besides, you're in shock, and drunk."

He was right about the last part. Nick seemed like he would drink forever, but I was done. Waves of blackness washed over me and I was falling asleep as I sat, my head tipping forward and awakening me with a start. "Crawl down in the focsle there with the sleepin' bag. I'll sleep up here on the day bunk. Not that I dare to sleep. Probably better keep an anchor watch tonight."

I slept real hard for a few hours, then hardly at all. The boat kept bucking and yawing; waves slapped against the hull inches from my head, and the anchor line squeaked and snapped in its roller. When I finally dozed off again I dreamed I was trapped in the claustrophobic focsle of the Marauder. It was filled with water and lying on the bottom of the sea. I was struggling desperately to keep my nose in a little bubble of air, way up in the bow.

# CHAPTER 25

## When the Horse Bucks You Off.

In the morning it was still blowing a steady 30, but the worst seemed to be over. Nick made good coffee, but my hangover was not tamed that easily. Besides the coffee, I drank cup after cup of water from his little sink. It tasted like fiberglass, but at least it was wet. "So, what should I do with you?" he asked me. "I put it out on the radio yesterday that I had you, you didn't drown, so I can't just throw you back now."

"Take me over to the Teal, they'll run me to town when they go."

"Yeah, OK, I gotta get rid of my fish anyway. I guess Uncle Merle can have this batch. It's just about low water right now, about as gentle as it's going to get for tying up out here."

The Teal left a little after noon and, whitecaps spanking its broad, flat stern, plowed slowly downwind through the cans and sticks which marked the channel across "the hump" to Point Whitshed, then to town. I sat in the warm galley with Walrus and Rob, a fisherman who had a blown engine in his skiff and was getting a tow to town. Ray, the Filipino boxer, was standing at the big diesel oil stove. Plate after plate of sourdough pancakes and crisp bacon came out of a couple of cast-iron frying pans and I drank coffee till I had the jitters.

Walrus shook his head. "For God's sake Matthew, put something on over those pink longhandles. I got a pair of Levis here ought to fit you." When he came back with the pants he said: "We thought we'd lost you there, Bud. A couple of guys said on the VHF that they saw that new guy, the Muskrat, go into the breakers out on the point, and you never came back out. Finally we heard Nick come up on channel 16 and say he had you."

"Yeah, I pulled a really swift move. Should of just cut my net and let it go."

"That was a bad blow last night." Rob said. "We don't usually get 'em like that until Silvers in the fall. Must have been some big-assed waves out on the point. Hey, you hear about Mikey Mills over at Grass Island?"

"No, what?"

"Oh, his anchor line parted around high water early this morning. Before he could get out of his bunk and get his engine started the wind pushed him backwards into a sandbar so hard he broke his outdrive. Then it pushed him way up on the flats over toward King Salmon."

Walrus chimed in: "Nobody could get to him to tow him, so with that big tide and that high wind he blew right up there by the grass banks. His skiff's gonna be stuck up there at least 'till the next run of big tides, in two weeks."

"You should always have a spare anchor on board," Ray concluded.

Walrus said: "But you, Matt, you need to have a spare boat on board! What are you gonna do now?"

"I don't know. Maybe I should quit, go with the flow. Insurance pays off the boat and I've made over a thousand after my gas and groceries. Maybe I should retire with my vast wealth." Even as I said it I knew I was just wallowing in embarrassed self-pity. I've been humiliated and scared, but I don't think I'm going to quit fishing, just like I wouldn't swear off picking my nose or masturbating just 'cause someone caught me doing it.

Ray looked at me funny. "You know, if I stayed down every time I got knocked down by a lucky punch I wouldn't have won very many fights. No, I got back up, even when I didn't really want to."

"You're right, Ray. But I'm a little spooked out right now."

"Well, you almost drownded, so I understand this. But when the horse bucks you off, you get right back on. Show him who is the boss."

The Teal let me off at the end of D float in the harbor. The rain was still blowing sideways as I stumped over to the Sally B in Walrus's Xtra Tufs, which were a couple sizes too big. I took a shower until all the hot water was gone. When I had finally rinsed off the salt water to my satisfaction I slept for a long time. Finally, someone woke me up, banging on the door of the galley. "We know you're in there, Witz. Open up."

"What do you want, Byron?"

"Come open the door! It's raining!" I stumbled down from the wheelhouse bunk and let them in. BD and Melissa. Melissa gave me a hug that lasted for a long time. When she finally let me go, she held me out at arm's length with a very stern look on her face.

"Don't you EVER do anything like that again!"

"OK."

Then BD started in. "Seriously Matt, it sounded on the VHF like you drowned in the breakers. You scared the shit out of everyone."

"Sorry. Didn't mean to be inconsiderate." We looked at each other, me with my hangdog face and both of them looking stern. Then the corners of Melissa's mouth started to turn up in a smile. BD burst out in a snigger. In a moment we were roaring with gleeful, relieved laughter, hugging and bouncing wildly around the little galley. When we finally settled down a bit BD smiled at me and shook his head.

"Clever monkey beats the reaper."

I felt my euphoria ebbing away, replaced by seriousness, sadness. "God, I'm glad I didn't drown. I'd miss you guys."

BD looked uncomfortable, changed the subject. "You wanna go uptown? I'm buying."

"No, I think I'll just stay here and lick my wounds for a while. I drank too much last night. That Nick drinks like a fish."

Melissa was not deterred. "Come up and eat a meal at least. Don't just stay down here and brood."

"I'm not brooding, I'm hibernating."

"Well, bears eat before they hibernate."

"OK! OK! Let's go have dinner."


It was prime rib night at the Elks. BD was an Elk, so we were good to go, not that it probably mattered who wandered in. The Elks was in the basement of a cement block building on First Street that housed the bank and overlooked the harbor. Another architectural triumph, it was built with the bathrooms and storage blocking the view. There were no other windows. But somehow an inch-thick slab of overly marbled beef slathered with horseradish, and a football-size baked potato filled with sour cream and bits of bacon, consumed in the troglodytic splendor of the windowless clubhouse seemed like good therapy. I washed it down with red wine that tasted like purple color crayons spiked with vodka.

Nick and Vicki were sitting at a nearby table, with another couple I didn't recognize. We exchanged a glance or two until I felt impelled to go over.

"Well, what can I say? Thanks for saving my life. And for the soup. I'll get your clothes back to you as soon as I get to the laundromat."

Vicki lit up in recognition. "Oh! So *you're* the hippy in the breakers? Thanks for saving him, Nick. He's cute!" Nick rolled his eyes. The other couple looked at me as if I had just landed from another planet.

"Hey, at least let me buy your table a drink here, Nick."

"Be my guest." I turned and walked toward the bar, glad to escape the awkwardness.

Overfull and somewhat drunk, we were thumping back up the stairs to street level as Martin Gauer, Arnie and another guy came down into the Elks. Martin caught my eye for a moment, snorted with contempt. As he passed me he mumbled "fucking longhairs" *sotto voce*. A miasma of whiskey sweat radiated off him.

BD must have heard him too, and bristled. "You talking to me, Shorty?"

"Actually, Clausen, I was referring to yer faggot friend there, the blind muskrat. But hey! Fuck you too!"

I wasn't in the mood for this, but I burst in anyway: "Look, I told you I'd pay to mend your net. Just give me the bill and back the fuck off!" He started puffing up like a toad. Arnie looked me in the eye with a cold stare as he and his running buddy grabbed Martin and dragged him down the stairs.

"Come on, Marty, before the Prime Rib is all gone."

Melissa looked at us in disgust. "What was that nastiness all about?"

"I don't know, ask the monkey here," said BD. "Not that Gauer needs a reason to be an asshole."

I shook my head. I didn't feel like revisiting another of my recent screw-ups.


It was a warm, balmy evening. We were half way down the hill to the harbor when it dawned on me. "Shit! I left my jacket on the chair. I'd better run back up and get it!"

"You want us to come back up with you?" Melissa asked.

"No, it'll just take a second." I'd turned the corner by the Lefebvre Apartments and was almost back to the bank when the door to the Elks' stairway swung open. Gauer's two pals staggered out, supporting him between them. His feet were dragging along the ground rather than walking. I thought he was passed out drunk until I saw the bar towel they were using to try to staunch the blood gushing out of his nose and from a big cut above his eye. The whole front of his shirt was soaked with red.

"Fer shit's sake, Arnie, sit him down on this bench and call the hospital! He's gonna frickin' bleed to death!"

"They already called the cops," Arnie answered, as they flopped Marty down against the wall of the bank.

"Whoah! What happened to him?" I asked.

"Your pal Nick Vasiloff happened to him!" Arnie replied. "Goddamn animal! He belongs in jail!"

The other guy said: "Marty started giving Nick a ration of shit about that money from their boat that sank, grabbed him by his shirt, so Nick just up and cleaned his clock! The bastard was remorseless! We finally dragged Marty up the stairs or Nick'd still be beating on him!"

The cop car pulled up then, with the red light going around, but no siren. Police Chief McKinley got out with a disgusted look on his face. I decided this was a good time to go down and get my coat. Downstairs things were in an uproar. Several tables were knocked over, plates were broken and beer was running across the floor. Nick's friend and another guy had their arms around Nick's shoulders, real tight, and one of them was talking into his ear. Vicki was sitting at the table sobbing, and the lady from the other couple was trying to console her. Nick just looked down at his fists, panting, then he picked a piece of something red off of the big gold nugget ring he wore on his right hand.

# CHAPTER 26

## Dream Demons

I'm standing at the window in horror. My net is festooned across the bushes and muskeg and up over little spruce trees as it snakes away, fathom after fathom, into the tangled woods. How will I ever get it back? "Oh! Oh no!" I must have cried out.

"What's the matter, baby?" Anna asked me gently. "You're having a bad dream. Come back to bed."

I was standing naked at her window, staring out through dream eyes at the hillside behind her apartment. "Oh, damn! I'm sorry. I dreamed the tide left my net up in the woods back there." I got back in bed and snuggled up against her with my eyes closed, my heart still drumming adrenaline rhythms in my ears.

"You guys and your dream demons. Arnie dreams he's being overrun by V.C. and your net gets washed up into the woods by a tsunami." The warm woman smell washed over me; her bed, her skin, her hair.

"How'd you stay out of the war, Matthew?"

"We shouldn't be in that war. It's none of our business."

"But you didn't get drafted?"

"No." I moved a bit to reposition my erection against the curve of her hip. Her hand slid along it in a slow caress. "A medical deferment."

"What for? Priapism?"

That made me chuckle. "No. Heart murmer. A hole in my heart only you can fill." I snuggled a little closer.

It was Monday morning. Everyone but me was out fishing. Last night I'd told Anna my tale of woe and she had fed me a nice dinner of baked halibut with sour cream, Parmesan and breadcrumbs, then took me to bed and consoled me several times until I drifted off to sleep. My dream had jolted me fully awake and now I lay in bed and watched the trees outside the window. Anna sat up and started reading a book she had on the bedside table. After a bit I craned my neck around to see the title. Anna Karenina, by Tolstoy. She was near the end. She gave me a look, then asked, "You ever read Tolstoy?"

"I slogged through about half of War and Peace. I've seen the Garbo movie of this one."

"You should read it. This is my second time. Tolstoy is the master. He understands everything."

"Are you afraid you will end up under the train like that other Anna? Is that why you won't leave him and be with me?" She looked at me with a blank expression.

"What are you going to do now, Matt? About fishing."

I was puzzled by her non sequitur. "I guess I'll try to find another skiff and net."

"You like fishing?"

"It's challenging."

"And what are you going to do in the fall? After silver season?"

"I don't know. Maybe go back to California for a while? Wanna come?"

"You see how you are? I live here. I have a job. I have a house. A life! Here! Maybe it isn't all I want, but it's all I have. You don't live here." She'd trapped me. Anxious bleakness knotted my stomach.

"I'd live here if I could live with you."

"That's sweet of you," she said dismissively.

"But someone else lives with you. And he must not be all you want, either, or I wouldn't be in this bed. So why not change it?"

"There is more to life than sex and romance, Matt. He's my security blanket." As soon as she said this, she tensed and her eyes got big. She'd said more than she wanted to. I tried to push the fear of what she might be telling me out of my mind.

She tried to change the subject with a joke. She touched my erection again. "If I lived with you, your priapism condition would take some getting used to," she laughed.

"No time like the present to start that therapy." I rolled on top of her and pinned her arms above her head. Anna K fell onto the floor.

I wanted to spend the day with Anna. I could tell I was being what girls call, with withering contempt, "clingy." But I couldn't help it. I felt clingy. It was probably a good thing that Anna had a date with her friend Paula for smoking a batch of fish at Paula's smokehouse. They were going to be cutting and brining fish all morning, and tending the fire in the smoker all day and all night. It sounded like an Alaskan excuse for a girl sleepover to me. I teased her about bringing her pajamas and a big stack of 45 RPM records, maybe making s'mores. She assured me that smoking fish was serious business, and that I would sing a different tune when I tasted the result. She made a breakfast of waffles with more of that great homemade jam, moose sausage and fried eggs, but then she gathered up her knives, put a bandana on her head, turfed me out the door and marched off to start the arcane smokehouse rituals.

So I went by the Union Hall to look at the "for sale" postings. Pretty slim pickings. With no seine season, anybody who had a gillnetter that ran was going to be fishing it, not selling it. Then I headed down to APA to face the music with Uncle Merle. He was standing at the counter with the bookkeeper looking at tender tally sheets when I came in. He pursed his lips and nodded his head. "Good to see you, Matthew."

"Good to be here, Mr. Wickett."

"Well put. Sometimes there is just no substitute for good luck."

"Good luck? That's a funny way to think about losing my boat."

"Oh no! You are one of the lucky ones. So, what now? Should I have Gloria here total up your season and cash you out? Or are you going to go back out and give the Copper River another try?"

"Well, I don't know that I can find another boat."

"Oh, there are always more boats. Let's see . . . You might talk to Bob Thoreson. His brother Whitey just went to fish Bristol Bay with their uncle. Whitey's building a new bowpicker down in Seattle for next season and I think he's planning to sell his old rig. It's a Charlie Mohr skiff with a little Volvo inboard-outboard. Bob would know the details. How about a net? You have a spare net?"

"No, but I think BD Clausen has one he would sell me."

"Well Matt, from what I hear you will be putting in an insurance claim for the total value of your vessel insurance. We got a call this morning from the Teal that some of the guys saw your Muskrat up on the outside beach in the Mousetrap, just around the corner from Egg Island Point. All rolled up in gillnet like a Havana cigar. I will need an affidavit of loss, and you might need to get some pictures of the pieces of your boat, so they don't try to make you salvage her. You could fly out and do it, or maybe ask someone who fishes there to sign a witness statement or take a couple of photos next opener, if they can get in close enough. You're going to need to talk to the Coast Guard as well, if you haven't already, since they were alerted that you were missing. It sounds like your boat's way up at the high water line, so no hazard to navigation."

"Hey, thanks Merle. I had some doubts about going fishing again, that maybe I've been given a message. But I keep thinking of what Nick Vasiloff said to me: 'What the hell's the matter with you? You think this is supposed to be easy?'"

Merle chuckled. "No, he's right, its not easy, but there aren't many enterprises left like this one. We're the last of the buffalo hunters. So, just let me know if there is anything you need to get back in business and we'll write you a purchase order. And we'll get that insurance processed ASAP."

"Thanks again."

"By the way, you know Nick's in jail? Actually, he's probably out on bail by now."

"Marty Gauer?"

"That's right. He's in the hospital. He's probably not out by now. Concussion, broken nose and cheek bone, and quite a few stitches."

# CHAPTER 27

## It Does All Make A Circle.

I was walking back from APA in a drizzly mist when the Happy Trails came rolling down the hill from town, no longer black, now dove grey with caked dust from the highway. The horn honked, the truck stopped, the passenger door flew open and Julie, arms spread wide and squealing with delight, crashed into me and hugged. We spun around a couple of times. "I can't believe we found you! Oh MY GOD! What a trip!" Reluctantly, I peeled Julie off me as Charlie came sauntering over. He gave me an elaborate soul handshake and an embrace.

"You guys made it! Welcome to Cordova!"

"Oh man, this place is so far out! When's summer, though?" Charlie asked.

I laughed ruefully. "This is it! Then sometimes it rains. How long have you been here?"

"We got here Friday," said Julie.

Charlie exclaimed: "Man. the wind blew about a million miles an hour during our ferry ride from Valdez! Big honkin' waves were crashing clear over the bow of the ferry!" That must have been the start of the big Friday night blow. I thought of my experience in that same weather and felt myself closing up like a clam in the face of their childlike enthusiasm.

"So, where are you guys staying?"

"Oh, we found this great place, Shelter Cove!" Julie explained. "It's almost like a little commune. We pitched the old army tent just down stream from that wrecked cannery, but sometimes I sleep in the Happy Trails. Lots of cool people are living out there. This place has such good vibes!" She got the dreamy expression I recalled from our French fry encounter, and her blue-green eyes twinkled.

"It does!" Charlie added. "We got jobs at a cannery, St. Elias, the first day we were here. This is Monday, Sockeye Sunday they call it, so no work today."

"But where are you going, Matt?" Julie asked. "Hop in. We can give you a ride."

"Just like the good old days, eh? I was going down to the harbor. I'm living on a boat there. Why don't you come down and check it out, maybe I can rustle up some lunch."

We sat in the galley of the Sally B, drinking herbal tea. I had some of the stuff with ginseng in it to keep me energized out fishing. Half a salmon filet from last closure was in the fridge and I made up some salmon salad sandwiches. Just like tuna salad, with mayo, pickle relish, some chopped onion, these were a staple at cannery lunches and mug-ups. For a real treat, I put in some cheddar cheese and buttered and grilled the outsides like grilled cheese sandwiches. Just as I figured, Julie was enthralled with the toasty brown, buttery treats.

"Matt! You can cook!" She enthused.

"You are going to make some lucky girl one heck of a wife!" Charlie added.

"So where's Peter?" I asked between mouthfuls. Julie's mouth compressed into a line.

"I dumped him. There should be more to life than getting stoned and watching the TV. He wasn't happy about it, though. That's one of the reasons we came here."

I felt a little guilty flutter of happiness at the news of Peter's ex-ness. "Sucks to be him, I guess."

Julie obviously wanted to change the subject. "What about you, Matt, what cannery are you working at?"

"No cannery. I'm salmon fishing. At least I was until last opener."

"You got a job on a boat?" Charlie was excited.

"No, I bought a boat, but I sank it last week in the breakers." I chuckled ruefully. So, I guess I'm unemployed at the moment."

"You sank it?" Julie's big eyes had gotten bigger. I told them the cliff notes version of the story. As I did, they asked a million questions, and I tried to explain the half a million things they knew nothing about. It made me realize how little most people know about boats, about commercial fishing, about the strange little world of a fish town. Not that I was the big expert after all of two months here. Still, I found myself giving the kindergarten versions because they had no way to process anything more, and I wasn't sure I could explain the inchoate mass of impressions I had about it any better even if they could have grasped it.

After lunch, they suggested we go for a ride. They hadn't really seen the town or anything else much in their three rainy, cannery-benighted days here. We loaded into the Happy Trails and I assumed the third place up front, in the middle. The thought flickered across my mind that I was in Peter's spot. We cruised around the half-a-dozen streets of town for a few minutes, then I recalled my walk with Anna and suggested we go out Lake Avenue and along the north side of Eyak Lake on the Power Creek Road. We passed Nirvana Park and the old cemetery, and then the floatplanes tied up at Chitina Air and Cordova Air Services' wooden docks on the lake. One of the old, reliable but extremely loud DeHavilland Beavers was taking off on the lake. Its prop-wash whipped the rooster-tail wake into a white mist that trailed it like the tail of a low-flying comet. Charlie pulled out a fat jay and lit it up with the glow from the ancient cigarette lighter in the dash. "Doobie doobie doo, let's smoke a doobie" he crooned in a passable Sinatra imitation.

The sun poked its snout out once or twice and lit up the lake like molten silver as we bumped along the narrow track between the gravel beach and the steep flank of Mt. Eyak. The first blooms of fireweed were just showing on their tall blossom spikes. In places, the uphill side of the road was a rock cliff 30 or 40 feet high, with little rivulets of rainwater trickling down its face and wildflowers and ferns taking advantage of every crevice where they could find a foothold. Several real waterfalls plunged down the mountain, ducking into culverts beneath the road and into the lake.

At the end of the road, Power Creek roared and pounded out of its canyon and then spread out into half a mile or so of shallow gravel riffles and meanders before entering the lake. Red salmon spawning grounds. A veritable sockeye seraglio. We stopped and got out. The shallow pools on either side of the road had fish by the hundreds. No longer the bright, iridescent flashers of the flats, the colors had morphed into opaque brick reds and olive greens. The males had developed a hunchback and a dogtoothed, billhook snout. The females had scoured out little dips in the gravel and they lay peacefully in their nests, tails gently stroking to keep their places against the current. The males engaged in occasional splashing scuffles to determine who got to snuggle up against one of the ladies. It was early in the season, but the place already had a ripe fish odor, and several well-gnawed carcasses lay up on the gravel. Big bear tracks were everywhere in the muddy places.

We watched the spawners in silent awe for a few minutes. Then Charlie said: "Boy, when nature does sex, she doesn't just fool around. This is really something!"

I grinned. "Yeah, and they're all dying for love, like some Shakespeare tragedy."

"They all die?" Julie asked. "Can't they go back out to sea when they're done?"

"Nope, its spawn and die for these guys. See how they've changed from the ones in the cannery? Once they hit fresh water they don't eat, and they transform into these new shapes and colors. They live off their fat until they spawn, then they die here and fertilize the lake so their babies will have lots of little creatures to eat when they hatch out."

"I guess it does all make a circle then," she said. "That's what we all do, really. Give up part of ourselves to try to nurture the babies we make."

"And no one lives for ever." Charlie added. "I guess there's worse ways to go than to die at an orgy."

"Once BD told me about the salmon cycle, I felt a little better about killing some of them," I said. "The individual doesn't count for much in the big scheme. What matters is that the species carries on, and that species fits with all the other species. There is no way all the salmon that come back in a good year could spawn here. Us and the bears and the eagles, we take the extra ones. Just don't get greedy and break the chain."

On the way back in, I had Charlie stop at the little Chitina Air Service office while I ran in for a minute. Ellen and another pilot, a blond kid who looked like he was about 14 years old, were lounging in the folding chairs in the waiting room, drinking coffee out of Styrofoam cups. A very round, middle-aged native woman wearing black, up-swept harlequin glasses sat behind the counter with a bank of radios on the wall next to her, a big AM set, two CBs and a couple of VHFs. One of the VHFs crackled as I came in: "3 5 Chitina 9 7 Tango." The woman fished a mike from the spaghetti of them on the wall and replied:

"Chitina Air back."

"I dropped off that starter, the last of the parts runs, at Softuk. Picked up one passenger at Grass Island. Inbound now, ETA 5 minutes."

"Roger 9 7, we'll have someone on the dock to catch you, Tom."

Ellen looked up at me. "Hi Matt, what brings you to this limbo of lost souls?"

"Ouch! Is it that bad?"

"No, but we wait, then we fly a little, then we wait some more."

The other pilot spoke in a tone of mock sincerity: "Ellen here is like an angel tethered to a Cessna 185 by an ankle bracelet. She yearns to fly free, far beyond Softuk." Ellen gave him a sour look.

"Not everyone gets to be Amelia Earhart, huh Ellen?" I quipped. "So, I might need to do a fly-over of my ex-skiff, up on the beach by the Mousetrap? Merle says I should take a picture or two for the insurance."

"Yeah, sorry to hear about that. Do you need to land, or could we just fly around it real low a couple of times? You could ride out on the parts flight tomorrow as a passenger and take your pictures. Cost you $20 bucks, right Mary?"

The lady behind the counter nodded. "Nobody rides for free. Be here around 11."

Now we heard the sound of the inbound plane, then the hollow thump as the aluminum pontoons hit the water. It dumped its speed 100 yards out in the lake, then kept under way with occasional short, snorting bursts of the engine and propeller. An amphibian, it was now in the awkward aquatic phase. No longer airplane; now an airboat burdened with great useless wings on its back. It steered with tiny vestigial rudders on the back of the floats, controlled with rope and pulleys like something that would guide a sea kayak or a soapbox racer rather than an airplane.

Back in the Happy Trails, Julie and Charlie invited me out to the Cove. The afternoon was turning into a nice evening and they thought we should sit by their campfire and swap tales about our adventures. "We'll take you by your boat to get yer guitar, maybe do some tunes?" We stopped off at the liquor store and I got a bottle of Charlie Krug Cabernet to take along. BD had bragged that the wine selection in town had grown, in just the last couple of years, from Blue Nun, Red Mountain, Annie Green Springs, and White Port to include a couple of drinkable wines with far more subtle colors. Cordova wasn't just a beer town any more.

# CHAPTER 28

## Hot and Wet.

We bumped our way into the Cove, followed a few moments later by Walrus in his VW bus. Julie and Charlie went into their tent and I walked over to Walrus, who'd stopped and stuck his head out the window.

"Brother Matt! How'zit goin', bro?"

"Good, I'm good!"

"Seriously, how is your battle fatigue? You know, shell shock?"

"I'm OK. I think I'll get back on the pony, like Ray said."

"Right on! Ray is a wise man, my friend."

"Hey, its Monday, what are you doing in town?"

"The skipper's kid, you know, Jonathan Livingston Seagull, took my spot on the Teal. I'm on the beach."

"Aww, yeah. Bummer, man."

Julie came out of the tent and Walrus dropped his voice to a whisper. "Oh man, Matt! Who is that peaches and cream red-haired girl?"

"That's Julie, a friend of mine from Washington. She just got here."

"I know their tent just popped up here. Wow! It's getting so that every time the ferry comes to town is like Christmas. You just don't know what sort of wonderful presents it will bring! Anyway, I'm going to fire up the sauna a little later. When you see the smoke signals, come on up. And bring your friend if she wants to." He popped the clutch on the bus and rattled on up toward the little cabin in the trees.

Charlie built a fire out of pieces of an old wood pallet he'd scrounged from the cannery, and unfolded some aluminum lawn chairs with plastic web seats. We sat by the blaze and I opened the wine with my Swiss Army knife. Julie brought three metal tumblers, blue, gold and green, just like the ones I drank cool-aid out of when I was a kid, and I poured the vino. We clanked a toast and sat looking at each other with self-satisfied smiles. Then the stories began. We recounted our various Alcan adventures. They'd spent a couple of days broke down by Fort St. John. My tale of the mad trappers and the big handgun was received with shivers. I told them about my vacant Visqueen palace off across the lagoon, and offered it to them if they wanted a little more space.

Then Julie changed the subject. "Matt, I should try to find my friend Anna. You know anything about her?"

"Oh yes! She works at Point Chehalis, right next door to your cannery. She lives in the apartments in the old high school building, at the end of Third Avenue."

"Far out! I can't wait to see her face when I show up." I didn't feel like going into any details about my situation with Anna. I let it slide.

I'd been checking the sauna now and then out of the corner of my eye. Pretty soon its rusty chimney was pouring white smoke, which then morphed to transparent funhouse mirror heat ripples bending the trees beyond the stack. "You know, we are invited up to the sauna. That was my buddy Walrus who came in in the VW bus. He lives in that little cabin across the creek from it."

Julie was on board immediately. "Ohh, that sounds good! I don't think I've been really warm since somewhere back in British Columbia."

"Man, I don't even have a towel." I grumbled.

"Don't worry! We've got, and shampoo too." She went into the tent and pawed around in a duffle bag, came out with towels and soaps. Charlie scrounged in a plastic cooler and found some beers.

We walked up the path along the creek. As it got steeper, someone had attached an old hawser between two trees to make a hand hold. The sauna had a large porch with walls on two sides, filled with big nails to hang clothes on, and a couple of benches to sit on for shoe removal. The creek went by within a couple of feet of the porch, and a large claw foot bathtub had been embedded in the gravel of the stream to make a cold pool.

A couple of people's worth of clothes were hanging on the nails when we arrived. I knocked on the door and called out: "The neighbors are here!" The door had a little diamond-shaped window. Walrus and Patty, his "old lady," were inside.

"Take yer clothes off and come on in!" Walrus shouted. A blast of steamy hot greeted me as I entered and sat on my towel on a bench. Patty was perched up on the highest platform, grinning like a plump and very sweaty Cheshire cat. The sauna was a hexagon shape, old wooden plank walls and ceiling, maybe 12 feet across. A little window looked down onto the Cove and the inlet. Worn wooden benches were built in to 3 of the walls, two tiers high in places. A 55-gallon drum stove dominated two sides and the last contained the door. Walrus was feeding a chunk of wood into the stove, which huffed and glowed with the extra air. Big drops of sweat dripped off the end of his nose and his droopy mustache. On top of the stove was a metal turkey-roasting pan filled with rocks. Very hot rocks. Several plastic buckets of water sat on the floor nearby. "She's just starting to get going good now," Walrus explained.

Charlie came in, his thin white body and cloud of red hair backlit for a moment by the light from the doorway. Then Julie opened the door and stood, another aura of red atop a cello silhouette. "In or out!" Walrus barked, "Yer dumpin' heat."

"Sorry!" She scooted in with a grimace, shut the door and settled onto the closest bench.

"Don't mind him, Walrus thinks he's the sauna fuehrer. Hi, I'm Patty."

"I'm Julie. Hey, thanks for having us up. I need some heat!"

Walrus put on an exaggerated scowl. *"Ich bin der Sauna Fuehrer! Sieg Heiss! Sieg Heiss!"* he chanted in a phony crowd roar hiss. At the second cheer, he scooped a ladle of water from one of the buckets and dumped it on the rocks, where it exploded into a burst of steam with a sound of ripping parachute silk. The cloud spread above our heads then settled down upon us, so hot you didn't dare take a deep breath. "Better!" he grinned evilly.

Charlie had brought in a couple of beers, and offered them around. Walrus accepted. "Patty 'n me, we'll share one, thanks! But first, a libation to the sauna goddess." He poured a little splash of beer onto the stove. It sizzled away to nothing, and the most wonderful smell of freshly baked bread and yeast filled the air. "May she always be hot and wet!" The evil grin reappeared. Charlie smiled and Julie let out an embarrassed giggle.

Patty grimaced. "Stop it!" Fortunately, Walrus and Charlie soon realized they were both dedicated Grateful Dead fans, and launched into an esoteric musicology conversation full of references to Pig Pen and Jerry.

Once we got to really sweating, we took turns ladling water over ourselves from the buckets, soaping up and rinsing off. Walrus tossed a few more ladles-full onto the stove, and the heat finally drove me out onto the porch for a breather. Patty and Julie came out behind me and Patty went straight into the icy creek-water tub with a shriek, immersed for maybe 30 seconds, then came rocketing out again. Julie and I stood, watching the vapor rise off our overheated bodies. I struggled to maintain my faux nonchalance when what I really wanted to do was blatantly stare at her naked, steaming loveliness. Patty clambered back onto the porch and shot us a serious look. "You NEED to do that, you know. Don't be a wuss!" she said as she went back into the sauna.

We still stood looking warily at the tub. "What do you think?" Julie asked.

"I think that water was snow about 5 minutes ago, but I don't think we will respect ourselves in the morning if we don't do it." So in I went. The shock of the cold gave me an intense little mini-panic-attack; a nasty *deja vu* of my salt water swim a couple of days ago. Shit, maybe I do have shell shock! I was back out in a couple of seconds, half-heartedly reassuring Julie, between shudders, that it wasn't so bad.

Julie went in gamely enough, with a full-throated scream. She doubled or tripled my immersion time, then came out panting with short little exhalations, covering her breasts with her forearms. "Owww! That's so cold my nipples hurt!"

"Let me kiss 'em better." Ohh, I can't believe I said that! Maybe I should claim to have Tourette's or something.

She winced with embarassment, but gave me a sly smile as she walked past and back into the sauna.

After the next rinse cycle Julie and I decided we were done. Another couple of cove-dwellers had showed up with pot, which was well received by Patty, Charlie and Walrus, who stayed to smoke it. I didn't want to fuzz out the good tingle from the sauna, so I passed.

Back at the Happy Trails, we got the fire going again and Julie got out her trusty teapot. I strummed the guitar aimlessly while she brewed up something that smelled like oranges. After the tea, she said: "Matt, do you do any Roy Orbison? He's so emotionally exposed for a rock-n-roll guy. I just love that." I played *Crying* and she sang with me, like we had actual broken hearts. Then she got up, poked the fire and smiled at me. "Let's do *Be My Baby*, Matt." We picked a key she liked and off she went.

> *You didn't know how much I needed you so*
> *And if I had the chance I'd never let you go.*
> *So won't say you love me*
> *I'll make you so proud of me*
> *We'll make them turn their heads, every place we go.*

About half way through she started looking straight in my eyes as she sang it, tarting it up hotter even than Ronnie Specter used to do. I sang the "*be my, be my babys*" on the chorus, while she did the fast syncopated *bemylittlebaby* riff, wiggling in time to it.

> *So won't you please. Be my little baby*
> *Say you'll be my darling. Be my baby now. Oh, oh, oh, oh.*
> *I'll make you happy baby, just wait and see.*
> *For every kiss you give me, I'll give you three.*
> *Ever since the day I saw you, I have been waiting for you, you know I will adore*
> *you 'til eternity.*

"God, Julie, you sang it like you meant it!" I said half jokingly and half hopingly. We locked gazes again and I set the guitar down. She didn't reply, just came over and kissed me on the mouth. We ended up in her little nest in the back of the truck, kissing and fondling until she pushed me away firmly.

"What?"

"I need to get my diaphragm."

Julie did sex with inward-directed intensity, single-mindedly pursuing climaxes like a huntress. She wasn't making love to me as much as making it *along with* me. At first her disconnected remoteness was disconcerting, but then the transcendent animal need of it was a liberating turn-on. Julie really liked to screw! And if she liked me too, then so much the better.

The next morning we woke up all warm and snuggly in the back of the truck. Actually, I woke up first and watched her sleep for a while. One arm was thrown up over her head, outside the blanket. The smooth skin on the inside of her arm was almost translucent and seemed to glow from within. A little tuft of hair in her armpit, then the swell of breast, rising with her breaths. God! Women are so much more beautiful than we hairy, malformed lumps of male clay! It's a wonder they deign to speak with us lesser beings, let alone mate. Julie's eyes flickered open. "Hi, Matthew. Why are you staring at me?"

"Because I want to. I've wanted to stare at you ever since I met you." I kissed her on the breast. She sat up, all businesslike, and said she would build a fire and make coffee. I recalled her forlorn morning at the campfire in Oregon. "No, let's go in to town, to the Pioneer Cafe. The coffee will be weak, but you won't have to make it. And the sourdough pancakes will be to die for."

"OK." Julie put on some clothes and started up the truck.

"What about Charlie?" I asked.

"He's my brother, but we aren't joined at the hip. I don't need him to help me gaze into your eyes over a cup of coffee."

"OK."

The pancakes at the Pioneer were world class, a little crispy around the edges and chewy and tangy from the real sourdough starter that had been in the Wiess family for decades. Julie's cannery job started at noon that day, so after breakfast, she swung me by the Sally where I traded the guitar for my 35-millimeter camera. Then she dropped me off at Chitina Air and gave me a little goodbye kiss. "Have a fun airplane ride, Matt!" It was going to be more like a funeral, laying the Muskrat to rest, but I was excited to fly in the little float plane and get a birds eye view of the flats.

# CHAPTER 29

## Who Needs The Misery?

Ellen was flying the parts flight. She had one other passenger, a little Jewish man. The guy was actually wearing a yarmulke. He was going out to one of the tenders down at Softuk, clear at the other end of the flats. He was buying fish for cash, and had an attaché' case clutched tightly in one hand, no doubt filled with stacks of twenties and hundreds. As we strapped into the metal seats, I made eye contact with him.

"*Shalom*," I said casually.

"*Aleichem shalom*," he replied with a guarded smile.

The weather was high overcast, but you could see a long way underneath. The first part of the trip, over the grass banks, looked just like the 'Nam TV footage of chopper flights over the Mekong Delta. Green and flat, with little ponds and sinuous tendrils of river snaking through it. Then we were over the grey-on-grey of the tide flats. The inside of Egg Island lay off to my right, and we flew right over Copper Sands. The Teal was laying with the others in the tender anchorage, perfect miniatures like the little ship models I used to build. It was just about low water, so the banks were showing. Dozens of Lilliputian gillnetters were hanging on the ends of their long strings of pearls in all the sloughs. I recognized Steamboat, and Duck's skiff. Ellen pointed way up by the grass banks to the north where a lone skiff sat forlornly on the sand. "Mikey Mills" she intoned. Then she winged over and lined up a landing in Pete Dahl slough, up above the markers where there were no nets. She gauged the landing so that we dumped our speed perfectly and only idled the last 50 feet. She stepped down onto the pontoons just as they bumped gently at the stern of one of the tenders, and handed over a tie-up line. A box of groceries and a coiled-up steering cable were passed across, then we were up again and off to Softuk. To the left we could see way up the Copper River. Ramparts of mountains reached into the clouds on each side, with glaciers slithering down the valleys. Between were braided the muddy channels of the river, pouring out of the interior laden with the silt the glaciers were relentlessly grinding off the face of the land.

"*Gezegenung* (farewell)," the fish buyer muttered shyly as he clambered down onto the plane's float at Softuk.

140

"*A gut yor,*" I replied with one of my few fragments of Yiddish. He nodded and climbed on the tender. Ellen dropped off another batch of parts for somebody's engine tune-up, and we were on our way back. We flew west along the outside beach on the return. Most of the bar entrances had rows of breakers barring the gates at low tide. We passed over Egg Island Channel, wide open except for the big hook of breakers on the west point, then came an indentation in the beach, with rows of white waves quite a way out. A couple of boats had their nets set in the deeper gutter between those breakers and the beach. The Mousetrap. Ellen winged the plane over into a wide circle, and descended until we were maybe 100 feet off the sand.

"Get your camera ready." There were a few big logs and sandy lumps along the high tide line. One of them was teal blue. She tipped us about 45 degrees and the inside wing, my side, pointed down as she turned the plane in a tight clockwise circle.

The skiff was half full of sand, the metal reel stanchions were hammered flat and one side of the hull only had about half the planks. The remaining ribs sticking up on that side looked like the old cow skeletons along the trail in a John Ford western. Net was draped everywhere. More net trailed across the sand, peppered with silvery lumps of fish. Seagulls and eagles, their lunch interrupted, took off in alarm. There was no sign of the outboard or the doghouse. I snapped some pictures while Ellen circled us around two or three times.

I looked over at her and shrugged my shoulders. "I guess I'm done." She nodded. I had an empty knot in my stomach as we flew back to the lake. I kept flashing on those eagles and seagulls pecking the eyes out of my sandy corpse up on the beach.

I was in a blue funk as I walked back toward town. Passing the native graveyard made me think of Anna. Anna my love. Queen of my heart. Until the next girl comes along and sings "Be My Baby" to me. I don't deserve either one of them.

The Sweetbrier, the Coast Guard's big black 180 foot buoy tender, was moored at the end of the city dock. I stopped by and filled out a bunch of forms attesting to the disaster wrought by my incompetence. Not an uplifting experience. I thought about trying to see Anna, just down the road at Pt. Chehalis, but I was too bummed.

I spent the evening on the Sally B. Made some dinner and played the guitar. Actually wrote a letter home, but left out the part about the near-death experience. They didn't need to hear that. I just said that I was trying to buy a better, safer boat.

Eventually I grabbed a book, thinking I'd read myself to sleep, when someone tapped lightly on the galley door. "Are you receiving guests this evening, Mr. Mankiewicz?" It was Julie, channeling her elegant-English-girl accent again.

"I'd be delighted by your company, Miss Vaughn." It was true. Just seeing her smile raised my spirits, and when she came into the galley and gave me a nice, juicy kiss, they rose even further. Then she pulled away. "I saw Anna today! (Startle response.) At her cannery. She lives with some fisherman guy. (Minor discomfort.) God, she's prettier than ever! (Pang of longing.) I told her about you, Matt. (Vague sense of unease.) She says she knows you. (Stronger sense of unease.) We're gonna get together tomorrow after work." (Sounds like trouble.) Then she shifted gears and asked me about my flight.

"It was actually kinda depressing," I told her. "But there's nothing to be done."

"I'm sorry, Matt. I was hoping you'd take me for a boat ride some day."

"Maybe I will yet. But where are my manners? Could I offer you a little something?"

"What have you got?"

"Brandy?" She made a scrunchy face. "Cookies, and milk?" The scrunchy face bloomed to a smile and she nodded. We sat at the table and ate Hydrox cookies, chocolate with cream centers. With rapt concentration, Julie twisted each one apart, dunked the half-cookies into her milk and then, with a blissful expression, consumed them.

"You eat cookies like a ten year old girl scout."

"Once you perfect a skill, why change? And you better hope no one finds out you've been having sex with a ten year old girl scout, Mr. Mankiewicz!" She smiled a devilish smile and grabbed another cookie.

When the cookies were all gone I lured her up to the big bunk in the wheelhouse. As I unbuttoned her blouse I asked her: "Didn't your momma warn you not to take cookies from strange men, young lady?"

"You're not so strange as you think. And I only take cookies from the cute ones."

The fleet came streaming back into the harbor at high tide early on Wednesday morning. Julie had to go to work, and so did I. I needed to go buy a boat and a net. I was walking up from the harbor when I saw Anna coming down the hill toward the canneries. I smiled at her and waved. She didn't smile back, but stormed straight up to me.

"You and Julie!" she growled. "What the hell is that?" She scrutinized my face as she said it. "What the fuck? You're screwing that hippie tart, aren't you"! A wave of hot shame rolled over me, but the blatant unfairness of her double standard pissed me off. My pent up frustration with her and Arnie bubbled over.

"Excuse me? Which one of us is living with someone else?"

"So you don't deny it?"

"You've got a lot of nerve! Let's be fair!"

"Fair! What's fair got to do with it? I won't have it! I won't put up with it!" She stamped her foot in frustration. Her face wrinkled as if she was about to cry, then turned cold and hard. Her voice took on a singsong, mocking tone. "Move in with me, Anna. I love you, Anna. We're soul mates, Anna. Bullshit!" She kicked the gravel with her boot, threw her hands up above her head. "What's the point of it all? Who needs the misery?" She brushed past me and walked away down the hill.

Part of me wanted to run after her and grovel at her little boots for forgiveness, but a hard lump of anger stayed me. I went the other way, walking with no particular destination for several blocks and muttering under my breath. "Thinks she's the center of the goddamn universe! Everything has to be Anna's way or no way! 'I won't have it!'" I mimicked. "Selfish little brat! Not liking the boot on the other foot very much, is she?" I ranted and raved about the lack of justice for a bit more; then the anger ebbed away, leaving only the sick feeling in my stomach and the sadness and guilt.

# CHAPTER 30

## You Have Some 'Splaining To Do.

**M**y mission was still to find Bob Thoreson and see about buying a damn boat. I pulled myself together a bit and walked out Whitshed Road, as it followed the edge of Odiak Slough. About a quarter of a mile along a big wooden barge, maybe 100 feet long, was moored against the steep bank of the slough, resting on the mud. Bob's skiff was tied alongside in a little channel. A two-story conglomeration of structures took up most of the barge's deck. I could almost leap down onto the roof from the road, but instead accessed by way of a slippery wooden staircase attached to the bank.

I knocked at a door with a big porthole. A voice called out. "It's open, abandon all hope and enter." I entered, into a shed-like anteroom of painted plywood, part fisherman's locker and part pantry. A chest freezer, shelves of canned goods and cases of paper towels, a workbench with engine parts, another bank of shelves with boxes and jumbles of fishing gear. An open door led off to the left into what looked like a garden shed or a warehouse, another led to the right down a long, dimly lit hallway. A set of stairs led up to doors on the second floor. I hesitated, not sure where the inhabited portion of the maze was located. The voice called out again. "Up, come up and to the right."

I found my way into the kitchen/dining room/living room/observatory. Bob, coffee cup in hand, was sitting at a table by a wall of windows, looking out across the slough to town, and beyond to Orca Inlet and the mountains on Hawkins Island.

"Ahoy, Bob."

"Matthew!" He flashed a wry smile. "I wondered who had wandered into my labyrinth for the first time. I can always tell the new ones by their confusion. Grab a cup of mud, the pot's on the stove." Once I was coffeed up, he gestured at the chair across the table from him.

"Funny you should arrive just now. I've been reading an interesting article in Journal of Clinical Psychiatry, about using psychoactive chemicals in cases of repressed traumatic memory. Some descendants of the Leary/Alpert Harvard Psych guys did the study. The problem is that as soon as someone finds a promising chemical cocktail, the government makes it illegal. Admittedly, these psychedelics are not for the faint-hearted, believe me, I know. But we don't make psychotherapy illegal even though it makes people cry."

This stuff was pretty far down on my priority list of problems right at the moment, but I waited while he explicated. We segued into politics for a while, the chances for reelection of President Nixon despite his dirty tricks, and then he asked about my family back in California. I gave him the thumbnail sketch of my boring suburban roots.

"How does the family feel about all this?" He gestured out toward the inlet.

"They aren't too happy. They worry too much." That comment curdled as I recalled that a couple of days ago I had almost died, but I blathered on. "They just don't get how amazing this is, this place, the chance to do something really primal and make money too. Nobody is giving it to me. I'm creating it myself. My father thinks I should be following in his footsteps, that it's all decided, my destiny. I'm supposed to be what he wants. He doesn't have room in his head for me to be anything else."

"Have you told them you feel this way? About what you are doing?"

"No, not really. I've been ignoring them, I guess."

"Hard to blame them, then, for not understanding."

"Hmm. I guess so."

Bob shifted gears. "So, speak. To what do I owe the singular honor of this visit?" I explained about my boatlessness, and the cause, and that I'd heard his brother might have a boat to sell. He watched me with a skeptical eye.

"You are perilously close to breaking the cardinal house rule concerning fish talk, or the lack thereof, in this salon. But, technically, we could call this a business discussion, and skirt the letter of the law. At some point you will also need to address your unresolved anger toward your father, and your narcissism, but this probably isn't the time or place."

In the end, we decided that I would buy brother Einar "Whitey's" skiff. We would go look at it and sign a promissory note in the morning. I could take possession of it with a substantial down payment, which, not coincidentally, was slightly less than the amount I had on the books down at APA. My insurance, whenever it came, would almost cover the rest.

I had no feeling of elation, or even accomplishment, as I walked back to town. I did have the feeling that I was being followed, however. I looked back and saw Skipper overtaking me, padding intently along. He fell in beside me and as we walked together he looked up at me with an occasional quizzical glance.

"What should I do, Skipper? About these women? I mean, it's fine for you to mate with as many bitches as you can; you're a dog! For us, it's more complicated. We expect things of each other. Commitments. And we can talk. Sometimes that just makes things worse. Sometimes we say things we can't un-say, and sometimes we don't say the things we should. Sometimes we say things we feel and then wish we hadn't said them. And if that isn't bad enough, sometimes we say things that aren't true, or we aren't even sure what true is." We got to the corner where Chase Ave. meets the Highway, by Odiak Pond, and Skipper gave me a long look, and then took off up Chase at a trot. "A lot of help you are. Jesus! I'm talking to a dog! You can never get a decent answer out of a dog."

Arnie's truck came rattling down Chase and stopped at the Highway stop sign. The window rolled down and he rested his elbow on the door and leaned his head out. He was a handsome man. Sandy blond hair and a strong, square chin. I wasn't really in the mood for whatever this was going to be about.

"Heard about you losing your skiff."

I nodded.

"I guess you are pretty lucky to be here."

I nodded again.

"So why *are* you here? Look, we don't really need outsiders coming up here. You don't know what's going on and you don't know what you're doing. You're just an accident waiting to happen. Why don't you take this as a sign and go on home. Go back to California and go surfing or something."

I could feel my face redden. I tried in vain to think of something to say. Finally, Arnie shook his head in disgust and drove off.

Back at the harbor, I kept going past the Sally B out to the Glacier Island. "Let's see if Clausen still has a net for sale." BD's skiff was tied to the seiner, but he wasn't there. Melissa was at the galley table, eating a bowl of cereal.

"Really late breakfast, Matt, care to join me? There's lots." She gestured at a huge box of Cheerios and a gallon of milk.

"I'm looking for BD," I said briskly. Melissa's lower lip stuck out in a pout.

"That doesn't make me feel very good," she pouted. I realized what I'd sounded like.

"Wait, I didn't mean it like that. I'm sorry! Let's start over." I took an exaggerated breath. "Why yes, Melissa, I'd love a bowl, thank you! I've been so distracted I've forgotten to eat. No, don't get up! I'll just help myself if that's OK." I grabbed a bowl from the cupboard. "What's with you and Cheerios, anyway? The whole time we all lived at the big house that was the only breakfast cereal I ever saw you eat. No Wheaties or Frosted Flakes?"

She gave me a deadly serious look. "Matt, I just really believe in cereal monogamy." She scrunched up her nose and giggled. Her self-delight made me smile despite my mood. "You're acting funny, Monkey. What's going on?" I sat down at the table with my bowl and spoon.

"I think I bought a new boat. And I think I had a fight with Anna."

"You think? Aren't these things you would know for sure? Why are you being so vague?"

"Well, I won't buy the boat until tomorrow," I said through a mouthful of "O's".

"And the fight?" I took another spoonful, just to postpone the answer for another instant.

"I've been spending some time with this other woman, and Anna isn't happy about it, even though, as you know, she spends a lot of *her* time with another guy, who she lives with fer crissakes!" My voice got louder and my anger came back as I plowed through this convoluted sentence.

"Oh, you foolish monkey! So you're trying to get back at her? If this was a ploy to make her love you more, it was very ill conceived. You're poking a hornet's nest."

"It wasn't a plan at all. It just happened."

"Guys!" she muttered dejectedly. "So, you're sleeping with this . . . what's her name?"

"Julie."

"Julie is the pretty redhead who's been mooning around the Sally?" It was more of a statement than a question. I nodded. "So how did Anna find out about all this? Did you tell her?"

"Julie talked to Anna. They're old friends from high school."

"Oh God, that's even worse! It's easy to hate a total stranger, it's a harder thing to be humiliated by a friend."

"I didn't do it to humiliate Anna! I like Julie!"

"Matt! It doesn't matter why you did it! Julie's counted coup on her old friend by bagging her guy. You drove a wedge between them." Melissa appeared exasperated by my stupidity. I was getting an uneasy feeling that I was in way over my head.

"Well, Julie doesn't know about me and Anna . . . I don't think . . ." I trailed off. The uneasy feeling intensified as I grappled with the nuances of that statement in light of what Melissa had said. She snorted derisively, then just rested her forehead in her hands and closed her eyes, shaking her head in despair.

"You are in sooo much trouble!" Then, in a Ricky Ricardo Cuban accent: "Lucy, you got some 'splaining to do!"

"But, who to?"

"That's what you are probably going to have to decide, pretty quickly. Or maybe you can just go on like this and hope that the two of them don't get together and tear you limb from limb like the Maenads did to Orpheus." She smiled at her clever classical allusion.

"'Lissa, you're not making me feel better," I said forlornly.

"I'm afraid that's not humanly possible at the moment, Matthew. If you were a Catholic, you could try lots of *Hail Marys*. Seriously, Matt, if I were either one of those girls I'd be pretty mad at you right now, not so much for what you did, but for what you didn't do. You blindsided them! They found things out the embarrassing way. Women are like cats. When we fall in the water, we hate it, but the first thing we do is look around to see who else saw. If no one saw, then maybe we can lick ourselves dry and pretend it didn't happen."

"I guess I better go talk to Julie, before she visits Anna."

"Is that a decision? Are you picking?"

"What do you mean?"

"Are you trying to keep Julie, not Anna?"

"Wait a minute! You're reading way too much into this. I just need to explain to her, like you said. Anna's already mad at me, why make it worse?"

"Matt, I've got a net to mend. I've gotta go." She got up and plunked the bowls into the sink, shaking her head in exasperation.

"OK. Thanks for helping me sort this out."

"I'm not sure we made much progress, but, you're welcome."

Julie was working on the slime line at St. Elias. The fish were headed and gutted with long knives by the butchers, who then slid them down the stainless steel tables to the slimers. The slimer had a spoon on the end of a little water hose to clean the blood out of the inside of the body cavity, and make a few passes over the outside to clean off the slime fish have on their skin to lube them so they can slide smoothly through the water. When a fish was clean, the slimer slid it off the end of the table into a tote to be taken away to the freezers.

I stood just inside the doorway and watched Julie in her boots and big rubber apron like they wear at the morgue. Rubber gloves and orange wristers (plastic sausage casings with elastic closures at the wrist and above the elbow) protected her arms. She had a bandana on her head with a plastic shower cap over that, and just a little frizzy ducktail of red hair stuck out at the back of her neck. Her hands were going through the ritualized motions of cleaning fish after fish, but her face had a faraway, Mona Lisa expression. Eventually she noticed me and flashed a radiant smile. She gestured at the clock on the wall and signaled two fives with her non-spoon hand. I waited out in the break room with a cup of coffee and some cookies off the big tray of them the cannery had set out for the next break.

At the break, fifty or sixty people trooped in, grabbed coffee or juice and cookies and sat on benches alongside the long tables. Julie grabbed a cookie and linked arms with me, escorting me outside onto the dock where the smokers congregated. The apron and gloves were gone, but the shower cap made her look like a Dutch woman in a Vermeer painting.

"Hi! What a nice way to break the monotony!" she chirped.

"These places can get pretty boring, all right."

"Tell me about it! I've almost run out of things to fantasize about" she said with a mischievous grin.

"We used to sing down at Morpac. Acapella crab serenades."

"Yumm, sounds like a fancy Italian seafood dish."

"So, Julie, I need to tell you some stuff. About Anna. About me and Anna."

"Like what?" She gave me a quizzical look.

"Well, like we're together, sort of."

"Hunh? She told me she was with that Arnie, that fisherman guy."

"Yeah, she is." Julie's quizzical look changed to annoyance.

"That little pig, always taking more than her share. I told you guys worship her. So, what are you saying? You dumping me?"

"No! I mean, I don't know. I guess that's up to you."

"Oh, I get a say, do I?"

"Look, I just thought you should know. It's only fair."

"No, fair would have been to tell me a couple of days ago. Before you jumped in bed with me."

I made the palms-up, hunchy-shoulder, scrunchy-face submission gesture.

"So, are you dumping her?" she asked.

"She's dumping me, more like." I blurted it out without thinking about the implications of it. That seemed to be my habit these days. She, of course, didn't miss the nuance.

"So I'm your back-up plan B? How flattering!" I shook my head in silent negation, not daring to say anything more. "I'll think about it," she said. "It's not like we're married or something. Still, it pisses me off! Why her?" She pursed her lips into a sour expression and looked me in the face. "Why don't you leave, Matt," she said disgustedly. "I don't want to look at you right now. We'll talk later." She turned her back and stared out at the mountains across the bay, tapping her foot and nibbling absently at the cookie.

# CHAPTER 31

## Everybody I Love Has To Die?

Buying Whitey's boat the next day was a no-brainer; a welcome island of certainty in the sea of confusion and doubts I had about the love triangle, or quadrangle, or trapezoid, or whatever erotic geometry it was I was tangled up in. The boat was clean and fast and everything worked. The unpainted plywood in the hold and aft of the reel had a clean smell of teak oil and floor hardener. A blue and white sister ship to BD's skiff, it had a little Volvo 4 cylinder engine and outdrive that purred her along at 18 or 20 knots. A fathometer and a VHF radio promised to make life a lot more secure. There were two bunks and a diesel stove with an oven in the cabin and a little Plexiglas windscreen on the roof at the steering station to dodge the wind and spray. Whitey even threw in an old Winchester shotgun with more rust than bluing on the barrel. Bob and I ran the skiff down to APA, got a check and signed a bunch of papers, and it was done.

As we were heading back, Marty Gauer's boat went by going the other way, down toward Morpac or the fuel dock.

"That guy seems to have taken a real dislike to me, Bob. What's his problem?"

"Marty Gauer? Interesting tale, there." Bob grinned. "My wife is friends with his wife Alice, so she's heard some stories. But Alice seems a lot happier with Gauer than she ever was with Black Nick Vasiloff. Anyway, Marty's an orphan. Grew up in an institution back east. Being small, he got pushed around a lot, probably was the tormented social outcast for a while. By the time he got out, he was street tough and ran with a rough crowd. There are even some rumors about mob guys. Once he got up here, though, he took to fishing like a duck to water. He's smart and shrewd and he gets what he wants. Bit of an overachiever. I don't know him too well, but he seems to have a classic small man syndrome. Fluffs up like a bantie rooster if he feels slighted. No one is ever going to bully him again. Why, what did you do to him?"

"Well, I ran into his net out fishing, but I offered to pay to mend it and apologized like hell. And his pal Arnie Swenson and I aren't on very good terms."

"So I hear. You know Alice Gauer is Arnie's sister? So you are crossways with Arnie the war hero and Marty the hoodlum. Neither one is probably too taken with your lefty hippie lifestyle, or your hairdo."

We were back to the harbor. I let Bob off at the head of the float, and tied up alongside the Sally. BD and Duck were on the deck of the Glacier Island as I came in, and they sauntered down the dock for a look.

"Well, tat's more like it!" Duck said. "Maybe you'll catch a fish or two this season after all."

"Yeah, nice rig Witz! But the reel looks kinda empty."

"I've been meaning to speak to you about that, Byron."

Duck looked shocked. "Uh oh! He called you Byron there, skipper, like yer mom does. You are either in big trouble or he wants something."

"I want something. You still have the spare red net you were going to sell me?" "Speak in haste, repent at leisure. But yeah, I still got it."

"All I've got left of Pete's gear is the silver net. Meshes are too big."

"If I sell it I'll be screwed if I trash my good one and need the spare."

"Oh man! You've got the prettiest net mender in town living on that boat with you, what are you worried about?

"OK, OK! I'll sell it to you."

"Pay after fishing, right?"

"God, Witz, yer killin' me here!"

"Sorry, but I need to get my shit together if I'm gonna get out fishing on this evening's tide. Where's the net?"

"It's in my locker at Morpac. If you run your skiff down there we can pull it out with the forklift and you can wrap it on your reel right off the dock. I had some other stuff to do, but I can see you're on a mission here, so let's go. I'll head down in Chuck the Truck and get started."

Duck got a serious look on his face. "I'm leaving. You guys don't need me to hold your hand while you do this net deal. But Matt, did you hear about Anna's mom?"

"No, what about her?"

"She's in the hospital. Some kind of liver failure. I think she's got the D.T.s too, the snakes. She drinks way too much, just like my dad."

"Ouch! Not good. How's Anna?"

"Anna's freaked out, is how she is. I saw her there this morning when I went to the hospital. She's in a panic."

"Thanks for telling me, Duck."

BD fed the net over the edge of the dock and made sure it didn't tangle coming off the pile. I took the end of the corkline aboard over the stern, then anchored the skiff about 50 feet out from the dock and wrapped the net onto the reel as it dropped down into the bay. As I was rolling it on I took stock of all the things that weren't ready for actually going fishing. No groceries. Only one end buoy for the net. No hip boots, no oar, no pike pole, no gaff hook, no flashlight, no sleeping bag.

I was coming up with a lot of excuses to stay in town and go see if I could make Anna feel better. Which is what I finally decided to do.

When I got the net aboard, BD took off and I ran the skiff back to the harbor. I went up to the pay phone at the harbormaster shack and called Anna's house.

"Hello." A man answered. I almost hung up.

"Is Anna there?"

"Who's calling?"

"Matt."

"She's pretty upset right now. This isn't a good time." His voice rose. "In fact, there's no good time!" he shouted. "Why don't you fuck off and leave us the hell alone!" Then I heard Anna yelling in the background.

"Who is it? You're not my goddamn social secretary, Arnie! Give me the fucking phone!" Then her voice came on the line, quiet and tearful. "Is it you? Oh God, Matt! I'm so scared! She's gonna die. She's finally gonna get her wish." She started to cry.

I didn't know what to say. "Anna, baby, Anna, she's at the hospital. The doctors know what to do."

"They don't! Her liver doesn't work and she's having hallucinations! They have her strapped into the damn hospital bed like Frankenstein's monster!"

"Honey, I'm sorry. I'm so sorry."

"Why does everybody I love have to die?" she wailed. "Daddy, Rick, now my mom. I almost lost you too."

"Anna, are you going back to the hospital this evening?"

"Yeah, after I eat something. I'm gonna make Arnie go fishing, then go back."

"I'll meet you there. I'll come there."

"OK."

I got to the marine supply store just before they closed, grabbed up a bunch of stuff I needed, paid for it on a cannery purchase order, dragged it all down to the skiff, then turned around and headed back up to the hospital. As I walked up the hill to Second Avenue I rolled the replay of the phone conversation over and over in my head. Her mom's situation sounded bad, but there was nothing I could do about that. Anna had been in a tiz, but she'd put me on the list of the people she loved. Distraught or not, she'd practically bitten Arnie's head off for trying to chase me away. I had no idea what I could say to comfort her, but at least she was willing to let me try.

Anna was sitting in the little lobby of the hospital with a plump middle-aged woman who looked at least part native. The place looked more like a small 1950's apartment building than a hospital, but there was a nurse on duty at the reception desk. Anna got up and came over to me. She had a horrible, vacant look on her face. "Visiting hours are over. They won't let me in to see her unless something happens, which I guess would be that she dies. And they've got her on so much sedative they probably won't even know!" As she said this, she crumpled into tears and leaned herself against me in a listless hug. I held her and rocked slowly back and forth, feeling completely helpless. She sobbed quietly for a few moments, then stepped back and wiped her nose and eyes with the sleeve of her sweater. She gestured at the native lady. "This is my Auntie Ruth, mom's sister. She is my rock. Ruthie, this is my friend Matt, from California."

Ruthie nodded her head, but her stolid expression never changed. "Hello" she said. The three of us sat together on the cold Naugahyde couch for a while. I couldn't think of anything to say.

I took Anna's hand and held it, gave it a little squeeze now and again. She looked exhausted. Finally, I suggested that she might want to go home and sleep. I offered to walk her up the hill to her place. She nodded mutely, then went over to the nurse. "I just live two blocks from here. If she wakes up and calls for me, you call me! Don't just let her die here all alone."

"No one's dying, dear. And I have your number right here on this pad."

Aunt Ruth said: "you go home to bed, Anushka. I'll stay here little bit more."

We walked slowly up the hill. I held her hand. When we got to the apartments I asked her if she wanted me to come up. "No, Matt. Thank you, but I'm bad company." She hung her head.

"That's not true," I mumbled. She ignored me and kept on through clenched teeth.

"I'm sorry I'm such a bitch. It seems like no matter how hard I hold on, everything I love keeps slipping away."

"Try to sleep, Anna. I love you." She gave me a tiny sad smile and touched my lips with her fingertips.

# CHAPTER 32

## An Etiquette Question.

I went out to the flats on the morning high water. Better late than never. I was at the Copper Sands anchorage in just over an hour! And no windburn on my face! Got there in plenty of time to get a high water slack set. With the fathometer, I even knew how deep the water was without having to poke down into it with the pike pole! I spent some time sonar-ing around looking for deep potholes and getting a 3-d sense of the bottom in the places that I had been fishing blind before.

Duck had said a little squirt of reds always came in to Eyak Lake the end of June or around the 4th of July, and some of them were there on that tide. I got maybe 20 on the high water set. BD's net was better than the one I'd gotten from old Pete, 60 meshes deep instead of 45, and almost no holes. The water that came dripping off the net into the bilge triggered the automatic float switch on the little 12-volt bilge pump. No more bailing!

As the weather was good I ran out into the ocean. I had to go past the Egg Island point, which gave me a case of the shivers as I recalled my last disastrous visit to that spot. I steered way wide of the breakers as I motored out and down to the east toward Pete Dahl, and set the net out in 40 feet of water. Again, I marveled at how much faster I could get around, and how everything was so much easier with better equipment. Once the net was out I went into the cabin and surfed around the channels on the VHF radio. Another luxury! I could communicate with others, and I could try to figure out where the fish were being caught. This was especially important when fishing out in the big ocean. There are a couple of theories as to how to do that. One is to determine the location where no one is talking. This is the radio version of the black hole in astronomy. The black hole appears black not because of the lack of anything there, but because the mass of what is there is so huge that not even light can escape its gravitational field. The radio black hole is black because the mass of fish in that area is so great that radio waves don't escape. The fishermen in that vicinity are too busy picking fish to talk on the radio, or they are maintaining radio silence because they are terrified that the rest of the fleet will come where they are and clean up the fish they are working on.

Another way to fish via radio is to find a channel that some radio group is using to communicate in secret code, and break the code. The key to catching lots of fish during any given opener is to find where they are as soon as possible. Since each fisherman only has one net and can only be in one place at a time, we form radio groups with other fishermen we think might be able to find a fish or two, and when one guy does he tells his group, they move there, and that increases the chances of the whole group getting onto the fish. The trick is to somehow tell your group but not the whole fleet. It also helps if the fleet doesn't even know who is talking and to whom. Hence the code. The code needs to enumerate in some way what each guy is catching. A 10 fish set for an hour may seem like pretty good fishing, but if another guy in the group somewhere else got 40, that is obviously better. So radio codes employ randomly generated words to stand for numbers. And random or goofy radio monikers for the identity of the speaker. Someone comes on the radio and says: "Afghanistan, Basutoland."

"Afghanistan back, switch to the other channel." They go up to "secret" channel 79 or whatever.

"Basutoland, you got me up here?"

"Roger."

"I had a Mai Tai on the last one and a Pina Colada before that."

"Yeah, OK. I'm getting about a Martini an hour down here. Maybe I'll move your way after low water." So, you now know that a Martini is probably fewer than either of the fruity tropical drinks in the tipsy drink code of the undeveloped country code group.

The down side of monitoring the radio is the inane and boring conversations one finds oneself auditing. In time, gillnetting, like warfare, can come to consist of long periods of boredom punctuated by occasional moments of excitement, or terror. Some relieve the boredom with long, pointless radio chats. They forget that they aren't talking on the phone, and that they are sharing their rambling musings with other hapless users of that radio channel.

After a while I tried giving Byron a call. My boat name was a problem, though. Whitey, in a fit of Scandinavian ethnicity, had named the boat the *Opna Havet*, which meant "open sea" in some obscure Norse lingo. So when I called BD on the *Hard Rain* the call went something like this:

"Hard Rain, Opna Havet"

"Hard Rain back to the boat calling."

"Opna Havet back, it's Matt."

"Up the Hobbit? What the hell is that? Man, you need a new handle there, Hobbit!" Now Duck came on the radio in a hissing, quavery voice.

"What's it gots in its pocketses, little hobbit? Give us the precious! Must have it! Nasty little hobbit steals the precious!"

"Screw you guys! I'm just checking to see if the radio works."

"It's booming in here in Mordor," someone else says. That was enough for me. I hung up the mike and went out on deck to pick up the net, desperately vowing to rename the vessel.

There was a flurry of activity about a third of the way down the net from the boat. Three or four corks were bobbing vigorously, like I was catching something big. Maybe a cluster of fish hitting all together? A moment later, a large black form broke the surface with a snort of exhaled breath. The sleek head and shoulders of the sealion stayed above the water as the massive jaws crunched down several times on the silvery fish, which was still trailing a tatter of green gillnet web. Then the whiskered mouth opened wide, and with a deft toss of the head the fish disappeared down his throat.

"Hey! Stop that you asshole!" I shouted at him. He gave me a brief glance, then dove back beneath the surface. Several gulls landed to gobble the last bits of sockeye meat floating in the oily patch of water where my fish had just been consumed. Now another part of the net began to jiggle ominously. "Oh, you bastard!" I was livid with anger and frustration, and dove into the cabin to get the shotgun. I was determined to defend myself from further depredations by this voracious pirate. When I came back out, he was down at the far end of the net. Clearly out of range. I picked the net as fast as I could, but several mutilated fish came aboard, and new tears in the net made it clear that the lion had worked me over pretty good. Who knows how long he'd been there, tearing the fish out and eating them or just ripping the bellies and eating the eggs or milt? At $4 a fish and hours of net mending a visit by a sealion was a painful experience. Sometimes a peppering of shot would discourage them, but when they got too thick you just wrapped up the net and left the area.

When I got back to town Nancy Vasiloff was dead. I heard about it from Melissa as soon as I tied up the skiff. "They were planning to fly her to the native hospital in Anchorage sometime on Friday, but she went into a coma and died before they made it happen."

"Oh no! Anna's gonna freak out."

"Yeah, she did! When they called her and told her her mom was gone she stormed down to the hospital and raised hell, screaming at the nurses and the doctor. Sheriff Mac had to come and take her home. Everyone in town is talking about it."

"Oh, geez. Oh no." I just stood there looking at the dock and shaking my head.

"Well Matt, I thought you should know. I'm gonna go mend some gear over on A float. See ya."

It was pretty early in the morning to be trying to see Anna or call her. Actually, I was dreading it, so I figured I'd wait a while. I'd been on short rations out fishing, so I decided to go up town and get breakfast.

The Pioneer was crowded with fishermen plowing into plates of sourdough pancakes, bacon and eggs. Most had just rolled off their boats and were still in their fish-smelling flannel shirts with the sleeves cut or rolled half way up the arms. On their heads were dirty ball caps or the flat beret-like "halibut hats" which had once been white cotton but were now a dingy, mottled brown, tie-dyed from fish-slimed gloves. The air was thick with cigarette smoke, coffee steam and loud, growly talk. I saw John and Duck at one of the tables. Duck's shirt had white salt rime at the cuffs.

"Join you guys?"

"Plunk it down. We just ordered." Duck started in on me right away. "Say, John, did you know Matt here was a hobbit?"

"Seems tall for a hobbit," John said thoughtfully.

"So I've been told," I replied. "I'm changing the name of the fucking boat."

"Ooh!" Duck was shocked. "That's not something one does lightly. That can be bad luck. Still, unless you are a Skandahoovian like Whitey, it could be a burdensome name you've got there."

"So, what chew gonna call it," John asked?

"I'm thinking 'Desperado,' like the Eagles' song."

"Good name," John nodded. "Hey, I saw Marty Gauer this morning. He's out of the hospital, but he still looks pretty dinged up. He's all pissed that they aren't going to press charges on Nick. Police report says Gauer initiated physical contact, so the rest was just yer everyday bar fight."

"Boy, if he started it he sure came out on the wrong end of it." I said.

"Yep," said Duck. "Nick doesn't lose 'em very often. The only time I even heard of a draw was when Arnie Swenson tangled with him for punching Arnie's sister Alice back when she and Nick were married. Everybody figured Nick backed away from that one a little bit, 'cause Arnie was in the right to call him on it. Alice is married to Gauer now. He may be a jerk, but at least he doesn't punch his wife."

The waitress came over with her apron and note pad. "Did I miss you, honey?"

"Yeah, I just crawled in here, but I'll take a short stack and a couple eggs over easy, coffee and orange juice." She scribbled, then bustled off. I looked over at Duck and softly asked: "Did you hear about Anna's mom, Duck?"

"What do you mean? I told *you* she was in the hospital!" As soon as he spoke it was clear that he realized I must have different news. Shit, now I was stuck. I'd suspected by the way he was acting that he didn't know his Aunt Nancy had died. Now I was going to have to be the one to tell him.

"She passed away yesterday morning, before they could fly her to Anchorage." Duck got a blank look on his face and pressed his lips into a flat line. He looked down at the table and didn't say anything. "I'm sorry, man." He nodded his head. His food came a minute later and he ate in silence.

I went to the men's room and washed up. When I returned, Duck was ignoring his half-eaten breakfast. He watched John eat for a bit then said: "Aunt Nancy was real good to me. She could always cheer me up. When I was a kid, her and Joe would let me stay with them any time I needed to get away from my dad. She knew how her brother was when he was bad drunk." He pushed a piece of pancake around in the syrup with his fork. "After Uncle Joe died, she just seemed to fall apart. You know, people try to drown their grief in alcohol. Problem is, the grief don't drown. It floats. Don't know why I'm sad now. She's really been gone for a long time already." We sat a while longer. My food came. "You seen Anna yet, Matt?"

"No. I'm scared to, Duck," I blurted. He got a little smile at that.

"Rightly so. She gets real emotional." He looked back down at the table for a while. "I guess I'll go after breakfast."

After I ate I went back down to the boat and tinkered with some things on the skiff that weren't quite right. Little stuff like greasing squeaky bearings on the stern rollers. Taking stock of what was in the tool kit. Tightening the guy wires that kept the stove pipe on. I was wasting time, trying to put off calling Anna. In the afternoon I finally walked up to the pay phone at the head of the dock and called her. Arnie answered, of course.

"Who is it?"

"It's Matt. Can I talk to Anna?"

"No. She's sleeping, I think. Leastways, she's not crying right at the moment."

"Look, I know I'm not someone you want to chat with, so let me talk to her, or at least let me know how she's doing."

"She's doing awful. In fact, if you give a shit about her maybe you should come try to talk to her. Let her throw things at you for a while. I'll go down to my boat."

"Door's open," she said in a muffled voice. Anna was lying on the couch in a rumpled cotton nightgown, looking out from some desolate place way behind her bloodshot eyes. Her unwashed hair was a tangled mass of flamboyant art nouveau spaghetti spread on pillows damp with tears. The carpet was dotted with crumpled tissues.

"Matthew?"

"Yeah." What do I say to her? "Anna. Sweetheart. I'm so sorry." Her face crumpled.

"Why doesn't everyone just shut up and leave me alone? You're all fucking useless! Just let me lie here."

"OK. I'm just going to sit here for a bit." I sat in a chair. She pushed her face into the pillow. She pounded it with her fist a couple of times and lay there with an occasional sniffle. After a few minutes she sat up, clutching the pillow to her chest.

"I'm a goddamn orphan," she said in a hollow voice. "They've abandoned me."

"I don't think they did it on purpose."

"Maybe he didn't. But her? Once he was gone, I wasn't a good enough reason for her to keep on living." That chilled me.

"Anna, you didn't make your mom an alcoholic."

"I didn't make her anything! I didn't help her. I stayed away from her while she got more and more miserable. I was ashamed of her. The crazy drunk native lady."

I didn't say anything to that.

"I couldn't even be bothered to try to keep her alive. I just went home and had a little nap while she died." She flopped back down on the couch and started to cry.

I sat there for a while longer. "Can I do anything, Anna? Make you food? Hot cocoa? I know those are pathetic suggestions, but I can't stand to see you like this and do nothing." She looked at me blankly, then responded in a monotone.

"Thank you, but no. There's nothing anyone can do. I'm just going to lie here and bleed for a while."

In a few minutes she seemed to go to sleep, or at least lie still with her eyes closed. I gave her a kiss on the cheek and left. As I walked through town I passed Duck's apartment. His light was on so I knocked on the door.

"I just came from Anna's, Duck."

"How is she?" I raised my hands in a gesture of befuddlement. "She chased me away this morning," he said.

"I know, she told me we are all fucking useless, and I guess that pretty much sums it up."

"Aunt Ruth is taking care of the burial things with Hollis, the town undertaker, and Father Vladimir. Other than that, we *are* all fucking useless. The time to do anything about Nancy Vasiloff was a long time ago, if there ever was anything we could have done once Joe died."

"But what about Anna?"

"I think she just has to grieve it out, man, like I did when my dad died."

"She seems so torn apart about it. One minute she's pissed that her mom didn't care enough to stay alive for her, and the next she's all guilt tripping herself that she didn't want to be around her mom cause of her problems."

"Man, that's how it is when your parent's a drunk! It's like he's your kid instead of the other way around. You feel guilty for not helping him but you feel ripped off and embarrassed 'cause he's weak and fucked up when he's supposed to be the grownup. I finally decided that you're stuck with the parents you got, so get over it. And you can't make someone be happy if they ain't."

"Well, I hope she figures that out. She's pretty miserable right now, herself."

"Once they die, your last chance to fix the thing you can't fix is gone forever. That's pretty hard."

Life during gillnet season is chopped into 36 and 48 hour chunks. Two days out fishing and a day and a half in town, then the other way around, like some sort of split personality disorder. I came back to town Wednesday morning after the Monday/Tuesday fishing period, which I had spent exploring around Steamboat and Paulson's Hole, and not catching a whole lot of fish. There was a folded note on the galley door of the Sally. "Matt—Come see me. Julie." The 'i' was dotted with a little heart. That bodes well, I thought, but I have other stuff to deal with. I went over to BD and Melissa's boat.

"Anna's mom's funeral is this afternoon. Should I go?"

"Why are you asking us?" BD replied.

Melissa jumped on him. "Byron! He's asking an etiquette question. He's trying not to be a total Neanderthal, unlike most of the guys in this town."

"Yeah, I guess that's it," I said. "Is it appropriate?"

BD got interested now. "I see. The question has nuances. It's going to make Arnie uncomfortable, for sure. And it's a Russian Orthodox ceremony at their church, then out to the pioneer cemetery, but there will be white people there too, so you won't be too out of place. But, 'Lissa, is it going to make Anna happy? That's all Monkey here really cares about, right pard?" He looked at me with a wry smile.

Melissa said: "She probably won't care too much right now with all her pain, as long as you don't engage in fisticuffs with her other boyfriend. But later on she'll remember that you showed her respect, that you cared."

"I'm not too keen on churches," I said. "My folks never made me go, seeing as how there weren't any Catholic synagogues. They both thought that their birth religions were anti-intellectual mumbo jumbo."

"You aren't into Theo-tourism then, huh Matt? You know, visiting different churches to check out the exotic rituals? But wait, you used to go with me to the Black Baptist Church now and then to hear the soul choir."

"That was the only time I've been in a Christian church.

"Well, don't expect the Russian Orthodox congregation to rock like that."

"I went to the synagogue for my cousin's Bar Mitzvah, and for my uncle's wedding, and that's it for the Judaism. The singing there wasn't that great either, unless you like tenor solos in a four thousand year old language."

"Just show up at the cemetery," suggested Melissa.

As I walked out Lake Avenue to the cemetery I heard the funeral bells from the Orthodox Church down in Old Town. High bell, then middle tone, then the low one, then all together. At the cemetery, I was early, or they were late, but the procession wasn't there yet so I kept walking out along the lake in the grey drizzle. Out past the air services I came to the ice skater's cabin on its little beach. Ducks were feeding in the shallows. Black buffleheads with their Mohawk crests and jaunty white flashes on the sides of the head were paddling around, then diving down with a little plop. I waited to see how long it would take them to pop back up again, and tried to guess where they would reappear. A raven flew into the hemlocks behind me, then dropped onto the beach. He hopped methodically along, inspecting each bit of litter, turning it over with his beak. He pulled open the crumpled paper bag he found by the cabin steps and fished out the piece of waxed paper inside. He cocked his head to one side and eyed it skeptically, then tossed it away, squawked once, and flew off.

I saw the white smoke and smelled the incense as I walked back. The burial ceremony was under way. The priest in his black cassock and odd cylindrical hat was droning on in Russian. A couple dozen people were gathered around the open grave. Arnie and Duck and Duck's brother Bill and sister Lily were standing by Anna and Aunt Ruth. Nick Vasiloff was there, with a striking-looking brunette woman who must be Aunt Sophia. I didn't recognize anyone else in the small crowd trampling the little area of freshly mowed grass around the grave. I stood in the back and watched Anna. Her face was frozen into a stony expressionless mask, like an ancient Egyptian sculpture. Her eyes flickered over to mine, then back into the raw hole in the earth.

The priest went on for a long time. The incense burned my eyes. After a while I walked a few yards into the tall grass to get out of the line of the smoke. I saw a couple of clusters of chocolate lily by one of the old crosses and bent and picked a stalk. Now, the family was dropping handfuls of earth into the grave, one by one. Anna dropped hers in and closed her eyes. Aunt Ruth put an arm around her shoulder. People started to file down the hill to the road. I waited to one side until Anna and Ruth came. I handed Anna the lilies. Her eyes wrinkled like she was going to cry again, but she just nodded. Then Arnie and Duck passed. Arnie glared at me. "Thanks for coming," Duck whispered.

# Chapter 33

## You Can't Screw Your Way
## Out Of This One.

On my way home I stopped by the Post Office. There was a letter from San Francisco, from Roach, and one from someone in Seattle, no sender name on the envelope, just the return address. I opened the one from Roach. He was starting a new band with less drugs and more rock-n-roll. He had a solid drummer and a bass player. He needed a rhythm guitarist who could sing harmony with him. He needed me, he said, so I needed to get over my "Old Man and the Sea" complex and get my ass down to San Francisco.

The other one turned out to be from Donna:

> "Dear Matt,
>
> As you can see from the postmark, I am in Seattle. I am going to start working for a temp agency here as a bookkeeper. It sucks to have no money, but it is better than a pop in the eye, as my Grandma used to say. Ha Ha. Sick joke, huh?
>
> I heard about your boat disaster from my friend Ellen. I am so glad you are safe!! I miss you. Now that you aren't fishing, why don't you come to Seattle? I have rented a little apartment. No phone yet, but write me at this address.
>
> XOXO—Donna"

Oh man, that lady is persistent fer sure! Still, for some reason I felt bad about how things had gone with her. When I got back to the boat I dashed off a letter. I told her about my new skiff as a gentle way of deflecting her "come to Seattle" idea, and I gave her the news about Nancy Vasiloff. I wished her the best with her new place and new job.

I sat at the galley table, feeling wrung out and empty, and hoping I wouldn't have to go to another funeral for a long time. I got out my guitar and played a couple of sad tunes. 'Daniel' by Elton John seemed to best fit my mood. Then I thought about my family. I considered going up to the pay phone and calling home, but I couldn't really face it. I ate a can of clam chowder with saltine crackers, and then walked over to St. Elias.

They were done running fish for the day, cleaning up the processing area, washing down the sliming tables. But they were still loading and unloading freezers. I saw Charlie in one of the crews and waved. He flashed me the peace sign with one of the heavy insulated gloves he was wearing. He was banging metal freezer trays to unstick the rock-hard fish, then sliding them into sleeve-like plastic bags. Another guy was putting the bagged fish into cardboard coffins, a couple dozen into each one.

"Hey, Charlie!"

"Hey, bro!"

"So, Julie's all done for the day?"

"Yeah, got off about an hour ago. They don't want us to work any overtime. Afraid we might make some money. We'll run the rest of the fish in the morning. Anyway, she took the truck out to the Cove, gonna make me walk home."

"I was thinking about going out to see her. What do you think?"

"Brother, she makes it pretty clear to me that she is in charge of her own social life. I know she was pissed at you about that Anna thing, but if you still like her you'd better let her know or she'll be cozying up to one of these cannery cats. A couple of them look pretty interested and she doesn't like to be alone."

"So she doesn't consider me the spawn of the devil? No shoot on sight order?"

"Naw, I don't think so."

I nodded my head. "Thanks, man!"

"Peace, brother. Oh! Hey, we took you up on your offer and moved our base camp into your plastic palace. Bourgeois luxury, baby!"

Julie was glad to see me. It was as if our chat at the cannery had never happened. I told her I had been at the funeral, but she changed the subject. I felt a flicker of guilt when I thought of Anna mourning her mom while I cavorted with Julie in the back of the Happy Trails. Anna knows how to find me if she wants to, I figured. Well, maybe not at this very moment she doesn't, I hope.

Julie awakened first and suddenly rolled on top of me, pinning my wrists to the mattress with her extended arms. Her determined face was inches from mine. "When do I get my boat ride, Matthew? You're not going anywhere until I get my cruise. I didn't come all the way to Alaska just for the scenery on the slime line."

I was enjoying the sensation of her warm body pressed onto mine, and undulated my hips a couple of times.

"Don't try to distract me! You can't screw your way out of this one. I want my ride!"

"OK! You win! I need to go down to the fuel dock this morning. Come with me, and then we can run up the inlet a way, maybe go around the corner to Deep Bay. But I gotta be back to head out fishing around 2:00."

"Good. I'll call in sick at the cannery. OK, now you can distract me."

On the Thursday evening opener I ran up to the Steamboat markers, then followed some skiff through the Racetrack to Pete Dahl slough. Someone had anchored an orange buoy every quarter mile or so to mark the bends in the narrow channel. Pete Dahl was another big drainage farther east, almost as big as Egg Island and Copper Sands but not as deep. I was truly thankful for the depth sounder as I explored the place. Even with the electronic help, I smacked into a sandbar so hard that I bent the hell out of my propeller. It vibrated so bad I was afraid it would shake the boat apart, so I had to put on the spare wheel. I didn't catch a lot of fish either, but felt like I was expanding my repertoire by learning a new place. I was in line behind John at the tender in Pete Dahl on Friday morning. He delivered a lot more fish than I had. Then he idled his skiff along side me as I pitched mine off. "So, Coghill River opens next week, that little sockeye run in the Sound over by Whittier. You goin' over, or staying out here on the Copper?"

"How am I supposed to know? What are you going to do, John?"

"Man! I'm tempted to go over there. The run forecast is OK this year, and it's so mellow! Deep, clear water, no sand bars, no breakers, easy fishing and beautiful scenery. Glaciers and trees! 'Course, you might not catch shit; there won't be very many pinks for sure, but you can make it up with time. It's 5 day a week fishing over there."

"Why would I want to fish 5 days a week to catch fewer fish?"

"Well, there you go! The flats runs are tapering off, but you can stay here and do just fine once half the fleet leaves. Some of these guys hate the flats. They just grit their teeth and bear it until Coghill opens, then they'll fish for one fish an hour over there to keep from having to come out here. I don't know, maybe I should stay here. Well, one thing I know, I better get the net back in the water. Catch you later."

As I pulled away from the tender my engine started to sputter, no power. I throttled up but it shuddered and missed. I circled back into the tender anchorage and threw the anchor. I had a sick, panicky feeling in my stomach. Here I was in a totally new place, now I had some mechanical problem. I opened the engine box and looked at the little 4-cylinder Volvo. Looked like a perfectly good engine to me. I checked the glass fuel filter, emptied it even though there was no sludge visible. I pulled the dipstick and the oil was transparent amber and right at the mark. I fiddled with all the sparkplug leads and the coil wire, made sure everything was attached. I started the engine again and revved it up. Still bad. Well, I don't know shit about mechanics. All I ever did with Brutus was change the oil and spark plugs once or twice. I wasn't that guy who spends the weekends putting a racing cam in his '56 Ford Fairlane.

What the hell was wrong? The terror of the unknown is the most debilitating fear of all. Ignorance is not bliss when your engine won't run. Shit! What do I do now? Call John on the radio!

John came over about half an hour later. We monkeyed around with this and that. Seems like a person is always a clearheaded mechanical genius when troubleshooting someone else's problem, and a panic-stricken toddler when it is his own equipment that has gone in the crapper. Eventually he held up my distributor cap triumphantly. "Broken. See the hairline crack in the plastic? See these burn marks? You've probably got moisture in there too now, and the spark is squirreling around going everywhere but to the sparkplug lead it's supposed to go to. Got a spare?"

"I'll have to check. Whitey has a box of spare parts, but I'm not sure what all is in there." Still, I had an overwhelming sense of relief. Now, at least, I knew what was wrong. I had a rotor, condenser, point set and spark plugs in the parts box, but I didn't have a spare distributor cap.

"Guess you are going to have to buy yourself a five dollar distributor cap for about $50. That's what your parts flight is gonna cost you, after Chitina runs down to Cordova Outboard and buys the cap for you, then flies it out here. Might as well have 'em send you a set of plug wires while you are at it. Those look kinda tired." He looked at his watch. "Call 'em quick and you can get it out here this afternoon on the regular parts flight. Otherwise, you wait 'till tomorrow or charter the whole damn plane."

# CHAPTER 34

## Something Better Than This.

On Saturday, back in town, I went up to the pay phone at the harbormaster building and called home, collect, so I wouldn't have to keep shoving quarters into the phone. Dad answered. He told the operator yes, he would accept the charges, then launched into me.

"Well, thank God you finally called! Your mother was about to call the Alaska State Patrol, or State Troopers, or Mounties, or whatever the hell they are up there, to look for you." Then he reined himself in. "How the hell are you, anyway?"

"Well, I'm OK, Dad. How are you guys?"

"We're fine, of course. So, how's fishing? Catching enough to eat?"

"I'm doing OK. Starting to figure it out."

"I hope you get it figured out soon, and head on home. Your mother is worried sick."

"I know, dad, but it doesn't do any good for her to worry."

"You know, that has never made her stop before." I heard a door slam on the other end. "Chela, it's Matthew! Calling from Alaska! You are still in Alaska, aren't you?"

"Yes, Dad."

"Well, she's grabbing the phone out of my hand, so, be safe."

"Matt? Are you OK? What's happened?" Palpable tone of panic.

"Nothing's happened, Mom, I'm fine. I'm just calling to say hi."

"Ay Dios Mio! What a relief! We're fine too. Your sister is talking about going to UCLA. Something about business school. I hate to think of her down there in all that smog, though. What do you think? She could go to Berkeley and be so much closer. Of course she got into San Jose State too, and she could live at home. But going away to school is half the point, isn't it?"

"I guess."

"How about you? Are you eating? I know you were learning to cook a little bit, but when you are busy you can forget to eat."

"Mom, you're not a Jewish mother, so stop with the eating!"

"I may not be Jewish, but they don't have a monopoly on loving their children. I worry about you. Up in that place. How is BD? And that sweet girl, Melissa?"

"They're doing fine, they say hi."

"You know, Matthew, I worry that you won't meet the right kind of girl up there. All those men, and hardly any women."

"That's not really a problem, Mom. There are lots of nice, interesting women up here."

"Well, that's not what you hear. So, did you buy that better boat you were talking about in your postcard?"

"Yes, I did. It's great! Much better. Newer and safer. I'm even gonna make a little money doing this. Don't worry."

"Well, you can't make me not worry."

"That's what Dad said. But I wish you wouldn't. Oh, by the way, Sandra is pretty interested in the taco business. You might drop some of your not-so-subtle hints to Moe that he should think about a place for her in the empire. You know, she is pretty smart. She says she could be the son Dad never had."

"What does that mean, Matthew?"

"Never mind, Mom, you know what it means. Well, this is costing a lot of money. I'd better say goodbye."

"We love you, Matt. Come home soon. And write more often. How hard is it to write a little post card?"

"I love you too, Mom. Bye."


Oh, God! Why is that so hard? Why can't I tell them anything real? It's all just a big whitewash to keep them from freaking out.

After the phone call, I stood on the dock looking out at the harbor entrance and across the little channel to Spike Island. A tender was getting ready to make the 90-mile trip to the Coghill fishery. He was idling along real slow, pursued by three or four skiffs like baby ducks following their mom. They were rigging up all in a row with bridles of heavy lines. The tender was going to give them all a free tow across the Sound.

My attention kept wandering over to my right, toward the St. Elias and Point Chehalis canneries, side by side. Like I told my mom, there are lots of nice, interesting women up here. At least two, anyway. Pretty soon I walked over that way. Julie was no doubt sliming fish in St. Elias. The Happy Trails was parked out front. I kept walking, to Point Chehalis, to the cookhouse.


Anna was in her usual kitchen goddess mode, bossing her helper, a young Filipina named Nita, who bustled around briskly and wore a heart-meltingly sweet smile no matter how short-tempered Anna got with her. Anna was stirring a steaming something in a humongous aluminum pot. Her hair was tied in a ponytail and she was wearing a white bib apron over her blouse and jeans, apron strings tied in the back in a little bow. She turned when she realized I'd come in, and blew a stray strand of hair out of her face. My stomach gave a tingly jolt. My heart still went over the high hill on the roller coaster every time I saw her.

"Soup's not ready yet, Matt." She gave me a wan smile.

"I see you are back at work, Anna. How are you doing?"

"OK, I guess. Life goes on, even for orphans."

I nodded agreement. Nita looked at us for a moment, then went out into the break room.

"Thank you for coming to mom's funeral. That was sweet of you. You never even met her."

"She had you; that puts her pretty high up in my book."

Anna dropped her eyes and pursed her lips at my ham-handed compliment.

"What am I going to do with you, Matt?"

"Is that a rhetorical question, or do you want me to answer? I've got some suggestions," I said with a leer. She chuckled and went over to the big industrial refrigerator and got out an industrial-sized can of butter. "There!" I said triumphantly. "A smile sighting! I made you giggle. You should keep me around just for that!"

She shot me an amused look over her shoulder, then scooped a gob of butter into a bowl and set it by the stove to warm. She reached onto a high shelf and took down a big plastic sack with about 10 soft-looking loaves of Vienna French bread. "The crap they call French bread up here is an embarrassment. A real Frenchman would fall on his boning knife before he would serve this stuff. The only thing you can do with it is make garlic bread."

"I've never been to France, but remember the good loaves they make down in San Francisco? The sourdough rounds?"

"Oh God yes!" she rhapsodized. "And that Laraborou Bakery that makes French bread that actually has crust! Hard crust, and chewy on the inside? It's heaven! I could eat a loaf of that every day, slathered with butter, or better yet, Brie. Or dipped in your coffee in the morning? I'd weigh 400 pounds, but I'd be happy. You know, Matt, I've been evaluating my life the last few days."

"Have you?"

"Yes." She held up a loaf of the soft bread by one end and squeezed it in her hand until the rest of the loaf broke away and fell onto the counter. With one hand, she kneaded the remainder into a pasty ball of dough, and then held it out to me with a look of disgust. "I want something better than this!" She turned back to the counter and began slicing the loaves in half horizontally and buttering each half. "I'm busy here, Matt. I've got to feed the hogs." Then she paused, turned back toward me, considering. "Arnie's going to Coghill. I think he's getting pretty sick of me. I'm mean to him. In fact, I'm a total bitch." She spat it out with a tone of contempt. "But he's boring. There has to be more to life than fishing and deer hunting." Her eyes locked on mine. "Come for dinner on Wednesday, and we can talk about better loaves than these."

"Can I bring something?"

"Bring red wine, something good. I'm going to cook you a meal I would serve in the restaurant I will never have in this stone-age village."

The meal turned out to be beef Stroganoff, over egg noodles. On the side was a salad and some carrots with a glaze of brown sugar and butter. Cloth napkins, candle on the table, it really was like eating in a fancy restaurant. All the flavors were intensified somehow, and everything looked so neat and perfect. There was a sensuousness to eating food with her. Watching her savor a bite, her rapt attention focused in on nuances of taste and texture, was almost like peeking in on a sexual act.

When we were finished eating, and I had run out of rapturous comments about how good it was, Anna said: "I haven't forgotten about you and Julie, you know. You are a dog. A bad dog!" She stood, picked up the dishes.

I started to launch into my "you do it too" defense, when she cut me off.

"There is a difference, Matt!" She set the dishes down and stood by the table. "I've thought about this!" Her voice was tight, tense. "I'm being unfaithful to Arnie because I love you. That's why it's making him so miserable. I can't help it. But you're being unfaithful to me because you are weak. You're thinking with your dick! I don't think you love her like you love me, and judging from our little sisterly chats, I suspect she doesn't love you either. That's why I haven't kicked your ass out the door. Correct me if I'm wrong."

My nerves were tingling and I had crumpled my napkin into my fist so hard my knuckles were white. It was clear that something important had just been said. Whatever I said next was probably going to be important too.

"You're right. I don't love her. I love you, but I get jealous, then I get mad at you. I feel like a fool."

"I guess love makes fools of all of us."

"Whoah, that's cosmic!" As soon as I blurted the snide comment I wished I hadn't. She recoiled a bit, then she laughed and said:

"Come here, baby. You just don't know when to shut up, do you?"

We hugged for a while, then I said: "Anna, I know I'm kind of a slut sometimes. If a girl chooses me, I'm so thrilled I don't usually say no. But with you, I feel like I did the choosing. You're the one I want."

"Baby, it's always the girls who do the choosing. Sometimes we just let you think it was you, for reasons of our own."

# CHAPTER 35

## Give Me Those Ruby Slippers!

$A$couple weeks later we were once again entwined under the sea otter, glowing and catching our breaths.

"Wow! I thought the Fourth of July was yesterday." She didn't react to my lusty joke.

"Remember the first day we met, Matt, when you went off on all that age of chivalry stuff and pledged to wear my token, and I said I would set you many perilous labors?"

"Yes, I do, Anna. I will never forget the first day we met."

"Well, I have another perilous labor for you." She said it with an air of grave seriousness.

"You mean more perilous than putting up with you?" I laughed.

"OK, forget it then," she said, a little taken aback.

"Anna, I'm teasing you. What is the labor?"

"Matt, convince Nick to give me my money! I want to go away. To the City. To the Emerald City to get a heart, or a life, or at least some goddamn ruby slippers and a job cooking in a real restaurant."

"Why don't you ask him?"

"I asked him weeks ago, right after my mom died."

"What did he say?"

"He teased me! He said he had no kids he knew of, and he'd never had a wife he wanted to leave a nickel to, so I'd get everything when he died. Then he pretty much admitted that he had money, from the Nancy. He said there was some money "for me," and he paid all the costs of mom's funeral, and a few of her bills around town. Then he said it was complicated and would take a little time. He wouldn't give me any more details, about anything. I haven't heard from him since, and I've called him and left messages, but he doesn't call me back."

"Well, it's the middle of fishing season, maybe he's over at Coghill."

"Whatever! He's a goddamn control freak. If he gives me the money then he loses his power over me. He's not the boss anymore."

"Why do you think I could get him to do anything, if you can't?"

"'Cause he saved your life! Now he owes you! You're linked."

"What? That's nuts! He saves *my* life, so now *he* owes *me*? What have you been smoking?"

"You'll see. Just talk to him."

"Anna, when I was on the Marauder with Nick, after he saved me, he told me the story of the Nancy V. I think it was the truth. I could never figure out why he told me, but it finally dawns on me that he must have wanted me to tell you." I recounted the story to her. By the end Anna was in tears. "He never told you, did he?"

"No. And I don't care! I still hate him! Even more! I always knew it was his fault! The greedy bastard killed my father!"

Now I was wishing I'd kept my mouth shut. She wiped her cheek on the bed sheet, pulled herself together. "Just get me my money, Matt. Explain how important it is to me. How important it is to you that I get to make my dream happen, some bullshit like that."

"Is it bullshit? Your dream? Because it isn't bullshit that I want you to have it."

"No, it's not, it's not bullshit," she said, a little chagrined. "I love it here, this place is my place, but how can I miss it if I don't go away? And it's so inbred and claustrophobic. The men are boring. Once you've knocked 'em dead in the Club Bar with an electric blue cocktail dress a couple of times, you run out of challenges."

"OK, I'll look for him, for Nick. I'll ask around about where he is."

"You're gonna be mad at me when I tell you this next thing."

"Then don't tell me. I feel great and I don't want to be mad at you."

"OK." She didn't speak or move for a minute.

"All right! Tell me! The horrors I imagine are far worse than any reality could be."

"On Wednesday I'm going over to Coghill for a few days to fish with Arnie. Nita will handle the kitchen for me. It's like a vacation over there. Then we're going to Anchorage for the weekend. Staying at the Captain Cook and shopping. Nordstrom's beckons to me and I can't say no. I'll be back on Sunday evening."

"Do they have busses in Anchorage?"

"I guess, why?"

"Then I have a favor to ask you, too. Push Arnie in front of one. He won't be expecting it."

"Matthew! That's awful!" She snorted with surprise.

"Does that mean no? Or will you think about it?"

# CHAPTER 36

## I Know You Think I'm A Fool.

I didn't enjoy the weekend when Anna was in Anchorage. I tried not to think about her with Arnie, but that was like telling yourself not to think about an elephant. The more I tried not to, the more I did. I thought about trying to find Julie, but something about it felt too sleazy, even for me.

I was walking up from the boat harbor, passing the Outboard Shop and the Anchor Bar, when I heard the sound of whirring gears. "Sounds like a piece of shit Ford starter grinding up a pound of coffee," I said as I walked up to John, sitting in his not-so-new baby blue Ford truck. While the body looked relatively intact, the truck had sustained a catastrophic injury at some time in the past. Contact with an irresistible force or an immovable object had twisted the frame and alignment such that, when it ran, the truck proceeded down the road in a diagonal, crab-wise fashion, like a Labrador puppy whose rear end was threatening to come up one side and overtake the front. Currently, however, the hood was up and John's window was down. John's seagull was perched on the pipe rack over the cab.

"They've been making electric starters for 50 fucking years!" he cried out in exasperation. "You'd think they would have figured it out by now!"

"Well, the other companies have, but these guys seem to have a problem with it." I pointed at the oval Ford logo on his steering wheel.

"So, Matt, tap on the side of the starter with this big wrench when I crank it. Tap hard, but don't shatter the housing." How the hell am I supposed to know how hard would shatter the housing until I hit it hard enough to shatter the housing, which is exactly what he doesn't want me to do. I decided not to discuss the phenomenological nuances of this paradox with him, as he was obviously in a foul mood already.

I tapped. The starter finally engaged the flywheel and the truck started. John's mood brightened immediately. "Dude, thanks for tapping! Just what the doctor ordered. Where ya going? Need a ride?"

"I'm just going up to Duck's for a bit."

"Hop in, I'll drop you." As we began to roll the gull jumped off the rack and began to fly along behind us. "Hey, I met your friend Julie at the Club Bar the other night." His thick black eyebrows rose like Groucho Marx's. "She told me about how she met you hitchhiking, and how she used to know Anna V, back in high school. Man, I don't get it! Why would a fox like that Julie waste her time with a lanky mutt like you?"

I couldn't see anything good coming from this conversation, so I changed the subject. "So, John, I see you didn't go to Coghill. Are you starving as bad as I am on the flats? Last couple openers I barely paid for my gas and groceries."

"I started to go across, but I changed my mind. Where're you fishing? Still down on this end?"

"Yeah. Egg Island and Pete Dahl."

"Man, you need to come down to Softuk! It's the end of July. There's nothing much left down at this end, but they're still trickling in down there."

"It's so far!"

"It's so far!" John mocked me in a tiny baby voice. "Get a note from yer mom! OK, here's Duck's. We're here."

"Thanks, John," I said as I jumped out. The gull landed and began picking at something in the truck's bed.

Duck was having a little venison feed at his funky, overheated apartment, and had invited me up. Ellen was there, and Kenny, and a friend of Ellen's named Linda, who Kenny called "Auntie Linda." It turned out she actually was his Aunt. Kenny's father Rick was her brother. As I came in, Duck was teaching Kenny how to open a beer bottle with a church key. Ellen and Linda were merrily reprimanding Duck for teaching Kenny bad habits.

"These aren't bad habits! These are crucial life skills every man needs to have! He's not going to have his mom or his aunt around all the time to open his beers for him."

"Let's open another one, Duck" Kenny pleaded.

"Now yer talkin'! But another man rule I have is I only drink one beer at a time. Otherwise, they warm up on ya, and go flat, no fizz. But maybe Matt here wants one, and we can open his?"

"You open 'em, I'll drink 'em" I replied. Kenny held the beer between his knees and levered up the cap, which fell onto the floor and rolled into the corner. A little stream of foam bubbled out the top and down the side. Kenny wiped it off with his hand and rubbed it into his coveralls. "Good job!" I said. "You don't want to hand a guy a slobbery beer."

Ellen groaned: "Not on the pants! You're gonna smell like a brewery!"

"And a noble smell it is, too!" Duck said. "Wear it proudly, lad."

"So, BD and Melissa must be fishing over at Coghill?" I asked. "I haven't seen them for a couple of weeks."

"That's right," said Duck. "I guess BD's dad is fishing over there too, and they probably spend the weekends at their island place, or up in Anchorage. It's easier to run into Whittier for the closures, and take the train up to Anchorage, than it is to get back here."

"So, how about Nick?" I asked. "Seen him around lately?"

"Yer buddy Nick Vasiloff? I think he might be over there in the Sound."

"I guess Anna Vasiloff is fishing over there too," Ellen added, glancing wryly in my direction. "Reeling her other guy back in. I flew her out to the Valhalla at Coghill River on the parts flight on Wednesday." She imparted this information with an evil grin.

"I know, Ellen. She told me. Look, I realize you don't like Anna very much, but I do. And I know you think I'm a fool. I do too. But I'd like you to reign it in just a little bit, for my sake."

Ellen and Linda's mouths both formed perfectly round "O"s. Then they looked at each other and giggled.

"Sorry, Matt! I'll try not to be so bitchy if you try not to be so serious."

"It's a deal, Ellen."

"I can't believe my ears!" Duck was incredulous. "Here's Ellen, usually as serious as a heart attack; telling someone else not to be so serious."

"Watch your step, Donald," Ellen replied, "or I'll start being bitchy to you too."

"Say, did I ever tell you the story about how I shot this deer?" Duck pointed to the big pot of stew on the stove, overtly changing the subject.

"Why, I haven't heard that story since the last time we ate some of your deer, Duck," Ellen replied.

"OK! Then you're about due again." The story revolved around Duck's travails last winter over on the other side of Hawkins Island, packing a slightly larger than expected deer a slightly longer distance than he had thought he had walked, through snow he described as "ass high to a taller Aleut than I am." He could walk on top of the crusty snow fine just carrying his rifle and little daypack, but carrying 70 or 80 pounds of deer made him plunge through up to his crotch. Dragging the deer didn't work either. It acted like a snowplow, creating an immovable berm after about ten feet.

"Did you ever get back?" Kenny asked in wonder.

"Nope." Duck shook his head seriously. "I'm still out there."

"You are not! Don't tease me." Kenny hung his head in embarrassment as he realized he'd been mocked for his dumb question.

"How did you get it out?" I asked. I figured one more dumb question couldn't hurt.

"How would you do it?" Duck asked.

"I don't know, Socrates, I'm just a city boy." Duck gave me a puzzled look. He didn't "get" the Socrates thing. "Snow shoes?" I suggested.

"Probably would of worked but I didn't have 'em. What I did was I cut the head off and left it back at the gut pile. Then I cut the deer into a front half and a back half. I strung the front half up in a tree so the bears wouldn't get it, then packed the back half out to the boat. Carrying less than half the weight, I hardly fell through at all. The next morning I came back and got the other half. Took a while, but there ya are." He gestured at the pot.

"I would have got my mom to come and fly it out with her airplane!" Kenny shouted triumphantly.

Duck slapped his forehead. "God! Why didn't I think of that?"

Dinner was hearty and filling. The deer meat was lean and mild, not gamey like I'd expected. Afterward, Kenny and Ellen and Duck sat cozied up together on the couch, like a real family. They all looked pretty happy. I felt good for them, but it made me feel lonely. I talked with Linda for a while, then excused myself and headed back down to the boat. Something about the evening had been a downer. I didn't know what.

I took a couple of puffs on a roach I found in the ash tray in the galley, but it just made me feel more withdrawn and sad. I started thinking about Anna. I though about how right, how warm and content I felt when I was with her, when she was bustling around cooking something or just walking with me somewhere. Doing nothing with her was like doing something. I felt full up, sufficient, when she was around, empty and yearning when she wasn't. Even when she was yelling at me I knew I was really alive. To stop moping I read for a while. *A Confederate General From Big Sur* by Richard Brautigan. It was funny and just demented enough to cheer me up a little.

# CHAPTER 37

## Short Fuse

I saw him from the back as he turned the corner in to the alley that ran back to the door of the Club Bar. But it was definitely Nick, moving leopard-like in his thigh-length black leather jacket. I followed him in, then almost bumped into him. He'd stopped just inside the door to survey the Saturday afternoon denizens of the bar.

"Hey, Nick!" He swung around toward me and gave a wan smile of recognition. "What are you drinking?" I asked. My air of forced joviality rang phony in my ears. He raised one eyebrow and walked up to the bar. I followed him over.

"Canadian Club and soda" he said, half to me and half to the bartender.

"I'll have a Bud." When the drinks came I put a $5 on the bar.

"You don't have to buy my liquor for the rest of my life, son." His steely blue eyes skewered me. Anna's eyes, but colder metal.

"I know, but I do owe you."

"You don't owe me shit! Rule of the sea is you assist a fellow mariner in distress." I nodded my head.

"Nick, I'd like to talk to you about something sort of, well, personal."

"If it's about my wife, I don't really give a shit." The bartender shot us a glance, then pretended he didn't hear.

"No, it's about Anna." A flicker of smile passed across Nick's face.

"If you're gonna ask me for her hand in marriage, better ask Arnie Swenson instead." He chuckled at his own joke. "I'd like to hear that conversation." This wasn't getting any easier, but I continued my patient diplomacy.

"You know, Anna is a gifted chef. She'd like to go to school and make it a career."

"It's her career now, ain't it? I never ate her cooking, but I hear she makes damn good salmon chowder."

"She wants to go away to school. To California."

"I bet you'd like that, wouldn't you? Arnie's supposed to crab with Marty this winter. Don't expect that leaves him much time to move to California and chauffer her back and forth to cooking school. What's this got to do with me, anyway? I ain't the boss of her."

176

"Well, the thing is, she hasn't got the money to do it. She's hoping to get her dad's share of the money from the Nancy V." Nick's face froze for a moment.

"You mean the money that don't exist? That's in 50 fathoms?" Something in me let go.

"We both know that's bullshit, Nick! You told me the story yourself. Why don't you give her her goddamned money!"

A strobe light flashed in my left eye. Something flat and hard smacked me in the back. Now I was looking up at the bottoms of the bar stools. Why do people insist on putting their gum there? My eye throbbed with achy pain behind spritzy stars of light.

I spent a couple of minutes on my back, then got to my feet with a little help from the bartender. He pressed a wet bar towel over my eye. Nick was gone. The barman had escorted him out the door. "Whatever you said really pissed him off."

I nodded. "Fucker's got a short fuse."

Back out on the street, I leaned against the wall, nursing my wounded eye and battered ego. After a while I gathered myself enough to start back toward the harbor. At the corner, I waited to cross the street. The field of vision in my left eye was narrowing, like I was looking through a telescope. I was gingerly touching the growing puffiness as John's blue truck sidled past. He gave me a curt wave and an odd smile. Julie was snuggled up next to him, looking adamantly in the other direction. Ouch! I think I've been dumped. I wish I hadn't seen that. Better if Nick had shut both my eyes. Then again, maybe Julie's made a decision for me that I should have had the will power to make for myself.

It was good to get out of town the next day. Bright sun sparkled on the inlet as I ran the can channel. A pod of sea otters, aquatic teddy bears, floated leisurely about on their backs like vacationers on air mattresses in some hotel swimming pool. I expected to see trashy paperbacks rather than clams clutched in their front paws. They lifted their heads and regarded me with expressions of apprehensive curiosity, then abruptly dove for cover.

Rounding the corner at Shag Rock, I had the mild westerly breeze at my back. The boat was running smooth and easy. My gas tank was full. I could see out of both eyes despite the blue-black ring around my left one. (They really do look like the ones in the cartoons!) Right hip braced against the side rail, left foot up on the step into the cabin, one hand on the wheel below the control panel on the back of the house, it was a pretty comfortable ride. At the Egg Island channel, I made up my mind to keep going out into the Gulf of Alaska and all the way down to Softuk. The ocean had a long, lazy lump rolling, just big enough to lug the engine down a bit as I climbed them, then speed her up a couple hundred RPM as I slid down the other side. It made for a gentle, rhythmical ride that rocked my insides. It felt good. The rock and roll of the seas wrapped me in a sweet syncopated sadness. I started singing the Neville Bros.

*If you want something to play with  go and find yourself a toy.*
*Baby my time is too expensive and I'm not a little boy . . .*
*Tell it like it is don't be ashamed to let your conscience be your guide*
*But I know deep down inside me I believe you love me, forget your foolish pride.*

After two or three times through the song I got a little self-conscious, even though I was all alone. Is it Anna, or am I the one ashamed to let my conscience be my guide? And it looks like we both have a healthy dose of foolish pride.

After a while I came up on the Pete Dahl can, a huge steel ball painted orange with a black "P" and anchored in about 40 feet of water off the bar entrance. I never did see the can at Grass Island, but I kept the compass pointed east and kept on going. The beach swung out at Kokenhenik and there was a big tide rip of muddy water from the main stem of the river pouring out there. I found that ball, with a big "K" on it. Softuk was just another six or seven miles now, but John had said that the bar made a big arc on the west and you had to go past and come in from the east at about a 45 degree angle. Once I got to the line of breakers on the bar I swung out and drove around in a couple of big circles until I saw the Softuk ball. It seemed like a long way from there to the land, but I put the ball on my stern and started to go in. The water shallowed up and the lumps started to get steeper. Pretty soon the fathometer was showing only 8 or 10 feet deep at the bottom of the swells and 14 or 16 feet at the top. Off to my left a wave would fold over now and then into a long breaker. "Hope it doesn't get any shallower. Hope I'm not missing the entrance hole!" After another half a mile I started getting a little more water, and the swells were flatter. I could see the masts of the tenders, and the radio antennae on the skiffs in the cozy anchorage on the other side of a sandbar off my starboard bow. I snuggled in among the anchored boats and dropped the pick, went in to the cabin, and started frying up a can of corned beef hash for dinner. I was pretty pleased with myself for coming in to safe harbor after my big voyage of discovery.

The fishing down at Softuk was pretty scratchy, as we were at the very end of the sockeyes and the fall Cohos hadn't really started yet. And I was just learning a new place. Delivering at the tender was often the familiar deflating experience of watching the guy in front of me deliver twice as many fish as I had.

On the last low water, probably due to lack of interest by the regulars, I managed to get the set at the markers of a channel called Charlie Mohr's Hole. It was good for half a dozen reds. In the last 20 fathoms, up by the beach, a couple of corks were bobbing. A big king, listless and red as a brick, was lying up against the corkline, just hooked by one strand on her lip. I hadn't seen a king for almost a month. That run was way done. "You're late for the ball, lady" I told her as I gaffed her aboard. "The carriage already turned back to a pumpkin." Still, it was a $20 bill I hadn't expected. The weather was balmy and the forecast was good, so at the end of the fishing opener I anchored my skiff at the Martin River markers and used my twenty to fly back to town with a bunch of other fishermen on the Chitina Air Beaver. Ellen was flying it. She smiled at me when I climbed aboard, and shook her head.

"Matt, that eye makes you look like that dog on the Little Rascals. I hope the other guy has one too."

"Nope, but I bet he's nursing a sore hand where I smacked him with my face."

# CHAPTER 38

## Crane Hunt.

It was the first of September on the Flats. The endless daylight and boundless energy of July was long gone. Now the nights were almost as long as the days, and early frosts had turned the willow and blueberry leaves up beyond the grass banks copper and gold. There was fresh snow, "termination dust," on the mountains. The fishing season was winding down with the light, maybe just a couple of weeks left. If you didn't have a season made by now, you were probably going to be pounding nails this winter rather than getting tan on some beach in Hawaii or Puerto Vallarta. Silver season openers were three and a half days long, so, by the inescapable logic of the 7 day week, there was a three and a half day closure from Thursday evening at 7PM until the following Monday morning at 7AM. I was planning on spending the last few hours of a slow Thursday afternoon making a couple of lazy sets flooding up the Softuk channel. Just going through the motions till the closure. One fish, two fish, red fish blue fish. A Doctor Seuss day.

Out of the low grey clouds came a strange throaty trilling sound. Many answering calls came from behind it to the west. Long straggling lines of great grey birds began dropping out of the clouds over the grass banks just inland of the channel. They circled down in lazy spirals and began disappearing into the tall grass on the salt flats, gargling out to the rest of the flocks still airborne. The VHF radio crackled.

"Desperado—Hard Rain"

"Yo, Desperado back."

"You hear that, Matthew?"

"Roger, weird sound, huh?"

"That's Sand Hill Cranes by the thousand. They look like the younger cousin of a pterodactyl, but still pretty good eating. They're heading to California for the winter; just like we would do if we had the brains God gave cranes. It's supposed to blow tomorrow so they'll probably stay around for a few days. Let's spend the closure up Cudahay Slough and do a little bird hunt."

"Well, OK. I wasn't too keen on running all the way back to town and then maybe getting stuck down on that end if the weather went to shit."

"Which it is very likely to do this time of year. So when you deliver at the tender make sure you get some groceries for the closure. Food is optional, but beer is mandatory. I'll give Duck a call on the 'Secret Channel' and see if he is up for it too."

Duck came on the radio as soon as BD clicked off. "I've been listening to you girls gossip. I haven't caught squat today. Let's bag it early and get up there while we can still see."

An hour later we were unloaded and the fish holds were clean. The three skiffs headed up the slough playing follow the leader, past the "Fishing Closed" markers and up toward the grass banks. The channel, which had been a narrow gutter between muddy banks at low tide was now, two hours before high slack, indistinguishable from the surrounding miles of submerged sand flats, covered with only a foot or two of opaque grey sea. Duck was in the lead in his wide white Tiedemann skiff. Like a blind man tapping from side to side with his cane he ran the skiff in a sinuous line, swinging left or right into the deeper water whenever it began to shallow up. His eyes flicked from his depth sounder to the subtle tiderips and nuanced currents that hinted at the deeper water of the channel.

The barrier island was a long grey hump on our right. In a mile or so, a sand bar began to show on our left, and it soon grew into a bank several feet high. Tufts of salt grass began to appear on the drier sand on its top. Then, the world began to morph. What had been a dark line on the horizon resolved into fir trees on a bank of actual earth, which reared up ahead. Old tree stumps and snags, slumping off the eroding banks, pointed their fingers accusingly out into the channel. Confined now by land on both sides, we were in a little river draining the Suckling Hills, which bind the Copper Delta on the East. The channel arced to the left, with the treed land on the right and miles of open salt grass flats off to the left, toward where the main stems of the Copper wind down from the glaciers and peaks of the Alaskan Range.

Duck, BD and I throttled back our engines and motored slowly into a wide spot in the slough. Duck scurried onto his bow and dropped his anchor. His anchor line snugged tight and his skiff swung around pointing back the way he had come. The current flooding up the channel rippled a tiny wake on either side of his bow. He flopped a couple of buoys out on his port and starboard side cleats and BD and I rafted up our skiffs on either side. I stood on my fish hold for a moment and looked at all the color around me, the greens and honey golds of late summer grass on the banks and the dark green line of trees toward the hills. The rich, warm smell of plant life exploded in my head after days of cold, salty ocean air.

"Let's take a little walk up on the banks and see if anything is flying around before we lose our light." BD suggested. We spent a few minutes gathering up our shotguns, pawing through boxes of shells and stuffing them in the pockets of our jackets. "What kind of loads have you got on board there Matthew?"

"I've got #4 for ducks and my buckshot for the lions."

"Well, I hope there's no lions out there this evening," said Duck, poking his head out the door of his cabin with a droll grin. "Those big cranes are scary enough."

BD said: "#4 is too small for geese or cranes. It'll bounce off 'em like hail. You need some of the #2. Here, take a handful of mine." Just then Duck came out from his cabin cradling his shotgun lovingly in both arms. "Holy shit!" says BD. "That's a fucking cannon!"

"No Clausen, that's a Remington 10 gauge pump action shotgun."

"So you're geared up for big game after all. A 12 gauge isn't good enough for you?"

Duck grinned. "I'm tired of trying to sneak up on birds that are smarter than me. Maybe now I won't have to get so close." While we were talking, BD was thumping away on a bellows foot pump. With a piff, piff, piff, a little yellow and blue inflatable rubber boat was taking shape on his deck. Diminutive blue plastic paddles were lying next to it. As the dinky boat reached firmness and expanded to its full 6-foot long splendor, I noticed that it had a vessel name painted on the stern in magic marker. It read "Arctic Challenger." The hailing port was listed as Cordova, AK. "Wow, was that the prize in a Cracker Jacks box?" Duck asked.

"You can walk to the fuckin' beach if you don't want to ride in my boat" he pouted, his voice filled with mock misery.

BD ferried us, one at a time, to the east beach. He tossed the inflatable up on the grass bank and tied its little painter to a miniature willow bush. "Don't want my mighty vessel to blow away!" We strategized for a minute and came up with a plan. No more cranes were flying, but we could hear them far off to the west, out on the grass flats, calling like a bunch of bassoons with broken spit valves. "Tomorrow for them." BD said. "Let's see if we can jump a duck or a goose."

I would walk down stream. Byron headed up and Duck moved inland to another little swale a few hundred yards away. As he walked away he turned his hound-dog face to me. "Don't shoot me now, you Cheechako. When I'm down in that swale you might just see my hat bobbing along and mistake it for a goose."

"Don't worry about it, Duck. I rarely hit anything I shoot at."

In fact, that was fairly close to the truth. As a kid, I had hunted pheasants a few times with my Portuguese grandfather and uncles down in Los Banos, never hitting anything. Tromping through the frosty stubble of last summer's cornfields while the pheasants sneaked around and got behind us was a Thanksgiving Day tradition. I guess it got us out of the house while the women cooked.

When I was about 10 I was entrusted with carrying a pheasant my grandfather had shot. I was toting the seemingly lifeless, surprisingly heavy bird by his cool, leathery reptilian feet. His ankles felt like snakeskin wrapped tightly around a pair of chopsticks. After 10 or 15 minutes we came to a barbed wire fence and I laid the beautiful bird down to open the strands and crawl through. The moment he touched the ground, the iridescent blue, green and brown wings exploded, propelling him into a flapping, gobbling, heart-attack inducing takeoff. He launched up and irretrievably away. Cackling hysterically at the cleverness of his ruse he escaped over the field we had just crossed.

My uncles' laughter burned my ears. "They sure scare the crap out of you when they jump like that."

"So Matthew, you think you're the President? Pardoning the Thanksgiving pheasant?"

When the chuckles subsided my Grandfather said: "Hey, *rapazim*, (little boy) it's not your fault. I should have wrung his neck to be sure." But my Thanksgiving turkey still tasted of shame and ashes that year.

So I was not wholly at home in the role of Hemingway-esque blood sport outdoorsman. Walking alone in the dusk with my shotgun at the ready began to give me a strange sense of unreality, as if I were acting the part of a hunter in some amateur theater company production. That was when two geese came flying up from down river as fast as anything has ever flown. They were barely 10 feet above the grass, going like the devil himself was after them. My shotgun came up and I thumbed the safety off. As they came abreast of me I put the bead on the end of my barrel out in front of the lead bird and squeezed off. Boom! In slow motion I visualized the pattern of shot fanning out in front of the bird's beak. Like some Roger Rabbit animated cartoon, the cloud of lead waited there in freeze frame as the goose flew into it. He folded up into a tumble and augured in to the tall grass. "Whoah, I got him!" I walked over toward where he must have crash-landed. I couldn't see him. I walked a little farther. Hmm. It's kinda dusky but it isn't dark. Maybe he went a little farther down range than I thought. I walked a few steps more. I was starting to get panicky. I know I hit him and I know he crashed. Where the fuck is he? Am I about to be humiliated by another fowl! Oh, the awful symmetry of it! Then I saw a wing sticking up out of the grass, feathers gently waving at me in the breeze. When I picked him up, the goose's bright black eyes stared blindly and his body was warm but his neck was strangely limp. I gave it a quick snap, just to be sure.

The sound of boat motors and anchor chains came up from the slough. I guess we won't have it to ourselves this weekend. I walked back toward the skiffs, carrying my surprisingly heavy goose. The familiar feel of reptile leather feet pulled me through a wormhole time warp; a tactile deja vu back to my California childhood. The sound of a floatplane, a Cessna 185, not the loud, nasty DeHavilland Beaver, dragged me back. It circled once, then came whiffling in to a landing on the slough with a hollow aluminum thump and a hiss of wake like red-hot steel doused in a barrel of water. Dodging the anchored vessels, it hydroplaned down the narrow channel on its torpedo-shaped pontoons. When it had dumped all its speed, it pirouetted about and came slowly back up the slough.

Four more boats were now anchored below us. The Cessna motored gingerly toward one of them. The plane gently nudged the stern of the Marauder. Nick

Vasiloff, like a cat burglar carrying a small duffel bag stuffed with some sort of loot, (or was it his laundry?) leapt onto the plane's float. With a wary eye toward the propeller a few feet from his head, he scuttled back along the aluminum float to the door on the side of the plane and climbed in. Below the Marauder, Arnie's Valhalla and Martin Gauer's boat were rafted side by side. Below them was another boat I didn't recognize.

I stood on the bank by our raft of skiffs. The Arctic Challenger, tied by its painter, nuzzled brightly against the flank of BD's boat. Somebody was back at the boats already. I called out in my most feminine falsetto. "Oh taxi! Taxi!" I sang, waving my goose-filled hand primly over my head like a rich lady shopper with her Nieman Marcus bags. BD came out from his cabin, slithered over the cap rail into the dinghy and paddled to the beach.

"Where to, lady?" he rasped in his best Brooklyn.

We climbed back aboard the skiffs and Duck came out from his cabin. His lower jaw thrust forward, and in his thick, phony Aleut/Tonto accent he marveled over my goose. "White man shoot straight . . . make big kill!"

Pleased at my success, I recounted the details. Duck relapsed into his normal speech. "I heard your shot. Mikey Mills coming up the slough jumped those geese for you."

BD, slightly miffed at coming back empty handed, cut us off. "OK, quit yer bragging there, Witz, clean yer goose and let's decide who cooks dinner tonight."

I drew the short straw on dinner. I had to pluck and clean the goose, then cook the food too! While I was at the stern, plucking, another 185 landed on the slough and taxied down to the boats below. We decided to let the gander age for a day or two, but I had bought a package of pork chops at the tender and threw some spuds into the stove. I fried up the chops with a sliced onion, and then poured a can of cream of mushroom soup and some Worcestershire sauce over the top for instant gravy, which we slathered over the potatoes as well. I opened a can of green beans to round out the menu. Pop open some beers, and we were dining in style. Nobody complained.

After dinner, BD got out a deck of cards and a bottle of George Dickel Tennessee Whiskey and I could see trouble with a beer chaser on the horizon. We played cards until the bottle was empty. Then I have a vague recollection that we were singing old Burl Ives sea chanteys through numb lips for a while before we stumbled toward our respective bunks. By then the wind had huffed up to a steady thirty knots and it was raining. Fortunately, the tide was dropping in the narrow slough so the worst of the wind blew over our heads.

"G'night. Crane hump, I mean, crame hunt at firss light boyss!" Duck drawled.

"We'll see," BD slurred.

I lay in my bunk. The planet whirled on its axis so fast that I feared I would be flung off into space by the centrifugal force. I breathed convulsively in and out through my mouth. Should drink water, I thought, as I spun off into blackness.

It was way past dawn when I heard scufflings and bumpings on the other boats. I opened my eyes. My skull throbbed, trumpeting the symptoms of what was surely irreversible brain damage. I put on my pants and dragged myself out the door. Duck's head was poking out of the door of his cabin like a turtle peering out from his shell. "Coffee, Witz," he whispered, and poured me a mug full from his metal pot.

"Oh, God yes!" I replied. He set the pot down on his deck with a thump and we both froze into a wincing posture, like we had been tazered. "No loud noises!" I pleaded in an adamant whisper.

A horizontal rain was blowing by and the boats were swaying in the eddying gusts of a howling 40-knot wind. The world looked pretty miserable and uninviting. I looked over at Duck hesitantly. "Hunting?"

He nodded unconvincingly.

"Look," I said as I slurped my first sip of coffee. "I'll go hunting if you guys absolutely promise not to discharge any firearms. I'm afraid the sound would drop me to my knees."

"Take aspirin, drink water. Some cranes are going to meet their maker today."

In the end, the cranes got a reprieve. We decided to wait out the awful weather a bit, and spent a lazy day just bunkered into our bunks reading, nursing our hangovers with a steady diet of cheap beer, or playing Pinochle over on BD's skiff. At some point in the afternoon, we heard a couple of muffled shotgun blasts from up the slough a way. BD stuck his head out the door. "Must be Marty and Arnie. Marty's inflatable is gone from the side of his boat. They're tougher than I want to be to be out in this shit." Our crane assault was planned for first light on Saturday instead.

"First light" was more like 9 o-clock when we finally ferried over to the west bank of the slough, scrambled up the muddy cut-bank and started stalking across the vast expanse of salt grass. We fanned out about 50 yards apart. We could hear cranes gargling eerily off in the distance. Tromping through the high grass in hip boots and long raincoats was a workout, and soon I was sweating recycled beer out of every pore. Occasionally, we would get close enough to a small group of birds that they would jump up, flap ponderously off another half a mile away, then settle awkwardly back down into the grass in what looked like a controlled crash landing.

Eventually, via some message known only to the cranes, they all decided to lift off from their grazing with a great cacophony of trilling. Hundreds of birds filled the sky. Clawing at the moist air with their huge wings to gain altitude, they began wheeling in a clockwise swirl, ascending into the grey clouds. One group of them jumped up close enough to BD that he got off his three shots before they were so high that they were out of range. One of the cranes gave a little flutter when BD fired, then stopped flapping. He coasted, dropping out of the flock and gliding downward. BD followed his trajectory, loping along through the grass. The bird landed and disappeared. The rest of the huge flock was now swirling around high up, several thousand feet above us and to the east, sniffing the wind to see if the conditions were right to continue their trip south. There was no sense in shooting at such long range. Duck came up next to me and we followed well behind BD as he tromped through the grass, trying to locate where his prey had gone to ground. His long raincoat was open now to cool him off, sailing out behind him in the wind, and the tops of his hip boots, well above the knee, made his legs look strangely disjointed as he moved. He was a gawky, awkward sight as he stalked.

Suddenly, the crane stood up right in front of him, neck and wings spread to their full extension in threat display. BD jumped back in surprise, his raingear flapping like the crane's wings. The bird seemed almost as tall as he was, and very angry.

"Ichabod Crane vs. Sandhill Crane" I intoned to Duck in the overly dramatic tones of a TV wrestling commentator.

"Softuk Smack-down" he replied.

BD raised his shotgun, preparing to dispatch the crane at point-blank range. The crane darted his head forward like a snake striking and pecked the end of the barrel. BD lowered it and stepped back a step. He clicked his safety on and held his shotgun by the barrel like a club. The crane darted again and BD swung and missed as the crane hopped back. BD took a couple of quick steps forward and swung again, aiming a little lower. The crane ducked his head, but not quite enough. The stock of the shotgun smacked him in the neck. The bird toppled over, wings flapping convulsively. BD whacked the head one more time.

We walked up. "What's up with the Tarzan shit" Duck asked, "your gun jam?"

"I couldn't bring myself to just execute him. Did you see how he squared off with me? He deserved a fair fight. To die like a warrior."

"Fer sure." Duck grinned. "Not that he's any less dead for all that." Then he looked up at the clouds. "I think this batch of cranes have skied out to greener pastures. Let's go back to the slough." I looked to the east, where the cranes were now just barely visible fuzz high in the grey sky. The wind was letting down, backing to the northeast, and the rain had stopped. It was quiet, except for the tweets of some little sparrows flitting around in the grass.

When we got back, something was different. "Looks like Arnie and Marty didn't care for the hunting." Sure enough, there were two fewer boats anchored up in the slough. That night Duck roasted my goose for dinner, and served it with rice cooked with chicken broth and butter, and a can of pears sprinkled with cinnamon for a side dish. The meat was darker than chicken, more like wild duck. He basted it with butter and its own drippings to keep it moist. BD and I drank a bottle of wine with it, but Duck stuck with the beer.

# CHAPTER 39

## No Smoking, Please.

I was trying to sleep in on Sunday morning. Fortunately, we had run out of beer fairly early Saturday evening, so my head was throbbing and my tongue had grown some sort of fungus layer, but neither symptom approached the seriousness of the terminal brain cancer I had had Friday morning. I was dragged rudely out of my muzzy dream state by the sound of the Beaver landing on the slough. Once down on the water, the flatulent idling went on interminably as it motored around and let off its passenger on one of the boats anchored below us. Finally, it charged past on its ear-shatteringly loud takeoff. A moment later its wake rocked us.

I gave up and got out of the bunk. I pulled my pants on and went out onto my fish hold to take a leak. The tide was coming up, so I gazed placidly out over the sea of grass toward Kokenhenik as I emptied my bladder over the side. The thud of the shock wave hit at the same time I heard the sharp thump of the explosion. My head snapped around to see the roof of the Marauder's cabin cartwheel into the air. Bits of window glass shrapnel splattered into the mud of the banks and rattled and ricocheted off our boats. Something like a wasp stung my ear. The windscreen on top of Duck's cabin shattered. A misty white cloud rose from where the Marauder's cabin had been. Things were splashing into the water, some big, some small. An orange life ring dropped from the sky and landed by my skiff with a slap, as if someone in heaven was coming to my aid. I realized I had spun around and was pissing on my boat. BD came scrambling out of his cabin.

"What the fuck!?" he asked.

I pointed past our bows toward the Marauder with one hand and put my dick back in my pants with the other.

"Oh Jesus! Where's Nick?"

"I don't know. He probably came back on that plane that just landed. What the hell happened, anyway?"

"Must have had a fuel leak, a bilge full of gas. You turn the ignition key or a switch, anything that makes a spark, and boom!"

Now Duck came onto his deck, pushing his feet into his hip boots and crunching bits of his broken windscreen. "Maybe he left his stove on and that torched the gas fumes off." He reached down and picked up a shattered compass in a brass gimbal housing lying on his deck. "Christ, it's raining marine hardware! I'd give it a minute before you go over there. That boat may blow again, or start to burn. All that gasoline and fiberglass will burn real fast."

"No!" BD barked. "Get your fire extinguishers, and we'll go over in my skiff." Now bits of debris started floating past us in the slow current flooding up the slough. A boat cushion with the plaid fabric I recalled from the bench seats in Nick's galley passed by. I grabbed the red fire extinguisher from the mount on my cabin wall by the stove and started to step across to Duck's skiff when I realized I was barefoot and went back for my boots.

"Check and see if you still have an ear, Witz," BD called out. "You're bleeding." My hand flew up to the side of my head and came away red. The shoulder of my tee shirt was red. I felt around with my hand, but the ear felt intact. Part of the outer edge, near the top, was divided in two. As soon as I touched it, it started to sting like hell.

"It's mostly still here," I said. I grabbed a sock off my bunk and held it against the ear. "Let's worry about Nick right now."

We jumped onto the Hard Rain. BD fired up, untied from Duck's skiff and motored cautiously over to the Marauder. Where the upper half of the cabin had been was just an open cockpit with wisps of thin white smoke rising out of it. The corner posts of the cabin framing stood up on each side like the legs of an upside-down chair. It smelled of fresh gas, but there was no fire.

"You see him anywhere?" Duck asked.

"No, but I can't see down inside." BD answered. Let me back down a bit and we'll look in the back deck, around the reel" "Nope, not back here. I'm not too keen to get on board there while she's still smoking. Smell all that gas? That white mist is gas vaporizing. No smoking, please."

I said: "Pull up forward and I'll get up on your cabin and look down into the house. See what I can see." Part of the front of the boot cabin, over the focsle bunks, was still intact. I craned my head and looked forward. V-bunks, a sleeping bag, no Nick. The rest of the cabin was open to the sky. The engine cover was gone and you could see the front of the engine below the galley floor.

"He's not here." I said. "If he was on board, he's in the water now." A panicky feeling welled up in me as I thought of him helplessly drifting, hurt, maybe unconscious. "Shit! We've gotta find him!"

BD came up with the next plan. "Let's call the air service and see if they actually flew him out. And somebody needs to let them know in town what happened."

"It doesn't look too lively down on Mike's boat, so who else would have flown in here?" said Duck. "I'll warm up your AM and call. But if he's drifting up the slough we don't have much time."

"I'll putt along real slow and see if we can find him. Maybe he's in the shallows, or pulling himself onto the beach. You look left, Matt, I'll look right," BD ordered.

"Man, this sucks! You can't see down two inches in this water, how are we supposed to see him if he's sunk?" I asked.

BD just looked at me with a grim expression on his face.

A minute later Duck was talking to Chitina Air. "3 5 Chitina Air, Whiskey Tango 2638 Hard Rain calling, pick me up Mary?"

"3 5 Chitina back to the Hard Rain, go ahead Byron."

"Its Duck, Mary, but I'm in Softuk, Cudahay. Was that your Beaver that just landed here?"

"Roger that, it was Andy on 6 8 Foxtrot."

"Who did you drop off, over?"

"I think it was Nick Vasiloff, I can check the manifest."

"There's been an explosion on the Marauder, Nick's boat, a gasoline leak we think. He's not on board. We are looking for him in the slough. Could you relay this information to Mac at the police department, and the hospital? If we find him, it is very likely he'll be injured. Maybe you could turn that plane around if we need to medivac him to town?"

"3 5 back. Affirmative. I'll contact my pilot and head him back. Please advise when you find Nick. I'll contact the police here in town. Break, 6 8 Foxtrot, 3 5 Chitina, do you read, Andy?

"6 8 back, Roger, I copied all that, I'll head back, should be at Cudahay in about 10 minutes."

Meanwhile, we kept looking. I grabbed BD's pike pole and started probing down into the water as we moved along, hoping to feel something that wasn't mud on the bottom. Five minutes went by. We got up to the corner where the slough makes a dogleg to the right and shallows up. BD ran close in to the outside of the curve, where anything floating along would wash up into the shallows. Nothing. Ten minutes went by. We heard the Beaver coming from the west, lining up for his landing.

"6 8 Foxtrot, WT 2638 Hard Rain. We haven't found him. I don't know if there is any point for you to land. I'm afraid it's too late anyway, if he's been in the water this long."

"6 8 back. Roger that. I'll circle around a couple of times."

"OK. Are you sure you let him off on his boat?"

"Affirmative, Duck, he's hard to mistake."

"Roger. WT 2638 clear." Duck came out of the cabin. "Goddamnit!" We headed back down the slough, against the current, hoping against hope that we had missed something.

"It's just been too long now, Duck. He's gone," said BD.

The plane circled for about 5 minutes, then came up on the radio again. We told him there was no point in his landing. Then Mary came on from the office.

"Hard Rain, 3 5 Chitina, I've spoken with Mac. He says you are in State Trooper jurisdiction. They'll be out on the 185 in about an hour. He's spoken to the Coast

Guard. They want to know if the vessel is on fire or is in imminent danger of sinking."

"Negative, Mary, but we haven't been able to find Nick. We'll keep looking."

"Mac also told me to tell you not to go aboard the Marauder until the Troopers get there. He doesn't want anyone else to get blown up."

We looked for another half hour, then BD threw up his hands. "Fuck it! I give up." We tied back up to Duck's skiff and sat on the deck, dejected.

"I wish we hadn't drunk all your whiskey, Byron," I whined.

"I wish you guys hadn't drank all my fucking beer," Duck added.

"Yeah, like you hardly got any of it."

"Let's have a look at your ear, Witz." They got a wet cloth and cleaned it up a bit. "You've got a nice clean slice there, Vincent, clear through, for about 1/2 inch in the soft part. Probably could use a stitch or two, or you're gonna look like an old Tom cat who's lost a few fights." We decided to put a band-aid on it on either side, to close the wound, and hope for the best. At least it stopped bleeding.

Our raft of boats began to rotate gently as the tide changed. First the tide went slack and we swung perpendicular to the slough, pushed by a northeasterly breeze, then, a few minutes later, we lay facing up river as the current began to ebb.

"This will be fun." Duck grumbled. "Now we can watch all Nick's shit drift back by us on the ebb."


The 185 landed and they taxied up to my stern. The trooper, a trim, 50-something guy in a blue rip-stop nylon jacket with a badge on the chest, stepped onto my engine cover. He wore a flat-brimmed "Mountie" hat and a revolver in a well-worn black holster rode on the hip of his blue wool pants. He had a leather attaché case in his hand, like a businessman would carry. Ellen came up on the other pontoon and handed Duck a line that he tied onto a cleat on his skiff, the middle boat.

"Pretty exciting mornin' huh boys?" the trooper said.

"Too exciting, Bill." BD replied.

"I'd like to ask you for a couple of favors, if I may. First, I don't walk on water, so I'd like to borrow one of your skiffs and a driver for a bit. I need to go take a look at the Marauder. Also, I assume you haven't found Mr. Vasiloff, so I'm going to have to proceed as if this were a fatality. I'm going to need to interview each of you at some point. Don't motor away for a bit, OK?"

"No problem."

"Is anyone else in the slough here? I see one other boat."

"That's Mike Mills. He's still in town," Duck answered.

Now Trooper Bill looked at me. "I know Duck and BD here, but I don't believe we've met." He stuck out a big, meaty hand.

"Matt Mankiewicz, sir."

"Bill Wrigley. This your skiff?" I nodded. "OK Matt, you want to be my chauffer for a bit?"

"Sure."

"OK, that'll work." Now he turned to the Cessna. "Ellen, I'll probably be an hour or two, do you want to wait, or come back later?"

"It's Sunday, Bill, so were kinda busy. Let me check with Mary and see how tight the schedule is." As I was warming up the Desperado, Ellen stuck her head back out of the plane. "I'm good for a 2 hour layover, Bill. I'll keep Duck and BD company for a while." A smile bloomed on Duck's face.

We pulled up to the stern of the Marauder. Trooper Bill had me tie on to the stern cleat with one line. "If anything happens, suddenly, fire or a boom, I'm coming back as fast as I can, but you just turn loose and be ready to get away." I watched as he climbed aboard, set his attaché case down and started snooping around, first at the stern, then working his way up to the cabin, and down inside. He turned the battery selector switch inside the cabin to OFF. He reached around the engine and turned the lever on the fuel supply line to OFF. He looked around for about 10 minutes, then came back to his briefcase. He took out a 35-millimeter camera and began taking pictures, mostly of the engine area and the back of the cabin, where the doorway used to be. Then he fiddled around with other stuff from his brief case, dusted for finger prints with a little brush. I was getting bored. I started watching half a dozen ravens arguing over a spawned out salmon carcass they had found up on the bank. Bill finally came back aft. He taped an official-looking sign to each side of the boat. "Police Investigation. Do Not Enter."

"There's still more gas sloshing around in here than I would like, but everything is nice and cool. I guess I'm done. She's the Coast Guard's problem now. Hitch a ride back?"

"Sure."

"Wait, before we go back, let's mosey down and make sure no one is on board Mr. Mills' skiff." We checked it out, peered in the window, banged on the side of the cabin and yelled. No one home. Then the trooper had me cruise up and down the slough again, looking. Finally, we tied back up in my old spot alongside the Bufflehead.

"Now, what about our missing fisherman?" Trooper Bill asked. "How about I set up my office in the stern here, and I'll take a short statement from each of you guys, one at a time, as to what happened? Let's start with you, Duck."

We each told Bill our stories. I realized as I told mine that there were a lot of assumptions. I had assumed it was Nick who came back to the boat; I had assumed there was no one on Mills' skiff; I had assumed that Nick was in the water somewhere, drowned or blown up. Then Trooper Bill asked me if anyone else had been here, who wasn't here now. I told him about Gauer and Arnie, that they'd left around high water yesterday. "No other planes landed," he asked?

"Not 'till the one about an hour ago."

"Did anyone, you or any of the other guys here this weekend, go aboard Mr. Vasiloff's vessel, before or after he left on the plane?"

"Not that I'm aware of."

"How about the two who left yesterday?"

"Not that I'm aware of, but we were off hunting part of the time, and sleeping."

"Mr. Petroff mentioned that a fair amount of alcohol was consumed over the last couple of days. So you might have been a bit impaired, might have missed something? A boat coming, a plane, someone going aboard the Marauder?"

"I guess it's possible. I wasn't watching the whole time, or listening either, for that matter."

"OK, fair enough. If you think of anything you haven't told me, even something unimportant, you let me know." He gave me a card with his name and phone numbers on it. "Let's hope we find Mr. Vasiloff duck hunting on the grass banks. Radio in if you do."

"Of course."

"Ellen and I will fly around the area again, low and slow, on our way out."


When they were gone, we all looked at each other.

"That was weird," Duck said.

"Yeah, he acted like it was a crime scene," said BD.

"He was dusting for prints," I added.

"This place is starting to give me the creeps," said Duck. "Let's go on down to the Martin River markers. We need to be there in the morning anyway to go fishing."

BD said: "Better get going then, while we still have enough water." They warmed up their engines, then BD and I turned loose while Duck pulled his anchor. Byron led the way this time, his bright little inflatable boat lashed upside down on top of his reel. I was in the middle. We got down stream about a quarter mile to a big turn where another slough comes in. BD slowed his skiff down and it came off the step. A bunch of ravens and seagulls were gathered by a bump just appearing out of the receding water, right on the edge of the wide, muddy beach maybe 50 yards away. I pulled up by BD and took my skiff out of gear.

"Those birds are mighty interested in something there," he said as Duck pulled up alongside us.

"It looks too long to be a dead seal," Duck said ominously as he bumped up to the other side of BD's skiff. I got a queasy feeling in my stomach, and we all exchanged grim looks.

"Damn! It's too shallow to get to it with the skiffs, and the tide's ebbing pretty hard. We'll go stuck." Now BD started strategizing. "Hey Witz, how about I drop my pick and you run me in to the beach up above 'till your outdrive bumps, then I'll get to it with the rubber boat, and my hip boots."

I got my binoculars out and the nasty sight leapt into view. He was lying on his back. Painted over with muddy silt. Still there was no mistaking. Open mouth and sharp profile. The ravens were picking at the eye sockets. "You don't wanna see this. It's not pretty."

"You sure it's him?" BD's anchor splashed off his bow.

"Unless it's some other dead guy."

"Not funny." Once his anchor grabbed we tied off on either side of him and I passed him the binoculars.

"Couldn't we just call the troopers back? Do we have to do this?" I asked. BD ignored me.

"After you drop me off, go down stream a bit. If I get screwed up in the current you can pick me up." Duck was quiet, and very pale. He kept looking off toward the mountains, in the other direction.

"You OK Duck?" I asked.

"I don't like dead people. I'm the one who found my dad at his cabin a couple of days after he died. I'm gonna try to call Ellen and Trooper Bill." He disappeared into his cabin. BD was bustling around, getting the Arctic Challenger ready. The vision of the sandy corpse was burned into my brain. I kept looking down at the binoculars as though they were the cause of my discomfort. That could have been me a couple of months ago, rolled up on the beach dead.

Duck came back out a minute later. "Bill says not to try to go to the body."

"Fine with me," I said.

"Bill will come back out in a wheel plane and land on the beach. He asked one of us to either wait here anchored or to anchor a buoy in the channel so they know where to look."

BD was aghast. "Jesus, we can't just leave him there! The ravens are pecking at him!"

"I think he's beyond caring about that, Byron," I replied. In the end, we all stayed there in the channel, waiting for the cavalry to come to the rescue.

# CHAPTER 40

## I Guess I'm An Heiress Now.

The tide was up. A really high one. From my perch in the Sally's wheelhouse, I could see over the riprap bank of the boat basin, right across the pier to the street. I watched Donna park the Bronco up on the pier. The wind was coming up and whipped her tan city-girl raincoat tight against her curves as she came down the ramp. The State Trooper's truck cruised slowly past. It was pretty obvious where Donna was headed. I came down from the wheelhouse and met her at the galley door.

"Hi Donna. Welcome back." I tried to keep my voice neutral, but inside I was less than thrilled with this development.

Her impish grin flickered with uncertainty. She locked eyes with me for an instant; then she threw herself at me and gave me a hug. "God! I've missed you! How are you? How did fishing go?"

"Pretty good, I guess. I'm getting the hang of it."

"What a weird deal with Nick! The troopers are saying that it may have been a homicide. How will they ever narrow down the suspects with all the people who wanted to kill that bastard! Oops!" Her hand came up to her mouth and her eyes mugged shock and amazement. "Better not speak ill of the dead. I guess I'm an heiress now. Better clean up my manners."

"What do you mean about a homicide?"

"Oh, they think someone set a booby trap on his boat to make it blow up. Clipped some wires onto the electricity. I don't know. As long as it isn't suicide, I get the life insurance. He had a policy through the Fisherman's Union. Matt, this is amazing! I was going to file for a divorce, but I hadn't got around to it, thank God! You know, Nick didn't even have a will? I talked to the attorney about it, on the phone, and since we're married, and he doesn't have a will, it all goes to me. He doesn't have much in the bank and most of the boat insurance money goes to the bank. He's got some money on the books at a couple of canneries. But he's got cash stashed all over that house. I'm gonna have to go through it with a fine tooth comb before I sell it."

"Donna, what about Anna's money? And Gauer's?"

"Well, if I find a big bundle with their names on it, then we'll see." She gives me her Good Witch of the North grin. I get a sick feeling in my stomach.

"Come on! You gotta do right by her, Donna, don't you think?" I could tell I wasn't being very persuasive.

Something hardened in her face. "I know you're sleeping with that bitch. I'm pretty goddamned sick of these young tarts screwing my men! So don't be surprised if Anna Vasiloff is one 'worthy cause' that I do not choose to contribute to. I won't be buying Vicki a pink Cadillac either, even if she thinks she earned it with all that time on her back." Then, almost like a switch had clicked, the anger left and the manipulative smile came back. "I thought you and me might have a chance to get together, Matt. Help me spend my money. Think it over. You know where I am." The galley door slammed after her.

Early the next morning, I was awakened by knocking at the door. I could barely hear it over the buffeting howl of the wind and the creaking of the boat working against the tie-up lines. "God! Hope it's not Donna again" I thought as I pulled on my pants. "I can't handle those mood swings before I have my coffee." It wasn't Donna. It was Trooper Bill.

"Good morning, officer."

"Good morning, Mr. Mankiewicz. Sorry to show up so early, but I have a lot on my plate today."

"No, that's fine, I'm up. Come in out of the wind. How can I help you? More questions?"

"Actually, yes. I have many questions. Can we sit?" He took off his dripping jacket and hung it by the door.

"Sure." I gestured at the galley benches and we slid in opposite each other.

"It seems someone wished Nick Vasiloff ill."

"A lot of people did, as I hear it."

"Well, yes, but someone seems to have done something about it. A little boat sabotage, it appears. Do you know anything about that?"

"No, just what we talked about out on the grounds."

"Mmm. So, I count six people who had an opportunity to go aboard the Marauder and . . . tinker with it, while Nick was in town. Mr. Wells possibly, Mr. Gauer, Mr. Swenson, Mr. Petroff, Mr. Clausen, and yourself. You know the three-pronged test we use? Means, motive and opportunity? Well, unless one of these persons who had opportunity steps up and tells me he did it, I have to look at the other two points of my trident. Motive and means. That brings me to the reason for my visit. This is a small community we live in here, Matt. People know other people's business, and rumors get around. There is a rumor that you were involved, romantically involved, with Mrs. Vasiloff, Nick's wife Donna. Is that true?" He took out a spiral notebook and started jotting. I was feeling a little queasy. This was disconcerting.

"Yeah, it was a while ago. When I first came to town. It's over now."

"Over?"

"Yeah."

"It's odd, then, that one of the first places she went when she came back to town yesterday, is this boat."

"Yeah, she came here yesterday afternoon. I didn't invite her, she just came. She didn't stay long."

"The other rumor is that Nick and you have had several confrontations, about Mrs. Vasiloff or something, one of which resulted in your being struck by Nick in the Club Bar. A violent confrontation in which Nick, as he usually did, came out on top."

"Yeah, he punched me in the eye. But that wasn't about Donna."

"No? Why else were you and Nick enemies, then?"

"We weren't enemies! The man saved my life! Why would I want to kill him?"

"Then why would he want to punch you in the eye? Aside from sleeping with his wife, that is." That really sounded bad. He was just stating facts, but it felt like he was twisting them all up. How would this sound in a courtroom?

"OK, here's the deal. I'm in love with his niece, Anna Vasiloff. That's Nick's brother Joe's daughter. The reason Nick punched me is because I demanded that he give Anna Joe's share from their boat that sank, when Joe died."

"Yes, the Nancy V. I know the story. I understand there is some question as to whether that money was saved or is on the bottom of the Sound."

"I'm pretty sure Nick has it, er, had it."

I was starting to have flashes of the old Perry Mason shows my dad liked. "Do I need to get a lawyer? Are you gonna arrest me?"

"Should I?"

"No, I mean . . . NO!"

"OK. To be fair, you are what we call 'a person of interest.' It's so neat and tidy. You have affair with the wife. You spend three days anchored by his boat while he's not there. Boat blows up. Husband dies. Looks like an accident. She gets the money. You live happily ever after. I get my trident, means, motive, opportunity."

I'm sure I had an incredulous look on my face. "What? No! No way!"

"What 'person of interest' means, Matt, is I would like you to stay in town for a few days. Don't get on the ferry. Don't go out to the airport. Don't go out the road, even."

"Can I go fishing?"

"Sure you can go fishing, in your skiff. Don't run it to Valdez, or Whittier, however. And I have a few more questions for you, if you don't mind."

"Do I have a choice?"

"Sure you do. Like I said, you aren't under arrest, and I couldn't make you answer any questions even if you were, if you don't want to. And you can get a lawyer if you want, but since you aren't under arrest, you don't get a free one from the State."

"OK, what questions?"

"Did you go aboard the Marauder that closure, for any reason?"

"No."

"Did you see anyone else on the Marauder, other than Nick?"

"No."

"You mind if I take a set of your fingerprints?"

"Sure, but look, my prints are probably all over the boat, 'cause I spent a day on it when Nick rescued me during that big blow during red season." He nodded.

"Was Nick opposed to your relationship with his niece?"

"Maybe a little irritated, but I think he was mostly amused by it. He laughed at me, about that and about Donna and me as well. The person opposed is probably Arnie Swenson." I smiled at my little joke.

"I expect so." Trooper Bill returned my smile.

"Can you think of anyone else who may have wanted to do Nick harm?"

"Hell yes I can! He beat the crap out of Marty Gauer a couple of months ago. Put him in the hospital. Over that same 'nonexistent' money." Bill nodded. "And I understand that Arnie Swenson had run-ins with Nick over Arnie's older sister, Nick's first wife. The one who's married to Gauer now."

"How well do you know Mr. Swenson?"

"I don't know him. I mean, I really haven't met him, but it sounds like he had no use for Nick. And he's tight with Gauer, he's his skiff man and they crab in the winter. Maybe they share their hatreds, too. I understand Nick's been known to pick other people's crab pots during Tanner crab season. That'll piss a guy off. Man, you've been here longer than I have, and seen the police reports. Probably wrote some of them. I bet you have a big list of people with grudges against Nick."

"Yes, he had more than his share. So, Byron Clausen is your friend? Did he talk about Nick?"

"Only to warn me he was not someone you wanted to get in a fight with. 'A bit of a sociopath', he said. And that he was a good fisherman."

"So, Duck, Mr. Petroff. He's your friend too?"

"I've only been here a few months, but I guess he's my friend."

"What was his feeling about Nick?"

"I don't know. He was pretty close to Nick's brother Joe. Nancy was his aunt. I think he would have liked to see Nancy get her inheritance while it could have done her some good."

The Trooper looked at me in silence for longer than was comfortable, then he said: "Anything else you want to tell me? How you rigged the boat to explode, for instance?" This totally caught me off guard.

"No! I mean; I didn't. I don't know how you would even do that."

"What would you say if I told you I've got a witness who says he saw you go aboard the Marauder during the closure, in Mr. Clausen's inflatable raft?"

"What? That never happened! Who told you that?"

He smiled at me pityingly. "If I decide to arrest you, you'll get to see all the witness statements." My hands were sweating and I could feel that my face was flushed. He watched me in silence for a while. "OK, Matt. Sorry to spoil your morning." He reached for his coat. "Remember, don't leave town. And if you decide you want to tell me anything else, just let me know. Sometimes cooperating with us helps you later on." He set a business card on the table as he put on the coat.

"Holy shit!" I put the coffee pot on. I'm totally flipped out. Bizarre images are crashing around in my brain. I'm a middle-aged man in a faded blue work shirt in my 18th year in the prison laundry at Eagle River. My father is reduced to penury purchasing high-priced lawyers to handle my appeals. My mother cries into the phone on the other side of the thick glass partition in the visiting room. I wonder if Alaska has the death penalty? Wait! I didn't do it! And it's not like I'm some poor Negro down in Texas, with a white jury winking at each other and sending me to the gallows for a crime some redneck did.

# CHAPTER 41

## A Person Of Interest

The coffee and toast with nagoon berry jam settled me down a bit. It wasn't me, so who did do it, then? And who made up that bullshit about me going over to Nick's boat? Very likely the same person. I can't imagine it was Duck or BD. Why would they? It would be pretty handy if it was Arnie, and he'll be the one spending the next 20 years up at Eagle River. Probably was Gauer, though. Just the kind of weasel-assed thing he would do. Rig the boat to blow up, slink off down to the markers; then rat me out for it.

I needed some sort of reality check. I got my long Helly raincoat on to go down the dock to Clausen's seiner. The wind almost tore the door out of my hand. Rain was blowing hard, like BB's, and scooting along the surface of the float in sheets of haze. I made a slipping, sliding run for it down the float and into the sheltering lee of the Glacier Island's cabin. I pounded on the door, then just let myself in. No one was in the galley.

"You guys here?"

BD's voice came up from the focsle. "Yeah, we're here. Whaddaya want?"

I could tell by the slight exasperation in his tone that I had caught them at a less than opportune moment for a social visit. I just bulled ahead.

"I was hoping to talk to you about something. I can come back later."

Melissa answered. "No, it's fine, we were just sleeping in, being lazy. Grab some coffee, the stuff in the pot is pretty new."

I got a cup off the wall and filled it up. I sat down at the galley table and waited for them to appear from down below. Out the galley window I watched the boats on the next float shudder and writhe against their tie-up lines as they were pummeled by the grey williwaws. The weather was so thick that I couldn't even see across the harbor up to town.

"What a shit day!" BD intoned as he came up the focsle steps buttoning his flannel shirt. "I don't even want to think about our rigs down there at Cudahay in this blow. We should have run 'em to town. I knew we were pushing our luck. This late in the year, and on this run of big tides, it was sure to blow. I hope they don't go dragging out of there. God knows where they would end up."

I hadn't even thought about my skiff anchored up in this storm with no one aboard. "You think they'll drag anchor?"

"Not much we can do about it now." He held his palms up to the heavens. "I think John and Julie might have stayed down there this closure, but I don't know how much he could do in this weather." I still got a little zing in my stomach when I heard Julie and John referred to that way, as a couple.

Melissa came up from the focsle, wrapped in a silk kimono-like robe, pulling a brush through her tousled hair, and slid in to the settee across from me.

"Hi Monkey. Enjoying the fall weather?"

"Don't know that I've ever seen it rain this hard, or blow this hard either."

"Weather radio says it's blowing over 90 at Middleton Island."

"Equinoctial storms" BD pontificated. "Tempestem Horribilis Equinoctialis. So, what is it you want to talk about? No, let me guess. You got a visit from Trooper Bill?"

"Yeah I did. Did he talk to you too?"

"Yeah, this morning early."

"Byron, I'm freaking out! He practically accused me of murder! I'm a 'person of interest.' He went off about me having means, motive and opportunity. What did he say to you?" Melissa's eyes got big. BD went over to the window and looked out. It was almost like he didn't want to look at me.

"He asked me a lot of the same questions again. And a lot more about who could have gone aboard the Marauder and rigged it to blow up. We went through the long list of people who hated Nick, and why. The rumor from the cop shop is that someone set up a simple electric spark trigger. Alligator clip a hot and a negative wire off the electrical panel. The wire ends pass each other, touch and spark when the door opens. Then the guy disconnects the bilge pump wire so it can't pump the fuel overboard, cuts the rubber fuel line so it runs a bunch of gas into the bilge and climbs out the galley window. Boat fills up with fumes. Next guy who slides open the door, boom! Probably figured it would burn to the water line and destroy the evidence, but the explosion was so sharp it blew the fire out. That happens sometimes. But, what makes you think he suspects you?"

"Man, he says he has a witness who saw me go aboard in your inflatable. Who told him that? Someone is setting me up. It's starting to feel like the Twilight Zone!"

Now BD turned to look at me. "Cool out, Matt! Maybe he just threw that out there to see if he could get you to freak and confess."

"Byron, I'm not gonna confess, 'cause I didn't DO anything!"

"We know! There's no way you could have walked across Duck's skiff and my skiff and gotten in the rubber boat without waking me up. I could tell every time one of you went on deck to piss. I wake up every time the goddamn tide changes and we swing around." He leaned against the side of the settee, next to where Melissa was sitting.

"You don't think it was Duck who told the Trooper that, do you?"

"Matthew," Melissa said, "you're sounding paranoid."

"I am paranoid! Someone's out to get me. Do you guys think I should get a lawyer?"

BD said: "If Bill really thought you did it, don't you think he would arrest you? I think he's fishing. But maybe you shouldn't have any more chats with him without a lawyer. And no, I don't think Duck told the cop he saw you go over there, and, just for the record, I don't think Duck or you did it, either."

"Well, thanks for the vote of confidence. That leaves Arnie, Martin, Mike . . . and you."

"Matt!" Melissa squealed.

BD cut her off. "If I was going to blow anyone up it would be Martin Gauer for fucking me out of ten thousand dollars of herring this spring. I bet you're hoping it was Arnie, huh Witz?" He gave me the wry smile he used whenever he zinged me.

Again, Melissa raised her voice. "Byron, this isn't funny! Someone's dead and someone is probably going to go to jail for a long time for it."

"I've been meaning to ask" I said, "does Alaska have the death penalty?"

"I don't think so, except maybe for claim jumping" BD replied.

"OK boys," Melissa looked serious now, but assumed a pedantic, kindergarten teacher tone. "Let's be Trooper Bill, or Sherlock Holmes, or Miss Marple for a minute here. I'm gonna assume, for the sake of our friendships, that neither Monkey or my cute little stud-muffin here blew Nick up."

"Jolly Good, Holmes!" BD was sniggering. "You've already eliminated a third of your suspects through your rigorous deductive reasoning."

Melissa didn't even look, she just shot out a sharp left jab that caught BD on the thigh and made him wince. "So, does anyone know when Mike Mills flew in to town? It was after Nick Vasiloff left, correct? You are certain that he didn't fly back out on Sunday until after the boat blew up, but he was there in the slough for a while after Nick left?"

I knew the answer to this one. "He left on the flight that landed right before it got dark. Cordova Air's last plane. We heard it land right after we came back from the hunt, remember, Byron?"

"OK" Melissa said, "that gave him, what, an hour after Nick left?"

BD warmed to the enterprise now. "Yeah, at most, but we were either on deck admiring Matt's goose, in the Challenger, or walking around on the banks, and I didn't see him move. He plunked his anchor down, and that was it till the plane came."

"I didn't see him go anywhere either," I added. "Plus, what would his motive be?"

"He's right, Melissa. He's one of the few people I can think of who hasn't had any sort of run-in with Nick."

"OK, he goes into the 'very unlikely' column. So, what about your friend Donald Petroff?"

"What, he doesn't get a free pass for being our friend, like Matt does?" The left jab shot out again and BD winced again and sidled over to the sink, ostensibly to get a glass of water, but more likely to get out of range.

Melissa continued." Duck was pretty close with Joe Vasiloff, and Nancy was his Aunt. He may have had a grudge against Nick for the Nancy V sinking, and for the fact that Nancy and his cousin Anna never got any money from it, if there was any. He had three days of opportunities to give you two the slip and go do the nefarious deeds on the Marauder. You guys were probably so drunk half the time that you would never have noticed."

BD was incensed. "Come on, Melissa! You can't be serious! Duck? Plus, we were only that drunk the first night, and Duck was as bad off as we were."

"OK, I'm putting him in the 'maybe' column. How about Marty Gauer?"

"Now there's a prime suspect," I offered. "He still has the wounds from his last ass-kicking by Nick. A public humiliation. He thinks Nick ripped him off for half a seine season, then lied to him about it, he's married to a woman Nick abused, and he's a small-minded, weaselly, gangster asshole to boot!"

BD laughed. "Don't beat around the bush, Matt, tell us what you really think!"

"So," Melissa summed up, "motive we've got in spades with Martin. Means—he probably knows enough about boats to figure out how to make one blow up."

"Yeah, and he's just dumb enough not to realize it will probably not burn up all the evidence of his tinkering" BD added.

"And opportunity, when did you say he left the slough?"

"He and Arnie left sometime on Saturday, while we were out on the crane hunt." I explained.

"Yeah, and they hunted on Friday in the shit weather, so they were out and about that day" BD added.

"So, there was Thursday night, when you were all drunk, Friday while you were sleeping off your hangovers, and Saturday morning when you were out assassinating innocent fowl. Lots of chances, for both of them."

"Hey, that's right! How about both of them together? If I'm gonna be paranoid, might as well think big."

"One perp at a time, Matt. So, I think we could put Marty in the 'very likely' category. That leaves Arnie Swenson."

BD took off on this one. "Arnie and Nick used to hate each other when Nick was married to Alice. Nick was unfaithful to her and beat her up, and it totally pissed Arnie off. They came to blows. I think it mellowed to extreme distaste after Alice divorced Nick. That was a long time ago, though. Why kill him now?"

Melissa had an answer. "If the Nancy V money is a motive for Martin, how about for Arnie? His girlfriend's inheritance. After all, that money was motivation enough for her other boyfriend here to take a punch in the eye." She gestured at me. My black eye was long gone, but no one had let me forget it.

"But now that he's dead, Anna may never get the money!" I was recalling Donna's delight at her inheritance. "He had no will, so Donna gets it all."

"Well, maybe they thought he had one, and that she was in it. Didn't you say he had promised her she would inherit, Matt?"

"Hey, are you suggesting that Anna put Arnie up to killing Nick?"

BD liked the idea. He mimicked a girly falsetto. "Arnie, if you kill my uncle and get my money, I'll love you forever, forsaking all others. It's Shakespeare, man! I'm just not sure if it's Hamlet, or Macbeth."

"That sucks, Byron. It's not funny," I snapped. BD's hands came up in a palms-out gesture of surrender.

Melissa said: "It is a possible motive though, even if she didn't suggest it to him. You add it in to the bad blood from Nick beating up Arnie's sister, and it might just make sense. I'm putting Arnie behind Gauer in my most wanted list. And he certainly has a good motive for saying he saw you on Nick's boat. Gets rid of the other boyfriend. He's a respected local boy and a decorated war veteran. People will believe him."

"What good does all this Agatha Christie shit do, Melissa? I'm still on the verge of being arrested for something someone else did, and largely due to someone lying about me. This is starting to feel like *To Kill A Mockingbird* or some damn thing.

"Much as some folks dislike longhairs, Matt, it's a stretch to compare yourself to an oppressed southern black man."

# CHAPTER 42

## Funeral Games.

I fought my way back to the Sally. The storm was just as bad as before. Inside, on the galley table, was a note from Anna. "Matt, I'm over at Pt. Chehalis. I need to talk to you." I hadn't seen her since the closure before Nick was killed. We were still in our mode of sneaking around behind Arnie's back, even though he was fully aware of what was happening. I had suffered a black eye, gallantly obtained in her service. I was no longer seeing Julie. Still, she hadn't left him.

The last of the silver salmon were hardly enough to keep the Pt. Chehalis plant busy, but they were running Dungeness crab caught right out in the inlet as well, hundreds of thousands of pounds already in the first couple of weeks of the season.

When I walked into the kitchen, Anna immediately stopped what she was doing. She gave Nita some quick instructions, and then grabbed my arm. "Come into the break room." Trestle tables were covered with floral print oilcloth. Towers of white soup bowls and rows of white coffee mugs were lined up by big stainless steel coffee urns on tables along the wall.

"Matt, they think you killed Nick!" She looked fiercely into my eyes, as if she could bore in to the truth with some sort of x-ray vision.

"Anna, I didn't kill anyone."

A flicker of relief flashed over her face, then she said: "I didn't think you did, but I'm not the one you have to convince."

"Who thinks I did? How do you know this?"

"Trooper Bill has talked to Arnie, several times."

"So it was Arnie who accused me?"

"Well, not exactly. Martin told Arnie he saw you go onto the Marauder when Nick was in town. So Arnie figures you rigged it to blow up. I don't really know what he told the Troopers. He's totally upset and freaked out about the whole thing. I've never seen him like this before. He's been having horrible nightmares, a couple of times a night even."

"So it's Martin who says it was me? Look, I haven't been on Nick's boat since he pulled me out of the breakers!"

"Well, someone told Trooper Bill they saw you."

"Bill has talked to me, too. He says I'm a 'person of interest.'"

"What are you going to do?"

"Well, if they arrest me, I'll get a lawyer. Until then, I'm going to hope they arrest whoever really did it."

"Matt, that sounds like a pretty lame plan, but I can't think of what else to do."

"Me neither." Now I looked her square in the face. "Anna, do you think Arnie could have done it?"

She looked completely surprised, taken aback. "Arnie? Huh?" She thought for a moment, shook her head. "I don't think so." I was relieved that she actually seemed to be considering it for the first time. If she'd plotted or put him up to it, she was an impressive liar. "Why do you think he did it?"

"Someone who was there did it. I just know it wasn't me. But hey, do I get a kiss before they haul me off to prison for a crime I didn't commit?" She smiled and gave me a perfunctory peck.

Her eyes roamed around the room, then settled on me again. "I think I may be well and truly fucked, Matt."

"You? What happened?"

"Donna happened. She's back in town to 'sort out her inheritance.'"

"I know."

"Matthew, there was no will! That goddamned Nick! There isn't as much as a note on a bar napkin to say that I should have any of Nick's money. No matter what he told me, Donna is still his wife. With no will, she gets his house, every penny he has at the cannery and in the bank, and every nickel she can winkle out of Nick's stashes and hidey-holes." She pressed her lips together in a tight line. She sniffed once. "It's so unfair!" she wailed.

I hugged her to me for a minute, then she pulled away. "I've got salmon chowder to make. Are you going fishing tomorrow?"

"Yeah, my rig is still down at Cudahay. One more week of silvers, I guess. If we can get down there with this weather."

"Arnie is fishing here at Egg Island and Pete Dahl. Just going through the motions till they close it." She looked at me with a mournful expression. "I'll try to come see you this evening. Will you be on your boat?"

I nodded.

"Nick's funeral is tomorrow morning," she said. "I'm not looking forward to it."

"No, I guess not."

"Arnie won't go. Says he didn't like the man, and doesn't want to go to his funeral. You know, it might look good if you went with me, Matt. Show you've got nothing to hide."

I made a sour face, but then I thought about it. "The man saved my life. I guess I could do that."

"Good. Be at the church at 10. And stay out of prison, Matt." I nodded.

The church service is a long ordeal of droning Russian prayers, bells and incense. There are quite a few people at the cemetery. At the graveside Donna is trying to look grief-stricken, but she can't keep a smirk off her face. Vicki, whose wardrobe is apparently short on black items, is garbed in an incongruous mix of dark clothing in questionable taste. Between her blubbering and sniveling and her low-cut blouse she is attracting a lot of attention. Anna and I, Sophia and Dickie Hansen, and Duck and his brother Bill and sister Lily are all standing together, watching the two of them. I can tell that Anna is getting more and more pissed off.

Finally, the ceremony is over, people are dropping handfuls of dirt in the grave and milling around. Vicki starts bawling and Donna snaps at her *sotto voce*. 'Give it a rest, you bimbo.'

Now Vicki comes completely unglued and starts yelling: "You didn't love him; all you ever did was make him miserable and take all his money!"

"That's what you're really crying about, you sleazy gold-digger, his money!" "You're not fooling anyone with your weepy act," Donna growls through gritted teeth.

To my amazement, Vicki emits a wail and launches herself at Donna, trying to rake her with her claws. Bill grabs her arm before she can get there, spins her around, and Lily envelops her in a hug, cooing something in her ear to calm her down. The priest is looking all nervous, and suggests we proceed back to town. Nick's sister Sophia is staring daggers at Donna. Then Anna starts toward Donna with a determined look on her face. This doesn't bode well. A vision of Anna pummeling Donna flashes in my brain. She's a Vasiloff, after all. She probably could kick Donna's ass if she wanted to. I step forward and lightly grasp Anna's arm, tense as a steel spring.

Anna doesn't touch Donna, but her voice is thick with barely suppressed rage. "Donna, since the subject of money has come up, when can I expect my father's seine money? My inheritance, which Nick was keeping for me?"

Donna looks startled, then turns on her brilliant smile. "Anna, this is not a good time to talk about that," she says condescendingly.

"No, it's the perfect time to talk about Nick's wishes. Here, in front of his family and friends." Donna's eyes flick from one scowling face to another. The only sounds are the wind in the hemlock trees and Vicki softly sobbing in Lily's embrace.

"Talk to my lawyer." She turns and walks down the hill to the road.

# CHAPTER 43

## No One Has To Go
## If They Don't Want To.

That afternoon, Melissa drove BD and me out to Chitina Air in Chuck the Truck. We passed the old cemetery. Someone in an orange raincoat was filling in Nick Vasiloff's grave up on the hill. It made me sad to think that Anna had been to so many funerals.

The wind had let down some, but it was still maybe 30 with higher gusts. The clouds were racing by, low and dark, but the rain had trailed off. Mike Mills, Duck and Buck Barnett were in the air service shack when we came in, shuffling about with little Styrofoam cups of coffee in their hands. Waiting. Buck smiled when he saw me.

"Gut check time, hippie."

"How do you mean, Buck?" I was hoping he wasn't going to start in about Nick's murder.

"Gettin' on that plane, boy, is what I mean. It's gonna take serious stones to fly out there in this weather, if the pilot'll even do her."

Just then, Ellen walked in from the back of the office. "I made one trip already today. The flying is do-able, bumpy maybe. It's the taking off and landing that scared the crap out of me."

Mike Mills closed his eyes and gave a little groan. "If it scared you, Ellen, I don't know if I want to go."

"No one has to go if they don't want to. If I didn't think we could do it, I'd say we aren't going. But it's up to each of you to get on the plane."

BD looked at Duck and me in turn. "I'm game."

Duck said: "I want my skiff. I miss it."

"I think I'll go in the morning," said Mike.

"There's room on the flight we bumped this morning, that will go tomorrow at 9. You'll miss the opener." Ellen told him.

"Openers are over-rated this time of year" Mike replied.

"If a girl has the guts to go, I'm goin," Buck muttered unhappily.

"OK, saddle up boys." Ellen grabbed the clipboard with the manifest, scratched Mike's name off.

The beaver idled into the lake, throwing up sheets of spray as the pontoons smacked into the whitecaps the wind was whipping up. I was the biggest, so I was riding shotgun to keep the weight up front. Ellen lined up into the wind and pushed the throttle forward. The plane jumped ahead, smacked the waves with 4 or 5 spine-jarring thuds, and bounded into the air. As soon as the pontoons were off the water, a swirling gust laid us over twenty degrees and the plane slewed sideways. She fought it back to level with quick snaps on the steering yoke and a tap dance on the foot pedals. We lifted up and through the slot in the bowl of mountains that contain the lake.

As we shot the gap out to the flats, the first stomach-wrenching drop took place. Over the top of the roller-coaster. We fell like a rock for several hundred feet until we thumped into a spot of sky that still had air in it. My face and palms began to sweat and I could feel I was wearing a sickly grin. Ellen smiled at me, reached around behind my seat and pulled out a couple of paper barf bags and waved them in the air. "Don't be shy about using these," she shouted over the scream of the engine.

Fortunately, we were all going to Cudahay, so we only had to make one landing. Ellen circled the slough once to figure out the wind and how the boats were laying. We breathed contented sighs to see our miniature skiffs were all still there, like little ducklings in a row. She lined up the landing below the turn in the slough, where it was a little wider and straighter into the wind. Down by where we had found Nick. Bucking and buffeting, she wrestled us down onto the water with a bouncy landing. We looked around with big grins. The air in the plane was thick with relief.

"That's the way ya do it!"

"Piece 'a cake, huh, Ellen?" As she was taxiing us up to the skiffs, she looked back over her shoulder.

"Thanks for not puking on my plane, boys. It's been a pleasure flying you on Chitina Scarelines."

When we got up to the skiffs it finally dawned on me. "Where'd the Marauder go?"

Buck explained. "Insurance company paid one of the tenders to get 'er. Salvage tow. Big money."

BD and I tied up to Duck's skiff again, for beer and frozen pizza heated up in his tiny oven a few pieces at a time. Things were a lot more subdued than during the crane hunt weekend. But after his beer, Duck looked at me with an irrepressible smirk. "That was a heck of a funeral there, Matt. Almost turned into a mud-wrestling match."

"Yea, something tells me Donna won't be staying in town long. I just hope Anna gets her money."

"I'll be very surprised if she does."

We fished the next couple of days with pretty poor results. On the flood tide I went down toward the bar to set the net. The whole entrance was a wall of huge white breakers, crashing and rolling one after another. It looked like high surf scenes from the North Shore of Oahu.

On Tuesday, Duck got on the radio. "Hard Rain, Bufflehead. I'm fed up, Clausen. I think the last of 'em went up the creek on that big storm and big tides. I think I'll head for the barn before the next typhoon strikes."

"Sounds good" BD replied. "I wanna be sure I get back to town for the Ducks Unlimited banquet Thursday evening. Break, Desperado, you copy? How about you, Witz? You wanna go home?"

"I'm ready to go home. I just can't figure out how to get there with those humongous waves out on the bar."

"No, don't try to go that way! That lump out in the ocean is still huge. No way you wanna go out that bar. We should run across the inside on this next high water. We've got a thirteen-foot tide. More than enough to get over the flat between Grass Island and Pete Dahl. We'll put the wind on our butts and squeak across the shallows. Don't go stuck, though, or you'll be out here until the big tides in October."

"Don't *you* go stuck! Cause I'm gonna be so close behind you I'll run right into your ass."

# CHAPTER 44

## Hens Unlimited

The Ducks Unlimited fundraiser was a big deal, and a good excuse for an end-of-the-season party. I barely got a ticket. It sold out.

BD and Melissa, Duck and Ellen, Matt and . . . Linda? Ellen's pal came unescorted, so we sat together. Kenny was spending the evening with Granny. The event was held in the Elks, as it was the biggest hall and thus the default venue for such things. The place was packed with booze-and-beer-swilling Cordovans. There was going to be an auction later, and some of the auction items were displayed or described on the walls, so people were milling around, drinks in hand, checking out the treasures. At some point, they started serving dinner at the buffet by the kitchen. BD and I sniggered when we realized it was broiled game hen halves. "Look at all those birds! Maybe they should call it 'Hens Unlimited." Still, we filled our plates and returned to our table.

Martin Gauer and his wife, Arnie's sister Alice, were at the next table. Marty's other seine crewman was there as well, and two more chair backs were tipped up against the table to reserve a couple more places for people yet to arrive. For Arnie and Anna? To complete the seine crew?

Marty shot me a sneer as he sat down. He finished his drink fast; probably not his first, then went and got another. As he returned to his table he feigned surprise at seeing me. "What's this? I figured you'd be in jail by now, hippy."

"What do you mean, Marty?" I said his name with a tone of contempt that was not lost on him. BD was making subtle no-no gestures at me.

"What I mean is, I can't imagine they'll let a long-haired freak like you get away with murder." My face and ears were heating up. "Why'd ya do it, weirdo? Trying to impress Nick's slutty niece by blowing him up?"

I launched out of the chair. I hadn't punched anyone since junior high school, but as I rose up I popped him real fast, square on the nose with a left to get the range, then, as he backed up in pain and surprise I stepped in and brought my right across as hard as I could. It made an awful crunch. Pain shot up my arm. Marty fell back onto the table and started making a howling, whimpering sound. Marty's wife was screaming, and I heard Melissa shout my name.

"Shit!" I thought, "I've broken my hand." But then I realized the crunch had been the sound of Marty's recently mended face breaking back into pieces again. "Uh-oh!" Duck and BD were on both sides of me now, holding my arms at my sides and telling me to settle down.

"You're going to jail, son." Mack, the Chief of Police, had come over from a nearby table and had handcuffs on me before I even knew he was there. I felt lightheaded and buzzy with adrenaline. I was watching the proceedings from a vantage point outside my body when I heard a man cry: "No! Don't arrest him!"

Anna and Arnie were just coming in from the entry stairway. Arnie had a terrible, agonized expression on his face. In a loud but hollow voice, he said: "Wait! That's the wrong guy. He didn't kill Nick. It was Martin."

Alice Gauer's eyes got huge and she turned away from Marty writhing in the food on their table. "What are you saying, Arnie? Why are you saying this?" Her voice got louder and higher pitched with each word.

"I'm saying it 'cause it's true. I'm not going to lie about it any more."

I spent the night in jail, but it was a strangely euphoric experience. I had not only punched out an asshole who richly deserved it, but it now seemed very unlikely that I would be spending years in jail for a murder I didn't do. I felt kinda bad about Martin's face, but when they let me out the next morning, Mack told me he was under arrest up at the hospital. Mack said Martin might still press charges against me for assault, but the DA wasn't going to do it otherwise. Marty had more pressing problems at the moment, like, Murder 1. When Bill told him his prints came back from the lab a match to ones on the boat, Martin didn't deny going aboard. All he said, through his wired-shut jaw, was: "the man needed killing."

When I came out onto the street, Anna, BD and Melissa were all there waiting for me. "Whoa, what a reception!"

Melissa said "we thought you could use a little company, Matt."

Anna came up to me and gave me a hug. "God! I'm so relieved. We thought they were arresting you for murder, not just a bar brawl."

"Yeah, I'm not usually the bar brawl type. I guess I kinda lost it there for a minute."

"That was pretty righteous of Arnie. He did the right thing by you."

"Say what?" I blurted. "The guy perjures himself, tells lies about an innocent man, and you call it righteous when he stops?" Melissa's eyes got big, and Anna recoiled a bit at my vehemence.

Anna tried to explain. "Arnie told me last night that he knew all along Marty had gone onto the Marauder. He admitted he didn't tell the troopers that until last night. Marty had said he was hoping to steal Nick's money. It was Marty who'd said he saw you sneak on there later, in BD's raft, during the blow on Friday. Then when Arnie heard about the explosion, he just put 2 and 2 together, and got 5. He blamed you."

BD jumped in. "Anna, are you gonna believe that self-serving crap? Arnie had a lot of reasons to want it to be Matt, who's desperately trying to steal his girlfriend, rather than Marty, who is his seine skipper, his hunting buddy, and is married to his sister."

Anna looked unhappy, trapped. "I know. I think he knew all along Martin was lying. Maybe that's why he was so miserable. Last night, after they arrested you, Arnie kept saying: 'those fucking alligator clips.' There were a couple of those wire clips on the table while they sat in Marty's galley before he went on to the Marauder. He kept rolling them around in his hand, like Captain Queeg with the steel balls." She looked away from BD, at me. "I hear that jail food isn't very good, Matthew. Why don't we go get breakfast at the Pioneer?" She looked hesitantly at Melissa and BD. "You guys want to come?"

"Thanks, Anna, but we ate" Melissa answered. "We're just glad to have the Jail Monkey out of the slammer." She gave me a hug. "Come by the boat later, Matt. I made a pie. I'll save you a piece."

At the restaurant, Anna was subdued. I was still bubbling with relief. "Never been in jail before. You know the weird thing? That place has no windows. You can't tell if it's day or night. It's disorienting, and creepy."

"I was in the old jail once. They don't use it any more. It was like a big box of iron. Made out of old military landing mats welded together. Like something from The Great Escape."

"Did you have a mitt and a baseball?" Then I thought about it a bit. "Anna, what were you in jail for?"

She looked embarrassed. "I was drunk and disorderly. It was a long time ago."

I let it slide, changed the subject. "So, they arrested Martin?"

"Yes, they did. They have his prints from Nick's boat, they have Arnie's statement, they have the alligator clips Arnie saw, and it sounds like Marty pretty much confessed." She gave me a sly smile. "Everyone's talking about you, Matt. They say you punched Marty out 'cause he called me a slut."

"Well, that was one reason."

"Thank you."

"You're welcome."

"I need to go to work now, Matt. I'm a poor orphan. Remember? Now I don't even have an uncle."

"Yeah, OK, I'll walk you down." Anna was quiet as we walked. Finally, I said: "Anna, I'm sorry about Nick. Even if you hated him, it must suck to lose your family. Too many funerals."

She looked at me with a sad smile. "Nick was a tortured soul. Unfortunately, tortured souls torture those around them."

# CHAPTER 45

## Have a Good Flight.

P t. Chehalis Cannery's work hours were getting irregular as the season wound down. They were closed the day after I got out of jail, so I tried several times to call Anna at home. First I got no answer. Then I got Arnie. I almost hung up when I heard his voice, but I asked for her instead. "She's not here. Hey, isn't it time for all you little snowbirds to head south for the winter?" Then a click as he hung up. He's waiting me out. Waiting for me to leave.

Anna's cannery was running crab the next morning. APA was going to pull my boat out later, but I got up early and waited outside Pt. Chehalis until Anna showed up. She looked harried and distracted. She gave me a quick hug.

"You OK Anna?"

"I'm not sleeping very well." She didn't elaborate. "We are shutting the kitchen for a while. Until Snow Crab starts up. I've got a lot to do."

"So here's the deal, Anna."

"Oh, there's a deal? What's the deal then?"

I ignored her testy tone and said: "Fishing's over, for me anyway. I'm not in jail. I'm putting my skiff up in the warehouse today. You're the only reason I have to stay here. But I can't just mope around here all winter waiting to be with you for a few hours every now and then. I'm thinking about getting on the southbound plane, day after tomorrow. I'm gonna fly to Seattle, then to San Francisco. I'm gonna get an apartment and play in a band for a while, with a college buddy of mine. Remember that bullshit dream of yours? That we tried to tell Nick about? San Francisco and cooking school and restaurants? It doesn't have to be bullshit. Come with me. Why don't you get on that plane with me?"

"I don't have the money, Matt. I've only got, like, a thousand dollars. That fucking Donna has all the money! She just blew me off. The probate attorney says I would have to sue Donna if I disagree with what she does with Nick's property. Since there is nothing written down, no will, no contract, not even a witness to a verbal agreement, I really have no claim against the estate."

"I've got half my season in the bank. I'll buy your plane ticket."

"No! I mean, let me think about all this."

"Anna, haven't you *been* thinking about all this? We've been talking about it for weeks."

She just looked at me, with the same far away, appraising look she had given me the day we met in front of the drug store and I had asked her to come have a drink.

Just then BD showed up in Chuck the Truck, which was grumbling a little louder than I remembered. "Hi Anna. Get in, Witz. If the beach boss is gonna pull your skiff at 11 o'clock you don't wanna keep the parade waiting. Other guys want to get up on this tide."

Anna kept looking at me. A smile crept onto her face. "We'll talk later. Better not call me at home, though. Arnie's getting really freaked out. He's making me miserable." She looked down at her feet, a little chagrined. "Well, we're making him miserable too. Now he's giving me ultimatums. I'm supposed to break up with you."

"Well, don't."

She shook her head. "He got a moose tag, for the other side of the Copper, so I'm hoping he'll go hunting out the road and cool off. Well, you better go before BD runs out of gas." She leaned up and gave me a quick kiss.

I got into the rumbling station wagon and BD started quizzing me. "Boy, that looked serious. I wondered why you told me to meet you here. What's going on?"

"I'm trying to convince her to go to California with me, but she's all messed up about the money she didn't get from Nick, and about Arnie, and she's kinda stubborn to boot. Still, I think she wants to go."

"Be careful what you wish for, brother."

"Gee, thanks for your support!"

"I just don't want to see you moping around like Arnie Swenson."


Two days later, BD drove me out to the airport. He had wrapped some tin cans around the worst holes in Chuck's exhaust system with wire and high heat tape, so he ran a bit quieter. Still, we were torn between keeping the windows shut to cut the noise and leaving the windows open to prevent the carbon monoxide poisoning. "Let me know if my lips turn blue" I told him.

"They'll be blue from the cold if you don't roll your goddamn window up some."

As we drove out the road I kept my eyes on the view out across the delta and up to the glaciers and mountains. There was red and straw and honey where green had been a month ago, and the snow had come down the gnarly mountains to the sides of the glaciers already. I was trying not to think about how Anna wasn't with me. Trying not to think about that elephant again. We passed a moose standing in a beaver pond. BD was talking about some graduate program in fisheries science he was interested in at a college in Southeast Alaska. They were on the quarter system there and he was going to try for admission for winter quarter. Fizzy bubbles of anxiety were making it hard for me to concentrate on what he was saying.

Why hadn't I heard from Anna? Why hadn't I pushed her more, convinced her? I'd walked by her place, and even called her phone number once or twice despite her telling me not to, but no one had answered. I'd tried the cookhouse at Pt. Chehalis, but they were done for the season. Eventually, I concluded that she was avoiding me. I couldn't believe she was taking such a cowardly way out. But my pride had stiffened up and now here I was, leaving town alone.

Once we got to the log cabin terminal building I pulled my backpack and guitar out of the back of the wagon. BD gave me a backslapping hug. "OK jailbird, I'm gonna boogie back to town. Have a nice flight." Then he tilted his head to one side and gave me a long look. "You did pretty damn good this summer, for a Cheechako rookie. See ya back here in the spring, if I don't see you this winter sometime. You know, there're fish to kill in the winter too, if the rock-n-roll thing doesn't work out. There's crabbing. Only highliners get vacations."

"You and 'Lissa should come down to California when the weather gets too shitty up here. Maybe Roach and I will be opening for The Who at Winterland."

"We'll see."

I carried my stuff inside and checked in at the Alaska Air counter, which was actually the only counter in the little terminal. Three or four other passengers were milling around. Nobody I knew. Certainly not Anna. What the hell am I doing? I should be looking for her right now rather than getting on the plane by myself. In desperation, I called her from the pay phone in the terminal. No answer. I was standing looking dejectedly at the Forest Service display about the Copper River Delta when the door burst open. A sealskin parka was backing in through the self-closing door, dragging an immense suitcase. Anna and her buddy Paula giggled as they manhandled, or womanhandled, two suitcases and another bag or two over to the counter. "Put me in a seat by that handsome Mr. Mankiewicz if you can" she told the counter agent, looking around and pointing back over her shoulder at me. A smile pulled up the corner of her mouth. She and Paula spent the next ten minutes alternately laughing, hugging and sniffling tearful goodbyes.

Anna and I got to our seats and belted in, side by side. I was surprised, delighted, giddy. I didn't really know what to say. I just sat there, grinning at her, letting the waves of happiness wash over me. When the plane took off, I reached over and took her hand. Finally, apropos of nothing, I said: "that's a lot of luggage you have, Ms Vasiloff."

She smiled at me and squeezed my hand. "Your hardest labor of all, Matt, will be putting up with me and all my baggage."

## END

**Discography**:

Portions of the lyrics of the following songs are reproduced in this novel. The author thanks the performers, writers and recording or publishing companies for the use of their work:

"Gimme Three Steps" recorded by Lynyrd Skynyrd
Written by Allen Collins and Ronnie Van Zant
MCA Records, Duchess Music Corp., 1972.

"My Cherie Amour" recorded by Stevie Wonder
Written by Stevie Wonder, Hank Cosley, Sylvia May
Tamla Records, 1969.

"Louise" recorded by Paul Siebel
Written by Paul Siebel
Elektra Records, 1970.

"Be My Baby" recorded by The Ronettes
Written by Phil Spector, Jeff Barry, Ellie Greenwich
Phillies Records, 1963.

"Tell It Like It Is" recorded by Aaron Neville
Written by George Davis and Lee Diamond
Par-Lo Records, 1966.

# Glossary of Fishing and Nautical Terms

Anadromous:     ADJ. All 5 species of Alaska salmon are anadromous fish, meaning they reproduce in fresh water streams and lakes. The juveniles go out to the ocean then return as adults after 1 to 3 years to spawn in fresh water. Pacific salmon die after spawning, and do not return to the ocean.

Bar:     NOUN. The shallow mouth where a river or channel enters the ocean, or a sandbar, a raised or shallow place in an area of sandy or muddy bottom.

Bow:     NOUN. The front of the boat.

Buoy:     NOUN. A float, a polyurethane ball filled with air, or a navigational marker, often of metal, anchored to indicate the location of a channel or shoal.

Brailer:     NOUN. A round metal hoop with a heavy mesh bag attached, used for moving fish once they are caught. The bottom of this bag can be pursed shut with a chain or rope to contain the fish, and then opened when swung over the hold to allow the fish to fall out.

Cleat:     NOUN. A metal device fastened to a boat or dock, with two ears or horns to which a line can be made fast.

Closure:     NOUN. A period of time when the fishing season is temporarily closed for conservation reasons, usually to allow for escapement so the run can reproduce.

Cork:
NOUN. A float to hold up the corkline.
VERB. To caulk a seam in a boat.
VERB. Slang fishing term for setting your fishing gear between another's gear and the fish, cutting the other person off from the fish.

Corkline:
NOUN. The top line of a gillnet or seine, strung with floats to suspend the net on the surface.

Dog:
NOUN. Chum salmon. *Oncorhynchus keta.* 6-15 lbs. Summer run fish in Prince William Sound. Also, a metal tab used to engage a gear to prevent it from turning.

Fathom:
NOUN. 6 feet, derived from the distance from hand to hand with outstretched arms.

Gear:
NOUN. Fishing equipment, a gillnet or seine.

Gillnetting:
NOUN. Drift gillnetting. A fishing method in which a net of fine twine tied in meshes of a specific size is drifted in the water in a substantially straight line. Fish swim into the meshes of the net. Their heads enter but cannot pass through and they are entangled. The net is then pulled aboard the fishing boat beginning at one end and the fish are cleared from the net one by one.

Highliner:
NOUN. A top-producing fisherman with catch numbers in the upper 10% of the fleet.

Humpy:
NOUN. Pink salmon. *Oncorhynchus gorbuscha.* 3-5 lbs. The most numerous species in Prince William Sound. Taken largely by seining, late June to September.

Kicker:
NOUN. Slang for an outboard motor. Also, a bonus or extra payment after the season is over.

King:
NOUN. Chinook Salmon, Tyee, *Oncorhynchus tshawytscha.* The largest of the 5 species of Pacific salmon. Usually 20-30 lbs on the Copper, but may get up to 100 lbs. Return to the Copper May and June.

Lazarette:
NOUN. A compartment below deck in the aftermost portion of a boat, aft of the fish hold, usually with the rudder post and steering gear.

Leadline:          NOUN. The bottom rope of a gillnet or seine, usually braided line with a center of lead shot to keep it down in the water.

Line:              NOUN. A rope.

Mesh:              NOUN. The diamond-shaped sections of a gillnet or seine, or the length of twine between the individual knots.

Opener:            NOUN. Also "a period." A period of time when fishing is legally open.

Pick:              NOUN. An anchor.

Pick the Net:      VERB. To reel the net back into the boat and remove the fish.

Port:              NOUN. The left side of the vessel. In ancient times, the preferred side to lay against the dock, as the steering oar was on the opposite (starboard) side.

Red:               NOUN. Sockeye Salmon, *Oncorhynchus nerka.* @6 lbs. Prized for its rich, dark red meat.

Run:               NOUN. As a noun it refers to the return of a species of salmon to their home river to spawn.
VERB. As a verb it is used to describe traveling by boat, or the movement of a school of fish.

Seining:           NOUN. Purse seining. A fishing method in which a net of heavy twine is used to encircle a school of fish. The top of the net (corkline) floats on the surface and the bottom line (leadline) has a series of rings through which a rope (a purse line) passes, by means of which the bottom can be drawn closed so the fish cannot dive out. The net is then brought aboard until the fish are concentrated into the bunt (moneybag) and then are rolled or brailed into the hold. This method requires a seine boat and a skiff or jitney to tow the other end of the net during the set, and a crew of 3 to 5 people.

Silver:            NOUN. Coho salmon. *Oncorhynchus kisutch.* 6-12 lbs, adults return to the Copper Delta in the late summer.

Skiff:             NOUN. A small flat-bottomed boat.

Slough:          NOUN. An inlet of the sea, a bayou, channel or backwater.

Starboard:       NOUN. The right side of the vessel. From 'steer board' side, the side that the steering oar was on in pre-rudder vessels.

Stern:           NOUN. The back of the boat.

Swale:           NOUN. A gutter or channel. A little valley or low spot in the sea bottom.

Williwaw:        NOUN. A powerful gust of wind.